To Caina'

BLOODLINES

Mariah Hayes '19

It was great to meet you in seattle!

Mariah Hayes

ISBN 978-1-64300-994-0 (Paperback)
ISBN 978-1-64471-523-9 (Hardcover)
ISBN 978-1-64300-995-7 (Digital)

Covenant Books, Inc.
11661 Hwy 707
Murrells Inlet, SC 29576
www.covenantbooks.com

To my sister, whose love of books matches my own and who was there with me every step of the way.

CHAPTER 1

The full moon shown bright, lighting a path through the dense forest. The wind whistled softly through the trees, and all was calm, or so it seemed. Then the beating of horses' feet on the hard packed earth could be heard. It got louder as the source got closer. Suddenly, five horses galloped over the landscape. Their riders were hunched low over their steeds' backs, their black cloaks blowing violently out behind them. The rider in the front was a woman. The wind blew her thick brunette hair around her stunningly beautiful and young face. Her hand rested on her swollen stomach carefully hidden by the folds of her maroon dress. The women silently beckoned to the four men behind her, then they slowly came to a stop.

"Your Highness," the man on the right got off his horse and hurried up to her, "I think they are far behind us."

"Yes, it seems so," the young queen said quietly. She got off her horse and beckoned to the other three men.

"Check the area," she ordered. She then carefully pulled her cloak around her and turned to look the man in the eye. "But remember, Fulcan, you can never be too sure."

"Of course, Your Highness," Fulcan smiled, then his face went back to a frown, "I knew that trying to make an alliance would be a wrong move. The Vampire King and Queen are just too violent." Then his face got sterner, and he began to raise his voice. "You could have gotten yourself killed. You almost did get yourself killed. You should have listened to my judgment. If you did we wouldn't be in this mess and the king would still be alive!" He bit his tongue. He knew he had gone way too far.

"I know, you were right," the queen almost sobbed. Then her face went soft again. "But we had to try. I just thought things would go better, be more graceful." The young queen looked at the ground, trying to fight back her tears.

"I'm so sorry," Fulcan said quickly. "The death of Richard was not all your fault. Who knew Queen Vallira had an ambush waiting for us, and Richard, her own son! They tricked us all. I, too, thought that this would finally bring peace between us. Those bloody monsters!" Lydia winced as he spat out the fowl word. Then Fulcan laid a hand on her shoulder. "Again, I'm sorry."

"No matter." The queen sniffed. "I'll be all right. We'll figure things out when we get back to Galatia." Fulcan looked up at the sky, trying to think of a way to change the subject.

"Well, the next question is what to do next?" The queen sighed then looked back up at him.

"I cannot ride much longer." She brought her hand to rest it on her stomach but then swiftly took it back. She quickly stole a glance at Fulcan's face, but he didn't seem to notice. "We'll have to make camp." She continued, heading toward her horse.

"Not here, it's too close to the Vampire's realm."

"Then where do you suggest?" The queen snapped. Fulcan sighed. The young queen could get so testy.

"I'm sorry, Fulcan. I know you're just trying to help." The queen looked back down at the ground again.

"Queen Lydia!" Two men came jogging up to them.

"What is it, Henry?" The queen's face was suddenly alert.

"There's a small cabin just ahead of us," Henry, a fairly tall man with a close-cropped beard said.

"Do you think it's safe?" Lydia turned back to Fulcan.

"It seemed quiet and peaceful enough," Henry answered.

"I think an old woman lives there," the other man added.

"It might be Serene, the old teller," a third man with a bloody cloth around his wrist, which was now a stump, insisted. "I heard she lives somewhere around these parts."

"Well, if it is indeed her, then it is probably safe to go," Fulcan answered. "We will have to be careful, though. You never know what could happen.

"It's settled then." Queen Lydia began to remount her black mare but only succeeded to get on with the help of Fulcan. "Thank you. I must be weak from the events of today." She panted, then straightened up again, trying to recover. "We will go at once." Her men mounted their horses and trotted after her as she pressed her horse forward.

As she trotted in the direction of the old cabin, Lydia felt a hot flow of tears coming again. Her mind wandered back to just before nightfall the day before when her husband, and true lover, Richard, was cut down by the Vampire queen's sword. She was just about to proclaim their alliance when Vallira, the Vampire queen, rose up into the air and let out an ear-splitting screech.

"Traitor!" she screamed at her son. The great hall came alive as Lydia and her party were surrounded. A battle broke out all around them. The hall was filled with the vampires' terrifying screams and the air was immediately filled with blood. She could still hear her own scream as she watched her lover fall to the ground. Then Jordee, the man with the bleeding stump, ran forward to help his king when he got his hand sliced off. Just before Lydia could avenge her husband, Fulcan grabbed her, and they fled down the entryway, vampire soldiers racing after them. Fulcan then threw her onto her horse, despite all of her protesting cries, and the five that were left out of about one hundred galloped out of the gates. They had ridden all the next day, through half the night up until that very moment.

She was pulled back into the present when she saw the cabin just peeking out through the trees. They rode up to the front of the house. Lydia got a strange feeling. It was like there was a force around the residence, pulling them closer and closer. The yard was decorated with all different kinds of statues from cute little fairies, their wings almost transparent, to terrifying goblins and monsters she had never even seen before. As she dismounted, it seemed as if every single glass eye of the strange creatures watched her and tormented her, begging her to come near them. Lydia hesitantly continued into the yard, followed closely by her men.

"Keep your eyes ahead of you," Jordee warned. "One look into the eyes of the Flaguns and . . ." But it was too late. Just then, Lydia looked up to meet the evil, red stare of a monster-shaped statue with fierce horns that jutted out of its head, batlike wings protruding from its back, and deadly fangs pointing out from its snarled lips.

"No! Your Majesty! No!" Jordee cried as Lydia raised a delicate hand to the monster's face. The monster statue's eyes seemed to go ablaze as Lydia got closer and closer. Just then, Fulcan seized his arms around Lydia's shoulders and yanked her away from the monster's gaze. The young queen dropped to her knees, still in Fulcan's grasp, and looked up, a terrified look on her face.

"I . . ." The queen choked, tears streaming down her face, "I saw Richard. I saw . . ." she began to sob and turned to hug Fulcan fiercely.

"It's all right." Fulcan soothed her. He gently stroked her long, brown hair, trying to calm her down. Then suddenly the torches surrounding the house burst into flame. Lydia swung around to face the cabin and the sadness was replaced with fear. The front door opened exposing a small old lady who looked as if to be at least 150 years old, or older. The strange woman peeked at them over the top of her small spectacles. Her eyes wandered around at each of them. When her tiny eyes came to rest on Lydia the woman began to squint even more and Lydia got an uneasy feeling. When she was just about to introduce herself, the ancient woman cleared her throat.

"I knew you would come." Her voice was weak and scratchy. It sent a chill down Lydia's spine as the woman peered hard at her, her spectacles inching down toward the bridge of her nose each time she took a wheezing breath. Lydia hesitated.

"I am Queen Lydia of Galatia in the north. I have come here to seek a shelter for the night. You see, the men that I have left are wounded and weary, as am I. We will leave at first light, but we can travel no longer tonight." Suddenly, the woman seemed to snap to attention.

"Awww," she sighed, "come in, come in. I would be honored to have you." The queen looked back at Fulcan with a worried look on her beautiful face. Seeing her look, he gave her a reassuring nod and she went in. The old woman beckoned to a chair. She only came to Lydia's waist and was as wrinkly as a prune. Lydia sat, her men being seated on either side of her.

"Tea?" the old woman insisted, pouring a glass for each person. Right as Lydia was about to take a sip the old woman spoke, her scratchy voice making Lydia jump and she put down her tea as to not spill.

"Excuse me for my rudeness, I am Serene," the woman began. Then her eyes grew wide, "I knew you would seek my hospitality . . . my help." Then her eyes came to rest on Lydia's growing stomach, hidden beneath her cloak. The look in her eyes made Lydia flinch, and she felt the other men shift uneasily beside her. Serene gave then a stern look, then her face softened.

"You don't need to fear me, child. I will not hurt you. I cannot hurt you for you carry something very special."

"I'm sorry," Fulcan cut in, "Her Majesty must rest." He gave Lydia a hard look.

"He's right," Lydia continued. "We have a long journey home and I should retire. Thank you for your hospitality."

"Do what you will," the woman said. "Right down the hall and to the left. Would you like me to take you there?" She slowly stood up.

"No, "Fulcan protested, "we will escort her there." The old woman stared hard at him and sat back down.

"Sleep well, dearie," she said. Then as Lydia and her escorts made their way down the hall she said again, "Sleep well."

"That woman creeps me out," Fulcan stated as soon as he was sure they were out of hearing distance. "Did you see the crazy look in her eyes every time she looked at you? I don't believe any of her nonsense. And what did she mean that you carry something special?" Lydia's eyes widened and she pulled her cloak more tightly around her.

"I . . . I don't know." Lydia swallowed. She wasn't ready for Fulcan to know about her secret pregnancy. The only ones who knew were herself, Richard, and of course her closest nurse, Martha. But she was worried; maybe it was wise to tell him. She was after all almost seven months pregnant, and she was surprised she had even hidden it for this long.

They soon came to a little oak door. Fulcan opened it for her, and she slowly went in. The room was fairly small, with faded, dark purple walls, and one small window, which was set very close to the low ceiling. In one end of the room sat a desk with an ancient mirror placed upon it, and on the other end sat a twin-sized bed, placed with two flat pillows and a scratchy, poorly handmade quilt. It was simple, and somewhat cozy, with a small fire already blazing straight across from the door.

"I guess it will have to do," Fulcan muttered. "The men and I will stay right outside your door if you need."

"Thank you," Lydia answered. He smiled and led the men out, shutting the door behind him. After she heard their footsteps grow silent, Lydia quietly took the couple steps to the bed and sat down. A tear trickled down her beautiful cheek as she looked down at her stomach and at the only part of her true love that still survived. Then she remembered the image of her happy, but secret past with Richard, which then led into the terrifying image of the event at the Vampire's realm that she had seen in the monster statue's eyes. She shut her eyes as tears came faster, and she slowly climbed into the hard bed. She then drew the scratchy woolen blankets around her and silently cried herself to sleep.

CHAPTER 2

A shadow cast over the walls. With each step the teller took, the floor creaked a bit. Fulcan stood up, seeing the old woman. His hand rested on the sword at his side.

"What do you want?" Fulcan asked hesitantly. Serene didn't answer but instead moved closer to the door.

"Don't come any closer!" Fulcan warned, drawing his sword. Serene hardly gave him a glance and put her hand on the doorknob. Fulcan swung down but was cut off before he hit his target. The teller spun around and her hand grasped Fulcan's throat. The woman was barely touching his skin and yet Fulcan's air was cut off. It was as if all the air was being sucked out of him. Serene half cackled as Fulcan crumpled to the ground. The other soldiers came rushing around the corner but were suddenly stopped in place. They struggled to pull free but couldn't move. Then, the teller turned slowly and went into the quiet room. Lydia woke to a dark figure looming over the bed. She tried to scream but no sound escaped her mouth.

"Hush, child!" the teller hissed, and she laid a fragile, deadly hand on Lydia's forehead. A tremble ran over the old woman's body and seemed to run down her arm to fill Lydia's head with an icy surge of electricity. She closed her eyes. Then, her stomach burned like fire. Lydia sat up in the bed, and her eyes flew open. The teller was nowhere to be seen. Lydia put a hand on her stomach. It had all been a dream. Lydia stared up at the ceiling of the room in thought. *The dream was so real.* She was a little lightheaded, and there was a tingling sensation lingering on her expanding stomach. She knew that she needed to get back to Galatia soon. Even though she was only almost seven months along, she had a strong feeling it was almost time.

When she sat up, she had prepared for the worst. She was expecting the teller to still come out of nowhere, but nothing happened. She slowly propped herself up and lit the candle beside her. She took it out of the holder on the wall and got out of bed. The hardwood floor was cold on her bare feet as she strode across the room. She looked at herself in the mirror and used her free hand to brush her hair back off her face. Then, she rested it on her stomach again.

What will my child become? She, of course, already knew, but she was still secretly hoping that somehow the child would be different. Lydia then heard a faint creaking noise and spun around to see the teller perched on her bed.

"Don't be afraid, child," the teller said, her face and body was relaxed.

"What do you want?" Lydia began, looking toward the closed door. "How did you get in here?" *Was the dream somehow real? How did the teller manage to get passed the guards?*

"It does not matter how I got in here," Serene said, her posture still relaxed. "What matters is the problem you will have to face not long from now."

"What?" Lydia stammered again. "How . . . What problem?" She was slowly making her way toward the door. Serene just looked at her.

"You can delay them, you know, her transformations." Lydia stopped in her tracks. "Yes, but not until the child is born. It will only take a quick spell, a quick remedy. You . . ." Suddenly the door swung open and Fulcan was standing in the doorway an arm's length away from Lydia, sword ready. But the teller had disappeared.

"Were you talking to someone?" Fulcan came in and carefully looked around. Lydia made her way back to the bed.

"You were probably just hearing things."

"I suppose so." Fulcan put his sword away. "Remember, if you need anything . . ."

"Right outside the door. I know." Lydia began to climb back into bed.

"Right." Fulcan took one last look around the room and closed the door silently behind him.

"Hello?" Lydia whispered as soon as the door was closed. "Are you there?" But the teller never came again that night. Lydia still saw no sign of her the next morning. Just a small platter of eggs and bread was laid out on the table. But as the small party left, Lydia heard the teller's voice in her head.

"Think about it, child. I will be right here waiting." Shortly after arriving back at Galatia, the queen surprised the kingdom, giving birth to a tiny, gifted, baby girl.

Seventeen Years Later . . .

"Nice shot!" An arrow sliced through the air and stuck into the small bulls-eye that had been carved into a tree. The archer was a slender, beautiful girl who looked to be about seventeen. She had fair skin and pinkish rose colored lips. Her thick, white-blond hair was pulled back into a loose braid that hung down to her waist, the loose strands blowing in the cool spring breeze. The most spectacular trait about her was her crystal blue eyes that shown as big and bright as a full moon.

"Perfect," the boy next to her said. He had dark brown hair and was tall, strong, and looked to be about the girl's age. "But I can do better," he teased.

"Shut up, Kaden," the girl shot back with a laugh, punching him in the arm.

"Hey, watch it, Nyla," Kaden laughed. "Or I might have to pound you."

"Oh, really?" She handed her bow to the servant girl next to her.

"Oh, come on," Kaden said. "Like you would ever get that dress dirty."

"Are you sure?" Nyla gave him a suspicious look and rolled up the loose sleeves of her sky-blue dress that matched her eyes almost perfectly. Although Kaden was a year older, and a whole head taller than her, she was feeling mischievous.

"I've known you practically my whole life, I know you better than you think," Kaden laughed.

"You never know," she said, giving him a little shove.

"Princess Nylina, Sir Kaden." A servant girl trotted up to them on a pretty brown mare.

"Yes, what is it?" Nyla asked.

"The queen would like to see you both."

Nyla sighed, mounting her own chestnut colored mare. "Too bad. I'll have to beat you next time." She grinned at Kaden.

"Not a chance!" Kaden laughed. "No way I'd let that scrawny little body best me!" She gave him a dirty look, teasingly stuck out her tongue, and cantered off toward the castle.

"Wait up!" Kaden laughed, loping off after her. In about a minute, Kaden's faster black stallion overtook Nyla's small mare. He laughed and looked back over his shoulder with a wicked grin on his face.

"Race you!" he called as he pushed his stallion into a full gallop.

"That's so not fair!" Nyla hollered back. She brought her mare into a gallop, but it was no match for Kaden, and before she knew it, he was nearly half a mile in front of her, grinning all the way.

"I win!" Kaden teased as they got into the courtyard. Nyla pulled her horse to a stop and jumped off. She led her horse toward the stables, Kaden hurrying after her.

"I'm sorry!" Kaden teased again when he finally caught up to her, "I should have slowed down a bit. You know, to give you more of a chance." Nyla handed her mare to a young stable boy, gently elbowed Kaden in the side, then started off toward the castle doors. Kaden snickered, also handed the stable boy his stallion, and quickened his pace to walk side by side with her.

They walked in silence for a while as they made their way up the palace steps. As soon as they reached the top, the huge stone doors swung open, and the two continued to make their way to the throne room. Nyla kept her eyes ahead of her as she thought. She was used to the silence these past couple weeks. Sometimes it was nice, and it gave her time to think just like it did now. But somehow the silence recently felt different. It seemed like they were always searching for things to talk about or the right words to say. For some reason, it was awkward, and she felt weird as she walked so close to Kaden. She looked down. Their arms were almost touching. Then she felt a feeling that had been creeping up on her the last few weeks. A feeling she never remembered feeling with Kaden in the past. A tingly happiness bubbled from her stomach to her chest. She had been feeling this way lately just at times when she would least expect it. Not that she had never felt happy around Kaden. He was always able to say, or do something to make her feel better when she was down and she could usually talk to him about anything. That's why he was her best friend. When they were little, Nyla had befriended Kaden, but he had always been different and not as outgoing as the rest. Then again, he had come from a different kind of family.

Kaden was the prince of Genora and the youngest of three boys. He was only ten years old when the kingdom was raided by a pack of werewolves led by Rothgar, the fiercest and least merciful werewolf alive. Genora's rulers knew that there was a large pack that roamed the parts near them and had, had a little trouble with them picking a few off of their best livestock, but they didn't suspect anything strange because the werewolves had no reason to attack. Unfortunately, they were wrong.

The king's best lieutenant, Shamus, had run into a couple werewolves while on a hunt. Although having the ability to transform into a big, oversized wolf, werewolves could almost seem to be mostly human. However, when a human is turned into a werewolf, almost all their human emotions and traits are forgotten and the animal nearly takes over all senses. Feeling threatened, the werewolves attacked, leaving two of Shamus's men dead, and Shamus himself bitten and horribly bleeding. But Shamus had managed to stab the werewolf that had bit him, and it had died a short while after. All might have been fine if it had been any werewolf, but it just so happened that the werewolf Shamus killed was not only the dominant female, but Rothgar's mate.

Genora was attacked in the middle of the night when they were least expecting it and was caught completely off guard. Kaden's father had led half of their small militia to the south end of the castle while the oldest brother, Kale, who was barely sixteen, led the other half of about thirty men to defend the castle gates. By the rising of the moon the next night, the castle was taken over. The king's dead body was found ripped apart and barely noticeable, Ganora was left in ashy ruins, and the queen had fled into the forest with only two of her sons, for Kale's body was never found.

But their troubles had not been over yet. The queen had fled into the Ieldra Forest, hoping to get away from danger. She knew that Galatia was not far, and she needed to seek refuge and safety there. After about three whole days of wandering, the small group had accidently stumbled upon a rogue vampire lair and were attacked by the unmerciful monsters. Kaden, being the young boy that he was, hid amongst the bushes and was not harmed. Kane, the middle brother, tried to help his mother as she was being swarmed by the hoard and had a long gash across his stomach from a vampire's deadly claws. The vampires eventually left a few hours later, leaving the queen dry and dead.

The two young boys continued to travel in the direction their mother had told them, but by nightfall of the next day, Kane's wound had begun to puss and he had come down with a fever. Kaden became desperate when Kane became unable to walk and Kaden, who was just a small boy, had to try to carry him. They traveled one more day before they came out into the daylight and could finally see Galacia's palace walls in the distance. By nightfall the two had made it inside the gates and Kane was cared for immediately by the best doctors in the Galatia palace. The most experienced healers had worked on Kane as best as they could, but to no avail. He died after three days of pain and suffering from a massive infection. Queen Lydia had then taken Kaden in with great sympathy and love. Nyla herself was only eight years old at the time.

The first time Nyla had heard of Kaden's past from her mother, she remembered crying for her friend and all his losses. She had only asked Kaden once about his terrifying time in the forest, but he was too young to really remember. It reminded her a little about her own father's mysterious death. Lydia hadn't told her daughter everything; she had always said that he had died in a great battle before Nyla was born. Nyla had asked about her father a couple of times—what he looked like, how he spoke, and how he laughed. Sometimes her mother would have long answers, but sometimes she barely told her anything, or once in a while, she would even shy away from the question and change the subject.

Once when she was little, Nyla had asked what her father's favorite food was, but her mother had just looked at her and began to change the subject, but for some reason, she began to cry. That's when Nyla's questions had stopped, for she hated to see her mother cry. Sometimes she would see her mother staring out one of the huge glass stained windows with a sad smile on her face. Sometimes Nyla swore she could hear her mother crying from her room late at night, but that wasn't very often. Her mother was strong and brave, and Nyla admired her greatly for it. She just wished that she could have gotten to know her father for at least a little while. He was probably a very great man.

Something caught her attention and Nyla looked up. Kaden had stopped walking and was looking at her with a sympathetic look on his face.

"What?" Nyla asked, puzzled.

"What's wrong?" Kaden turned to face her and slowly lifted a finger to her eye. When he brought it back, it was glistening with a tear.

"Are you all right?" Kaden asked, putting a hand on her shoulder.

"Oh, yes. I . . ." she stammered. For some reason, she began to feel embarrassed. She swiftly looked away and started walking again.

"It's nothing I . . ." What was she doing? She never felt embarrassed in front of Kaden before. "I was just thinking about something and . . ." She probably sounded and looked like an idiot! Surely he must notice! The big wooden doors started to open before she could say anything more and she began to walk in, relieved.

"Oh no, My Lady." The servant girl must have followed them in. "The queen is in the council room." Nyla gave Kaden a puzzled look, all embarrassment forgotten. They followed the girl back the way they came. Then they went up two flights of stairs, through another corridor, and finally came to a big black door.

Kaden didn't say another word the whole way and was lost in his own thoughts. *What is she thinking? Is she too embarrassed to tell me? She never gets embarrassed. I don't want her to be embarrassed. I want her to be able to tell me anything.*

"This must be pretty big," Nyla interrupted Kaden's thoughts. "My mother usually doesn't have meetings in the council room. Only for the more secret information. I usually never even go in here."

The room was dark and shadowy. At the front of the room hung a huge map of Galatia's few neighboring kingdoms in the north. Next to it hung another map of the southern kingdoms. The walls were lined with two rows of seats. In the center was a raised platform where the queen usually stood in an important meeting. Around the platform was a circular table where Queen Lydia now stood. Beside her stood a short, little man that had puny eyes, which hid behind his thin spectacles. This was Jamin, her most trusted advisor, and much to his dismay, Nyla's tutor. Next to him stood Fulcan, her top lieutenant. He was a bigger and stronger man with short red hair and a trimmed beard. Standing beside Fulcan was Samuel, the head of the guard, a young, very handsome man that was just a few years older than Nyla and only a year older than Kaden. He and Kaden had been friends for years, and although Kaden hung out with him a lot, Nyla hadn't really ever gotten to know him.

"Nylina, Kaden." The queen smiled at them.

"You wanted to see us, Mother?" Nyla began to move toward the table.

"Yes, we have just gotten word from Jordee." Jordee was the queen's messenger and spy since he had lost his hand in a previous battle. He had often gone to spy on the Southern kingdoms, more importantly Ridia, which was the main ruling kingdom of the South and Galatia's main enemy since the battle of the MaRidias when the land was still one kingdom. On the fourth, and final day of the harsh fighting and mass killing, Nyla's grandfather, and Lydia's father, King Hubert, had succeeded in killing Ridia's king, therefore splitting the land in half and creating Galatia, which was the North's main ruling kingdom. The two lands had been enemies ever since.

"There is disturbing news," the queen continued. "It seems that Ridia has been building a huge army all these years. Even bigger than our militia."

"Where is Jordee now?" Kaden asked, moving to stand next to Samuel.

"He will be on his way here as soon as he gets as much information as he can get. For now, I don't know what's going to happen. If Ridia's army is indeed much bigger than ours, we can only hope that luck will be on our side and our neighboring kingdoms, here in the North, will join and help us."

"I'm sure they will," Jamin added.

"Why would they?" Fulcan objected. "The other kingdoms haven't really trusted us since our king and queen tried to make an alliance with . . ." He quickly glanced at Nyla and swallowed his words. Jamin was now fidgeting with his spectacles, and the queen was looking down, clearly avoiding her daughter's questioning gaze. The room was filled with an awkward silence. Nyla caught Samuel's eyes, but he shrugged his shoulders. Fulcan suddenly cleared his throat and continued.

"Another issue would be if we even had much of an army left, since half of it was wiped out in the battle nearly eighteen years ago." There was an awkward silence again as everybody looked around the room, not daring to look at each other, especially not Nyla. She was beginning to get annoyed, and as the silence continued, she got even more frustrated. What weren't they telling her?

"I'll just have to wait for Jordee to return. Then we can make our decisions." The queen snapped to attention. "So Fulcan, Samuel, I want you two to keep lookouts on duty for Jordee. He will probably be coming in from the southeast since the west is practically off limits and forbidden from the Ieldra Forest. Jamin, I would like you to try and contact our closest neighbor, Ganea, for a meeting. We may have a war before us yet."

CHAPTER 3

CHAPTER 3

"Why is Jordee not back yet?" Queen Lydia scanned the landscape from one of the balcony like lookout towers facing the South, "It's been almost two weeks. This is very unlike Jordee. There's not even word from him."

"This is strange," Fulcan said. "I trained and worked with Jordee for over twenty years. Not once was he late. He always did a good job on getting to his destination faster than most men I've seen. I hope nothing has happened to him."

Lydia sighed, "I knew we should have sent somebody with him." She gently banged her fist on the stone ledge.

"I'm sure everything is all right," Fulcan tried to reassure the queen. "He's probably just . . . um . . ."

"How can you be so calm?!" the queen scolded, throwing her hands up into the air. "We could be an inch away from war here and you are just . . . ugh!" She ran her fingers through her shoulder-length brunette hair and walked to the other side of Fulcan to look to the east.

Fulcan just sighed. He was used to the queen's slight temper by now after serving her for longer than he could remember. Lydia's mother had died when she was only ten years old, and after that, she had become more like her father every day. Stubborn, and at times hotheaded, but mostly very kind and gentle. Lydia had been very young when her father had died from malaria and left her the throne. Many people had thought she was too young for she was only sixteen. In many ways it seemed to Fulcan that she was still that young, and still just as stubborn, but he had faith in her. He would always have faith in her even though she lost the faith of many, many people when she married Richard. Sure he was handsome, daring, kind, and great leader, but what he was had given him a bad reputation. Fulcan's thoughts were interrupted when the queen came back to stand beside him.

"By the way, how is the training going?"

"Good. All is going well. Nothing to report."

The queen nodded. "Good . . . how's Nylina doing?" the queen crossed her fingers.

"Samuel and Kaden have really been working with her. She moves just like her father. If she keeps this up, she is going to do great. She might even out reach some of my best warriors her age." Fulcan looked down upon the group of training troops, somewhat proud of what she had accomplished. Nyla was a hard student. Although she was very bright, she had always had a hard time standing still, or focusing. She was also very spirited and liked doing her things her own way, much like her mother. However, she worked hard and was definitely a fighter. When she had a challenge in front of her she was determined to overcome it no matter what.

"She reminds me of Richard so much." Lydia smiled weakly. She sighed slowly. "How much like him do you think she will be? I mean, mostly the special part."

"You're going to have to tell her sooner or later. She knows something is up. She's a smart girl. She is bound to find out that Vampire blood runs through her veins." Fulcan spat the word Vampire out.

"Don't get me wrong," he recovered quickly. "That's not a bad thing. She could do great things. She will do great things."

"I really hope so." The queen looked down upon the troops, trying to spot out her daughter.

"She will," he reassured her. "She just needs to get a hold of herself and realize who she really is . . . what she really is."

The queen hesitated, "I just don't think it's the right time. I don't know how well she will take it. Besides, Serene's little spell has kept her good for this far hasn't it?"

"Yes, but you should still tell her. Soon, before something happens."

"I know. I just . . . will she be able to take it? I mean, she used to be so scared of Vampires when she was little." Fulcan chuckled, remembering how many times he had stayed outside her open door when she was a little girl. But he choked back his laughter when the queen turned around to glare.

"I'm serious!" She hissed as she gave him a disapproving look.

"I'm sorry," Fulcan looked hard at her. "But I'm serious too." The queen huffed a sigh and made to turn around again.

"Tell me if there are any signs of Jordee and inform me if anything happens."

"Yes, Your Highness." Fulcan bowed, secretly rolling his eyes and watched as the queen left the tower. Then he turned once again to look down upon the young princess.

∽o∾

"Something strange is going on," Nyla told Kaden as their dull swords clashed together.

"What do you mean?" Kaden asked, dodging her swipe. They had been training men and soldiers ever since they had received word from Jordee weeks before. On this day especially, Nyla was in one of her moods. She had insisted on training with the soldiers. Fulcan had not taken this with great enthusiasm, but since she was the queen's daughter and heir to the throne, he didn't refuse.

"I know there are things they're not telling me. Things that I should've known a long time ago. They've been having meetings every so often ever since the first, and I haven't been able to go to a single one of them. Neither have you. Hey, Samuel's been to every one of those meetings and he's your friend. You should talk to him, see if he'll spill anything." She sidestepped Kaden's attempted blow to her shoulder then came around and thrust her sword toward his side. He blocked it and swung toward her, hitting her in the back.

"Ow!" Nyla sucked in a breath between clenched teeth. Kaden snickered, and she swung at him, but he dodged it.

"Concentrate, Nyla!" Samuel called from the sideline. He had been overseeing their training sessions and was normally a great teacher, but right now, he was starting to annoy Nyla. She gave him a glare just as Kaden hit her playfully in the arm with his sword.

"What are you doing? You're getting distracted." Kaden laughed. Nyla turned back to him and swung at his knee, only for it to be blocked again, but this time, he managed to wrench the dull sword out of her gloved hands.

"I won again!" Kaden raised his sword in the air, cheering for himself.

"Congratulations," Nyla mumbled sarcastically, sitting down on the bench behind them.

"Guys, come on!" Samuel called again. He started to head toward them, but Kaden waved him off.

"We are just taking a small breather." Samuel gave him a look but turned away anyway, going over to two other guards that were sparring. Kaden walked over to Nyla and sat next to her. "Come on, Nyla. What's wrong?"

"I just feel so unimportant," she sighed.

"You got to train, didn't you?"

"Barely," she said, looking at the ground. "However, if Samuel keeps telling me to concentrate, I'm going to whack him a new one with my sword."

Kaden chuckled.

"That's just Samuel. He takes what he does seriously and he actually does think you are doing well. He tells me all the time."

"Really?" Nyla looked to where Samuel stood practically shouting orders to the two men sparing a few feet away.

"Well, he's told me a few times. Okay, maybe once when I asked him how you were doing, but still it's a compliment. Samuel's tough, but he's good, probably just as good as Fulcan. He's tough on trainees because he pushes them to work harder in order to get better. That's why he's like the youngest captain of the guard in history, because he's good. Believe me, he's really a nice guy."

"Oh, I don't doubt that he's a nice guy. I just don't like him barking orders at me. That's what's distracting." She paused when Kaden chuckled again. "I'm just being a wimp. I'm distracted because I hate not being in the loop. I feel like my mother, Fulcan, Jamin, and

Samuel don't trust me or something, or think I'm not up to doing my part to help."

"They just have a lot to do that we can't help with right now. Your part is to train with the rest of us and become great, so maybe in the future, you can lead an army of your own. Of course I'd be right there with you." He slipped his arm around her shoulders and she stared into his stunning, dark green eyes, momentarily lost for words.

"I just wish they would be honest." She quickly tore her gaze away and looked down again.

"I've got an idea," Kaden said, standing up. "Let's go out for a ride. To cheer you up." Nyla looked up at him again.

"You sure Trainaholic over there is going to be okay with that?" She looked past Kaden. Samuel had moved past the next group and was surveying a couple of archers shooting at targets.

"I'll talk to him later and take care of it. It'll be fine." Nyla gave him an unsure look. "Please?" Kaden said. He suddenly grabbed her hand, and warmth shot through her body. He smiled at her pleadingly. Nyla was a little startled. Even though they were close, Kaden had never grabbed her hand or was never this irresistible. She smiled back and slowly stood beside him. She began forward, looking down at the ground. Then she noticed that their hands were still linked together and smiled. She glanced at Kaden, and he was staring at her with those impossible eyes. *Could his eyes be any more beautiful?* He smiled at her crookedly and, after a second, let go of her hand, but she stumbled and his hands shot out to steady her. She looked up at him again and he was grinning, visibly trying not to laugh. She looked away again so he wouldn't see her blush. *What is wrong with me?* she thought.

They watched in silence as the stable boy saddled their horses and brought them over. *Kaden's my best friend*, she thought to herself. *I've known him my whole life. Why do I suddenly feel different around him now?* She heard somebody clear their throat and noticed that the stable boy was holding out the reins for her to take.

"Oh, thank you, Jimmy." She took the reins from the freckled, nutmeg-haired boy and mounted her horse without looking at Kaden. Out of the corner of her eye, she could see him also mount his horse and silently look at her. Nyla didn't say anything. She began to nudge her horse but then hesitated and looked back.

"After you," Kaden said, pushing his horse slightly forward. Nyla started her horse into a trot, and they were soon out of the castle gates and were heading toward the archery shoot.

"Let's go somewhere we haven't," Kaden yelled. He turned his horse and led the way up toward the hills. They rode over fields and meadows passing cottages and farmers. They had been riding for almost an hour and a half when they came to a small stream.

"How much further?" Nyla asked as her horse drank from the clear water. She crossed her fingers behind her back, hoping that she could ride alone with him a little longer.

"Your call," Kaden said, jumping off his own horse and also drinking from the cool stream.

"Well, we could ride a little longer. It's not that close to dark," she said hopefully.

"Fine with me," Kaden said, remounting his horse. He smiled at her then grinned even more when she smiled back.

"Let's go then!" she laughed, heading into a canter. She galloped to the right, leading their horses over a pure green meadow sprinkled with flowers of almost every color. Nyla smiled and looked up at the sky, spreading her arms out beside her like she was flying. She hadn't felt this good in weeks.

Kaden smiled as he silently watched Nyla up ahead of him. He sighed. She was so beautiful . . . Then he frowned. A huge, fallen tree was blocking her path. Could she not see it? She wasn't pulling back!

"Nyla!" Kaden yelled, pulling back on his horse. She opened her eyes and looked back down, just getting a glimpse of the obstacle blocking her path. Before she could react, Nyla's small mare leaped into the air, trying to make it over the fallen tree. She looked down. They were going to make it! Then suddenly, her horse tripped practically in midair on a huge branch. Nyla was thrown forward off her horse, arms outstretched. She cried out in pain as she sliced open her upper arm on a spike sticking straight out from the log and closed her eyes as she hit the ground. She heard Kaden cry out her name

25

again and her eyes flew open. She quickly rolled out of the way just as her horse was about to fall on top of her.

"Are you okay?!" Kaden jumped off his steed and sprinted over to her, climbing over the log as he went. Nyla sat up, and seeing Kaden's horrified expression, burst out laughing.

"What happened?" Kaden asked, bewildered as he crouched beside her.

"I have no idea!" Nyla giggled. "I must have looked crazy." They both looked at each other and burst out laughing. Kaden stood up and walked over to her horse.

"Seems okay. Just has a little scratch on her right foreleg, but luckily no broken bones for either of you," he said, examining the cut. Nyla giggled and began to push herself up. She gasped when a shot of pain surged through her arm as she remembered her own cut. She brought her hand up and it was dripping with blood.

"What next?" Kaden said, checking the horse's saddle. There was no answer. He turned around. Nyla's face was pure white as she stared at her bloodstained hand.

"Are you all right?" He swiftly walked over to her and grabbed her shoulders. She looked up at him. Kaden jumped back as he watched Nyla's pupils slowly dilate, consuming the whole color of her iris. Her breathing quickened and became louder. She felt like her heart was going to explode.

"Kaden." Her voice was desperate. Her eyes continued to darken as she looked at him in panic. "Kaden!" She urged. "Help me!" The two horses behind them suddenly spooked and galloped away, but Kaden stared at her, frozen in fear.

"I can't breathe!" She outstretched an arm toward him. Then her hand flew to her heart. Something was happening to her! Her heart ached and then burned like it was on fire. Her breath was coming in quick gasps as she gulped for air. Her whole body began to shake and her vision was blurring. Her eyes flew to Kaden's once more before it went dark.

CHAPTER 4

Kaden's body shook as he stared down at the ground. His head was resting in his hands, still stained with Nyla's blood. After she had passed out, he had just stood there staring at her. Part of him was telling him to turn and run away, but a bigger part of him told him to help her, to get her safely home. Nyla's upper arm was bleeding badly, and Kaden kept pressure on it as best as he could. He had carried her a good mile and a half when he finally found the horses. He then tied Nyla's mare to his stallion and cradled her in his arms the rest of the way back to the castle, quietly whispering to her to hang on and though she was unconscious, reassuring her, and himself, that it was going to be okay.

About a half hour after nightfall, he rode through the castle gates and rushed her into the safety of the castle and its healers. He hadn't been able to see her at all since he brought her in. He had so many questions to ask, but only hoped that he would get a chance to ask the queen herself when she arrived.

A hand suddenly touched his shoulder and he jumped. He slowly raised his head to see the queen looking down at him with a soft look on her face. It was obvious that he was frightened and stressed. Kaden quickly stood up and took a deep breath to say something.

"Hush," the queen said softly. "We need to talk." The queen led him down to the council room that he and Nyla had entered together only a few weeks before. Again the room was occupied by Fulcan, Jamin, and Samuel.

"You need to tell me exactly what happened. Every detail. Leave nothing out!" The queen walked up to the platform on which she formally stood in a meeting and looked him straight in the eye.

"I . . . I don't know exactly what happened," Kaden stammered. "We were just riding, and we took a path that we normally don't travel. Nyla was ahead of me a little ways and there was a fallen tree ahead of her. Her horse tried to clear it but couldn't make it. Nyla was thrown off. She said she was all right, but she must have cut herself. I went to help her, but—"

"What, boy, what?!" Fulcan urged.

Kaden quickly looked up, his eyes filled with fear. His gaze switched to Samuel's and Samuel gave him an encouraging nod. "Her eyes became black. It was as if the pupils had completely consumed her irises, there was no color left. She said she couldn't breathe. She started shaking and she just . . . she just passed out. I . . . I couldn't help her. I . . ." He ran his hand through his hair and closed his eyes. He hated reliving that moment. He was so helpless, how could he let this happen? How could he let her get hurt like that?

"It's all right, Kaden. It's all right." Lydia put her hands on his shoulders as she tried to calm him down.

"What?" Fulcan said fiercely. "It's not all right! I told you something was going to happen and it has, Now—"

"What?!" Kaden burst out, opening his eyes. "What did happen? What's going on? What . . . what's happening to her?!" The queen sighed and let her arms drop.

"I knew I should have told her earlier. And . . . I should've told you. I should have warned you."

"About what?" Kaden asked impatiently.

"Calm down, Kaden. Let her speak." Samuel gave him a stern look. Kaden dropped into the nearest chair and waited for the queen to say more.

"Nylina is . . . well, she . . ." The queen was at a loss for words. She sighed as she thought of another way to say it. "Nylina's father was the prince and heir of Valdora."

Kaden sat up straight. "So he was a . . ."

The queen stared Kaden straight in the eye. "Richard was a Vampire." Kaden's eyes widened and his jaw dropped.

"So he . . . you . . . Nyla." Kaden was stunned. The only vampires Kaden remembered were the ones that had killed his mother and brother. The queen must have been crazy!

"So that means Nyla . . ." He couldn't bring himself to say the horrible word.

"She's a vampire, yes, or at least half. We're not exactly sure yet. The accident triggered her shift and she's turning now," Jamin spoke up from the corner of the room.

"You're telling me that Nyla's been a vampire this whole time and nobody's bothered to let me know about it?" Kaden gawked at all of them. He looked at Samuel. "Did you know about this?" Samuel said nothing and looked away.

"Samuel was sworn to secrecy just like the rest of us. We only told him because he's the captain of the guard and he needed to know." The queen moved to block Samuel from Kaden's view, but Kaden stood up and walked over to him.

"You knew about this the whole time and never said anything to me?! I thought you were my friend!"

"Kaden, I'm sorry, but—"

"I don't want to hear it, just leave me alone!" Kaden spun around and strode angrily out the door.

"Well"—the queen ran a hand over her face—"that was a disaster."

"I'll talk to him." Samuel gave her a reassuring look. The queen nodded.

"Let him walk it off. He might be ready to talk later." Just then, a nurse walked into the council room.

"Your Majesty." The young nurse gave a curtsy toward the queen, Jamin, and Fulcan and then gave Samuel a smile.

"Yes?" the queen asked impatiently.

The nurse snapped her attention back to the queen. "Your Majesty, your daughter is waking up."

The queen, followed closely by Fulcan, Jamin, and Samuel, made her way to the infirmary wing in uneasy silence. She kept her gaze down and Fulcan looked straight ahead of him while Jamin fiddled silently with his spectacles again. After what seemed like an hour of hearing nothing but their footsteps echo in the wide halls, they finally arrived at the big white doors. The queen reached for the door but then let her hand drop. Fulcan put his hand softly on her shoulder.

"I don't know what to say." The queen had tears in her eyes. She turned to Samuel and Fulcan. "You've come up against many vampires. What will she be like? What if she . . ." She took in a deep breath.

"It'll be all right," Samuel reassured her. "She'll still be Nylina no matter what. Trust me."

"You're right." She took another breath and opened the doors.

The light was bright in Nyla's eyes. She turned her head and noticed she was lying on something soft. *Am I dead? What happened?* Then she remembered her day with Kaden.

Kaden! She opened her eyes, but immediately regretted it and quickly shut them again. It was so bright! Where was she? Nyla sniffed and crinkled her nose. It had a weird smell, like plastic, and sterile. *What am I doing in the infirmary?* Then she heard voices.

"Oh, look at her, Fulcan!" She heard her mother's voice. "She's already changing!"

Changing?! What did she mean by changing? Is there something wrong with me?

"She hasn't changed that much. You're overreacting," Fulcan replied.

"She's completely fine." There was a new voice. "She's stable and completely healthy. Her pupils are still a little dilated, but they will return to normal in a couple of hours. However, she came in with a red mark running from her shoulder down to her elbow. She never had that before, and it looked as if it had just healed. Her healing abilities and senses are getting stronger. It's completely gone now, not even a scar."

What?! Then she remembered the cut and the blood on her hand. How had it healed by itself? She felt a hand on her forehead.

"Nylina," Lydia said quietly, "can you hear me?" Nyla nodded.

"What happened? Where's Kaden? Did he get hurt too?"

"Kaden's fine, honey." Nyla tried to open her eyes again but shut them right away. The light was blinding!

"Where is he? Can I see him?" She longed to see his face and make sure he was okay. Her mother hesitated.

"He's getting some rest. Can you open your eyes?"

"The light is too bright. It hurts my eyes." Suddenly the room got darker as someone covered the windows. Nyla slowly opened her eyes and looked around. Her mother was sitting right by the bed, her hand still resting on Nyla's forehead, and Samuel was standing behind her, but Fulcan was across the room leaning against the wall next to a fidgeting Jamin, a frown on his face.

"What's going on? What happened?" Queen Lydia sighed then slowly explained to her daughter about her past and what she really was. When she was done, Nyla had her eyes closed again and tears were rolling down her cheeks.

"So all this time, I've been a dangerous monster"—her voice was shaky—"and you didn't bother to let me know?! I could've hurt somebody!" The thought made her sick to her stomach.

"I should have told you a long time ago, but I was scared. I didn't know how you would react." Nyla opened her eyes again, looking into Samuel's sympathetic face, but looked away.

What is he doing here anyway? How had he known? There was a long silence, as nobody knew what to say.

"So what now?" Nyla asked in a stern voice, still avoiding eye contact. "What will happen to me now?"

"You'll just have to work on controlling it. Serene's spell has kept you from turning for this long, but the accident must have triggered something. You are beginning to change, but we'll get through this. It will be all right." She sat down on the bed. "But for the meantime, we are upgrading your guard. Samuel will now be guarding you at all times and once in a while another guard will be with him."

Nyla sat up. "What?" She looked at Samuel, who kept his face impassive. "Mother, is that really necessary?" There was no way she was going to be babysat all day and night! The queen looked her daughter in the eye.

"Nyla, I love you and I want to keep you safe. Samuel is the head of the guard, and he can be trusted more than you know." Nyla looked at Samuel again, but he stared uncomfortably at the floor. She glared at his head for a moment before shifting her gaze back to her mother.

"Mother, I know you want to keep me safe, but I really think I am more than capable of taking care of myself and you have guards all over the castle. Why can't they just watch me safely from afar like every other day?"

"Nylina, I will not argue with you about this." She leaned in, her voice low. "Please, just give it a try."

Nyla closed her eyes and sighed, "Okay." She might as well appease her mother; besides, she could always ditch Samuel and sneak off later. She moved to get up and her mother stood, holding out a hand to help her up. She sat there stubbornly, not taking her mother's hand. She kept her gaze down. "I'm feeling better now. Can we go?" She looked toward the door. "Is Kaden around? I want to talk to him."

The queen looked away from her daughter's gaze. "Honey, he's heard a lot of information today, I think we should just let him process everything for a little bit." Nyla looked at Samuel, but he was frowning at the ground. Nyla's heart gave a small, painful squeeze at the look on his face. *Kaden doesn't want to see me.* Nyla bit her lip, emotions clutching at her chest.

"Fine." Nyla stood up, pushing the feelings down. "I'm tired. Can I go back to my room now?"

"Sure, honey." Lydia put a gentle hand on her back. "Samuel will escort you to your room."

Nyla exited the infirmary, refusing to acknowledge the emotions threatening to squeeze her breaking heart. Her mother had lied to her all her life, and not only that, but others close to her had known and kept it from her. Betrayal bit at her heart like a rat gnawing at a piece of cheese. She took a deep breath and forced the thoughts out of her mind, needing distraction. She forced herself to peer at Samuel from the corner of her eyes as he walked beside her. Although he was "tough" as Kaden had described him, Samuel was definitely handsome, with his relaxed brown hair, sexy gray-blue eyes, and tall, toned build. Any girl in the whole kingdom would love to be in her position right now; however, in her mood, his heart-stopping good looks didn't faze her.

"So how'd you get roped into babysitting me? Was it just because you're Kaden's friend? I assure you I don't need supervision." She swallowed, hearing the bitchiness in her voice. It wasn't his fault he had to follow her around. He was only following orders. She breathed, taking the edge out of her voice. "I'm sorry by the way. I would hate to have to be at my aid night and day."

"It's no problem. I volunteered . . . in a way." He kept his gaze forward.

Nyla stopped, giving him a surprised look. "You did? You would rather babysit me than have the chance to yell at your troops?" She breathed in through her nose, hearing the rudeness creep back. "Sorry." She apologized again. "Why would you do that?"

"I don't know." He looked her in the eyes. "I guess I just want to keep you safe."

"Oh . . ." Nyla accepted the answer for the moment and kept walking. She was too exhausted to press the subject further. They were silent as they made it to her room.

"So"—Nyla stood awkwardly with the door open—"does being my 'watcher' day and night entitle you to come in or stay outside?"

Samuel tried not to laugh, which only fueled Nyla's temper further. "I can stay outside the door tonight."

"Okay," Nyla relaxed, relief washing over her. She definitely wouldn't be able to sleep with someone watching her, especially Samuel. She started to go in to her room but stopped, remembering her manners. She looked back at him. "Um . . . good night." Nyla gave him a fake smile and shut the door.

As soon as the door clicked shut, she took in the inviting surroundings of her room and every emotion crashed into her body, threatening to explode her heart. She leaned against the door, balling her hands into fists. She didn't even try to stop the tears as they spilled down her cheeks. Her knees gave out from under her as she choked back a sob and she slid to the floor. Waves of betrayal from her mother and who she thought was her family, along with the hurt from Kaden's rejection, collided with the loss of her father. If he were here he would know what she was going through, be able to comfort her and tell her everything was going to be all right. *Is it going to be all right? What am I going to do? How am I supposed to deal with this and get through it alone?*

Her hands raked through her hair. She had never felt so alone in her life. Her whole body shook with grief, and she wrapped her hands around her torso, needing to ease the pain. Feeling herself losing control, she forced herself off the floor and ran to her bed. She fell onto the mattress and buried her face in the pillows, allowing the sobs to overtake her.

CHAPTER 5

Nyla felt numb as she laid in bed staring at the ceiling. Although she was exhausted, she had not slept a wink. After she had cried herself dry, she had numbly stared into the darkness, tossing and turning, as her worries would flow into her mind whenever she would start to nod off. She suddenly sat up, looking toward her door. She had been worrying for hours on what Kaden was thinking and why he didn't want to see her. She had finally had enough worrying, and she was determined to see him. She stood, still fully clothed in her bloody dress, and started toward the door. She pressed her ear to the smooth wood, praying that Samuel was doing a round, or something, and not still be outside her door. Hearing nothing she slowly turned the handle and opened the door a crack. To her relief and surprise, she didn't see Samuel along the length of the hallway outside her door. She stepped out and silently closed the door behind her. She headed toward the direction of Kaden's room, walking as silently as she could. Every few seconds, she would check behind her to make sure she wasn't being followed. When she reached Kaden's door, she stopped and stared at the dark wood. Up until this point, she had been determined to speak to Kaden, but now that she was outside his bedroom door, she had no idea what she was going to say. She shook her head, angry with herself for being so nervous. It was going to be fine. This was Kaden for goodness sake!

She raised her fist to knock on the door and almost screamed as a someone cleared their throat behind her. She whipped around, her heart almost leaping out of her chest and running away for dear life.

"Princess, what are you doing?" Samuel raised his eyebrows at her.

"I . . ." she stammered, catching her breath, "I need to talk to him, Samuel."

"It's the middle of the night, Princess."

"I know. I just . . . This can't wait. I need to talk to him and find out what he's thinking and feeling about this . . . about what I am. He's my best friend, Samuel, and I need to know, or I won't be able to sleep at all."

Samuel sighed. "I understand, but you need to give him time."

"Samuel," Nyla said, beginning to get angry, "you can't tell me what to do."

"I'm not trying to tell you what to do, Princess. Kaden is my good friend too and I know he probably needs some time to process everything. He . . . he didn't really take everything well. That's why he wasn't in the infirmary wing when you woke up."

"Oh." Nyla's heart gave a painful squeeze.

"Listen," Samuel tried to reassure her, "Kaden will be fine. You can probably talk to him tomorrow. He just needs to sleep it off. It'll be fine."

Nyla nodded, feeling defeated. Kaden really hadn't wanted to see her. They walked back to her room in silence. Nyla didn't want to talk or even think anymore. She opened her door and shut it behind her, without a word, before flopping herself onto the bed.

∽∘∾

Nyla frowned as she stared at herself in her bedroom mirror. After she had returned to her room, she had stared numbly into the darkness for what seemed like hours before finally falling into a restless sleep. Surprisingly, her face looked just as refreshed as if she had slept like a rock the entire night, and although her face was pale with weariness, she still looked pretty with her young, beautiful features that many people said resembled her mother, and her father's soft, golden hair. However, she definitely looked way better than she felt, the sting of betrayal still weighing down her heart. Nyla looked into her emotionless eyes, like empty pools of clear blue water. She sighed and plopped back down on her bed. She wished she could just lie there forever and let everyone else worry about the cares of the day.

She frowned down at her stomach as it growled, betraying her with hunger. Clenching her teeth, she forced herself to stand and walk to her closet. She grabbed the first riding outfit she saw, threw it on, and pulled on her riding boots. She quickly twisted her hair into a loose braid before pausing at the door. She took a deep breath, dreading the moment she would leave the solitude of her room and walk into a world where she had to pretend everything was just fine. Straightening her posture, she opened the door and was startled to see her mother just outside, with her hand raised, about to knock.

"Nylina." The queen gave her daughter an overly bright smile, obviously trying to make up for lying the past seventeen years of Nyla's life. Nyla didn't return the smile and turned back to her bed. She sat down, keeping her eyes on her hands, clearly ignoring her mother. The queen entered the room, leaving the door open, and sat beside her.

"Nyla, we need to talk . . . about yesterday. What happened was—"

"With all due respect, Mother, I don't really care to talk to you about this right now." She kept her eyes down.

"Nyla, I know what I did was wrong. I should have told you, but—" Nyla stood up, her body rigid with hurt and rage.

"Yes! You should have told me, Mother! How could you keep something like this from me?! It's my life, *my life*, and you had no right to let me believe that I was normal my entire life! All my life I have hated vampires because of what they did to Kaden's family and here I find out that I'm actually one of them?! I hate what my father was and what I am! You just sat there and let me believe that Vampires were so horrible when my own father was one! How could you?! If Dad were here—"

"Nyla, if your father were here, it would be a whole different situation." The queen stood, her face reddening, but she tried to keep her voice even.

"Well, he's not! He left me alone in this world to deal with my lying mother and family! He left me alone to deal with what I am becoming, and I can't stop it!" Nyla turned and ran out of her bedroom, slamming the door behind her. She suddenly realized that there was a presence beside her and she jumped.

Crap! For a moment, she had forgotten about her dutiful body-guard. Great, it was going to be a lot harder to escape from the world and be alone with a guard following her around.

"Good morning." Samuel nodded a small smile at her, clearly ignoring the fact that she had just had a yelling match with her mother! Well, really the yelling was one-sided, but Nyla didn't feel guilty. Her mother needed to know how much her betrayal had hurt Nyla. Nyla's face heated and she tried to force a smile back but quickly turned her face away when she failed. Instead, she turned and began to walk down the hall toward the kitchen and dining hall. Samuel looked from her to the closed door, wondering what to do. The bedroom door opened and the queen stepped out, her eyes slightly puffy, but her face composed. She gave Samuel a small, fake smile.

"I'll be all right. Just follow her. Please make sure she's all right." Samuel nodded and gave the queen a short bow with his head. Then he went in the direction Nyla had disappeared down the hall.

Sensing her silent request to be alone, Samuel hung back a few feet as he followed her. Nyla tried to ignore his presence as she entered the dining hall. She stopped dead in her tracks when she spotted Kaden sitting alone in the corner. Other than a few maids cleaning here and there, he was the only one in the room. His attention stayed on the pastry he was eating as she entered. She filled her plate with fruit and small, jam-filled pastries then turned, deciding her next move. *Should I approach, or should I just give him space?* She decided on the first option. She was going to need to talk to Kaden sooner or later, and she might as well get it over with while they were alone, or at least almost alone. She looked back toward the door to where Samuel stood dutifully. He averted his gaze when she caught his eyes and he looked forward to the opposite wall. She appreciated his attempts to give her as much privacy as he could and she sensed that he didn't want to cause her any more discomfort than she was already feeling.

Nyla took a deep breath, preparing herself for the conversation ahead, and started toward Kaden's table. Kaden looked up as she approached and his eyes widened. He was so not ready for this conversation. He had no idea what he was going to say. He had stayed awake all night going over and over what the queen had told him about Nyla's past. He still couldn't believe the fact that Nyla was a vampire. The thought made him slightly sick. Up until now, the only opinion he had about the creatures was that they were twisted and vile abominations. They had killed his mother and brother, he hated every one of them with everything he had, and he was not about to admit that to Nyla. He dropped his mostly eaten pastry back onto his plate and rubbed his suddenly sweaty palms on his pants.

"Hey." Nyla gave Kaden a tentative smile as she sat down across from him.

"Hi." Kaden avoided her gaze, looking down at his plate. *Nyla can't be one of those revolting creatures, she just can't!*

Nyla picked up a pastry and bit into it, wracking her brain with what to say. She swallowed and took a sip of her drink. She looked up at Kaden, but he was glaring past her. She turned, looking for the subject of his angry stare. When Samuel was the only one standing in that direction her brows knit together in confusion. She turned back to Kaden.

"Kaden"—she hesitated—"I . . . my mother, she . . . she told you everything? About what I am?"

"Ya." Kaden still didn't look at her but instead looked down. She waited for him to say more.

"Kaden"—dread started to fill Nyla's chest—"look at me." Her voice sounded small and weak, her chest starting to compress when he didn't look up from his plate. "Kaden, look at me!"

"I . . ." Panic filled Kaden's body. He didn't know what to say, what to feel. "I can't, Nyla. Not yet. I'm still processing things. I . . . I don't know what to say. I don't know how . . ." He trailed off, closing his eyes, trying to shut out the hurt in her voice and face.

"Kaden, it's still me." Her voice quivered as her hands trembled in her lap. "I'm still me." Her voice was a whisper now. She drew in a slow breath as she willed Kaden to look at her. "Kaden?" She started to reach her hand across the table, but he moved his hand back. He looked up at her then, his eyes filled with sorrow and uncertainty.

"I'm sorry, Nyla. I have to go." He quickly got up, leaving his plate, and walked out the door. He had to get away. He had to work through the chaos in his heart before he could speak to her.

Nyla turned, watching him leave. Samuel stepped in front of him and put his hand on Kaden's shoulder. He said something to him, but Kaden angrily pushed past him. Nyla's gaze connected with Samuel's and she turned away. She looked down at her plate, tears beginning to fill her eyes. She picked up a piece of fruit, her hand trembling, but she put it back down, her hunger suddenly gone. She wiped a tear away and sat up straight, composing herself. She rose from the table and started toward the door. She kept her eyes down, avoiding Samuel's gaze as she walked past him and into the hall.

Samuel continued to keep his distance as he followed Nyla out of the castle, but as she headed toward the stables, he quickened his pace to walk just behind her. Nyla didn't even care. First her mother, and now Kaden, and she couldn't take it. She just needed to get away from the castle. She needed to get away from everything and everyone and just be alone.

"Princess Nylina, I'm sorry, but I have to go with you."

Nyla ignored him and kept walking. She motioned for Jimmy, the stable boy, as she neared her horse. He hurried to saddle her horse while Nyla kept her eyes forward, fighting to keep her emotions inside. Samuel saddled his own horse and brought it out of the stall just as Jimmy handed her the reins of her own horse. She led her horse out of the stables but suddenly turned, letting go of her horse, but it stayed dutifully in place.

"Can't you just leave me be for an hour?! I need to be alone!" She didn't even try to keep her voice down, all her strength going into keeping her swelling emotions from reaching her heart.

"I'm sorry." Samuel gave her an apologetic look but stood firm. "I will keep my distance, but I have to go with you."

"Ugh!" Nyla let out a frustrated groan and spun around, mounting her horse and immediately pushing it into a gallop. She didn't check to see if Samuel was behind her or not. As far as she was concerned, she was going to be alone. She kept her horse at a gallop until she reached the edge of the woods. She pulled it to a stop and jumped off, leaving her horse to graze on the tall grass. The tears had already started to fall and she wiped at them furiously with the palms of her hands. She groaned when she saw Samuel galloping toward her and she turned, bolting into the forest. She only got a few yards when her tears were blinding her way and she stopped, dropping down behind a tree. She pressed the palms of her hands into her eyes and tried to stop crying as she heard Samuel's footsteps approaching. She hated when people saw her cry, especially guys. It made her feel weak and she did not want to seem weak, especially in front of Samuel.

"Princess Nylina." Samuel stopped beside the tree. He hesitated before crouching beside her, thinking of what to say to comfort her. Nyla kept her head forward, letting the loose strands of hair that had escaped her braid shield her face.

"Listen, I know you don't know me very well, at least not on a personal level, but if you need to talk, I'm here for you." He frowned and moved his hand to touch her shoulder, but then drew it back, setting it on his knee.

"I'm fine." She lied, her heart squeezing painfully as she fought to keep her emotions concealed. She let out a jagged breath, hating herself for not being stronger. When Samuel didn't move, she leaned her head back on the tree, scowling up at the sky. She stood, suddenly angry. Samuel stood with her and she got in his face.

"I said I'm fine! Leave me alone already!" She pushed his chest, and although she didn't even faze him, he took a step backward. She glared at the calming look on his face and huffed as she dropped back to the ground again. She sat there for a moment, trying to calm herself down. She felt Samuel kneel beside her again, but she didn't look at him.

"It's just, my whole life has been a huge lie. My own mother has lied to me since I was born, and all this time, I've had no idea who my father was, or who I am. What I really am." She closed her eyes and a tear slipped out, but she quickly wiped it away. "Now Kaden is scared of me. He won't even talk to me." She let out a small sob. "Who could blame him, right? I have no idea what I am and what I'm capable of. I'll probably end up being just as bad as the creatures that slaughtered his family." At that the tears started to fall again, but she didn't bother to stop them. Samuel gave her a sympathetic look. He put his hand gently on her shoulder. His touch felt warm and comforting and Nyla didn't flinch away. She looked at him through her watery eyelashes.

"Nyla, Kaden is an idiot. Kaden's been my friend since I joined the guard and I don't want to say anything bad about him, but it's true. I know that what happened to his family is horrible and he has a right to hate vampires, but the way I see it, he shouldn't see you in that way. He's been your friend way longer than he's been mine and he should realize that you are still you, no matter what you are. I'm sure he will realize that in time." Nyla looked away, nodding helplessly even though she didn't believe what he was saying. He continued, "Plus, I'm sure he's probably more mad at me than he is at you. So don't worry. I know he'll come around."

"Why's he so mad at you?" Nyla sniffed.

"I knew you were a vampire. You're mother told me when I joined the guard and she made me swear to secrecy. He's mad that I didn't tell him."

"You too, huh? Did everyone in the kingdom know besides me?"

"No, just your mother, Fulcan, Jamin, your nurse Martha, and myself. Nyla"—he paused when she looked up at him, a few tears still escaping her lids—"I'm sorry that I didn't tell you. Your mother made me swear and I respected her wishes, but I am sorry."

"It's not your fault. You're not the one who decided to make everyone swear to secrecy."

Samuel shrugged. "Listen, I know that you're feeling hurt and betrayed, but your mother didn't mean you any harm. She really did have good intentions. Yes, maybe she should have told you sooner before you had to find out this way, but she had her own reasons for not telling you." Nyla thought for a moment and nodded her head.

"I just don't know if I'm ready to forgive her yet. I'm so angry with her and Fulcan. I'm sure they thought they had their reasons, but right now I just don't see them."

"You have a right to be angry, you do. You had no choice in what's happening to you. Just try to forgive them in time. Talk to your mother and work things out. She will always be there for you. We'll all help you through this."

"That's easy for you to say. Why are you even bothering to try to help me? You aren't the one having to go through this. I hate not having any control over this." Nyla frowned at her tone, realizing how childish she sounded wallowing in her self-pity. She sighed, looking into his deep, blue-gray eyes. "I'm sorry. I shouldn't be taking this out on you."

"It's okay." He gave her a small smile. "I'm not just here as your guard, but as a friend. Just talk to your mother. You won't regret it."

"Okay." Nyla gave him a half smile, feeling her fear and hurt lighten a bit. "Thank you." Samuel nodded and gave her a small, comforting smile. "Do you mind if we just sit out here for a while?"

"Sure." Samuel nodded and leaned back against the tree. After what must have been an hour of Nyla sitting in the same spot, holding her knees in silence, while Samuel fidgeted, was distracted by a lady bug, and walked around, seeming to survey nature, Nyla looked over to where Samuel now stood petting the horses. She was thankful that he never once got impatient, or asked to leave, while she sat there sorting out her issues. She watched him for a few moments before he caught her eye and smiled.

"You ready?" He walked over to her and held out his hand. She nodded and took his hand, letting him pull her up. She took in a quick breath, surprised at how warm and strong his touch was. She quickly let go of his hand, trying to ignore the tingling sensation shooting up her arm, and looked up at the sun overhead. "We should go back. I'm sorry I made you miss lunch."

"No worries." Samuel smiled at her. "I don't have a big appetite anyway." She gave him a thankful look and walked back to the horses.

"Where to?" Samuel asked as he mounted his horse.

"To find my mother. I need to talk to her." She gave Samuel a small smile before mounting her horse and pushing it into a walk.

☙◦❧

As soon as they put their horses safely back in the care of Jimmy at the stables, Nyla headed toward the castle. She walked at a quick pace, eager to find her mother, who she thought would most likely be in the council room, or the library with Jamin. Her mother loved to read, which was why the castle library had such an extensive collection of books and scrolls. Whenever the queen had free time, she could always be found sitting in one of the big, open window seats in the library. When Nyla got to the library doors, she turned to Samuel, who was reaching to open the door for her.

"Do you mind if I go in alone? I need to talk to my mother."

"Of course." Samuel gave her an encouraging smile, glad that she was taking the first step toward forgiveness. He opened the door for her and she stepped through, taking a deep breath when she spotted her mother on the second story window seat overlooking the maze-like garden.

"Mother?" Nyla took a few steps forward, wringing her hands together with anxiety.

"Nylina." The queen gave her daughter a small smile. She put her book down and hurried down the staircase. "Nylina, I'm sorry. I should have told you. I know now that I was wrong to keep this from you, but you have to believe me when I say I was just trying to protect you. I didn't know if you would ever turn, but I was wrong. I should have told you."

"Mother, I'm sorry." Nyla took her mother's hands in hers. "I was wrong to judge you and get so angry. I shouldn't have yelled at you and I'm sorry. I know that you had your reasons, and while I may not understand them right now, know that I am sorry." She looked her mother in the eye. "But I can't forgive you completely right now. I will in time, just I'm not quite ready yet, but I will try." The queen smiled and hugged Nyla.

"That's all I'm asking for. I don't expect you to fully forgive me, but I just don't want this to come between us. I love you, Nyla, and I will always be here for you to help you through this." Nyla hugged her mother back.

"I know." She let her mother go and smiled at her, a weight lifting off her shoulders.

"Dinner is about to start. Would you like to take a walk afterward? We'll talk about your father." The queen gave Nyla a hopeful smile.

"Sure, okay." Nyla followed her mother out of the library. The queen nodded at Samuel and mouthed a "thank you." He nodded and followed them to the dining hall.

After dinner, the three of them headed outside toward the back gardens, Samuel following from a distance. As they wove through the maze of rose bushes and other sweetly-smelling flowers, Nyla and the queen walked side by side.

"So my father . . . he was a good man?" Nyla hated to ask the question. Of course he was a good man. He had loved her mother and she had loved him back. Nyla shouldn't have even questioned her father's goodness, but she had been believing he was human her whole life, so who knows what else her mother might have hidden.

"Yes, he was a great man." The queen looked at her daughter. "Not all vampires are monsters, Nyla. A lot of them, okay, most of them are, but there are a few good ones. Your father didn't love what his kind were and what they did, but he accepted and embraced who, and what, he himself was. I won't lie to you. Before your father and I met, he had his 'bad' days. He didn't tell me everything, but he wasn't proud of what he did in his past. He learned from his mistakes and learned to control himself." She smiled, looking off into the distance. "I loved him very much, and I know he loved me and how much he loved you. He would be proud of you, Nylina. You have grown to be a beautiful young woman, and this is just a bump in your path. You'll get through this just like your father did. You're strong and I have strong faith in you, Nyla."

"I hope I'll be as strong and great as he was."

"You will be." Her mother sighed at the sky. "Nyla, there is another reason why I hid what you are. I can't even imagine what Valira would do if she found out. You are the daughter of who used to be her favorite son. Who knows what will happen if, when, she finds out." Lydia looked at her daughter, worry plain on her face.

Nyla shook her head. She hadn't even thought about the other side of her family and the thought terrified her. All the stories of Valira and the rest of the vampire ruling family were the worst. They were cruel and ruthless and out of all the unknown reasons they didn't venture out of their lands, Nyla was sure that fear of the other kingdoms wasn't one of them.

Lydia looked her daughter in the eye when Nyla didn't say anything. "That is a bridge we will cross if it comes." She gave Nyla a small, reassuring smile. "Right now, I should probably get back to the castle. I have another meeting with Jamin and the council members."

"Okay. I think I'll just stay and walk for a while." Nyla smiled at the queen. "Thank you, Mom." The queen smiled and gave her shoulder a loving squeeze before turning back toward the castle. She nodded at Samuel as she walked by and he moved to walk just behind Nyla.

"Say it." Nyla slowed so that Samuel was walking beside her.

"Say what?"

"Say I told you so. As much as I hate to say it, I admit that you were right."

"Oh, really?" Samuel grinned down at Nyla.

"Okay, now don't let it get to your head." Nyla stuck her hand out, making him stop. "It was probably like a one-time thing." She laughed at his surprised smile.

"Hey, I made you laugh. I must be doing something right today." She smiled shyly at his bright grin and looked down. *Wow, he really is gorgeous!*

"Okay, now you are letting it get to your head." She smiled at the ground and he chuckled. She looked up at him, meeting his blue-gray gaze. "Really, though, thank you."

"You're welcome, Princess Nylina." He continued to grin at her and she looked down again, blushing.

"Just Nyla. No need to be so formal." She bit her lip as she looked back up at him, her cheeks still rosy.

"Okay." Samuel nodded, not taking his eyes off her. There was silence between them for a moment.

"Nyla!" Nyla turned and smiled when she saw her friend Julia hurrying toward them. Julia, a short, red-haired girl with pretty freckles that dotted her face, was Nyla's lady in waiting and one of the best friends Nyla had ever had. Nyla had never really seen Julia as her lady in waiting, and they told each other everything.

"Hey, Julia." Nyla smiled as Julia approached. She hadn't spoken to Julia since the day before the accident, and she was eager to see how her friend was taking the news. "How are you?" Julia hugged her friend and then gave Samuel a shy smile. Samuel smiled back and gave Nyla a nod before walking a few yards away to give them some space.

"I'm doing all right, all things considered. What about you?" Nyla prepared herself for disappointment. Seeing Nyla's worried expression, Julia gave Nyla another hug.

"Nyla, I will never back out on you. You are my best friend and you are just like a sister to me. I don't care what you are. You will always be my sister."

"Thank you, Julia." Nyla hugged her tighter. And Julia let out a strangled huff. "Sorry." Nyla smiled. Julia shook it off, giggling, but her face became serious.

"Nyla, Kaden told me what he said and how he ran out on you. He'll come around, Nyla, he will. He's just . . . he's just freaking out a little bit right now. I know it's stupid of him and I'm so sorry. I know he's sorry too, he just can't tell you that right now." Nyla nodded. "Come on." Julia started back toward the castle. "I know where we can score some of the cook's personal stash of chocolate." She gave Nyla a mischievous grin, and Nyla laughed.

"I'm in. I always love sneaking in there and hiding it in different places." They both giggled as they headed back toward the castle. Julia kept her eyes low as they passed Samuel. Nyla turned to him, a new excitement in her mood.

"We're going to sneak some of Gert's chocolate and snag some before we hide it in a different place. You in?" She smirked and raised her eyebrows at him.

"Hell, yes!" He grinned and started to follow them. "I haven't done that in a long while. Kaden and I have been doing that for years."

"Ah! That rat!" Julia exclaimed. "I'm the one that showed him that!" She blushed when Samuel started laughing.

ᗍᘮᔓ

"See, deep down, I knew that you were cool," Nyla teased Samuel as they sat in the Nyla's room, passing the bag of chocolate between them. "I mean, it took quite a lot of convincing to get you to distract the maids and the young cook on duty, but I knew you'd come through. What was her name again?" Nyla grinned at Samuel.

"Daisy." Samuel squinted at Nyla as she and Julia laughed.

"That's right. Daisy. She was really entranced by you." Nyla giggled as she shoved a big piece of chocolate in her mouth.

"Jokes on you, guys, because I got her to agree to sneak me Gert's chocolate herself. So I can get it whenever I want and I don't have to do the dirty work to get it." He raised his eyebrows mockingly at Nyla.

"Pshhh! That's the whole fun of it," Julia chimed in.

"That's true," Nyla added. "Sneaking around is the fun part. Getting to actually eat the chocolate is just the reward." Nyla beamed triumphantly at him.

"Mmm, true." Samuel nodded, passing the chocolate to Julia. "Fine. You girls win. All I got was another adoring fan." He rolled his eyes.

"You don't like girl's fawning all over you?" Julia piped up, suddenly interested. She handed the bag to Nyla and leaned her elbows on her knees.

"Not particularly," Samuel said, taking the bag from Nyla.

"Oh, come on," Nyla interjected. "I've seen you flirt with girls plenty of times."

"Well, I'm not going to be rude." He gave her an accusing look, but then smiled. "Don't get me wrong, the attention is all right. I just think that when girls act all bubbly and fake just to get a guy it makes her look foolish. Just be yourself and let the guy come to you." He shrugged. Nyla and Julia both nodded.

"Well," Julia broke the silence. "It's a little warm. I think we should go hide the bag of chocolate somewhere cool before it starts to melt." She held the bag in her hands, squishing the semi-soft chocolate inside.

"I think you're right." Samuel stood up from where he was sitting on the floor, propped up against Nyla's bed. "I'll take it back." He held out his hands.

"No way. I want to help find a good hiding spot." Nyla stood, stretching her legs.

"Me too," Julia agreed as they walked into the hallway.

They returned the bag into the cellar and were headed outside to get some air. The three of them talked and joked around as they exited the main doors. Nyla's troubles were forgotten for the time being and the mood was light.

"I can't believe we put the bag between the bags of potatoes." Julia laughed as they sat on the front steps. "It is going to take Gert forever to find that!"

"Ya," Nyla snickered. "Good move on that one." She bumped Samuel's arm with hers.

"I would love to see Gert trying to find it." Samuel smiled. He looked up and his smile faded when he spotted Kaden approaching them.

"Kaden." Nyla stood up. "Can we talk?"

"Not now, Nyla," Kaden said, walking right past her.

"Kaden, I need to talk to you." Samuel stood, a frown on his face.

"Later, Samuel." Kaden reached the door.

"No, now." Samuel took a step forward.

"It's fine, Samuel. Let him go." Nyla turned and sat back down.

"No." Samuel didn't take his eyes off of Kaden's back. "He's your friend and he needs to treat you like one." Suddenly, Kaden spun around and strode toward Samuel.

"Who are you to defend her? You've never been her friend. I have!" Kaden backed Samuel down the stairs, but Samuel stopped at the bottom, standing his ground.

"Well, I'm her friend now, and if you are the friend I know you are, you will accept her for who she is and not what she is." Samuel looked down at Kaden, standing at least a head above him.

"Oh ya?" Kaden's voice rose to a yell. "Where was your friendship when she didn't know what she was and everyone was keeping it from her, including you?!"

"That wasn't my choice!" Samuel was now yelling.

"Okay, enough!" Nyla got up and marched over to them. "This is not the time. We all need to calm down here and just let it go. I can defend myself, neither of you have to do it for me."

"Nyla, Kaden's acting like he doesn't even know you! You are a vampire. So what?! Kaden needs to get over his issues and grow up!"

"Grow up?! I'll show you grow up!" Kaden slammed Samuel in the face with his fist, snapping Samuel's head to the side.

"Kaden!" Nyla shrieked. Julia stood up, astonishment on her face.

"Seriously, Kaden?!" Samuel roared, but he kept his arms to his sides, his body rigid as if the punch didn't even faze him.

"Dammit!" Kaden shook his hand and bent over, inspecting his fist.

"That's enough!" Nyla stepped in between the two men, facing Kaden, fury plain on her face. "Back off, now!" Kaden stepped back, glaring at Samuel over Nyla's head as she placed her palms on his chest, backing him up.

"Stay away from me, Samuel!" Kaden glowered at him before turning toward the castle.

"Gladly!" Samuel glared at Kaden's back as he opened the doors and disappeared inside. Julia stood there for a moment, unsure of what to do.

"I'm going to make sure he's okay." She looked at Nyla before going after Kaden. Nyla watched the doors close and spun around to face Samuel.

"What were you doing? I told you to let him go!" She scowled at Samuel before turning and going into the castle. Samuel followed her as she headed to her room.

"Nyla, I was trying to protect you. He's hurting you, Nyla, and if he was your friend he wouldn't hurt you like that. He would realize that not all vampires are bad and that you certainly aren't the abomination he thinks all vampires are!" She stopped at her door and spun around to face him.

"I don't need you to defend me, Samuel! I am perfectly capable of doing that myself! Now you just made things worse!"

"Fine, Nyla." Samuel took a deep breath, calming himself. "I won't defend you anymore. You can fight your own battles."

"Thank you!" Nyla turned, opened her door, and stepped into her room, shutting it behind her. She threw her hands up in the air before running to the bed, grabbing a pillow, and screaming into it. *How could they just fight over me like that?! Neither of them had the right to defend me! They were both in the wrong; Samuel had agreed to keep what I am from me my entire life, and Kaden was acting like I myself had killed his family! How dare they?!* Nyla felt like she could punch something. She turned, throwing the pillow onto the bed just as she caught her reflection in the mirror. She stopped dead in her tracks and stared, her mouth open. At first she thought it was somebody else staring back at her, but she rushed up to the mirror, staring at her face. Her pupils had dilated, completely blocking out any trace of bright blue. She squeezed her eyes shut and opened them again, her face paling when her eyes didn't change back. She stared, open mouthed, into the black eyes of the creature that had taken her place. She jumped as Samuel threw open the door. She stood straight, not even realizing that she had screamed his name. His mouth dropped open when she turned to face to him. Nyla turned back to the creature's reflection and brought her shaking hands up to her face.

"What's happening to me?" She started to panic as Samuel rushed toward her. He took her face firmly in his hands, forcing her to look at him.

"Nyla, it's okay. Relax. Breathe."

"What?" She tried to look back at the mirror, but he kept his hands firm.

"Breathe." Nyla stared into his blue-gray eyes, concentrating on how the colors in his irises swam together, like a cool, clear river.

"Breathe," Samuel whispered calmly, rubbing his thumbs softly back and forth just under her eyes. She closed her eyes, listening to Samuel's low, whispered voice. She concentrated on Samuel's soft breath on her face, then at her own, slow breathing. She relaxed her body and opened her eyes to Samuel's soft, blue gaze. Samuel gave a small smile.

"See?" He slowly let go of her face and she turned, looking at her normal reflection. She stared into her own, crystal blue eyes staring back at her and gave a sigh of relief.

"How did you do that?" She met his eyes as he stood behind her in the mirror.

"You were panicking, which would have only made it worse. You needed to relax." He went to turn toward the door. "Do you want me to get the Queen or Jamin?"

"No." Nyla thought for a moment. "There's no need to worry them. It won't happen again." She shook her head. "It won't happen again," she repeated, more to herself.

"Are you sure?" Samuel looked concerned. "They should probably know about this."

"No, Samuel." She hurried to shut the door before he escaped the room. "Please. I don't want them to know. It won't happen again."

"Nyla—"

"Samuel, please." Her voice was stern this time. "Please don't tell them." She said more urgently. Samuel let out a sigh.

"Okay, Nyla." He went to open the door.

"Samuel."

He turned toward her, letting go of the handle. "Would you mind staying inside my room tonight? Please?"

Samuel hesitated, but then nodded his head, taking in her scared expression.

"Thank you." She hurried to her closet and changed into a knee-length, loose nightgown. She peeked her head out from her closet, eyeing Samuel at the door.

"Will you turn around please, or close your eyes, or something." Samuel gave a small laugh.

"Yes, Princess." He turned around and Nyla hurried to her bed, pulling the covers up to her chin.

"Okay. You can turn around now. And please, call me Nyla. My friends don't call me Princess."

He turned and she gave him a small, nervous smile. "You know, you don't just have to stand there. I can get you a chair or something. You can maybe get a few hours of sleep?" Samuel smiled.

"I'm okay, Nyla."

"No, really. It's okay if you sleep. I don't mind. You're inside my room anyway you'd be able to protect me if something came bursting through the door." A thought occurred to her. "Or stop me if I tried to get out. That's why you're guarding me 24-7, isn't it? To make sure

I don't go crazy and hurt someone. After tonight, I can see why." She frowned up at the ceiling.

"Nyla." Samuel hesitated. He went to move closer to her but stayed by the door. "You're not going to hurt anyone. I know you won't. I'm just here as a precaution, just to ease the minds of some people."

Nyla nodded, turning on her side to face him. "It's the council, isn't it? Bunch of old crones." She heard Samuel snicker and looked up to meet his eyes from across the room.

"You happen to be correct. Jamin is the only one who trusts you won't do anything. The others obviously don't know you very well."

Nyla nodded her head. Out of the three selected council members backing the queen, Jamin was the only one Nyla liked. The others, Rumagen, a tall, spindly, balding man with a long nose like a hawk, and Melrose, a short, fat woman with probably just as much hair (Nyla and Julia suspected she always wore a wig); both had about the same sense, which was nothing. However, just like the royal family, the council members also came into position through family, something Nyla meant to change when she took the throne. She looked back at Samuel, who was leaning against the wall with his arms crossed.

"Samuel, please get a chair."

"Oh, fine." Samuel grabbed the nearest chair, which happened to be the felt one from her vanity, and set it down by the door before plunking down onto it. "Happy?"

"Yes." Nyla smiled, satisfied. "You're welcome."

Samuel gave a quiet laugh. "Good night, Nyla."

"Good night, Samuel." She blew out the candle beside her bed and rolled over, closing her eyes.

CHAPTER 6

Nyla squinted at her reflection in the mirror. She hadn't changed much in the last couple of days, but it was enough. Her face was a little more pale, but still just as pretty, her eyes now glowed an intense, light blue. Her hair was the same thick, white blond that it had been, but her lips were a deeper pink than they had been before. Although she had her mother's beautiful face, many people had told her she looked more like her father, with his same blue eyes and blond hair. She wondered how much like him she really was now that she was changing into what he was.

The most changes, however, weren't with her physical appearance. She was more graceful when she walked and she was faster. By now, she bet that she could outrun a horse. Her senses had also gotten stronger. She could hear things from miles away and could even hear through walls and doors. She was also much stronger than she used to be and had to watch what she did. Her eyes were more sensitive to light, and she could now see almost better in the dark. She could also smell more things, knew where they came from, and exactly what they were. Her reflexes were also faster, much faster.

The changes weren't bad; she actually liked most of them, especially when she could sneak around and attempt to ditch Samuel, which never worked, by the way. But she felt her life had slowly changed within the past two days as well. She was still always watched day and night by Samuel, and sometimes another random guard took over for an hour or two a day, when Nyla supposed Samuel actually needed to eat or sleep. She did suspect that Samuel slept when she did, on her vanity chair by the door, but she was never really sure.

She had tried to talk him into moving to the couch the night before, but of course, he had refused, claiming that he "didn't need sleep." She had rolled her eyes at this remark but didn't push the issue further. He could sleep in a sitting position on her vanity chair every night if he wanted to for all she cared.

She hadn't trained since the accident, but at least she could get out for a walk every now and then. She had resumed her regular tutoring lessons from Jamin every day, but Kaden had stopped coming to them. The worst part was that she hadn't really seen Kaden since his little fight with Samuel a couple days before. She barely ever saw him at meals and only really saw him randomly in the hallway, but he never even talked to her and barely made eye contact. She didn't know why he was acting this way, but it hurt, and she longed to see him. She was worried. Kaden, her mother, Samuel, Julia, Fulcan, and Jamin, along with Martha, her maid, the council members, and her nurse were the only ones that knew what she was, but Kaden was the only one that refused to have any contact with her. *What if he doesn't like me anymore and won't talk to me ever again because of what I am?* She couldn't bear that thought and looked away from her reflection, erasing the thought from her mind. She caught the eye of the young guard standing just inside her bedroom door beside Samuel and gave him a glare.

"Excuse me," she said, turning toward him. "I know you're following orders, but do you really have to watch my every move? I do need some privacy, you know, or are you planning on helping me pick out my wardrobe, and going to the bathroom too?" The guard looked down, embarrassed, and Samuel tried to hide a smile. Nyla huffed a sigh.

"It's all right, I've got it from here." Samuel chuckled and opened the door for him, nudging the nervous guard out. "You don't have to be so mean, you know. He's just following your mother's orders."

"He was literally staring at me! Like, totally checking me out. It was creepy. It's a good thing he's only a couple years older than I am, or else I would feel even more violated. I know my body's changed, but have some self-control." She gawked at Samuel as he started to laugh. "What?"

"Vampires have a natural pull and lust to them, especially when they're already attractive. Not everyone can control themselves around you Nyla. Especially a horny guy like Nigel." Samuel leaned against the wall, crossing his arms.

"Did you just call me attractive?" Nyla grinned teasingly at Samuel and he looked away, grinning at the ground.

"Okay, now you're going to get a big head," Samuel teased and Nyla rolled her eyes and smiled.

"But seriously, couldn't you be my only guard? You're just fine without any other help. You're the head of the guard, and I don't think you'll mess up, and no offence, but having you as a twenty-four hour guard is enough, I don't need more."

"Ha! Oh, thanks." Samuel laughed.

"Besides, you seem to control yourself around me." Nyla clamped her mouth shut and blushed. She turned, so that Samuel wouldn't see her coloring face.

Samuel smiled but dismissed her last comment, not wanting to embarrass her. "Yes, I could probably be your only twenty-four hour guard, but your mother's just worried about you. Cut her a little slack."

"Okay, okay." She turned and went to her huge walk-in closet across from her bed in her bedchamber, shutting the door behind her before undressing. Samuel had been ordered to guard her at all times since the accident, and Nyla was surprised her mother even though she needed the head of the guard to watch her. She hadn't really known him before, except for when he hung out with Kaden, and was not happy at all to have a permanent "babysitter," but she was definitely warming up to him.

Samuel had joined the guard at age fifteen and he had come a long way, being the captain of the guard at only age twenty. She always had an odd feeling of comfort and strong trust around Samuel and felt like she knew him and could trust him almost as much as Kaden or Julia. She smiled. She used to be able to tell Julia and Kaden anything. She couldn't understand why he was the only one of her friends that had completely avoided her since their confrontation in the main courtyard of the castle, but Nyla couldn't really blame him. He despised all vampires. Nyla sighed, shifting aside dress after dress. Jordee, the royal scout, had arrived just a few days before and was sent straight to the infirmary wing to recover from heat exhaustion and fatigue. That night a celebration was to be held for his safe return. All the council members and their families were invited, and she wanted to look her best. She was also determined to speak to Kaden. Suddenly, there was a knock at her door.

"I'll get that. It's probably Martha." Nyla came out of the closet in only a thin, form-fitting slip.

"Nyla, get back into your closet!"

"Samuel, there's someone at the door, are you going to get that, or am I?" She took a step closer and then noticed that Samuel's eyes were closed. "What's with you?" Samuel took a deep breath.

"Nyla, please get back into your closet." He opened his eyes a bit and then quickly shut them again.

"But—"

"Nyla!" Samuel interjected. "Just because you think I can, as you say 'control myself' around you doesn't mean that I can keep my eyes to myself when you are literally wearing next to nothing."

"Oh!" Nyla's face turned beet red as she looked down at her half-naked body. "I apologize, I totally forgot! Don't answer that until I have something on!" She rushed back into her closet just as another knock sounded at the door. "Just a second!" she called, shifting through her dresses.

She decided with a pearly, light magenta–colored dress that hung low off of her slim shoulders. She completed it with necklace of small pink tinted pearls tied snugly around her neck. She heard a third knock on her bedroom door and came out of her closet, trying to ignore the approving stares from Samuel. He had always had the reputation of a flirt and his strikingly good looks, along with his amazing body, didn't ward off any girls either, but he had never been arrogant. Nyla had secretly always had a small crush on him but had avoided pursuing it. Because she was the princess and future queen of Galatia, Nyla could technically marry almost whomever she wanted, especially if that someone was close to the royal family, like the captain of the guard. However, because of all the girls Samuel tended to attract, Nyla had always felt like she didn't have a chance and had given up a long time ago. Plus, she wanted to attempt to pursue whatever kind of relationship she could have with Kaden. That was if he ever talked to her again or not. Before Nyla could reach the door, Martha, Queen Lydia's favorite nurse, burst into the room, followed closely by Julia.

"Must you always evade the poor girl's privacy?" The plump woman got in Samuel's face. "I know you are doing your duty, but really, she doesn't need a babysitter every second of the day, especially if you're not going to answer the door!"

"Martha! He's fine in here, and I told him not to answer the door, because I didn't have any clothes on." Nyla clamped her mouth shut and her face reddened again as Samuel's eyes widened. Julia gave Nyla a surprised look and Martha gasped.

"What were you doing in here, Nylina Galatianti?!" Martha gave Samuel a stern look.

"Oh my . . . Martha, it's not like that at all. I was getting dressed in my closet and . . . it's not like that!"

"Mhmmm." Martha gave Samuel a disbelieving glower and Nyla's face grew an even deeper shade of red. Martha waved her hands at Samuel. "Now, shoo, or I'll beat you with a brush! I think I can handle things from here." Nyla suppressed a giggle as Samuel gave her an alarmed, disoriented look and shot out the door. Martha turned toward Nyla with a stern, concerned look on her face.

"Martha, really, it's not—"

"I'll keep my mouth shut, dear. It's none of my business." She looked Nyla up and down. "Oh, dearie, you look just stunning!" Martha turned Nyla around in a slow circle to scrutinize her carefully. "Now what to do with that hair? Nothing too fancy. Oh! I know just the thing!" Nyla smiled, letting go of her embarrassment. Martha had been her mother's nurse back when she was a child and had then looked after Nyla when she was born. Despite her old age, Martha could still work her round fingers to create the prettiest hairstyles and always seemed to know just what to do. When she was done, Nyla's blond hair was in loose curls that cascaded down her back and just passed her waist. A simple band of the same pink tinted pearls were placed low on her head. She stepped back and examined herself in the mirror.

"Perfect!" Julia smiled, and Martha's wrinkled face shone with pride. Julia had been assigned to be Nyla's lady in waiting from when they were the age of twelve. They had immediately become great friends and Nyla could confide in Julia about anything. She didn't seem to care at all of what Nyla was, and she was glad. It was nice to have people that would be there for her no matter what, besides her mother anyway.

"You better be off to the main dining hall, dear. Come along." Martha turned and started to head toward the door.

"Um, Martha?" Nyla bit her lip. "Please don't embarrass Samuel any more than he already is. He really didn't do anything."

"Okay, dear." Martha still didn't look convinced, but she nodded her head as she opened the door, ushering Nyla and Julia out. They joined Samuel outside her door.

"Ladies"—he smiled at them—"don't you two look quite . . . stunning." His eyes widened as Martha eyed him suspiciously. Nyla cleared her throat and nodded at Martha, who glared one more time at Samuel before she left down the hallway.

"I'm sorry, Samuel. Martha can be a little overprotective."

"That's an understatement, I think." Samuel gave a cautious glance in the direction Martha had headed. He looked back at Nyla and smiled when she giggled at his nervousness. "Really, though, you do look beautiful." He smiled at Julia. "Both of you."

"Thanks, Samuel." Nyla smiled into his light-gray eyes and a heat rushed over her as it did to all the girls Samuel smiled at.

"You do know I look almost the same as I do every other day." Julia blushed.

"Yes, Julia, but you look a little less grungy today than usual." He grinned as Nyla playfully elbowed him.

"Okay, shoo." Julia shooed Samuel with her hands just as Martha had done. "I can escort Nyla to the great hall. We need some girl talk."

"Oh, that sounds like fun," Samuel joked sarcastically. "Maybe I should stick around."

"Hahaha." Nyla smiled, rolling her eyes at him. "Julia's got it, but thanks."

"If you say so." Samuel smiled at the two of them and turned around making his way toward the direction of the side entrance to the great hall.

"So," Julia began as soon as they were out of earshot of Samuel, "how's having Samuel as a personal guard? Personally, if I were you, I would just secretly stare at him the whole time. And just so you know, sometimes I catch him staring at you too."

Nyla laughed. "I'll take note of that, but I don't think so. Just . . . a guard thing. He takes his job seriously," Nyla said uncomfortably. She didn't want to think of other guys right now with Kaden rushing in and out of her mind.

"Okay," Julia said, but like Martha, she didn't look convinced. Nyla dismissed it with a shake of her head.

"You look rather nervous for a simple dinner party." Julia gave Nyla a wondering look and Nyla smiled.

"I'm planning on talking to Kaden again today. I'm just nervous."

"He'll come around." Julia put a hand on Nyla's slim shoulder. "After his fight with Samuel, I went up with him to his room and talked to him. He felt bad for the way things happened, although I don't think he felt bad for punching Samuel in the face, besides the regret for hurting himself. I really think he hurt his hand more than he hurt Samuel's face." Julia paused, relaying the scene in her mind. She looked back at Nyla. "He did tell me he felt bad. He'll come around. He is your best friend after all. Well, besides me." She gave Nyla an encouraging smile and winked. "Don't worry."

Nyla sighed. "I don't even know why I'm worried about this. Jordee fully recovered yesterday and we had a meeting in the council room. There are so many things that are far worse right now than my situation."

"I wish I could help in any way and give encouragement, but I just can't. I don't know what to say, war is so scary."

"Ya. Jordee told us Ridia has doubled its army in just a couple weeks. There have been outbreaks amongst the people and many are evacuating. They don't want to be caught up in another destructive war."

"Where are people running to?" Julia asked.

"All over. Many are fleeing into the Ieldra Forest. This is just getting to be too real."

"Well," Julia thought of the best thing to say, "we can only hope for the best I guess."

∞‍∞

Kaden stood outside the dining hall doors and took a deep breath. He hadn't spoken to Nyla or Samuel since their fight. He didn't care much about talking to Samuel at this point, but he did want to talk to Nyla. He was just nervous, but it wasn't because he was afraid of what she was, he didn't think. He sighed, slipping his hands into the pocket of his formal trousers. Suddenly he heard footsteps echoing from around the corner and he smoothed his clothes down. He sucked in a breath as he heard Nyla's familiar voice.

"I don't really know why this has to be such a big deal. With everything that's going on, I don't think that my upcoming birthday is that important. I . . ." She stopped short as she spotted Kaden staring at her from the dining hall doors.

Kaden looked down, feeling heat rush to his face. He had thought of a thousand things to say to Nyla, but now that she was standing right in front of him, his mind was blank.

"Excuse me, My Lady, Kaden." Julia shot him a small grin, respectfully bobbed her head, and turned back the way they had come to go into the side entrance to the great hall. Nyla slowly approached Kaden, an uneasy smile on her face. Kaden's heart pounded as he glanced down and then back up into Nyla's intense, crystal blue eyes as she came face-to-face with him, barely a foot apart. He opened his mouth to speak as the big wooden doors began to open before them.

Nyla tried to smile as she walked toward the main table in the middle of the dining hall. Her thoughts kept wandering back to Kaden. She could almost feel the heat radiating off him as he walked just a couple feet behind her.

Why hasn't he talked to me since the fight? Is he really afraid of me and doesn't want to accept me? She felt a pang in her chest. She hated the thought of Kaden fearing her for the rest of their lives. *What was he about to say right before the doors opened?*

Nyla politely nodded to the female member of the high council, Melrose, but she didn't even smile inwardly at the bouncy red hair that Nyla knew was a wig. It was hard to concentrate with thoughts of Kaden flooding her mind and the many smells wafting from the kitchen. Nyla could tell that her senses were quickly growing; she could perfectly smell the salty, rich sent of ham, mashed potatoes, and freshly baked bread. She sniffed the air again, her mouth watering as the smell of hot apple crisp pie filled her nostrils. Then she almost sneezed as a strong flowery perfume tickled her nose from somewhere around the room.

Somebody cleared their throat, and Nyla noticed that she was already at the table, Kaden holding out her chair. She sat down, looking up into his green eyes. He gave her that crooked smile and her heart skipped a beat. She longed to get him alone and talk to him about what happened; she just didn't know exactly what to say. What if her fears were correct and he couldn't stand to be around her? *But he did hold my chair out for me,* she reminded herself. That had to count for something.

Kaden pushed Nyla's chair in and sat across from her. He peeked at her across the table, but she was looking down, fidgeting with the silky material of her dress. He rubbed his palms against his trousers and thought of what to say and how to begin. He cleared this throat.

"Sooo," Kaden began but trailed off when Nyla looked at him with her clear blue eyes. He stared back, unable to grasp what to say next. *How lame,* he thought, smiling sheepishly. Nyla looked down and bit her lip. Her heart pounded.

"So?" She looked up at him from underneath long eyelashes.

"Listen, I . . ." He was cut off as trumpets sounded. The queen came in, followed by Fulcan and Samuel, then Jamin, and finally Jordee. Everyone stood as the queen approached her seat at the end of the table to the far left of where Nyla and Kaden sat. Kaden caught Samuel's eye, and it gave him a pang of anger, but he looked away.

He didn't want anything to ruin his mood. While they stood, waiting for the queen to take her seat, Kaden took in Nyla's appearance. She looked gorgeous in her light maroon dress that molded to her body and then flowed down from her mid-thigh. He wanted to walk straight over to her and take her in his arms, telling her how sorry he was for avoiding her the last couple of weeks. He felt horribly guilty. He couldn't imagine what Nyla must be going through. She had just found out that she was a vampire, her whole past was revealed to her, and she had learned the real truth behind her father's death. Then there was the part where he had deserted her.

Nyla caught Kaden staring at her and her cheeks flushed. Apparently she had picked the right thing to wear. She turned her face away, hiding behind a cascade of blond curls and smiled, but she was still unsure. She needed to talk to Kaden alone, only then would she be sure everything was all right. The queen came to stand beside her chair and grabbed her golden goblet.

"We are all so relieved that Jordee has made it back to us safely. He has had a long, hard journey and we owe him great thanks. He is a great man, and without him, we would be lost without the knowledge we now possess. To Jordee!" She raised her full cup in the air and took a sip.

"To Jordee!" the dining hall rang. Everyone sat and a steady chatter filled the dining hall as soft, festive music began from the small court band in the corner of the room. Samuel sat beside Nyla and she gave him a cheerful smile, ignoring Kaden's glare from across the table. She needed to talk to Kaden and try to get him to make up with Samuel, but right now her attention was caught by the smell of food. Great platters of food were set on every table and the people began to dig in, happy in the joyful atmosphere, the threatening war almost forgotten. Nyla listened to the many conversations taking place around her as she chewed a mouthful of ham and mashed potatoes. To her left, her mother was talking with Fulcan and Samuel about the training exercises and how things were going. Nyla sighed. She hadn't been able to train since her accident and she hoped that she could resume her training soon, although she would be a bit behind. However, she figured she could always ask Samuel to continue to train her.

She suddenly jumped as she heard a loud, shrieking laugh amplified in her ear from a large female guest across the room. She accidentally elbowed Jamin beside her, causing his small, round spectacles to go askew on his long nose. Fixing his spectacles, he gave her a look and slightly scooted his chair another inch or two away from hers. She mumbled a short apology and turned her face down, hiding a smile. She heard a soft, familiar snicker across from her and looked up, surprised. Kaden was looking at her with amusement on his face. *Oh, great,* she thought. She had managed to embarrass herself, but at least Kaden was smiling at her. She blushed but smiled back, relieved that at least some of the awkward tension had disappeared. She never felt this way around Kaden, but something was different somehow. She had been feeling it for weeks even before the riding incident and Nyla didn't know why. Her eyes glued to his flawless face. Why hadn't she ever felt this before?

Kaden and Nyla had always been close since the day they became friends, but they had been little kids then. As Nyla was growing up, she mainly hung out with the boys around the court, the girls were too gossipy for her, but she had never really taken a great interest in many of the boys she hung out with. She had never really had a real boyfriend before. Nyla first noticed a change a couple months ago on Kaden's nineteenth birthday. She had noticed how good he looked in the formal attire he wore to the party the court held for him, and how mature his face and body had become. His green eyes had suddenly become more intense, shining from underneath sexy, low-set eyebrows and long eyelashes.

Her gaze turned to his gorgeous lips. When Nyla was about twelve and Kaden thirteen, he had almost kissed her experimentally. Back then, it had just been playful; they stopped before their lips even met, and they laughed it off, but now Nyla wished she could touch his lips and soak in their taste. She felt a soft breath in her ear as Samuel turned his head toward her. It tickled and sent strange, pleasant chills down her neck.

"After dinner, I'm going to go over training with Fulcan for a bit. You'll be fine?" She nodded at him and looked into his eyes a second too long before she realized what she was doing. She quickly looked away, surprised at how quickly her attention was turned away from Kaden. She bit her lip, and her eyes flickered to Kaden's again. He had a slight frown on his face, but this time, when their eyes met, he didn't look away.

CHAPTER 7

Nyla stood on the huge balcony hanging off the dining hall. She leaned against the railing, looking out into the darkness. With her changing eyesight, she could almost see every detail perfectly. The balcony overlooked a huge garden. There was an elegant stone angel that stood atop a fountain, water flowing all around her. Around the black-and-gray-stoned path, rainbows of flowers bloomed in colorful patches. The white and yellow daisies, although simple, were her favorite, along with the small pink and purple flowers they called Shooting Stars that dotted the ground in random places. She loved how the daisies opened and closed with the sun, as if they were honoring it. They were a sign of love and devotion, and when the soldiers would go to war, they would wear strings of them around their necks as a symbol from their loved ones. Nyla loved flowers and she used to spend many hours reading books of poetry, or attempting to read one of the numerous textbooks Jamin had given her to study, amongst the garden flowers. Although she liked Samuel's company, she was almost never alone and didn't get much opportunity to have that time to herself anymore.

She decided that she would start to read there amongst the company of the flowers again, even if she needed to ask Samuel to give her space from a different bench, which she knew he would do. Nyla sighed, looking at the full moon. The last couple of nights she had been tempted to sneak out of her bedroom window to be alone, even if Samuel was there sleeping on her chair. She was sure that she could make the nearly two-story jump to the ground, but the thought scared her. She was fine with sneaking out; she had done it numerous times with Kaden before, but she didn't want to have to sneak out at night just to get outside by herself for a while.

"Is this what I am to become? Some kind of animal, sneaking about at night?" she wondered aloud. She closed her eyes as the faintly chilled breeze, signaling autumn, softly tousled her long blond hair.

Kaden stood leaning against one of the columns opening to the balcony. He readied himself as he watched Nyla's back at the balcony railing. He studied the way her blond curls cascaded down her back, stopping just below her hips. His gaze lingered on the smooth curves of her waist and down her hips. He ran his hand through his hair, taking a deep breath, and slowly made his way toward her.

"Nyla?" Kaden said softly. Nyla turned her head, startled, and gave a small smile as Kaden came to stand beside her. She kept one hand on the balcony railing as she turned to face him. Kaden hesitated, thinking of what to say. "I, um . . . Would you like to take a walk with me?"

"Sure. In the garden?" Nyla gave him a soft smile and made her way to the winding steps on the right side of the balcony that led into the garden.

They walked silently side by side, making their way down the gray stoned path. Nyla let her hand hang loose, softly touching the tips of the flowers with her fingertips as they passed by. Kaden looked down at her other hand at her side. He longed to take her hand and hold it in his. They stopped at the fountain and he looked up at the stone angel's peaceful face. As a boy, Kaden had once heard a tale that the statue was once an angel sent to Earth from Heaven to protect the people from evil. She befriended the faithful, noble royals of Galatia and aided them in a giant, ancient war. Once her deeds were done, she turned to stone to be a guardian angel over all of Galatia. This legend gave him sudden comfort, as if the angel was urging Kaden on, and he took a deep breath.

"Nyla." Kaden took her soft hand in his and looked in her eyes, stopping her heart with his emerald gaze.

"Kaden." Nyla stared back, barely able to breath. "What happened with the fight with Samuel? Why did you stop talking to me and why did you just run out on me the other day in the dining hall? It seems like you're avoiding me."

"I . . . I haven't been avoiding you." Nyla gave him a disbelieving look. "Okay, maybe I have, but . . . it's not what you think." He looked down at their intertwined hands and realized he had held hers tighter with each word. He loosened his grip, preparing what he was going to say. He couldn't possibly tell Nyla what he had been feeling. She would be hurt and there was no point in telling her. He was going to work through his issues somehow. "I . . ." He struggled to find the right words.

"Are you really afraid of me?" Kaden looked up and winced as Nyla's expression turned to pain.

"No! No, I'm not afraid of you," he blurted. He took both of her hands now, desperate to reassure her.

"Well then, why won't you talk to me, or barely even look at me? I felt like you completely abandoned me." This time, Nyla looked down at their hands.

Kaden's heart nearly stopped. No matter what he had felt about her being a vampire, he had abandoned her, especially when she needed him the most. "Wow, I'm an ass," he said aloud.

Nyla looked up at him, startled. "I'm so sorry, Nyla, I didn't want to make you feel that way. I was just processing everything and I had to work out my own issues my way."

"It's . . . fine." Nyla shrugged and looked away again.

"No. It's not fine. Nyla, I was just scared." A sudden pain cut through Nyla's heart. *So he is scared of me.* Almost reading Nyla's thoughts, Kaden lifted his hand and tipped Nyla's chin up with his finger.

"I'm not scared of you." He looked into her big, crystal blue eyes. "It was just a lot to handle."

"And the fight with Samuel? What's going on with you two?"

"Samuel made me furious the other day. He's been my friend all this time and he kept such a big secret from me, and from you." Kaden sighed. "I lost control."

Nyla nodded. "Kaden, don't blame Samuel. It's not his fault he didn't tell you. He swore an oath of secrecy to my mother and he couldn't tell you. Please, you have to talk to him and set things straight."

"I really wish you wouldn't defend him." Kaden frowned but then sighed, letting it go. "I don't want to talk about Samuel right now." Kaden looked away. "Nyla, I didn't know what to say to you in the dining hall that day, or in the hallway since then. I didn't want to say anything stupid." He paused. He drew in a shaky breath, the memory of that horrible day flashing through his mind. "And I was so scared, Nyla. I couldn't do anything to help you. You looked like you were so terrified and in pain and there I stood helpless. I hate that feeling. I'm supposed to always be there for you and protect you no matter what. And . . ."

"And what?" Nyla barely breathed as she stared back into Kaden's eyes. They were so close she could feel Kaden's breath on her face. She was suddenly aware of the quick pounding of Kaden's heartbeat. "And what?" she softly said again.

Kaden took a deep breath. "And at that moment, when I was carrying you back to the horses and to the castle . . . When I was hoping, you would make it through and I wouldn't lose you . . . I realized . . . how I felt about you. Nyla, I always want to be there for you, I don't want to just be your friend."

Nyla's eyes grew wide and her heart pounded gleefully in her chest. She tried to contain the grin that threatened to consume her face and managed a sweet, small smile. She barely dared to breathe as she leaned in. That familiar crooked smile lit up Kaden's handsome face as he leaned toward her, almost closing the few inches between their faces.

"Nyla?" Julia's voice was heard in the distance. Startled, Nyla and Kaden snapped their heads in the direction of the sound. "Princess Nylina?!" She was coming closer.

"Um . . ." Nyla looked back at Kaden.

"We should go," Kaden whispered, letting go of her hand.

"Okay." Nyla tried not to show the disappointment on her face.

"Nyla?" She could hear Julia's footsteps coming closer.

"Yes? I'm here!" Nyla passed Kaden and was about to step out of the shadows.

"Wait!" He grabbed Nyla and leaned in, giving her a soft peck on the cheek. He drew back and grinned at the smile on her face.

"Nyla." Julia stepped around the big rose bush by the fountain. Nyla gave Kaden a grin and turned toward Julia.

"Julia. We were just taking a walk through the garden. Is something wrong?"

"There's a disturbance at the main gate. The queen requests your presence on the west tower immediately. Kaden, you are to meet Fulcan and Samuel by the main gate."

⌘

"Mother? What is it?" Nyla strode up the last few steps of the tower and came to her mother's side on the balcony. She looked down into the darkness and spotted a group of people approaching the castle gates on horseback. "Were we ever notified of anyone coming to Galatia?"

"It's a small party. We weren't expecting any visitors, but Fulcan said they seem pretty harmless. Just a few travelers seeking refuge."

"Are those draft horses?" Nyla hesitated, looking closely at the sturdy horses. "Mother, these people are from Ridia. They are wearing the king's mark."

"You can see that in the dark?" Lydia looked at Nyla in surprise.

"Yes." Nyla looked down. "I can see them as clear as day."

Lydia stared at Nyla for a moment then looked back into the darkness. She huffed a sigh. "Well, that does change things a bit." She turned to Nyla, trying to hide the worried look on her face. "We have to warn Fulcan and the others before they open the gate." She began to walk toward the spiral staircase at the tower's entrance.

"But what if they aren't dangerous?" Nyla strode after her mother. "Jordee said there were going to be many people trying to get out of Ridia before they get caught up in a war. Maybe these people are just seeking refuge."

The queen hesitated, contemplating her daughter's words. "Well, let's go and join Fulcan at the main gate. We'll see for ourselves just what these people are up to."

Nyla listened to their footsteps reverberate off of the walls all around them as they made their way to the main gate. Her mind was filled with jumbled thoughts of Kaden, the possible upcoming war, and now the newcomers at the gate. As they entered the main courtyard, the gate was still closed and they heard Fulcan's voice from the top of the wall.

"Who are you and where do you come from?" Fulcan called down to the party.

"We are humble travelers from the kingdom of Ridia," a man's voice answered. "We are seeking refuge from the pointless, upcoming war."

"Stay here," Lydia told Nyla as she made her way up the stone steps to take her place beside Fulcan and Samuel. Nyla spotted Kaden standing with Jamin, Jordee, and a couple of armed guards. She joined them, coming up beside Kaden.

"Why would you come to Galatia when it is common knowledge that Galatia and Ridia are mortal enemies?" Lydia looked down upon the travelers that were now lit up by torchlight.

"We couldn't stay in Ridia any longer. We had to get away from the merciless king and his new second, Rothgar."

Nyla's heart leapt in her chest and a dread surged through her body. She looked at Kaden, whose face had transformed from seriousness to a sudden hatred and a ferocity Nyla had never seen on Kaden's face. Nyla could hear the party's horses on the other side of the wall. She closed her eyes and listened closer to the newcomers' breathing and their heartbeats. She opened her eyes and almost ran up the steps toward her mother, Fulcan, and Samuel where they stood with their heads close together in an intense discussion. Lydia looked up at Nyla and straightened, an unreadable expression on her face.

"They're telling the truth," Nyla said. "I can hear their heartbeats and sense their emotions. They're telling the truth." She caught Samuel's eye and he gave her a small smile.

The voice from below spoke again. "We only need refuge. In return we offer information and our help." Fulcan looked at the queen, and then at Samuel, who nodded in agreement.

"Let them in," Fulcan announced.

The queen nodded. "Let them in."

There was a squealing groan as the gate slowly creaked open. Nyla made her way down the steps followed closely by Samuel, the queen, and Fulcan, just as the travelers entered through the gate. The party was led by a tall, thin man perched high on a black stallion. His long, dark hair blew slightly in the breeze and Nyla shivered as his cold, silver stare swept over her. He was wearing armor and a war tunic the green and black colors of Ridia's kingdom. With a closer look, Nyla noticed that instead of an attacking bear, there was a black wolf embroidered across his chest. A young man and woman followed him. The last was another young man. He kept his head down, nearly hiding his face beneath the drawn up hood of his black cloak. He suddenly looked up, gazing into Nyla's blue stare with his deep emerald eyes. His stare was intense and made Nyla feel uncomfortable and vulnerable and she looked away, shifting closer to Samuel standing beside her.

"Your majesty, Queen Lydia." The leader jumped off of his horse, walking toward the queen with a polite smile. "My name is Lamar." He held out his hand.

"Lamar." Lydia ignored his hand and he let it hang against his side. She eyed the others as they dismounted their horses and came to stand beside Lamar. Lamar cleared his throat.

"This is Felix." He motioned to the young man on his left. He had blond hair that hung to his shoulders and gold, yellow eyes that looked so inhuman he could have been an animal. "The young lady next to him is his sister, Adrian." The two were so alike with their blond hair and gold, animalistic eyes that Nyla guessed they were twins. "And this is Lucas." Nyla didn't even dare to look at the young man on Lamar's right. His intense emerald stare had been trained on her since the moment they walked through the gate. He took down his hood, and Nyla glanced at him taking in his short, spiky, dark chestnut-brown hair.

"Welcome." The queen gave a small cautious smile. "This is Fulcan, my top commander, Jamin, my advisor, and Samuel, the head of the guard. Beside me are the gentleman Kaden, and my daughter, Princess Nylina."

"My lady." Lamar bowed his head to Nyla and she nodded in acknowledgment.

"Why have you come?" Fulcan stepped forward now, looking Lamar straight in the eye.

"As I said, we are trying to get away from Ridia and the king's coldness. You have no idea what they are doing to the people."

"Yes, you did say that, but why have to come to seek refuge in Galatia?"

"Well," Lamar seemed to consider his next words, "Galatia is Ridia's biggest enemy, of course. We've wanted to be rid of Ridia for years."

"Why do you wear battle attire in the king's colors, and his new emblem no doubt?" Lydia kept her head high, eyeing Lamar.

Lamar didn't even blink, keeping eye contact with Lydia. "Yes, I was in Ridia's army, a part of the first infantry, actually." Fulcan and Samuel tightened their grip on their swords, but Lydia motioned for them to calm.

Lamar cleared his throat, his eyes now on Fulcan. "King Gafna is brutal and vicious. He's more of a coward than a leader. We'd rather be a part of a merciful and kind, but strong kingdom than one that's destined to fall apart."

"So"—the queen took a step forward—"you've come to betray your kingdom. How do we know we can trust you when you are already traitors?"

"You are a smart and great queen, Your Majesty. We have much information to bring you about Ridia's plans in exchange for refuge."

"Is it true that Rothgar has joined Gafna and combined their armies?" She squinted at Lamar, searching for any sign of a lie.

"Yes, it is true." Nobody spoke and Nyla closed her eyes again, listening to the soft, even pounding of the newcomers' hearts. The queen glanced at Nyla and she nodded to her mother.

"Very well." Lydia beckoned to the party. "Come, it's late. Get some rest. We will talk in the morning. Fulcan"—she motioned for him to come closer and spoke to him in a hushed tone so the newcomers couldn't hear—"let them stay in a couple of the rooms on the second floor of the west wing. They are high enough off the ground to keep them trapped if needed and far enough from our quarters to not cause any harm." She turned to Samuel. "Station guards outside their rooms so we can keep a close eye on them."

"Yes, Your Majesty." Samuel nodded. He beckoned at a couple guards to follow Fulcan. Fulcan dipped his head at the queen and motioned for the newcomers to follow.

"Thank you, My Queen. We are forever in your debt." Lamar bowed his head as he followed Fulcan and a couple of Samuel's guards into the castle. After they were out of earshot, the queen spoke to Nyla, Samuel, and Kaden in hushed tones.

"It's worth a shot letting them in. Maybe we can get more information out of them." She turned to Nyla. "They seem calm and trustworthy?"

"Yes, I could hear their heartbeats and sense their emotions. It's still too early to tell, but it doesn't seem like they mean any harm to us. They might be telling the truth."

"Well, we'll see. However, for the time being, I want neither of you to go anywhere alone." She pointed to Nyla and Kaden. "Don't go anywhere with them unless you are with a guard and you have my, Fulcan's, or Samuel's permission." She looked Nyla in the eyes. "Under no circumstances can they find out what you are. The last thing we need is putting you in any danger until we figure this thing out." She turned to Samuel. "Double your guard." He went to nod, but Nyla interjected.

"Samuel is just fine guarding me himself, Mother. Please, no more guards." She looked at her mother pleadingly. The queen looked at Samuel, who nodded.

"It's your call, Your Majesty." He shrugged and Nyla shot him a look. The queen looked at her daughter.

"Fine." She gave Nyla a stern look. "But please, be extra careful."

"I will, Mother," Nyla agreed.

"Come on, let's get some rest." The queen turned, satisfied.

"Yes, Mother." Nyla kept her head down as they entered the castle. She felt like more of a burden than ever. The queen gave her a quick kiss on the forehead and bid her good night before heading down the hallway. As soon as she was out of earshot, Nyla turned to Samuel.

"It's your call, Your Majesty?" she mocked him, a frown on her face. "What are you doing? You know I hate being guarded and you are more than fine with guarding me yourself." She put her hands on her hips.

"Hey." Samuel held up his hands in surrender. "Your mother is the queen."

"I don't care!" Nyla shot off. She glowered at Samuel. "Samuel, my room is crowded enough with just you and I sleeping in there. I don't think anybody else needs to join in!" Nyla paused and blushed, hearing the words in her head. Samuel tried not to smile, making Nyla blush more. Kaden cleared his throat, and Nyla remembered that he was standing behind her. She composed herself and turned toward him. She rolled her eyes as Kaden glared silently at Samuel, obviously uncomfortable with the conversation. He turned back to Nyla, putting on a smile.

"I'll see you tomorrow, okay?" He stepped closer, enjoying how uncomfortable Samuel looked standing behind Nyla. "Good night, Nyla." He leaned in and gave Nyla a kiss on the cheek. Her body stilled in surprise as his lips lingered a second longer than necessary.

"Night," she mumbled, disoriented. He stepped back and a flicker of annoyance sparked in her when Kaden grinned at Samuel triumphantly. She watched him leave, conflicting emotions battling in her mind. *Did he really just kiss me because Samuel is standing there? Why is it such a competition as to whom is a better friend to me?* Shaking her head, she turned back to Samuel. He smiled at her.

"Should we head up?" He nodded his head toward the stairs.

"Yes"—Nyla started walking—"but our conversation isn't over. As I was saying before, you should be on my side. My mom's the queen, but I'm the princess, and you're guarding me." She looked at him expectantly, hoping he saw her logic.

"Yes, I do guard you. However," Nyla rolled her eyes at his extra emphasis on the word, "she's your mother. As long as she's the queen, she technically does overrule you."

"Ah, fine." She crossed her arms grumpily.

Samuel laughed. "Sorry, but that's just the way it works."

Nyla gave him a half-serious glare and continued walking. A small smile spread across her lips as she rounded the corner, spotting Julia waiting outside her bedroom door. After the crazy events of the day, she desperately needed someone to confide in. She turned to Samuel.

"Sorry, but you get to stay outside the room tonight . . . but you can still use my chair if you want. I know how much you secretly love it," she teased.

"Oh, thanks!" Samuel rolled his eyes, smiling.

CHAPTER 8

"So he finally told you how he felt!" Julia clapped her hands in joy, rocking back slightly on Nyla's gigantic bed. "I just love fairytale true love."

"Oh, Julia, you're such a silly romantic. And overdramatic by the way." Nyla sat on the stool at her large golden vanity, combing her fingers through her hair. She caught Julia's brown eyes in the mirror and spun around on the stool. "It's definitely too early to tell if it's 'true love.'"

"Okay, well, why wouldn't it be? The tragic story of a young boy who lost his family, but is brought in by a kind queen and her beautiful young daughter. They become close, doing almost everything together, until one day they fall madly in love, knowing all along it was meant to be." Julia grinned proudly and Nyla couldn't hide her own smile. "You'll know it's true love when you share his bed." Julia added with a giggle.

"Oh my goodness, Julia!" Nyla got up, picked up a pillow from her couch, and tossed it at Julia.

"Hey!" Julia squealed as the pillow hit her square in the face.

"I haven't even kissed the guy and you're already talking about me sleeping with him?!" Nyla laughed.

"That's right, he'll be you're first kiss too! How romantic!" Julia squealed. Nyla picked up another pillow and Julia put her hands up in surrender. She laughed. "I say give it a shot." Julia giggled and got up, heading toward the door. "Well, I better get to bed."

"Actually, I was hoping you could stay here and we could have a sleepover like we used too. You could stay on my couch, or whatever."

"It's okay, I can have Samuel walk me back." Julia winked at Nyla and she rolled her eyes with a grin.

Nyla hesitated. "I just don't really want you sleeping in your room by yourself with all that's going on right now."

"Oh . . ." Julia turned, now serious as she slowly went back to sit on the bed. "What do you think about them? Do you really think that they are telling the truth? Their story is kind of suspicious, isn't it?"

"Well," Nyla sat across from Julia, "it is kind of coincidental that they happen to show up right as there is a war brewing, but I'm not sure. I mean, I could almost feel every feeling out there in the courtyard. It was like they were confident on everything that they were saying. So I don't know, I mean I don't exactly have a handle on this thing, but they seemed okay. My mother agrees that we can't trust them yet. She doesn't even want any of us walking around the castle or the grounds by ourselves. I guess we can't be too sure why they are here just yet."

"Right. I just hope they are who they say they are. I hate all this talk of war." Julia brought her knees up to her chest, hugging them tightly, silently thinking to herself. "So you could really hear their heartbeats and sense exactly what their emotions were?"

Nyla drew in a breath. "Yes. It's really crazy, but at the same time kind of fun, you know? It was so exhilarating to hear their hearts pounding, and breathe in their emotions. Lamar was so proud, almost arrogant. Like he was so impressed with himself for betraying King Gafna, or something." She paused. "Except for the dark, brown-haired boy, Lucas." She said his name wonderingly. "His feelings were hard to sense. It was almost fear, or nervousness, but wonder and hatred at the same time." She looked at Julia. "That sounds weird, doesn't it? I don't know it was probably nothing, like I said I don't quite know how to control everything yet." She gave a small laugh.

"Um," Julia hesitated, "how are you feeling, Nyla? I mean, are you doing okay with, you know, what's going on with you right now?" It irritated Nyla when people tried to wander around the word. Why didn't they just come right out and say it. Yes, she was half vampire and there was nothing anyone could say or do about it. She shook it off, though, needing to talk to her best friend.

"I'm all right. Yes, it's a little scary, just because I don't know exactly what's still going to happen. Jamin said that I'm kind of still in mid-transformation, so we still don't know what all I will be able to do yet. I guess he asked my mother if it was okay that he teaches me things about Vampirism that I can't really learn from everyone else. Apparently my father let Jamin study him a lot and now has some kind of a journal with all the information he learned. I guess it's good for me because I can learn things about my father, and myself, and at the same time Jamin gets to sort of study me in a way. I guess that as far as any history books go nobody has ever heard of a half human half vampire hybrid." Nyla managed a small smile, trying to show Julia she wasn't worried. However, the thought of not knowing exactly what she was turning into terrified her. Then there was what happened the other night with her eyes, but she wasn't going to reveal that to anyone! It was just between her and Samuel.

"Okay. That's good." Julia gave her a small smile, failing an attempt at hiding her sympathy and worry.

"Really, it's not that big of a deal." Nyla got up, pacing in front of the bed. "So far, everything has been good, so I'm actually excited to have lessons with Jamin. So . . . ya." She sat down again but didn't face Julia. "Plus," she added, trying to add light to the subject. "Kaden is talking to me again, and right now, that's all I care about."

"Good. I'm supporting you all the way. I'm not going to leave you now. So whatever you need, I'm there." Julia had obviously missed the Kaden part. "Just, be careful. Okay? With all that's happening and now the newcomers, we can't be too careful."

"Right." Nyla sighed. "Well, I'm tired. Let's go to sleep." She helped Julia pile rich blankets and pillows onto her lush couch and settled into her own bed.

∞∞∞

Nyla stared up at the maroon canopy over her bed. Julia had asked if she could sleep on Nyla's couch like she had the night before and Nyla didn't protest. She liked Julia's company and felt safer for Julia's safety when she was here, especially because Samuel could guard them both this way. She tilted her head toward the balcony doors, seeing a faint line of light blue starting to rise on the horizon. She had been lying awake all night, like most nights the past couple days, and her thoughts were racing around in her head from the recent events, bumping into each other. *Are Kaden and I really meant to be together like Julia had suggested? Will I inherit all my father's vampire traits, or just some of them? And what about that boy, Lucas? He seemed so mysterious.* And then there was the new problem that they had thrust upon them. Her thoughts turned to earlier that day.

Nyla was walking through the stone hallways of the castle with Samuel following dutifully behind her. She turned and walked down the winding staircase to the second floor where the west wing of the great library was. She reached the huge oak doors and thanked Samuel as he opened them for her. Jamin stood in his normal spot at the big oval table that sat on the balcony of second level. This is where they always had lessons, but it felt different this time. Nyla was actually excited for her time with Jamin now that she was learning more about her father and herself. Jamin looked down at her at the sound of the closing doors, still managing to peer over his tiny spectacles.

"No lesson today, Nyla, there's been a change of plans. You and Samuel are to meet your mother in the council room." He looked upset for not being able to study his new 'patient' and Nyla was surprised that she was upset as well. She hoped that being excited for classes wasn't going to become too much of a habit. He looked down at her again.

"Go on, you better get going. Your mother is waiting for you. I'll be along shortly. Kaden's already there." With those words, Nyla's disappointment disappeared and she spun around, so eager to get to the council room that she barely waited for Samuel to open the door for her before she shot out of it, walking hastily down the hall. When she had gotten into the council room, she found her mother, Kaden, Fulcan, and a few others standing around the table in conversation.

"Nylina, Samuel." Her mother smiled to her as she made her way to the table. "We were just discussing this morning's events with Kaden." Lydia, Fulcan, and Samuel had talked to Lamar and the others alone that morning. Nyla had wanted to be there, but the queen had insisted that she wait. No matter how much she asked, Samuel hadn't told her

much, because her mother had asked to tell her herself, so he was no help to her for information either.

"After talking with Lamar this morning, we have decided that they are giving us pretty good reason to trust them. They gave us more information than we hoped for. Gafna and Rothgar have been building an army like Jordee said, but it's far worse than we expected. They have been gathering everyone they can throughout Ridia and the surrounding lands, taking males, above the age of ten and forcing them to join Ridia's army. They have been attacking the nearest villages and they are planning an attack on Galatia."

Nyla expected this much from the gruesome king. "Well, we have the biggest military in the land. We can handle them as long as they stay beyond our walls. Didn't we send a scout to Genea to request a meeting for their help?" The queen nodded, but her face was solemn.

"Nyla, they are making an army of werewolves." Fulcan could barely hide the worry behind his expressionless face.

"What?" Nyla could barely believe her ears, "But . . . how could this happen?"

"Somehow Gafna got Rothgar to join him, promising fortune, safety, and a kingdom of his own . . ." Samuel trailed off, going to stand beside Fulcan. Nyla looked at him questioningly.

The queen took a shallow breath. "Gafna agreed that if Rothgar helped him to conquer our kingdom, he could take the thrown and have Galatia all to himself. The wolves would rule this land."

This time, Kaden spoke. "Yes, but what Gafna obviously fails to realize is that once Rothgar takes this kingdom, he'll turn right around on Ridia, claiming his kingdom as well."

"So what are we going to do? We have to make preparations, build a bigger army of our own." Nyla started to pace the room, "But how? Even if we draft all the able men in Galatia, we still might not have enough to go up against the wolves. We definitely cannot stoop to Gafna's level and recruit little boys. The thought of it makes me sick." She stopped pacing and returned to face her mother at the table as a thought crossed her mind. "What if . . . would the vampires—"

"Absolutely not!" Fulcan cut her off, his face in a ferocious frown. "Never again will we ever trust those beasts! They are nothing but monsters, pretty much every single one of them!"

"Fulcan!" Lydia scowled at him, and he quickly looked at Nyla in shock. "I'm sorry, Your Highness, I forgot my place. I didn't mean to . . ."

"It's no matter." Nyla's heart stung at his harsh words, reminding her of the "monster" she was quickly becoming. She turned to her mother again, clearly trying to dismiss Fulcan's fallacy. Lydia looked at Nyla for a moment, considering her words.

"No, Nyla. I'm afraid we cannot ask Vallira for her help. It's not an option right now."

"Well, what other choice do we have? We have to figure something out and fast."

"Yes, we know. It is just a lot to decide right now. We'll find a way. We'll defeat them somehow. We have too."

Samuel cleared his throat. "In the meantime, your mother has requested that we assigned you more escort permanently." Nyla's head snapped toward the queen in protest, but the queen shook her head.

"With what's going on right now and Lamar and his group showing up, we can't take too many chances. You will continue your day as you normally would, but Kristi and Dominic will join Samuel in guarding you." She beckoned to the other two guards in the room and Nyla realized she had forgotten they had ever been standing there. Kristi, a girl with short, dirty-blond hair that was always in a bun, was about Nyla's age and a pretty good fighter, having joined Galatia's army when she was only fifteen. The other man, Dominic, had buzzed black hair and the fierceness with which he fought matched his rugged, somewhat barbaric looks. He was the older than Samuel at about twenty-two or so. Nyla figured her mother chose guards so close to her age to bond with her and warm her up to the idea of more guards watching her like a caged mouse. Even Samuel was only twenty.

Nyla looked at Samuel and he gave her an insistent look, asking her not to argue with her mother. Nyla's brows furrowed, but she didn't object to this idea, although she hated the thought of being watched by not just one, but three pairs of eyes day and night. With all that her mother had to deal with, at least she wouldn't be worrying about Nyla's safety.

Nyla sighed, the thoughts of her knew escort reminding her that two of them were right outside her door. Dominic and Kristi took turns, but Samuel always stayed. He normally would have stayed inside the room, with the other guard outside the door, but since Julia was spending the night there, he wanted to give them privacy. Nyla threw off her covers and got out of bed. She didn't even notice the cold, hardwood floor as she walked to her bathroom and put on her deep red, velvet robe over her silky nightgown. Although she no longer felt the chilly cold of the approaching autumn nights, it was a habit to cover up the short, thin material. She stopped, listening for sounds outside her door. All she could hear was the even breathing of Samuel, and a guard she guessed was Dominic. She smiled, listening to Samuel breathe and was surprised she could even recognize what his breathing sounded like. She walked silently past Julia and smiled at her best friend, sound asleep, and continued toward the double glass doors opening to the balcony. She had recently taken on the habit of always keeping the right door slightly ajar, letting the faint aroma of the garden flowers waft in from below. These were the things she liked about her transforming body.

Nyla came to the balcony, resting her hands on the smooth marble and looked into the darkness below. She spotted a guard making his rounds at the edge of the garden, but he would never detect her. She hadn't snuck out of her chambers in a while, not since Samuel had started to guard her, but tonight she needed to get out. She had been feeling caged inside lately, and was becoming claustrophobic. She was irritated that her mother felt so strongly that Nyla couldn't handle herself.

She peered over her shoulder to where Julia was still passed out and looked forward again, taking a deep breath. She was feeling unusually fearless tonight and wanted to try something. In one quick movement, Nyla grabbed the balcony with one hand, swung her legs over the edge, and was hurtling down toward the ground. The ground rushed up from below her and she landed in an easy crouch on the earth. She smiled, feeling the soft green grass beneath her bare feet and stifled an exhilarated laugh. The blood pumped fast through her veins and her heart rushed. She felt the adrenaline and took off in a sprint, zipping past the rows of colorful flowers. Her footsteps and movements made no sound at all; it was as if she turned into a ghost. She came to a sudden halt by the tall, wall like rosebushes lining the path that lead to the center of the garden where the stone angel took her watch. She heard footsteps and crouched, scooting into the shadows of the rose bushes.

She saw the source of the footsteps walk past the path she was on. She couldn't make out who it was until she noticed the long, black cloak and the hood hiding the young man's face. It was Lucas. Her heart did a small flip. *What is he doing out here?* Staying low in the shadows, she followed Lucas through the remaining rose bush path and stopped when he reached the fountain. Lucas looked up at the moon. It was three-quarters full, lighting up the night sky. She followed his gaze up to the moon; it was almost calling her, a true daughter of the night. She wanted to join Lucas and bathe in the moon's light, but she came to her senses. *What am I thinking?* She didn't even know, or trust this boy for that matter. She could just sense something odd about him. The way he was holding his arms out, letting the moonlight light up his face, made it seem like the moon was embracing him. He tilted his head back, whispering something to the sky, but she couldn't concentrate enough to hear what it was. She started to move forward to get closer when she heard a noise behind her in the distance. One of the guards on duty must be coming their way. She looked back toward the fountain, but Lucas had mysteriously disappeared. Not wanting to get discovered and in deep trouble, Nyla turned and smacked right into a muscled body. She looked up, wincing as she recognized Samuel's stern face.

"Nyla," he said calmly, "what are you doing?"

"Um . . ." Nyla tightened her robe around her, searching her mind for an answer. "I, um . . . I was just enjoying a nice walk. Yep . . ."

"Well, I know that you think you can handle yourself, but it is still dangerous sneaking out here by yourself in the middle of the night."

"I wasn't sneaking! I was . . ."

He gave her a look.

"Okay, I was sneaking out, but hey, you have no idea how nice it is to have some alone time to myself. I feel like a caged bird!" She strode past him, making her way back in the direction of her balcony.

"I understand," Samuel followed her. "But, Nyla, it would really make me feel better if at least I was with you."

"Samuel, like you said, I can handle myself."

"I said you think you can handle yourself. Okay, the point is you may be able to handle yourself against other people, but can you protect others from yourself?" Nyla stopped in her tracks, Samuel never said anything to make her feel dangerous and out of control. "Nyla, I know about the hunger that vampires can get and it can be dangerous. I just want you to be careful."

She spun toward him. "I will be careful! I would never hurt anyone! How could you not know that?" She turned, but Samuel grabbed hold of her arm.

"Wait. Nyla, I know that you would never purposely hurt any-one, I do. It's just, for your safety, just no more sneaking out please?" He looked her in the eyes.

"Okay." She sighed and he let go of her arm, leaving the spot he had touched her tingling with a strange warmth. "No more sneaking out."

"Thank you. Now, you better get your rest, it's getting late." He put his arm gently to the small of her back and began to steer her toward the castle.

"When do you even sleep?" she asked him, not resisting his touch on her back.

He chuckled. "Oh, I have my ways."

Nyla smiled, nodding her head. "Are you really going to make me walk all the way back to my room?" He nodded his head. "In my pajamas?" she continued. Samuel took in the short robe that just barely hid her figure. He looked forward and breathed slowly through his nose.

"Yep." He nodded. "It would make me feel better that way, plus we are going to the same place."

"I could just sprint to my window and jump up onto the bal-cony. It's really easy."

"What if someone saw you do that?"

Nyla ignored his remark and continued. "We wouldn't have to walk through the castle together with the chance of meeting people in the hallway that may get the wrong idea. God forbid Martha hears that you and I were outside together, in the middle of the night, with me in nothing but a skimpy nightgown and a robe. I'm just saying that it might give people the wrong impression is all." Nyla looked hopefully at him, smiling as Samuel thought this through.

"Well, I guess we'll just have to sneak around and not let anyone see us then, won't we?"

"Now, that would make people get the wrong impression even more. We'd become the castles biggest scandal." Nyla raised her eyebrows at him.

"Nyla . . ."

"I'm not going to win this, am I?" Nyla looked defeated.

"Nope." Samuel gave her a grin. Nyla gulped as they reached the steps where two guards stood. She grabbed Samuel's arm and turned him to face her.

"How are we going to get in without them seeing us?" She gave him a begging look, widening her eyes in an attempt to make herself look extra cute.

"This is your punishment for sneaking out on us." Samuel grinned and she squinted her eyes at him. He laughed. "Nyla, I'm joking. It will be fine. They will not say anything to anyone. I am their captain and they know not to spread rumors about me." He started to walk toward the guards and Nyla reluctantly followed, trying to hide herself behind him. As they passed, the guards looked from Samuel to Nyla.

"Gentlemen." He nodded at them and the guard on the left raised his eyebrows as he took in Nyla's attire, the hint of a smile playing at his lips. Samuel cleared his throat and squinted at him, and he composed his face.

"Captain." The two guards nodded at Samuel and tried to keep their eyes forward as Samuel and Nyla entered the castle doors.

"Oh my gosh." Nyla turned to Samuel when the doors were shut. "Okay, that's not happening again. We avoid people, okay?"

"You don't want to be seen with me?" Samuel asked innocently.

"What? I don't care if I'm seen with you. I didn't mean it like that. I just—"

"I'm joking, Nyla. I know what you meant." Samuel gave her a smile and they started walking.

Even after having to hide a couple of times as a maid or guard walked by, Nyla still wasn't prepared and quickly jumped into an open doorway, pulling Samuel in with her. She shushed Samuel as the maid's footsteps got closer. She heard a noise behind them and she whipped around to see Martha snoring in a chair with a pile of clothes in her lap and in a basket beside her. *Of all the people we could have run into!*

"Oh my gosh!" Nyla whispered. She pointed to Martha's body, slumped in a chair. Samuel's eyes got wide.

"Seriously?!" He mouthed. Nyla stifled a laugh and held a breath as the maid in the hallway walked by. Nyla let out her breath and Samuel peered out the doorway. Suddenly, the maid stopped. Samuel pulled his head back into the room just as the maid turned around.

"Crap!" he whispered, looking around for somewhere to hide inside the room. He jumped behind the door and grabbed Nyla's hands, quickly pulling her against him just as the maid entered the room. Nyla craned her neck to the side to see what was going on, but the door blocked her view.

"Martha? Martha?" the maid said. Martha jolted awake with a snort. Nyla clamped her mouth shut and closed her eyes, trying not to laugh.

"What happened?" Martha's voice croaked.

"You must have fallen asleep while folding clothes. Why don't you go to bed, Martha. You can finish these tomorrow."

"Okay." There was the creaking of a chair as Martha rose. Then Nyla heard footsteps and looked through the crack by the door hinges. Martha and the maid exited the room and Nyla waited a few seconds before she let out a breath.

"That was close. Could you imagine if—" Nyla broke off as she looked up, coming face-to-face with Samuel. She suddenly realized how close they stood to each other. Her chest was pressed up against

Samuel's toned body and he still held her hands close to his chest. Samuel smirked at Nyla and she sucked in a breath, pulling away from him. She cleared her throat, composing herself and smoothing out her nightgown and robe.

"That was close," Nyla repeated again. "Could you imagine if Martha would have seen us? She would have been so mad." She looked up at Samuel, who was still looking at her with a crooked grin on his face. Nyla looked away and went through the door, feeling her face heat up. She heard him follow her out the door.

"She would have skinned me alive, for sure," Samuel replied, his voice light.

"Oh, ya." Nyla laughed. They walked in silence for a few minutes. They turned the corner and Nyla's door came into sight. Suddenly, Nyla grabbed Samuel's arm and jerked him back behind the corner when she spotted Kaden coming down the hall from the direction of his room. *What the heck!* Nyla put her finger to her lips. Samuel gave her a confused look.

"Kaden," she mouthed.

"What?" Samuel whispered. He went to look around the corner, but Nyla grabbed the front of his shirt and pulled him back. His face came back inches from hers and she quickly removed her hand from his chest, gently pushing him back a couple of inches.

"He cannot see us!" Nyla whispered. *That would definitely not be good.*

"Can I see Nyla?" Kaden asked Dominic. Samuel raised his eyebrows at Nyla and she shrugged.

"No, she's . . ." Dominic paused. "Do you know what time it is?"

"I know it's early, but I was standing on my balcony and I saw a light coming from her room." Nyla frowned. *I hadn't left a lantern or candle lit. That must mean Julia had woken up. Crap! She was going to be furious!*

"Well, I'm afraid I can't let you go in."

"What? Why not?" Kaden sounded annoyed. "Where's Samuel? I thought he's never supposed to leave Nyla's side." Kaden paused. "Is he inside with her?" Anger crept into Kaden's voice. Nyla panicked and she shoved Samuel out from behind the corner.

"Do something! Talk to him!" Nyla hissed, waving her hands in the air. Samuel shook his head, but it was already too late.

"Samuel?" Kaden called from down the hall.

"Hey, Kaden," Samuel said casually and started to walk toward him and Dominic. "I was just doing a quick check around the, um . . . main hall."

"Can I talk to Nyla?" Kaden didn't seem too happy to have to ask Samuel's permission.

"Afraid not. You realize it's super early, don't you?"

"There's light coming from her room. You can't tell me she's sleeping. Is she even in there?" Kaden's patience were starting to thin.

"Of course she's in there! I'd be with her if she wasn't."

"And you're sure she's in there? She could have snuck out."

"Oh, believe me, I'm a hard ass about stuff like that. I've known where she was the entire night." Nyla smacked her palm to her forehead.

"Uh-huh." Kaden sounded annoyed again. "Listen, Samuel. I need to talk to you." *Oh, please not now!* Then Nyla smiled as she remembered their conversation from earlier. She felt a sense of pride for him. He was actually going to talk to Samuel and make up like she had asked.

"Um . . ." Samuel hesitated. "We'll talk tomorrow."

"No, I need to do this now."

Samuel sighed. "Okay, let's head back that way." He motioned away from Nyla toward the direction of Kaden's room. Nyla heard footsteps heading away from her door And she peeked out from behind the corner. Her curiosity took over and she stepped out, following them. She knew she probably shouldn't eavesdrop, but she really wanted to know what Kaden wanted to say. As Dominic spotted her he raised his eyebrows in surprise. She held her finger up to her mouth, silently urging Dominic to stay quiet. He gave her a disapproving look but kept his mouth shut. She nodded in thanks and hurried toward Samuel and Kaden's direction. She stayed low in the shadows and was silent as a mouse.

"So listen"—Kaden stopped outside his door—"I'm sorry for getting so angry at you and . . . punching you."

"It's all forgiven." Samuel shook his head. "You have to know that I would've told you. I just couldn't. I swore to the queen."

"I understand." Kaden shrugged his shoulders. "I was just in a bad place. I mean, Nyla is a vampire? I can't believe that. I know it's Nyla and I know she wouldn't hurt anyone, but I'm having a hard time accepting that there are good vampires out there."

Nyla's heart squeezed painfully. Kaden had to know that she was good.

Samuel thought for a moment. "There are a lot of bad ones out there. Vampires are not . . . good by nature. Most of them are evil, but there are occasionally exceptions. Nyla is one of the good ones." Nyla smiled at his words. At least maybe he could make Kaden see things in Nyla's favor.

"I know that and I feel really bad about how I treated her. I do, I just had to process everything."

"She knows that." Samuel nodded his head in reassurance.

"I hope so. I know I've messed some things up and I want to make it up to her. Will you let her know that I am sorry? I told her, but I want her to know for sure that I do mean it."

"I'll let her know, but something tells me she already knows." Samuel looked over Kaden's shoulder to where Nyla crouched in the shadows. *Crap! How did he know I am here!?* At least Kaden didn't know she was spying on them.

"Thanks." Kaden paused. "I have to admit I'm a little jealous. You get to spend all day and night with Nyla."

Nyla's heart gave a delightful flip. Kaden wanted to spend more time with her!

Samuel nodded, unsure of what to say. "You don't have to be jealous. I'm just guarding her."

Kaden nodded. "I was just being an ass because I was annoyed and jealous. It looked to me like you guys have been getting pretty close. Then there were the rumors spreading around the maids that you've been staying in her room and it just made me upset." Nyla frowned. *Damn maids!* She had no idea they'd been talking about her and Samuel.

"We're friends," Samuel assured him. "I'm just guarding her."

"Okay." Kaden nodded but still sounded like he wasn't totally convinced.

"It's late. I should get back." Samuel looked uncomfortable.

"K. Well, will you tell Nyla I went to see her?" Kaden still didn't look totally happy, but he was going to let it go.

"Sure." Nyla watched as Kaden opened his door and went inside. Once the door was shut, she came out from the shadows and walked toward Samuel. She was already caught, and there was no sense in pretending she wasn't there.

"Did you have fun, eavesdropper?" Samuel raised his eyebrows but gave her a smile.

"You're right about what you said before. You are a hard ass." Nyla gave him a teasing grin.

"Hey, you're welcome. I could've told him where you were." Samuel came to walk beside Nyla as they made their way back to her room.

"Yes, but then he would have been angry and he might have tried to punch you in the face again," Nyla pointed out. "Especially with the rumors going around." She ran her hand over her face. "I cannot believe the whole castle has been talking about us! You're lucky he didn't seek you out and punch you again. Well, or try to punch you again," Nyla said, looking at Samuels face as they reached her room.

"Well, getting hit doesn't bother me anymore." Samuel shrugged.

"You don't even have a bruise." She stretched on her tiptoes, checking his face. "Not even a mark."

"What can I say? Kaden's never been a strong puncher." Nyla stepped back, noticing how Dominic tried not to look at her scarce clothing. She didn't even bother to hide herself behind Samuel anymore.

"Hey, Dominic." Nyla gave him a nod.

"Princess." Dominic acknowledged her while making it obvious he was trying not to look at her.

"Okay." Samuel rolled his eyes. "You should get back in your room now." He paused, looking her in the eyes. "And please no sneaking out again. As fun as this was, I don't feel like doing it again tonight." He squinted his eyes but had smile on his face.

"Nice job on that, by the way." Dominic nodded in her direction. "I would have never realized you had left. I don't know how he even knew you left your room." Samuel gave him a silencing look and Nyla suppressed a giggle. Samuel looked back at Nyla expectantly.

"Okay, I promise I won't sneak out again . . . tonight." She gave him a smug grin. Samuel rolled his eyes with a smile.

"Good night, Nyla." He leaned past her and opened the door.

"Good night, Samuel." She returned his smile as he shut the door.

"Don't say a word." She heard Samuel say to Dominic after he closed the door. Nyla turned, expecting to see an angry Julia standing there, but Julia was sound asleep on the couch. Nyla frowned at the dimly lit lantern. Julia must have lit it when she noticed Nyla was gone, but fell asleep while waiting for her to get back. She crept silently across the floor and snuffed out the flame. Nyla sighed. It had taken her and Samuel twice as long to get back to her room with them having to rush behind a pillar or into the shadows every time a maid or guard walked by. *Doesn't anyone ever sleep?*

Nyla crept to the bathroom and closed the door behind her, not even bothering to light a candle as she could see perfectly in the darkness. She turned on the faucet, splashing cold water onto her face. She looked at her feet, noticing they were filthy with dirt and she just decided to take a whole bath. She turned the water on and stripped her clothes off. She tested the water with her hands and watched as the steam floated off of the surface. She stepped in and sighed, the hot water not even bothering her skin. After about a half hour or so of soaking in the tub in complete darkness, she washed herself and got out. She grabbed a clean nightgown from her closet, the exhaustion starting to take over her body and mind. She slipped under the covers, still not completely dried off, her hair dripping all over the place. As soon as she settled into the bed, she fell into a well-needed sleep, completely relaxed and forgetting about all the troubles that lay in her not-too-distant future.

CHAPTER 9

Nyla woke hours later to sunlight peeking through her windows and the sound of the waking world coming in from outside. Her eyes snapped open, wide awake, and Nyla was pleased that she didn't need as much sleep in order to feel refreshed. She heard a rustling around the room and she lifted her head off the pillow. Julia was already up, dressed and ready for the day, folding the blankets and arranging the pillows on the couch like she did the other morning.

"So how was your night last night?" she said, not even looking up from the blanket she was folding.

"Um"—Nyla got out of bed, putting her velvet robe on—"it was good." She wasn't even going to try to lie to Julia. She looked at Julia, trying to read her mood, and pulled the covers up to her pillow, making her bed.

Julia looked at her, a disapproving look in her eyes. "I know what you did last night, Nyla. There was a draft coming from the open glass doors and I got cold. What were you thinking? You know we aren't supposed to go wandering around at night by ourselves!"

"Julia, please don't tell anyone. You have no idea what it's like. I feel like I'm caged up here! No one even saw me, it's fine! Well, except Samuel, and believe me, I got a talking to, so I won't be doing it again." She walked up to Julia and took the blanket she was folding. "Please don't tell anyone, please! Especially not my mother, she'd lock me in my room."

"Fine." Julia took the blanket back, folding it the rest of the way. "What were you doing out there anyway?"

"I just went for a run around the garden. I was enjoying the night." She decided not to tell Julia about seeing Lucas for fear that she might insist on telling someone and how would Nyla be able to explain to anyone else why she had seen Lucas all the way out by the fountain if she "wasn't outside"?

"Okay, well, just be careful. Not only would you be in huge trouble, but something could happen to you and no one would ever know it. It's a good thing Samuel found you."

Nyla huffed a small sigh. "Okay. I'll be careful."

"Thank you." Julia nodded to a plate of food on Nyla's vanity. "I had Samuel go down and grab you a plate of breakfast earlier." Nyla's eyes widened.

"It's after breakfast already? I was supposed to meat Jamin an hour after sunrise!" She started undressing as she ran to her closet.

"I'm sorry! I didn't wake you up, you never sleep in this late, so I thought you needed your sleep." She followed Nyla into the closet. "Honestly, though, you could wear anything and you would look fine. You don't even look like you slept. I could run my fingers through your hair right now and there wouldn't even be any tangles." She pulled out a plain, light green dress and shoved it at Nyla, "Here, put this on and eat!"

Nyla threw on the dress and ran out of the closet, looking at herself in the mirror. It was true; she looked as if she had never slept with her hair wet or had been up half the night running around. Her blond hair ran down her back in waves and her face glowed. Satisfied that she could approach Kaden without looking like she had gotten up only five minutes ago, she looked at the plate of eggs, bacon, toast, and glass of orange juice that Samuel had gotten for her. She shoved a bite of eggs in her mouth, scarfed down a piece of toast in three bites, and grabbed a piece of bacon, shoving it into her mouth. She gulped down the glass of orange juice and ran to the bathroom, brushing her teeth hurriedly.

"There." She smiled as she looked at herself in the mirror one more time before heading toward the door.

"Nyla, Jamin is going to be furious. You are already late, and it's a long walk all the way down to the library."

"It won't take me long at all to walk down there." She opened the door and came face-to-face with Samuel. She sucked in a startled breath and took in Samuel's amused expression.

"Good morning, Nyla. Have a good rest of your night?" Samuel gave her a smirk.

"Yes, I did. Thank you." Nyla slightly squinted her eyes at him. "Now, if you'll excuse me, I'm late." She stepped around him and then bolted past Dominic and Kristi, disappearing down the hall in a matter of seconds. Julia looked at them apologetically, not knowing how to explain.

She smiled at Samuel. "She's headed to the library." Kristi and Dominic looked at each other before hurrying in the direction Nyla had disappeared.

"Thanks." Samuel gave Julia a smile and headed after them.

Nyla sped down the hallways in record time, but almost had a heart attack as she saw Lucas and Felix standing at the end of the hallway. She quickly ducked back behind the corner she had just sped around and smoothed down the skirt of her flowy dress. Peaking back around the corner first, she headed toward the two.

"Princess Nylina." Lucas smiled at her. "What an honor to see you this morning."

She nodded. "Lucas, isn't it?"

"Yes, and this is Felix." He motioned toward his blond friend beside him. Nyla nodded at him uncomfortably. She didn't like the look of his animal like eyes even more up close, and they made her feel uneasy.

"Well, you'll have to excuse me, gentlemen. I'm late for a meeting with . . . the queen's advisor." She passed them, glad to get out from under Felix's stare.

"Wait." Lucas caught up to her, and Nyla could sense Felix following not too far behind them. "May we walk with you? We happen to be going this way as well."

"Do you?" Nyla kept her eyes ahead, wishing they would go away.

"Yes. So we've been taking the liberty of entertaining ourselves in the history and maps of this castle. We were hoping you would show us around sometime and fill us in a little more about Galatia's secrets." Nyla stopped walking and looked at him suspiciously. "We just want to get to know more about the kingdom we are joining. We've told you secrets about Ridia and we still have more. We are a very intellectual and eager to learn group, and we feel it would be right to get some information in return. We heard you had a very great father." Nyla suddenly felt threatened at the tone of his voice. *Why would he ask about her father?* She began to get a bad vibe.

"How was your little stroll through the garden last night?" She shot off, not thinking. She looked into his eyes and smiled when she saw she took him off guard.

"Spying on me were you?" He grinned at her. *Dang it!* Nyla wondered if she had just given the wrong information. Then she got an idea. If he was going to play the polite gentleman, she might as well lead him on.

"Maybe just a little." She started walking again. "I was just curious about you. Maybe I'm eager to get to know you more and see what kind of allies we gained." She forced a smile at Felix.

"Yes, we'll see." Lucas returned her fake smile. "Maybe this afternoon?"

"Maybe." She made a show of giving him a flirty smile. She spotted Samuel, followed closely by Kristi and Dominic, head around the corner. "Well, if you'll excuse me." Nyla turned and walked in the direction of the library doors, leaving the two men behind.

Nyla smiled at the library doors. Although she was late, the fact that she sped down there so quickly put her in a good mood. She opened the doors, not wanting to waste any more time, and looked around the room, expecting Kaden to be standing with Jamin at the table on the second level, but Jamin was standing alone, flipping through one of his notebooks. She joined Jamin at the table, looking toward the door. There was still time. Maybe Kaden was running late as well.

"Let's get started, shall we?" Jamin sat down and Nyla took the seat across from him, still looking at the door. Reading her thoughts, Jamin said, "Kaden won't be joining us. He has his own lesson now. You two have pretty much reached the point of graduation anyway. I figured that our lesson times would be just us now, that way you can tell me whatever you want and it would just stay between you and me if you wanted. Well, of course your guards will be standing down by the door too, but they're sworn to secrecy." He looked at the door. "Where are your guards anyway?"

"Um," Nyla was still disappointed that Kaden wouldn't be joining them, "I left them behind. They couldn't keep up." Almost as if on cue the three guards came through the door, looking at Nyla in disbelief.

"You left them behind?" Jamin looked at Nyla with raised eyebrows. Then he smiled, realizing what she had done. "Oh! Of course you have vampire speed. You can run up to speeds of over one hundred miles per hour, that's faster than the cheetahs in the south."

"Yes, we noticed." Nyla heard Kristi mumble from down below. She shot Kristi an apologetic look and turned back to Jamin.

"Now, have you noticed any other changes? Super hearing, strength, increased sense of smell?"

"Yes. All of that." Nyla paused as Jamin wrote something down in his notebook.

"Go on." Jamin grinned excitedly, pushing his spectacles up higher onto his nose. Nyla smiled to herself; the brains in Jamin was starting to take over. When it did, almost nobody could damper his ecstatic mood.

"Um . . . well, I can smell everything, even the flowers from the garden, and right now, I can smell the chicken salad for lunch cooking from the kitchens on the first floor."

"Excellent!" Jamin continued to scribble into his notebook.

"I can also jump long distances and impossible heights, and I have to watch my strength. Wow, I'm almost like an animal." Nyla looked at her hands folded on the table. Even her nails looked longer, sharper, and stronger. Maybe that was just her imagination. Jamin looked at Nyla, noticing her worry.

"Yes, Nyla. You are like an animal." Nyla looked at him in confusion. Wasn't he supposed to be making her feel better? "However," Jamin continued, "That's who you are, Nyla. That's who your father was. Your animalistic instincts help you survive." He gave her a reassuring look. "I studied your father for quite a long time and everything you are telling me is normal. We just need to figure out if you will have all the aspects of a vampire, or if you will only gain some of those abilities."

"The light stopped hurting my eyes after that first day in the infirmary. I can see really well at night now."

"Right, right." Jamin wrote more in his notebook. "You can see great in the daylight, but even better at night. Night is the domain of the vampire." Nyla rolled her eyes at Jamin's scientific attitude.

"I can also hear almost anything that I focus on. I can hear the faint sound of the fountain of the angel statue from my bedroom. I can hear the birds chirping outside the windows and the beating wings of the hummingbirds in the garden." She paused, focusing.

"The guard, Eli, standing outside the library doors . . . I can hear his even breathing. He just came back from pacing the corridor down the hall. I can also sense feelings—fear, anger, eagerness. Kristi doesn't like me very much. I can also hear every heartbeat in this room and the blood pumping through every one of your veins." Her eyes focused and she realized she had been staring at Dominic's chest, right where his heart was. She looked at Kristi, who was silently glaring at her. She felt Samuel's gaze on her and looked into his blue-gray eyes, but couldn't quite read his emotions. His gaze made her nervous and she turned back to Jamin, who was also staring at her, his mouth slightly open.

"Yes," he cleared his throat, "that's all normal too." He paused, drawing a deep breath. "So have you noticed any other . . . signs of vampirism?" Nyla knew exactly what he was talking about.

"No! I would never! I've never . . ." She couldn't even finish the sentence.

"Well, good. That's good." Jamin could barely hide his relief. "Maybe that's something that you'll never have to experience." But in his heart, he feared that the day would come when she would. Nyla remained silent.

"Well"—Jamin closed his notebook and stood—"I think that's enough for today. We'll come back tomorrow. Same time?"

"All right." Nyla stood, still lost in her own thoughts.

BLOODLINES

Everyone remained silent as Nyla walked down the hallway, followed by her escorts. Nyla was actually grateful that her guards didn't want to talk to her at the moment. Focusing on her abilities in the library had put her in a weird mood. She felt jittery and the adrenaline rushed through her. *What had just happened?* It was as if Nyla had lost herself and that thought scared her. *What is happening to me?* She found herself heading toward the training grounds. She yearned to be outside in the open air.

"Nyla." Samuel put his hand on her shoulder. "I have to go oversee some of the trainees as they duel today. It won't take too long, but Dominic is going to guard you alone for a while since I can't leave the training grounds." Nyla nodded. She hadn't even noticed that Kristi had left.

"Okay." Samuel gave her a small smile before walking ahead of her.

Nyla continued to walk forward. Her body screamed to run and get away from everything, but she needed to see Kaden and see what he wanted to talk about the night before. She figured he would probably be there and he always knew the right things to say to make her feel better.

Nyla smiled as she spotted Kaden dueling with Leonard, a young guard-in-training who was at least twice Kaden's size. Nyla came to a stop, leaning against the stone wall. Her eyes glued to Kaden's body, he was wearing simple brown pants and a tight shirt that showed every muscle curve of his upper body. Although he was thinner and lankier than Samuel's toned build, he still had quite an attractive body. Leonard swung in Kaden's direction, but Kaden was quick, coming up and quickly hitting Leonard across the chest. Leonard grunted, but continued to advance on Kaden, making him back up until he was up against the sword rack.

Kaden got distracted as he noticed Nyla standing there. He staggered as Leonard jabbed, but Kaden dove into a summersault just in time and, in one fluid motion, sprang to his feet and had his sword against the back of Leonard's neck. Nyla pushed off the wall, walking toward Kaden and Leonard, who were laughing and shaking hands, discussing the events of the duel. She clapped her hands together, and her heart warmed as Kaden's smile grew brighter as he saw her proceeding toward them.

"Very nice. You're getting better, but I could still kick your butt." She gave Kaden a teasing grin and nodded a hello to Leonard as he put his sword back, grabbing a bow from the rack in the corner and joining a few others as they were being watched closely by Samuel at the targets.

"Oh, could you?" Kaden laughed as he came toward her. "Shall we test that?" The jittery, electrified feeling rose up in Nyla's belly again and her heart picked up pace. He suddenly grabbed her hand.

"I need to talk to you. Did Samuel tell you that I stopped by your room last night?" Kaden's hand felt wonderful in hers and she nodded. "Um . . ." Kaden smiled back but looked to where Dominic was standing in the corner, ready to jump if anything was to happen. "What are we going to do about him?" Nyla looked back, the spirited smile still glowing on her face, and Dominic eyed her suspiciously.

"Do you trust me?" She turned back, squeezing his hand gently. A hint of confusion sparked across his expression, but he continued to smile.

"Um, sure."

"I have become quite good at sneaking off." Excitement rushed over her as adrenaline pumped through her veins. She slowly started to walk toward the edge of the training grounds and Kaden followed.

"Follow my lead," she whispered. They slowly walked along the edge of the rose bush maze at the edge of the garden. Nyla looked back, seeing that Dominic hadn't started to move toward them yet.

"Now!" Nyla took off into the maze. She could hear Kaden following just behind her, but she didn't stop. They zipped through the paths, Nyla swerving into random paths so that it would be almost impossible for Dominic to know where they went. She stopped suddenly, looking back and smiling when Dominic was nowhere in sight.

"Okay, I'm impressed. You can run for a long time!" Kaden panted, looking somewhat dazed. He looked around, trying to focus on where they were. "Why are we here?" he asked, taking in the rows of red and white rose bushes that surrounded them.

"I know where we can go to be alone." She beamed, leading him through the paths of roses and to a wall of huge bushes. She bent down, pushing back a curtain of branches, revealing a small tunnel through the plants.

"Come." She beckoned to Kaden as she knelt down, crawling into the tunnel on her hands and knees. The tunnel opened up to a room size, meadow-like cave inside the bushes. Tiny flowers dotted the soft grass that mixed with the moss-covered ground, and small beams of sunlight peaked through cracks in the ceiling of the branches above. The space was comfortable and there was just enough room to stand while bending at the waist. Nyla turned and sat on the grass-blanketed ground. She smiled at Kaden as he made his way in, coming to sit beside her.

"This is amazing," Kaden said, taking in the view. "How did you find this place?"

"My mother had Fulcan clear this whole space out for me when I was really little. I still clip the branches every once in a while so I can come here to just be alone and think. I'm sorry I never shared it with you. I've only ever brought Julia in here. It's just been my sort-of haven, and it was somewhere I could always come to be alone whenever I wanted to."

"No, I understand. It's your place. I wouldn't want to disturb that."

Nyla smiled, running her hands softly through a patch of colorful flowers beside her. "When I was little, I used to pretend that I was playing hide-and-seek with my father and he was searching for me. Other times I would be a princess locked in a tower or kept in a dungeon, and he was coming to rescue me. Obviously he would never come, but it was my own little fantasy anyway."

Kaden didn't know what to say. He scooted closer and put his hand over hers, stilling it over the flowers. Nyla caught her breath as Kaden scooted even closer so that his arm touched hers. The skin on her hand tingled where Kaden's was placed and warm excitement bubbled up through her chest. She looked up into Kaden's emerald eyes, barely remembering to breathe. The jittery feeling crept back, filling her veins with adrenaline, and before she knew it, his face was so close to hers that she could feel his hot breath against her lips. She hesitated. *Do I really want to kiss Kaden?* She thought about their friendship. Before she could think anything more, Kaden brought his hand up and put it gently on the back of her neck, drawing her face closer. Suddenly, before their lips could touch, Nyla drew back, feeling a weird burning in the pit of her stomach.

"What?" Kaden removed his hand from her neck.

"Um . . . nothing, it's just, a little . . ." She didn't know what to say.

"You're right." Kaden ran his hands through his hair. "This is completely wrong.

"What?" Nyla looked at him. He was the one who had almost kissed her.

"Oh no." Kaden grabbed her shoulders, reassuring her with a smile. "This is what I want. It's just . . . this isn't how it should happen. I should be a gentleman and court you first. I mean, it's proper I guess." He rocked back to a crouch and sat beside Nyla, his hands sitting safely in his lap.

"So." Nyla smoothed her hair and dress, taking a deep breath.

"So." Kaden turned toward her. "I talked to Samuel last night."

Nyla smiled. "Oh, and?" Nyla pretended to be surprised. She leaned back on her hands and looked at him in interest.

"Well, I think it went well. I apologized for punching him and we talked it out. I think we're good now."

"Good." Nyla smiled at him. "I'm glad you're making an effort to forgive him."

"Well, I'm mostly doing it for you." Kaden looked down at the ground. Nyla nodded, taking that in.

"Right now, I don't care what your reason is as long as you're trying. Samuel's really a nice guy, Kaden, and he's been your friend a long time. He didn't want to lie to you, but he had to and I'm glad you're getting past it." She smiled. "I can see why you're friends with him. He's a good guy." He nodded, his attention on a white flower he was twirling between his fingers.

Nyla closed her eyes, lost in her thoughts of her almost first kiss. Suddenly, her thoughts switched to last night when her and Samuel were hiding from Martha behind the door. She remembered the way his hot breath on her face had sent pleasant tingles up her spine and the way his deep, gray-blue eyes stared into her own.

Her eyes flew open. *Why am I all of a sudden thinking about him now?* She heard Kaden stir beside her and looked down at him. He was lying on his back, eyes closed, with his hands behind his head. She smiled, but guilt seeped into her stomach. Here he had almost kissed her and a few minutes later she was thinking of Samuel. *What's wrong with me?*

❦

"So your daughter will not be joining us tonight, I presume?" Lamar cut his ham delicately with his knife, taking his time.

"Well, she should be here any moment." Lydia glanced across the table to Fulcan, who slightly shook his head and shrugged. "I'm sorry, Lamar. I know how you all wanted to get to know her. I just don't know what to say." She put a spoonful of mashed potatoes into her mouth, looking down at her plate. Nyla wasn't one to completely ditch dinner and disappear without telling anyone about it. Of course she had to pick today to take on the habit.

"Yes, I was hoping that the Princess Nylina would like to spend some time with Felix, Adrian, and Lucas. After all, they would be spending a lot of time with her and the young, Sir Kaden when they start training with the militia." Lydia almost choked on the piece of ham she had been slowly chewing.

"What?" She quickly swallowed and cleared her throat. "I wasn't aware of the information that you would all be joining our militia."

Lamar looked taken aback. "Well, your majesty, I only assumed that we would be training with your troops because of the information we have given you. We have proven ourselves loyal enough I think."

Fulcan put his fork and knife down. "So you're just expecting us to welcome you into our kingdom, after you betrayed yours, and let you learn all of our secrets and battle strategies?"

Lydia shot him a warning look. "It's not that we don't think you are not . . . helpful to us, Lamar. It's just that we wouldn't want to put you in a position to be fighting against your own kingdom. Just because you could walk away doesn't mean you can stand to go up against all your friends and the place you have lived your whole life. You might find it too much for you, or change your mind."

Adrian stood up abruptly, all eyes shooting to her rigid form. "Make no mistake in thinking that we are weak. Don't doubt that we will not kill every last one of our enemy when the time comes. It will be a pleasure." Lydia shuddered at her brutal expression.

Lamar looked as if he wanted to strike her. "Adrian! Sit down this instant! How dare you be so disrespectful!?" Felix grabbed his sister's long sleeve and yanked her back down onto her chair. She looked down at her clenched hands.

"I'm sorry, Your Majesty. I meant no disrespect."

"It's all right." Lydia hesitated. "You were only expressing your emotion and . . . hatred for the ones that mean you harm." Lydia put another bite into her mouth, looking sideways at Jamin, who raised his eyebrows in unease. She cleared her throat.

"I'm sure Nylina just got held up. She will join us soon and then we will discuss your requests."

CHAPTER 10

Kaden lay there watching Nyla make a small bouquet of the tiny flowers that dotted the ground around them. He was definitely taking in every sweet moment. With all that he had felt and said to her, he was grateful that she didn't hate him. He looked up into the bushy canopy above them. The light that seeped through the branches was just a dim, blue hue.

"Well, shall we?" Kaden sat up next to her, beckoning to the way out.

"Oh, ya. Actually we're probably late for dinner. I'm starving! Mother wants me to start getting familiar with Lamar and the others. She doesn't want me to seem like I'm avoiding them. She thinks that they might grow suspicious, or something. I don't know." She followed Kaden out and smiled when he held his hand out for her and helped her up. Since Lamar, Felix, Adrian, and Lucas had shown up at Galatia's gates the whole castle had been a little uptight. Lydia had wanted to speak to the newcomers alone before formally introducing Nyla to them. As a result of this, Nyla had been eating at different times than her mother and the rest of them.

"Well, I don't want you spending too much time with them. I still don't trust any of them, especially that Lucas guy. I don't know what it is about him, but something just doesn't sit right." Kaden shook his head.

Nyla thought of last night when she had seen Lucas in the garden. He was mysterious, but at the time, Nyla hadn't gotten any bad feelings from him. Even so, she didn't really want to be alone with him either. She shivered, remembering his interested expression when he had first laid eyes on her in the courtyard the night they had all shown up. She contemplated telling Kaden about the encounter in the garden and in the hallway earlier that day but decided against it. There was no sense in causing any more suspicions without huge cause.

"I'll be careful, Kaden. It's not like I'll be spending all day with them or anything. Plus, I'll have Samuel with me the whole time. He'll protect me." The thought of Samuel made her feel warm, but she shook it off.

Kaden frowned at the thought of Nyla, Samuel, and Lucas all walking side by side. "I wish I were the one guarding you."

Nyla smiled at him, but it faded as they rounded the corner of the rose bush path and she spotted Dominic and Samuel standing by the main castle doors.

"Oh, crap!" She quickly crouched behind the rose bush.

"What?" Kaden remained standing, looking toward the castle. Nyla pulled him down with her, shushing him.

"Samuel and Dominic are by the doors. We completely ditched them, and I know they're not going to be too happy about it. Samuel is going to be furious." She felt guilty as she thought about last night. She had really meant it at the time when she said she wouldn't sneak off again. Her stomach grumbled. "We have to find another way in. Act like we've been in the castle the whole time."

"Ugh, why do you even have to have them watching you every second of the day?" Nyla shook her head and Kaden sighed. "Okay, but where can we go in without being seen by anybody?"

Nyla thought for a second. "Hmmm." Her face lit up. "My bedroom window?"

Kaden laughed. "Oh ya, I'm sure your mother and Fulcan would just love it if we had been missing for a couple of hours and we both just waltzed out of your bedroom together." Nyla looked away, blushing at the thoughts that flooded her mind.

"Well, what other choice do we have? I know there won't be anybody in there so we won't be seen. We can sneak out of my room. Samuel is waiting by the castle doors, so nobody will be guarding my room."

"Okay, fine. Lead the way." Kaden followed Nyla as they stayed in a crouch, hurrying in the opposite direction toward her bedroom.

"So how are we going to do this?" Kaden looked up to the marble balcony two stories above them.

"Oh." Nyla thought to herself, a puzzled expression on her face. "I didn't think about that. You can't just jump up there can you?" She gave a nervous laugh. "Well . . . you could just hop on my back and I'll jump us both up there." She looked over at Kaden with a guarded expression.

Kaden's face went red with embarrassment. "Um, no, I don't think so. I'm not going to let you carry me around. I'll just climb up the vines leading to the balcony. They look thick enough to support me." Nyla snickered to herself. Okay, the image of Kaden just jumping onto her back like a little kid was definitely unrealistic and ridiculous to imagine. She looked at the cover of twisting vines that blanketed the entire sidewall of the castle.

"Okay, well, let's hurry up. My stomach is literally eating itself. I'll go first." She was antsy with excitement at the thought of scaling the walls like a spider. Before Kaden could respond, Nyla jumped onto the wall, grabbing onto the green vines. Kaden was amazed, mouth open, at the speed and agility that Nyla climbed the vines. Within maybe a minute, she was pulling herself over the balcony railing with a grace and ease Kaden didn't understand.

"Okay, here goes nothing." Kaden grabbed onto the vine, pulling himself up and hooking his foot into a notch in the vines. Hand after foot he pulled himself up, occasionally avoiding thorns, or loose vines that hadn't seemed to affect Nyla at all. Nyla peeked over the balcony rail, surveying Kaden's progress.

"Hmmm. Not bad." She smiled as he reached the bottom of the balcony. She reached her hand down. "Here." Kaden reached up, grabbing her hand, and almost lost his breath as she swung him up and over the railing with no trouble at all.

"Wow." He breathed, smiling down at Nyla in wonder and amazement.

Nyla giggled. "Now all we have to do is wait here until dinner is over and sneak down to the kitchen for a sna . . ." Her words trailed off as she stopped dead in her tracks, coming face-to-face with Kristi as she stepped out of the shadows of Nyla's bed.

"Well, hello, Your Highness." Kristi scowled with obvious distaste in her malicious voice. "Now that I've finally tracked you down let's go see the queen shall we?" She stepped behind Nyla, placing her hand on her back, giving her a slight nudge.

"Now, just a minute." Kaden grabbed Kristi's hand, taking it off Nyla's back. "Nyla doesn't have to listen you. You are guarding her, not controlling her. You guys are crowding her, she can protect herself."

"Listen here." Kristi seemed to grow a couple inches, as she got right up into Kaden's face. "We were asked, by the queen, to guard her. We have a duty to our kingdom to keep her safe, and no matter how much I dislike it, I will do whatever I can to make sure she stays safe. If that means that I have to watch her day and night, never leaving her side, then I will. Keeping her safe also includes keeping her safe from herself." She turned her warning glare to Nyla. "Even though Samuel thinks you won't lose control. I know better. You have no idea what you are capable of and if you aren't careful, you could do something you could regret." Nyla was taken aback by Kristi's fierceness, but the blood still boiled in her veins. She was starving and she was so not in the mood to deal with this bitch.

"How dare you?! I may not know exactly what I am and what I am capable of, but I do know who I am. I am a good person, not the monster you, and everyone else thinks I am!"

"Nyla!" Kaden stared at her wide-eyed. She had Kristi backed up into a corner, her hand around Kristi's throat. Kristi whimpered as she stared, horrified, into Nyla's, black, colorless eyes. Nyla stared at Kristi, but she didn't even see her. Nyla's vision became thermal and Kristi's body turned into a colorful silhouette of heated flesh and blood. Her stomach burned with a hunger so powerful, she felt nothing else.

"Nyla, stop! Stop!" Kaden forcefully grabbed her arm, trying to force it away from Kristi's throat.

Nyla snapped to her senses, aware of what she was about to do. She let go of Kristi's throat, stepping back, her eyes on her shaking hands. She looked at Kaden, taking in his thermal body. She could barely make out his red and yellow expression, but his eyes stared into her own black, consumed ones. Her heart ached, and there was a horrible, burning of hunger in her stomach. She could sense every wave of fear radiating off of Kaden. She tried to remember what Samuel had said about breathing. She took a deep breath, but it didn't help.

"Kaden." Nyla reached toward him, but he stepped back, flinching away from her hand. Kaden moved to stand in front of Kristi, who was sitting on the floor, glaring with anger and fear at Nyla. The hunger sent a searing pain from Nyla's stomach to her chest and throat. Without a word, she spun and darted past Kaden, onto the balcony, and disappeared off the railing. Kaden stared at the spot Nyla had jumped off, not knowing what to say or think. He looked at Kristi as she cowered on the floor, breathing heavily.

Nyla ran as fast as she could away from the balcony and Kaden. She had no idea where she was going, just that she had to get as far away from him as possible. The dark, blue and purple world rushed by her as she ran into the darkness. She stopped, surveying her surroundings. She was standing by the steps at the castle's front doors where Samuel and Dominic had been earlier. She looked around, but Samuel wasn't anywhere to be found. Another jolt of pain plunged into her stomach and she started panicking. She knew that she could easily climb over the stone wall that guarded the castle, but where would she go? Suddenly grief and hunger overcame her and her whole body shook as she broke out into sobs. She stumbled over to the stables, looking for a horse, but the stalls were empty. She entered a stall and slid down the wall into the straw below her. Her hands flew to her face as she tried to block the thermal world around her. Her fingers moved to her mouth and she let out a scream as she felt the sharp fangs.

"No, no, no, no, no!" She wrapped her arms around her knees and rocked her body back and forth. "What's happening to me? I'm a monster." The whispered words sounded weird coming from her mouth, but in her heart, she knew it was true. She had felt the fear rolling off of Kaden back in her room. *Why wouldn't he be afraid of me, though?* He had hated vampires before and why should he change his mind now? *I wouldn't have really hurt Kristi, would I?* Still, Kaden had doubted her. He had flinched away from her touch. She thought of Samuel's calming, blue-gray eyes.

"Breathe! Breathe!" she told herself. She would not believe that she was a monster! The ache in her heart subsided as the colors started to fade and her vision began to return to normal. She felt the fangs melt back into her gums, returning to their normal size, but the throbbing burn in her stomach and chest continued to pound her body.

"I'm not a monster," she whispered again and again as she stared, not blinking, into the darkness of the stall.

"Hello?" a boy's voice called. Nyla heard footsteps entering the stables, but she stayed where she was, still staring ahead. "Who's there?" The boy rounded the corner of Nyla's stall.

"Princess Nylina?" The boy came closer and crouched in front of her. Nyla's eyes shot to the boy's and she recognized Jimmy's worried face. A pang shot into her heart.

"No. Jimmy, you need to leave." She tried to scoot away in the straw as the burning hunger in her stomach started to overwhelm her. Her heart pounded painfully and Jimmy's body turned colorful. She let out a small cry as she felt her fangs growing out from her gums. Jimmy reached out a hand and Nyla stood up, stepping past him, but she stopped. Tingles ran up her spine and over her body as the sound of his beating heart and the rush of blood filled her ears, making her mouth water.

"Princess? What's wrong?" She felt Jimmy's hand touch her shoulder and the burning in her stomach and chest crept into her throat and mouth. She turned, inhaling his warm, succulent scent. Her body shuddered and she let out a small moan.

"Princess, you're starting to scare me." Jimmy started to step back, but Nyla's hand shot to his arm.

"No, stay." Nyla had no idea what she was doing, but she couldn't take it anymore and she let the hunger and power take over her body. She ran her hand up his arm to his shoulder and leaned in. "Stay," she whispered in his ear. His body relaxed as he calmed to her voice. She drew back and looked into Jimmy's calm eyes. The hunger seized her body and she gave in.

She squeezed his shoulder and sank her teeth into the soft part of his neck. Jimmy's body stiffened and he struggled, but that just urged Nyla on as she drank deeply, letting the sweet blood run down her throat, filling her body with strength and power. Blood ran down her chin and stained Jimmy's shirt. The hunger surged, urging her to appease it, but she cried out, letting Jimmy's body slump motion-lessly to the ground. A strange power and ecstasy surged through her body and she stumbled back into the wall, her fingernails digging into the wood. She let out an inhuman scream as pleasure surged through her body, tingling from her stomach, through her chest, and over her skull. Then it was gone as suddenly as it came. Her heart relaxed and all at once Nyla came in control of her body, coming back to herself. Her vision returned to normal and her fangs receded back to almost normal size.

Nyla took a deep breath and her body relaxed a bit, but the hunger still burned angrily in the pit of her stomach, begging her for more. She smiled, relieved that the hunger had subsided a little, and looked down, her smile fading as her eyes fell to Jimmy's still body.

"Jimmy? Jimmy!" Nyla fell to her knees beside his body and rolled him over onto his back. "Jimmy!" She put her ear to his heart. The tears started to fall as she heard no heartbeat and she realized what she had done. "No, no!" She shook his shoulders, and her hand found the wound in his neck. "Jimmy, no!" She let go of him and fell back against the wall beside his body, staring at her bloodstained hands.

CHAPTER 11

"Queen Lydia!" Kaden burst through the doors to the great hall.

"Kaden, Kristi?" Lydia stood up from her chair across from Lamar. "What is it?" She looked from Kaden's terrified expression to Kristi's furious one. She met Kaden as he rushed toward the table. Kaden hesitated as he looked at the table to where Lamar, Lucas, Felix, and Adrian sat, all eyes on him.

"It's Nyla." He kept his voice low. The queen's eyes widened, but she guarded her expression as she looked at Fulcan. He stood, coming to join them. Kaden and Fulcan walked over to the doors, talking in hushed tones as the queen turned to Lamar.

"Forgive me, I'll be back in a minute." She turned to Kristi, guiding her across the hall to a chair along the wall. Fulcan rushed over to the queen, whispering something into her ear that Lucas couldn't hear. He squinted over to the doors where Kaden paced, running his hands through his hair. He looked over to Lamar and their eyes met, conveying some kind of message. Lucas nodded and Lamar stood, starting toward Fulcan and the queen. Lydia turned to Lamar and the others.

"I'm sorry, but we must excuse ourselves. We have a bit of an issue with the guards by the castle gates." Fulcan joined Kaden back at the door and they went into the corridor outside the great hall.

"Is it anything that we can help with, My Queen?" Lamar gave her a reassuring look, but she kept her face serious.

"I'm afraid not, but I thank you for the offer. You may retire or explore the library, whatever suits you, but please, stay inside the castle for your own safety." She turned. "Jamin." She beckoned to Kristi.

"Your Majesty?" Jamin crouched beside Kristi, still shaking with fury in her chair.

"Please take her to the medical wing. She's had a bit of a shock," the queen instructed.

"I have not had a shock!" She scowled at the queen. "That monster tried to kill me!"

"Watch your words," the queen warned, a threatening look on her face.

"I'll take her, your majesty." Jamin helped Kristi to her feat, escorting her out the side door. Lydia began to head toward the doors.

"My queen." Lamar stepped in beside her. "I really think . . ."

"No." Lydia gave him a small smile. "Thank you, Lamar, but no." She turned away and hurried after Kaden and Fulcan. Lamar turned back to his group with a suspicious look on his face.

Lucas stood up. "I'll follow them and see what they're up too. I won't be seen. The rest of you retire to your rooms. I will meet with you later."

"But . . ." Adrian started to protest, but Lucas shot her a warning look.

Lamar turned to Lucas. "That guard looked as if she wanted to kill someone."

"Or something." Lucas gave Lamar a grin before he went out the doors after Lydia, Kaden, and Lucas.

He snuck behind them, always staying a couple yards away in the shadows. He was as silent as a mouse, choosing his steps carefully. They stopped ahead of him. Lucas cocked his head to the side, listening to their conversation intently.

"Where could she have gone?" The queen's voice was worried.

"I don't know. She just took off right after . . ." Kaden trailed off, not wanting to relive what he had seen Nyla do.

"Right after what?" Lucas said to himself.

"Where was Samuel during all this?" The queen frowned at Kaden.

"Nyla and I . . . kind of ditched her guards. Samuel was overseeing some of the trainees and Dominic was watching us." Kaden shook his head. "It wasn't all her fault. I wanted to sneak away too. Don't blame Dominic . . . or Samuel." The queen looked furious.

"I don't blame Samuel, or Dominic. You should have known better, Kaden! Now my daughter is missing, doing God knows what, because you two decided to sneak off and be alone!"

"It's going to be all right," Fulcan reassured the queen. "She's probably just scared. She's going through a lot. Samuel is probably still looking for her. I'll send out guards to look and I'll find Samuel and Dominic. We'll find her."

"I shouldn't have kept this from her for so long. How stupid!" She started pacing impatiently. "I wish her father were here. She needs him! Now she's gone and . . ." She stopped. "Fulcan, she could kill somebody! She may have no control over herself; over her hunger!"

So she is a vampire! Lucas smiled to himself.

"We'll find her, Lydia!" Fulcan put his hand on her shoulders. Kaden didn't know what to think. All he saw in his mind was Nyla threatening Kristi, and then jumping off the balcony and away from him. He saw her eyes and her fangs in his mind and shuddered. Kaden couldn't think about that. They needed to find her.

Kaden approached the stables and held his breath. He had heard the whimpering and knew right away where Nyla was. What was he going to see? He hoped for the best, but feared the worst. As he entered the stables, he walked as quietly as he could.

"Nyla?" Kaden gasped as he saw the crimson blood smeared around her mouth and on her dress. Her hands were also covered in blood. Kaden moved slightly, trying to get a better look at the body lying on the ground next to her. In the darkness of the stables, he couldn't make out who the dead body was, but the fact that Nyla had killed anybody sickened him. The bloody images of his mother and brother as they were being attacked in the woods by the vampires flashed in his mind. He moved again, crunching the straw under his feet and Nyla's eyes snapped to his. They were red from crying and looked empty. Kaden took a couple quick steps back as her pupils dilated, turning completely black. Fear rushed into his veins and all he could see were the faces of the monstrous vampires years ago as they slashed and bit at his mother and brother. Nyla opened her mouth to say something, but all that came out was a small sob. Her breath sounded jagged and had an inhuman rasp to it. Kaden winced as he noticed her sharp fangs and he backed up.

"Stop . . ." Nyla didn't recognize her own voice. It sounded more alluring and persuasive. She tried to fight the hunger as it started to creep into her throat and mouth like a blazing fire. She closed her eyes against the enticing, thermal image of Kaden's trembling body. "Kaden . . ." She tried to calm her breathing.

Kaden bumped into the wall and ran out, and Nyla let out a sob. Kaden crouched outside the stable doors, feeling sick to his stomach, his body shaking. He heard footsteps and looked up, seeing Samuel and Dominic approaching him.

"She . . . she's in there." He didn't dare stand, his legs feeling weak. Suddenly, there was a crash. Samuel hurried past Kaden, disappearing into the dark stables. He came out, alarm on his face.

"She's gone. We need to find her." There was a scream from the training grounds and Dominic and Samuel took off.

Kaden leaned against the stable wall, taking deep breaths. He still couldn't get the sick feeling out of his stomach. His head snapped to the left as he heard another terrified scream. He stood on shaking legs and started to run after Samuel and Dominic. He caught up to them as they crouched over something on the ground. Kaden's stomach lurched as he saw it was a dead guard. Blood covered his throat and body.

"Dammit, Nyla," Samuel whispered as he closed the eyes of the bearded man at his feet. He turned toward Dominic. "We need to hurry."

Nyla stood crouched in the shadows at the edge of the rosebushes. The hunger still blazed in her stomach and chest and fueled her body. All she could think about was blood and danger, her survival instincts fully kicked in. She sniffed the air, catching the scent of another approaching guard. She heard him slowly approach and she got ready for the pounce. She was the predator and he was her prey.

She saw him come into view, but instead of pouncing, she stood up gracefully. Seeing her, the guard stepped back in fear. Blood dripped from her mouth and covered the front of her dress. She started to approach him, a malicious, but seductive look on her face. She smiled, exposing her fangs, and the guard pulled his loaded crossbow up, aiming it at her.

"Stay away," the guard warned with a shaky voice.

"Why would I want to do that?" Nyla purred. She took a step toward him.

"I mean it!" He moved his finger to the trigger. Just then, Nyla heard a noise behind her. Her head whipped toward the source and she saw someone running toward her. She turned back to the guard and took another step toward him. The guard pulled the trigger, sending a heavy, crossbow bolt toward her.

"No!" A familiar voice cut through Nyla's senses and she looked back right as the bolt plunged into her side. She screamed in pain and lunged at the guard, catching ahold of his shoulders and clamping her jaws down into his flesh. The guard screamed, which only fueled Nyla on. Suddenly, someone grabbed her and she was pulled off the man. She struggled but was pinned to her back on the ground. She tried to throw the weight of the person off of her, but she couldn't get her shoulders off the ground. She opened her eyes and stopped struggling immediately, seeing Samuel sitting on top of her, pinning her to the ground.

"Samuel?" The world returned to normal as she came back to herself. She tried to sit up, but he held her there. "Samuel, I . . ." She looked past him to where Dominic tended to the man who was sitting on the ground. She caught the scent of blood and realized what she had just done.

"No!" Nyla closed her eyes and started to sob. "No, no, no! What have I done?!" Samuel let go of her shoulders and pulled her into his arms. She buried her head into his chest, her body shaking with sobs. She clutched at his shirt with her bloody hands.

"Shhh." Samuel stroked her hair. He caught Kaden's eye as he walked up, surveying the scene. Kaden turned away and sunk down against the rose bushes. Nyla continued to sob into Samuel's shirt as he gently stroked her hair.

"Breathe," he whispered softly to her. She took a couple deep breaths and began to calm down. She pulled back slightly and hissed in pain. She looked down at her side to where the end of the bolt stuck out from her skin. Blood oozed around the wood.

"Samuel . . ." Nyla began to panic, pain spreading through her torso. Samuel's eyes widened as he inspected the wound.

"It'll be okay, Nyla." He tried to calm her, but her eyes became black again as she stared at Samuel in pain and horror. He swept her up into his arms and she gasped in pain. "Dominic!" He looked to where Dominic crouched next to the bleeding guard. "I'm taking her to the infirmary. She's been shot." Dominic nodded and Samuel took off toward the castle.

Kaden sat, leaning against the rose bushes. His body felt numb as he stared ahead of him. He looked up, seeing Lydia and Fulcan approaching them. Dominic stood from where he was crouched next to the guard, who was now lying down with his hand pressed against his neck. Dominic went up to them with a grim look on his face. He whispered something to Lydia and Fulcan that Kaden couldn't hear. Lydia gasped and Fulcan turned white. Dominic stepped back, speaking louder.

"The stable boy's body is still in the stables, and the other body is by the training grounds. Silas is bleeding profusely. I don't know if he'll make it." Kaden watched as Fulcan ran over to the guard on the ground.

"He's still alive, but we need to get him to the infirmary immediately." Fulcan beckoned to two guards and they rushed over to him, helping the guard up and carrying him toward the castle.

"Where's Nyla now?" The queen looked around frantically.

"Samuel took her to the infirmary. Silas shot her with his crossbow."

"What?!" Lydia took off toward the castle. Kaden looked up at Dominic.

"She was shot?!" He stood up when Dominic nodded his head. Kaden hurried after the queen.

Kaden heard the screams as he approached the infirmary and he stopped outside the doors. He hesitated, deciding what to do. He had seen enough blood tonight and he didn't know if he really wanted to see more, especially if the blood was Nyla's.

"Kaden?" He looked over and spotted Julia sitting in a chair next to the wall. She wrung her dress in her hands, worry scrunching her face together. He sat beside her, looking at the ground. "What happened? They said it was best if I stayed out. I've been asking, but nobody will tell me what happened."

"I . . . Nyla . . ." He swallowed. "She killed somebody." Horror struck Julia's face and she shook her head.

"She . . . she'll be all right. She didn't mean anything, I know she didn't." Julia looked at Kaden, searching for reassurance, but all Kaden could see was the image of Nyla's bloody face and black eyes boring into his.

"Julia, she killed two people. One of them was a guard and I don't know who the other one was. She injured another guard."

"She did?" A tear slipped down her cheek. "I saw them bring in one of the men. He looked like he was still alive. Why is she screaming in the infirmary? Is she still out of control?"

"The third guard, the one they brought in, shot her with a crossbow." Kaden's voice was like lead.

"What?!" Julia got to her feet. "Why aren't you in there?!" She gave Kaden an alarmed scowl.

"I . . . I can't Julia. I can't see that." Kaden didn't look at her, ashamed of himself.

"Well, I can." Julia turned and burst through the doors. Nyla screamed, her back arching off the table she was laying on as Samuel stood over her, barking orders at the nurses. Julia gasped at the bolt that stuck out of her torso.

"Oh my God!" Julia's hands flew to her mouth. The queen rushed over to her, her face as white as a sheet.

"Julia, you shouldn't be in here." She tried to nudge Julia out.

"No." Julia stood firm. "I can help." The queen nodded and moved to stand beside Samuel.

"Julia, put pressure on this!" Fulcan waved her over to the other end of the infirmary where he stood over the injured guard. She hurried over and pressed a bloody cloth onto his neck.

"Will he turn?" Julia looked at Fulcan with a worried expression.

"No. Only a pure-blood original has the power to turn a human into a vampire. They have to bleed the body dry to the point of near death and feed them their own blood. Then the 'fledgling,' as their called, needs to feed on a human to complete the turn."

Nyla stared at the ceiling, her torso burning with searing pain. Spots dotted her vision and she gasped for breath, whimpering as the breath alone made pain shoot out from the bolt lodged in her flesh.

"Someone grab me a towel!" Samuel ordered. Somebody handed him a clean, white cloth and Nyla turned her head to the left, looking into her Mother's upset face.

"Nyla." Samuel's concerned voice drew her attention away from her mother. She looked at Samuel. Her eyes connected with his and his eyebrows knit together, his mouth in a firm line. "I have to pull this out. It's going to hurt like hell, but I have to do it." She shook her head fiercely, clenching her teeth together so hard she felt they could shatter in her mouth. "I have to." He turned to the queen. "Hold her down." He turned Nyla's face toward him with a bloodstained hand and stared hard into her eyes.

"Don't take your eyes off mine. Concentrate on me. Don't take—" He yanked the bolt out of her with his other hand and she screamed. Samuel threw the bolt to the ground and pressed the towel onto the wound.

"She needs blood!" Samuel looked around the room. "She needs human blood now, or she can't heal. It's too deep of a wound." Julia ran forward.

"I'll do it!" She rolled up her sleeve. Samuel nodded to the nurse beside him and she hurried to a drawer where she pulled out a syringe with a long needle at the end. She grabbed an empty blood bag and attached a tube from it to the needle. Julia sat down in a chair as the nurse cleaned the crease of her arm with a cotton swab. She inserted the needle into her arm and Julia watched as crimson blood trickled into the bag.

119

"Why can't she just drink from me? Wouldn't that be faster?" Julia looked up at the nurse.

"I don't know if she would be able to stop." Samuel kept his eyes down, still locked with Nyla's. She focused on the deep, river colors in his eyes, not daring to look away from him. She felt her mother take her hand and squeeze it gently, trying to comfort her. Nyla blinked, white spots starting to cloud Samuel's eyes from her view.

"How's the blood coming?" Samuel called. He stroked Nyla's cheek gently with one hand while he kept pressure from her bleeding wound with the other.

"Am I going to die?" Nyla croaked. Her whole body burned.

"No." She saw the pain in Samuel's eyes. "Dammit, where's that blood?" He tore his gaze away from Nyla's face just as the nurse pushed the warm bag of fresh blood into his hand. He held it to Nyla's mouth and a few drops splashed onto her parted lips. She suddenly took the bag, her pupils dilating. She greedily drank from the bag, feeling a warming sensation spread out from her wound. She sighed as she sucked the last few drops from the bag and laid her head back onto the table. Samuel removed the blood soaked towel from her stomach. Nyla pushed herself onto her elbows and gave a sigh of relief when she didn't feel any pain. Samuel put his hand on the spot where the bolt had been a minutes before and he ripped the fabric slightly wider. He ran his fingers over the smooth skin of Nyla's stomach. There wasn't even a scar.

"All healed up." He gave her a small smile. She looked down at her dress. It was hard to tell what blood was hers and what was the other men's. There was also blood still smeared on Nyla's face and around her mouth. She looked at her red hands and her heart throbbed painfully as the images of what she had done rushed back into her mind all at once.

"Thank God!" Lydia crouched until she was level with Nyla. "Nylina?"

Nyla's gaze turned to her mother. "Mom . . ." Her voice was faint. "Mom . . . I . . ." She turned her gaze to the still body of the guard across the room. "Is he . . . ?"

"He's gone." Fulcan walked up to them but kept his distance.

"No, no, no, no," Nyla moaned in agony she started wiping at her tears, smearing more blood on her face. Fulcan nodded to the door and exited the room, giving them privacy. Julia gave Nyla a sympathetic look before following him out the door. Samuel nodded to the nurses and they left through the opposite door.

"Oh, Nylina, I'm so sorry. This is all my fault." Tears sprang to queen's eyes as she took in the sight of Nyla closing her eyes in agony. Lydia turned to Samuel.

"Thank you for finding her and bringing her here. I don't know what I would have done if . . ." The queen looked at the hole in the stomach of Nyla's dress.

"I would do anything for her," Samuel said, looking at Nyla with sympathy. Nyla didn't hear a word they said. She was lost in her own thoughts.

"I'm a monster," Nyla whimpered. She pulled her knees to her chest and buried her face in her hands.

"You're not a monster." Lydia reached a hand out to touch her knee, but Nyla flinched away. Seeing the pain in the queen's face, Samuel gently grabbed Nyla's hand, pulling it away from her face.

"You're not a monster, Nyla." He smoothed her blood-crusted hair away from her face with his hand and she looked up at him.

"Samuel, you had to pull me off of that guard. I killed Jimmy and I couldn't control myself. That guard shot me in order to save his own life and it still didn't stop me. I could have killed you!" She turned away, shame tearing at her heart. The queen looked at Samuel with wide eyes. He looked back down at Nyla.

"No. I know you wouldn't have killed me. You stopped when you saw me. You can learn control, Nyla."

"I don't know if I can." Nyla shook her head. "You should have just let me die before I can hurt anyone else."

"Nylina!" The queen exclaimed in shock. Nyla broke into sobs. "Nylina, my love"—the queen lowered her voice—"we'll get through this. We'll all help you." She looked at Samuel for encouragement.

"I will do anything that I can to help you, Nyla." Samuel gently pulled her chin up with his hand, letting her see the truth in his eyes. She blinked through her tears.

"I don't want this." She sobbed. "I don't want to be this . . . thing!" She hugged her knees tightly, her body and mind numb. She wanted to shut it all out.

"Nylina . . ." The queen tried to comfort her daughter. The doors opened and Dominic entered, followed by four guards carrying the bodies of the other guard and Jimmy inside the infirmary. A tear slid down the queen's cheek as she watched them pass. Nyla looked at Jimmy's limp head as it slumped backward. Droplets of blood splattered the floor from the wound on Jimmy's neck.

"I don't want to be here." Nyla looked away, her head spinning, as she felt sick. She jumped off the table, holding the side for support, but her knees gave out and she crouched, vomiting blood all over the floor. Samuel crouched beside her and pulled her hair away from her face, gently rubbing her back.

"Let's get you to your room." He slowly helped her stand, but she moved out of his grasp.

"I need to take care of things here." The queen wiped a few tears from her eyes and turned to her daughter. "I love you, Nyla. I will be up as soon as I can."

"No! I want to be alone." She shook her head.

"Okay, Nyla," the queen said sadly. She turned to Samuel. "We need to take care of the bodies." She walked past them and Nyla followed her mother with her eyes. She looked to where Dominic was wrapping the three bodies up in bloody sheets. Nyla turned and grabbed the side of the table again as she felt another wave of sickness. Samuel put an arm around her waist, pulling her gently back against him.

"Breathe. It will pass," he whispered in her ear. She closed her eyes and took deep breaths.

"Please don't leave me." Okay, maybe she didn't want to be all alone.

"I'll stay with her." Samuel turned his head toward the queen but kept a hand around Nyla's waste. She nodded, her mouth in a thin line. Samuel turned back to Nyla. "Better?" he asked softly. Nyla nodded her head she looked toward the door, remembering all the people standing outside the doors.

"Can we go the other way?" She turned, keeping her eyes on the floor as they passed the wrapped bodies of Jimmy and the other two guards.

Kaden had calmed down and was pacing nervously, ignoring Julia, Jamin, and Fulcan as they all sat in chairs next to the wall. He stopped as he saw the doors open and the rest stood. Kaden looked up and expected to see Nyla but was a little relieved when the queen stepped out. His heart leapt when he saw she was covered in blood. Lydia approached them all with a solemn look.

"Where's Nyla?" Julia asked in a small voice. "Is she okay?"

"She's distraught and unstable right now." The queen's pretty face was flushed with pain and worry. She looked tired and seemed to be ten years older than she was. "But she's going to be all right. You're blood healed her perfectly." She gave Julia a pat on the shoulder. Kaden grimaced as he looked down at Julia's arm where a bandage was fastened to her skin.

"What can we do to help? Where is she?" Julia asked earnestly.

Kaden looked around the queen and his face turned white when he spotted the blood that covered the table and the floor underneath it.

"Samuel took her to her room." The queen sighed. "I think it's best if you two keep your distance from her for now. You can go up to her room, but she wants to be alone right now." Julia opened her mouth to protest, but Lydia put a hand on her arm. "I know you want to be with her right now. We all do, but please. She needs to adjust. She just killed Jimmy and two other men. She's horrified with herself. She thinks she's a monster." The queen's voice broke and Julia gave her a hug. Kaden closed his eyes remembering the way Jimmy's head had drooped as the guards had taken him through the infirmary doors. Sympathy for Nyla nudged its way beside his fear. He wanted to be strong and not abandon her like he had before. He looked at the queen with a guarded expression.

"It'll be okay. She'll be all right." Kaden didn't believe his own words, but he hoped they would at least comfort the queen. He looked to where Fulcan was talking with the guards who had wrapped the bodies in the sheets. "Come on. I'll take you back to your room."

"No." The queen gave Kaden a grateful look. "I need to get things cleaned up and ready for a burial. Fulcan or Dominic will escort me back."

Julia looked at the three bodies. "I want to stay with you. Jimmy was . . . my friend."

"Very well." Lydia turned and walked back to the infirmary and Julia followed her in. Kaden stood there for a second, thinking of what to do. He decided to see if Nyla was all right. As he walked down the hall and turned up the stairs he heard a noise and looked behind him into the darkened hallway. Too distracted to investigate further, he took off up the stairs leaving Lucas peering out from where he was hidden behind a column.

CHAPTER 12

Lydia watched as Jamin and Mary, the head nurse, unwrapped the three bodies and started to examine them. She started with Jimmy.

"There are two puncture marks in his jugular. Obviously fang marks. It's a clean wound, but unfortunately not unpainful." Lydia winced as she looked at the two perfect holes in Jimmy's neck. "She almost drained him of blood, and he was unconscious when he bled out the rest of the way. It looks like the same happened to the other two."

"We will give them all a proper burial, but cover up the story." Lydia turned to Fulcan. "We shouldn't cause panic and fear when this can be controlled. I should have taken action right when she started to change, I just didn't want to believe that it was happening."

"None of us could have predicted that she was going to kill, Lydia . . . My Lady." Fulcan corrected himself in the presence of others.

"No, but we should have taken precautions. We need to take action to prevent this from happening again. If Nyla feeds regularly, she won't get bloodlust. She'll be able to control herself." Lydia sighed thinking to herself. "She healed so fast when she drank Julia's blood."

Jamin stepped forward. "I don't know too much about her changes, but I think she has completed the turn. She was shot with a wooden bolt from the crossbow, right?"

Lydia nodded. "Well, if my theory is correct, then Nyla was still technically in the fledgling faze before she gave into the vampiric hunger. She is completely vampire now. Look at who her father was. The human part of her was only Serene's spell. The vampire side of her was too powerful and magical, and it consumed her whole being. It's who she is. It's in her blood." He paused. "It's a good thing she was shot after she had fed on the other two bodies first. Now she's almost invincible, but because it was a wooden bolt that struck her, she still might have bled out. It's good that Samuel rushed her here and Julia was willing to give up some blood. We're lucky Samuel found her before anyone else did."

"Well, Kaden found her in the stables," Dominic cut in.

"Kaden found her first?" The queen looked at him.

"Yes, but he was sitting outside the stables when Samuel and I got there. Kaden looked . . . terrified. Like he had seen a monster." Dominic looked away from the queen's teary eyes.

Jamin hesitated before speaking. "Well, assuming Kaden's reaction wasn't handled then it only made her worse. That's probably why she went on a killing rampage and got the other two guards." Jamin gave the queen a sympathetic look. "She might take a while to get over this. She's a different person now. She'll eventually go back to the Nyla we know and love, but right now, she's too mortified with what she did and she's fully introduced to her whole self now. Her brain is overloaded and she's not thinking clearly. She's fighting who she is. We don't know how long it will take her to fully adjust." Lydia sat down, overwhelmed with all the information Jamin had loaded on her.

"Okay," Fulcan said, "but we still have two present problems at hand. What story do we fabricate to explain the deaths? If it was just one body it wouldn't be as bad, but covering up three deaths is going to be a challenge. The second problem is what Nyla is going to feed on."

Dominic stepped forward. "Well, as for Jimmy, we can just say he had an accident with the horses getting spooked. He was kicked in the head. The other two guards were run over by the stampede when the horses ran out. Nobody besides us needs to look at the bodies. Most of the horses were out to pasture anyway, so I'll go let some of the horses loose. We should say there was a fire. We'll burn the stables down and cover up the blood." He gave them a shrug.

"I think that just might work." Fulcan nodded his head. "Now, what are we going to do to keep Nyla's hunger contained until she can control it?"

"Well," Jamin put in, "I would prefer that she doesn't get used to human blood and drinks animal blood instead. Samuel's a good hunter. He will just have to take her to the woods every so often. We'll save extra animal blood in bottles from any cattle or sheep we butcher."

"Perfect." The queen pushed her hair back from her face. "Dominic, will you go check on Lamar and the others? Absolutely no word can get out about this, especially not to them. We just gained helpful allies and we can't afford to lose them." She went over to Julia, who was leaned up against the wall, her hands covering her mouth, and tears running down her face.

"Julia, you should go check on Nyla and comfort her. I know she doesn't want to see anybody, but she might let you in. Can you do that?" She put her hand on Julia's shoulder.

Julia straightened, wiping tears from her face. "Of course, she's still my best friend. I'll go." She took a last look at Jimmy's body and exited through the doors.

As they spoke, Lucas made his way to his quarters, careful to avoid any guards. He smiled at the new information he had just gained. This would help their cause so much if he could make it go the way he wanted. He saw Julia hurrying from the hallway leading to the medical wing. There were tears on her face.

"What are you doing here?" Julia gave him a suspicious look, trying to hide her tears.

"I heard a commotion and wanted to make sure everything was all right. I couldn't find anyone, so I'm just going back to my room."

"Oh." She considered his words. "Well, it's nothing, just Jimmy, the stable boy . . . he had an accident. There was a fire. I have to go." She hurried off in the direction of Nyla's room.

Kaden stood outside Nyla's bedroom door. He leaned against the wall, lost in his own thoughts. He hoped Nyla wouldn't be furious with him. He shouldn't have acted like he did. He hated himself for hurting her further. Suddenly the image of his mother flashed through his memory, but he shook it from his mind. He couldn't even imagine what Nyla had gone through and what she was feeling. He couldn't blame her for wanting to be alone and shutting the world out; he just hoped she wouldn't shut him out too.

A hint of jealousy filled him as he thought of Samuel in there with Nyla. He knew it was completely selfish, but he wished that it were him who had comforted Nyla and rescued her instead of running like a coward. It wasn't fair that Samuel got to be the one to be there for her in her greatest time of need. *What if she doesn't even want to look at me?* His thoughts were distracted as Julia came running up to him from behind.

"Kaden!" Kaden pushed himself off the wall as she approached. "Is she okay? How's she doing?"

"I haven't gone in yet." He stared at the door.

"Why not?" Julia looked at him in confusion.

"I don't know." Kaden frowned down at the ground. "Queen Lydia said she wanted to be alone. I don't know how she'll react to seeing me. I didn't respond well when I first saw her in the stables."

"Really?" Julia gave Kaden a sympathetic look.

"Well, I . . . I couldn't handle myself when I saw her. Samuel was there for her in the infirmary and I don't know what he said to her, but she feels like a danger or something to everyone else."

"Well, we can't just stand here and wonder at the door." She moved to the doorknob and turned it, slowly entering the room. Nyla sat on the bed, her knees to her chest, while Samuel sat beside her.

"I don't know what to do." Samuel stood and walked toward Julia. Julia moved to get a better look at Nyla and gasped.

"She's still covered in blood." Julia swallowed hard, looking away. "We should get her into a bath. I can take her if you want." She moved toward them, but Nyla panicked, scrambling backward on the bed.

"Stay back!" Nyla's expression was unreadable and dangerous as she crouched on the bed like an animal in defense. "Don't touch me! I might hurt you." Tears filled her eyes and started running down her cheeks as the image of the three, lifeless bodies in the infirmary flooded her vision.

"Shhh." Samuel knelt beside the bed, touching her hand softly. "It's okay."

"Nyla, you would never hurt any of us. Both Kaden and I know that." She went to stand beside Kaden, who was still planted by the door. Kaden stared to where Samuel's hand covered Nyla's. He willed Nyla to look at him, to say that it was all right. He wanted to be the one to hold her and comfort her. He was the one who had almost kissed her just a few hours before she had attacked Kristi. Then dread filled his heart as a thought hit him.

What if it had been me that she had targeted? What if we were alone when the hunger overtook her? What if she had attacked me in the stables too and Samuel had to pull her off me? He shook the horrible thoughts from his head. He couldn't afford to think like that. He had to do anything for her, no matter what the cost.

"No, Julia. We can't help her right now. She's too distraught." Kaden looked into Nyla's eyes, filled with pain and misery. "She's suffering right now. The fewer people are around, her the better."

"Well," Samuel hesitated, looking at the two of them, almost begging for help. "So I have to get her into the bath?"

Horror and jealousy filled Kaden's chest. He was the one who had confessed his feelings for Nyla and he was going to be damned if anyone else was going to see her naked, especially Samuel.

"Absolutely not!" Kaden started forward but stopped as he saw Nyla's warning expression. "No, Julia. You have to do it." He hesitated. "It's not right if Samuel or I do it." He hadn't spoken to Samuel about his feelings for Nyla, not that it mattered, but Samuel had been spending a lot of time with Nyla and what if he had feelings for her too? If the rumors were true, then Kaden didn't know what he was going to do. He wasn't about to confront that issue right now with Nyla in the state that she was in.

"Kaden," Julia came to stand in front of him, guarding her expression from Samuel and Nyla. "Nyla doesn't want anyone here besides Samuel." She lowered her voice so that only he could hear. "I know that you don't like it, but you're going to have to deal with it, for Nyla."

Kaden looked behind Julia to where Samuel crouched in front of the bed, next to where Nyla sat. Tears ran down her face, which had twisted again in agony.

"Okay." He took a deep breath. "We'll go. Samuel, take care of her and please let us know if there is any change."

"I will." Samuel nodded, not looking away from Nyla, keeping eye contact with her. She started to calm down as she stared into his stunning eyes.

Kaden sighed and turned, leaving the room with Julia trailing behind him. Once they shut the door behind them, Kaden groaned, letting out all the frustrated feelings he had been holding back.

"Dammit!" He ran his hands back through his hair and leaned with his back against the wall.

"Kaden"—Julia put a hand on his arm, but he shook it off—"it's going to be all right. She's going to get better."

"Is she?" He turned to Julia, pain on his face. "Besides Samuel, she doesn't want anyone to be around her, not even me! She killed people Julia! She killed Jimmy and I . . . I can't forget what she is. I'm scared of thinking that she's one of the monsters like the ones who killed my mom! Now Samuel is the one in there with her and I'm stuck out here helpless and . . . I am terrified Julia! I hate it and I hate that I can't make the feeling go away!"

"You are not helpless! Come on." She pushed him off the wall. "Keep it together. If you care about her that much, then you will have faith in her. You cannot give up on her, Kaden! She's not the monster you think she is. She's nothing like the inhuman creatures that killed your mom. If you give up on her then what hope does she have?"

"She has . . . I don't know . . . him!" Kaden turned and stalked off, leaving Julia alone in the hallway. She looked at Nyla's door.

"Oh, Samuel, make her better." She took a last look at the door and ran down the hall toward where Kaden had disappeared around the corner.

Samuel sat beside Nyla and stroked her hair, as she lay curled on her side. Her tears had stopped, but her whole body still shook.

"Nyla." Samuel leaned down slightly, placing his hand on her back. "We should get you cleaned up now. Can I get you in the bath?"

Nyla took a shaky breath. "Ya."

"I'll be right back." He started to get up and she grabbed his arm. "I'm not going to leave you. I'm just going to run the water." She let go of his arm and curled into a tighter ball. She squeezed her eyes shut, but the vision of Jimmy's still body, and empty, lifeless eyes haunted her. She felt sick to her stomach at the fact that she had not only killed two guards, but had killed her friend as well, and she hated the fact that she had liked drinking their blood. Her stomach lurched again and she clamped her mouth shut, not wanting to vomit on her bed.

"Nyla." She jumped as Samuel touched her side. "The water's running." She nodded and slowly sat up. With Samuel's help, she stood and walked over to the bathroom. He stood by the door, unsure of what to do until Nyla turned, her empty, sad eyes begging him in. He entered and shut the door, letting the steam from the hot water warm the room. Nyla fidgeted with the buttons on the front of her dress.

"Screw it! It's ruined anyway!" Nyla hooked her fingers in the hole where the bolt had pierced her and ripped the fabric. Samuel gasped and whirled around as Nyla let the dress fall to the ground.

"Samuel?" Nyla's small voice sounded from behind him, but he didn't turn around.

"Nyla, I couldn't 'control myself' around you when you came out in that slip remember?" He tried to joke. He flinched as she touched his shoulder.

"I trust you. I just need you to see me. I need you to know that I'm not a monster." Her voice was pained.

"Nyla, I know you're not a monster." He turned but kept his eyes closed.

"I'll get into the water first. Then will you stay? I just don't want to be all alone right now." Samuel nodded. He waited until he heard her get into the water and opened his eyes. Nyla sat deep in the big, round tub with her knees up to her chest, soap bubbles hiding her body. Samuel sat in a chair but didn't scoot it close to the tub, keeping himself an arm's length away. Nyla reached her hand out of the water, grabbing his hand, and holding it tightly.

"Thank you." She tried to manage a smile, but her face remained empty. Samuel was just glad she was holding a conversation.

"Thanks for finding me, and . . . pulling me off that guard." She gulped back tears and took a deep breath. "Thanks for saving my life even though I . . ." She couldn't bring herself to say the words.

"It's okay." Samuel gave her a small, reassuring smile. "You're going to be just fine."

"Samuel . . ." Her eyes were scared. "I'm evil."

"What?" Samuel looked at her confused.

"When I was . . . drinking Jimmy's blood . . . and when I attacked the other two men, I felt the power surge through me. I was stronger. I enjoyed it." The tears came again and she covered her face with her hands. "Ugh!" She stared, mortified, at her hands. "I still have their blood all over me!" She let out a small sob.

Samuel reached over, grabbing a washrag from the cupboard beside the tub. He crouched beside the tub, dipped it in the water, and began to dab at Nyla's face. He washed all the blood away from her hands and face and smiled at her.

"There. There's the beautiful Nyla I know. You're going to be just fine. You're strong." He was relieved as Nyla succeeded in a smile.

"Samuel." She leaned in, her breath hot in his ear. Her voice contained a seductive tone. He sucked in a breath.

"Yes?" His heart pounded.

"Thank you. You saved me." She pulled back, her face inches from his. He gazed at her, lost in those mesmerizing eyes. Before he knew what was happening, Nyla leaned in, but he pulled back, realizing what was happening. She was trying to lure him in. Her vampire side was still hungry and she was trying to push down her misery with lust.

"Nyla, no." He sat back on his heels, but stayed a safe distance close enough to the tub as not to upset her.

"Why not?" Nyla looked confused, but then her lips curved into a sweet smile. "I want you, I need you." Her eyes went black and she reached for him, but he pulled away.

"Nyla, I'm sorry, but you aren't thinking clearly. You're not yourself right now. This isn't really what you want." His heart ached as she sat back with a pained expression on her face. He sighed. "Come on, let's get you washed up." He watched her face as she washed her hair and looked away as she scrubbed the rest of the blood off of her body. She looked down at the red water and started to get out of the tub.

"I'll go change your sheets." Samuel stood up and waited for her to approve him to leave the room. She nodded and he stepped out, grabbing new sheets from the big wardrobe-like closet on the wall beside the bathroom. After having guarded her for a while, he pretty much knew where everything was.

Samuel turned as there was a knock on Nyla's bedroom door. Samuel opened the door and looked toward the bathroom, making sure Nyla still had the door closed.

"Dominic." Samuel spoke in a hushed tone, careful that Nyla would hopefully not hear them.

"This is from the queen." Dominic held out a silver tray. On the tray was a cup of steaming, brown liquid and a note. Samuel unfolded the note and quickly read it. His brows knit together, but he nodded in understanding. He took the tray from Dominic, crumpled the note, and handed it back.

"I'll be here when you're ready." Dominic turned, keeping guard in the hallway as Samuel closed the door. Samuel set the tray on the table and stripped the bloody sheets off of Nyla's bed.

As he changed the sheets, his thoughts turned to Kaden. He knew that Kaden had feelings for Nyla. He sighed. Samuel didn't know exactly what his own feelings were for her. She was surely amazing, but either way, he couldn't let her come between him and Kaden. After the bed was made, Samuel turned around and spotted Nyla in the doorway of the bathroom, watching him. She was cloaked in a short, white robe, her long, wet blond hair piled into a loose bun, the shorter, loose strands flowing around her neck and face. He gave her a small smile and she crossed the room, sitting on the bed. He sat beside her.

"What is that?" Nyla nodded to the steaming cup on her bed-side table.

"Your mother sent up some tea to calm your nerves." Samuel handed the cup to Nyla. "Drink. It will help you."

Nyla nodded and took a sip, sighing pleasantly as the warm, sweet liquid ran down her throat, warming her whole body. Nyla looked at Samuel, frowning.

"Please stay with me. I don't want to be alone. I'm afraid of what might happen if I'm alone." So that was why she didn't want to be alone. She was afraid of what she might do if she got the chance and lost control again. Samuel knelt in front of her, coming eye level with her.

"I will never leave you unless you ask me to." He stared into her eyes and found gratitude and complete trust, making them a little less empty. "Drink." He nodded to the cup and Nyla took another sip.

Pleased, Samuel stood up, sitting in the big felt chair beside her bed. "I'll be here all night."

Nyla set the cup down on the bedside table an stood up, facing Samuel. She desperately wanted a distraction from her thoughts. A burning feeling, different from the hunger she felt before, bubbled in the pit of her stomach. She untied her robe, letting it drop to the floor around her feet. Samuel sucked in a breath, but got a glimpse of her body before he could look away fast enough. Her body was perfect. No flaws whatsoever. He cleared his throat and continued looking the other direction.

"I know you don't think I want this, but I do." He could hear the hunger in her voice, but he didn't dare look at her.

"Nyla . . ." He heard her sigh and the bed creaked. He looked back at her, trying to keep his eyes on her face. She gave him a small, less empty smile, patting the bed next to her.

"Nyla."

"Please." Her face became sad again. "I need someone to be with me, to love me. Please."

"Nyla, no." He picked up her robe and handed it to her. She sadly looked away from him, taking the robe and covering herself. Samuel also picked up the cup of tea and handed it to her.

"Nyla, this is just a reaction to the power you feel from feeding. It happens all the time. Feeding is like an . . . aphrodisiac to vampires, but we can't. It wouldn't be right." Nyla still looked hurt as she gulped down the contents of the cup. She closed her eyes as the liquid sent another wave of warm tingles down her throat. Suddenly sleepy, Nyla got under the covers, staying in a sitting position. She pulled the covers up, but took off her robe, tossing it to the floor at Samuel's feet.

"Nyla." Samuel tried not to think about Nyla's naked body just under her blankets.

"I can sleep anyway I want to." Nyla shot off at him, yawning. There was a small silence between them. Nyla laid down and turned on her side. "Samuel, will you please just lay with me a while? I'll keep my hands to myself."

Samuel sighed and stood up, unhooking the belt that held his weapons and placed it on the chair. He took off his boots and looked down at his bloody shirt.

"Nyla—" Samuel went to sit back down on the chair.

"Just . . . take off your shirt . . . I said I'll keep my hands to myself . . . We are friends." Nyla's voice began to slur with fatigue.

Samuel sighed and stripped off his stained shirt. Nyla took in the sight of the smooth muscles rippling over his arms, chest, and stomach. She tried to keep her eyes open, but her lids felt like lead.

Samuel lay on top of the covers, careful not to touch Nyla's body, but she slowly rolled him on his side to face her. She pulled the covers around her body and lay facing him, her lids closed.

"Samuel." Nyla's breath was sweat in his face. "I'm not . . . evil, am I? I tried to . . . control myself . . . I . . . just . . ." She trailed off, sleepiness taking over her body.

"Shhh." He brought his hand to her face and softly rubbed her cheek with his thumb to comfort her. "Nyla, I know in my heart and soul that you are not a monster and definitely not evil. I promise I will help and protect you. We'll get through this." Although Nyla couldn't open her heavy eyelids, she listened to Samuel's voice with a slight smile on her face. After everything that he had seen, after everything she had done, he still had faith in her. Her breathing became heavy as she drifted off.

Samuel was completely aware of how little was between her smooth, naked body and him, but he knew it was wrong. *She isn't herself right now. She will probably wake up tomorrow and go running back to Kaden.* Samuel wasn't sure of his own feelings, but the need to protect her was pounding him. He would help her, no matter what the cost.

CHAPTER 13

Kaden lie awake in his bed, watching the growing dawn cast pink and orange shadows onto his walls. He had lain awake all night, his mind never straying from Nyla. *How is she doing? What are her and Samuel doing right now?* The thought of Samuel and Nyla together made him sick to his stomach, but deep down, he knew that Samuel was one of the best guys he knew. He was his friend and it made Kaden feel guilty that he would even doubt Samuel. Yes, he flirted, but he would never take advantage of anyone. Kaden wasn't even sure Samuel had those kinds of feelings for Nyla.

Kaden huffed a sigh, sitting up in the bed and running his hands through his hair. He got out of the bed and strode to the bathroom, careful not to wake Julia curled up on the couch next to his bed. She had refused to sleep in her own room, even though Kaden had offered to walk her there. Kaden understood, though. He didn't really want to be alone either. So much had been happening the past few hours that they all just needed time to process things and think.

He looked at his disheveled appearance in the mirror. His dark brown hair was messy and his green eyes appeared to be faded from sleep deprivation. He splashed cold water on his face, brushed his teeth, and got dressed, still not feeling any better. By the time he was fully clothed, and a little more awake, Julia had woken up. She sat on the edge of the couch, staring at the floor.

"What should we do now?" She looked at Kaden with a worried expression. "I mean, should we go to see how she's doing, or should we just give her some time?"

Kaden longed to see Nyla, but he knew better. "Let's go speak with the queen and see what her thoughts are." He waited for Julia to get ready and they made their way down to the grand hall to get some breakfast.

When they reached the grand hall, Lydia, Jamin, and Fulcan were sitting down, eating what looked like oatmeal. Jamin looked less like his usual, scholarly self, and Fulcan had a big mug of black coffee and a five o'clock shadow on his face. The queen still looked radiant, as usual, but even she had an exhausted quality about her. Apparently nobody had gotten very much sleep.

"Kaden, Julia." The queen gave them a small smile as they joined her at the main table.

"Any news on Nyla?" Julia asked anxiously.

"Not yet." Fulcan took another sip of his coffee. "No word from Samuel yet either. But Samuel's a good guard, he'll check in with us one way or another."

Kaden couldn't wait for Samuel to decide to check in. "Shouldn't we send a doctor, or Jamin, or somebody to check on her?"

"Not yet. Right now we need to give her time. She is safe where she is." The queen frowned down at her hands.

"Well, she doesn't really need a doctor. Her wound completely healed on its own when she drank Julia's blood. Nyla's a vampire, so she'll probably never need a doctor again," Jamin explained. Kaden hid his frown.

"She's also stronger than a normal vampire," the queen added. "Her father didn't tell me too much, but I know he was an original, pure-blood vampire. She'll be more powerful than a regular, turned vampire because she was born with it in her blood."

"Wait." Kaden let this information process through his head. "So her father was one of the first vampires? He was a pure blood?"

"Yes." Jamin took off his spectacles, cleaning them on his shirt. "We have no idea what she is capable of. I got to study King Richard, but he wouldn't give me much information on his . . . pure-blood abilities. Only the original, pure-blood family have those abilities, so Nyla may inherit them, and she may not."

"Well, what are these abilities?" Kaden leaned his arms on the table, getting a better look at Jamin to his right"

"Like I said, the king didn't give me too much insight to his abilities. I don't know. I do know that he was able to be out in the sun while regular vampires can't."

"Well, what do we do?" Kaden looked from the queen to Jamin expectantly.

"I guess just wait." The queen slumped a little in her chair. "This was her first kill. She's scared. Her heart and mind need to heal first, and then she'll be ready enough to talk about it. Until we know if she can control herself, we can't risk the safety of others." Just then, Lamar entered the hall, followed by Felix, Adrian, and Lucas. The queen looked at everyone, shushing them silently.

"My queen." Lamar did a small bow and sat down next to Kaden. The others sat across from him, next to Fulcan. "I assume all was settled with the commotion last night? There is talk amongst the maids about a poor stable boy and two guards dying last night." The queen shot Fulcan a small, panicked look. *Damn those gossipy maids!* Fulcan cleared his throat.

"Yes, it was an accident. The horses were spooked from a stable fire, and he got kicked. He died instantly and it was quick and painless. The two guards tried to help, but they got trampled by the horses as they ran out of the stables."

"Hmmm, quite unfortunate. You would think that a stable boy would know better than to get in the way of a panicking animal."

"Yes"—Lydia gave Lamar a shrug—"it is unfortunate, but an accident."

"Yes, so it seems." Lamar stopped talking as Lucas shot him a warning look.

"Yes, well"—the queen shifted uncomfortably in her chair—"there's to be a burial for them tomorrow before sunset. You are all welcome to join if you want to."

"And where is Princess Nylina?" Lamar asked, looking around the hall. "She was to be here today, was she not?" He ignored Lucas's stare.

This time, Jamin spoke. "She . . . has fallen ill. Just a small cold I'm afraid, but with the war brewing any day now, we need her to rest and gain back her strength."

"Ah." Lamar nodded his head. "Yes, we do need her to be as strong and healthy as she can be."

"Yes." The queen stood. "She will hopefully be well in a day or so." She turned to Fulcan and Jamin. "Shall we? We have a lot of business to attend to." She turned back to Lamar. "You can explore the castle grounds if you wish and join us this afternoon in the council room to discuss battle strategies that Gafna and Rothgar have been working on."

"Yes, My Queen." Lamar gave her a polite smile.

Kaden stood as well. "I should get to the training grounds. Julia?" She stood with him and they followed the queen, Fulcan, and Jamin out of the great hall. As soon as the doors closed behind them, Lydia turned to Fulcan and Jamin.

"Do you think they suspect anything?"

"I wouldn't see how they could, unless they were snooping where they shouldn't." Fulcan looked at Kaden and Julia. "Will you two keep a close eye on them in the coming days? Nothing too obvious, just whenever you get the chance. Maybe get to know the younger three a little bit."

Julia sighed unhappily. "Yes, I will do my best to deal with the girl, Adrian. She seems like a fun one to hang out with," she said sarcastically and Kaden chuckled. She turned to him. "Kaden, you can get to know Felix and Lucas." She gave him a smug smirk.

Lydia gave them a grateful look. "It would help us out greatly. Plus, it would also take your mind off Nyla for a while. At least until she adjusts and surfaces."

"Yes, Your Majesty." Julia turned.

"I will do my best, Your Majesty." Kaden followed Julia out to the training grounds.

"You're not going to train, are you?" Kaden gave her a teasing smile.

"No. Well, maybe I'll give it a shot. I've got nothing else better to do." She picked up a big sword and grunted at its weight. "Okay, maybe something a little smaller." She put the sword back on its rack and picked up a dagger. "This should do." She smiled at Kaden. "Okay, teach me what I can do with this thing."

⌒∽о∾⌒

Nyla stirred, flickering lights creating orange shadows from under her eyelids. She crinkled her eyes shut tighter, trying to block out the light. She breathed in deeply, frowning. The air was filled with dirt and the faint scent of smoke. Keeping her eyes closed, she rolled onto her back, her hands rubbing against her sleepy eyelids.

Samuel stood from where he was sitting beside the bed and pulled the blankets up to cover her more.

"Last night . . . was that a dream, or did that really happen?" Nyla kept her eyes closed, waiting for his answer.

"I'm sorry, Nyla . . ." A small pain ripped through his heart as a tear trickled down from her closed eyes. "Nyla . . ."

"I'm so sorry, Samuel, for everything I did. I'm so sorry!" She squeezed her eyes tighter, not wanting to open her eyes to the world yet.

"Shhh. Nyla, it's okay." He sat beside her on the bed.

"Thank you for staying here with me all night. After what I did . . ."

"Nyla, I told you I would never leave you. No matter what."

"I don't know what happened. I was just so angry and . . . hungry. I couldn't help myself. I . . . I didn't mean to kill them, I swear!" Nyla opened her eyes and frowned up at the dark ceiling. *This is not my bedroom.* She turned her head to the side, looking at Samuel. He sat in a chair beside her, torchlight creating an orange halo of light around him.

"Where are we?" Nyla sat up, clutching the covers around her.

"Nyla." Samuel looked at her cautiously. "This is for everyone's safety, including your own."

"Are we in the dungeon?!" Nyla frantically looked around her. They were in a dark, stone cell. Half of one wall was made up of thick, steel bars placed close together so that a person could look through the bars, but barely fit an arm through. Nyla was in a bed covered in her own sheets, and around the room there was a table and two chairs, a wardrobe, a silver vanity, and a small, silk couch. Nyla grimaced when she spotted the chamber pot sitting on the floor in a sectioned off corner of the cell. There was also only one small window, close to the ceiling, on one of the walls, letting in a little fresh air.

"Why am I in a dungeon, Samuel?!" Nyla looked at him, demanding an explanation.

"Nyla," Samuel remained calm, "these are the queen's orders. Because of what happened, the queen and the council decided that we have to take precautions and keep you here until we know for sure that you can control yourself."

"Are you serious?" Nyla didn't know if she was angry or heart-broken. "How did I get here?"

"The tea . . ." Samuel looked guiltily at the ground.

"You drugged me?" Nyla gasped, balling the blankets up in her fists.

"I'm sorry, Nyla. It was the only way. While we were in your bedroom, the queen had furniture brought here. This is the biggest cell and we wanted you to be as comfortable as you could be." Nyla shook her head in betrayal and Samuel continued. "This is only tem-porary, Nyla. We will work on controlling your blood lust and when we are confident that you can control yourself you will be out of here, I promise."

Nyla's breath shuddered as she tried not to cry. Although she was furious that her mother had put her in the dungeon, deep down she knew it was the best decision.

"Okay," Nyla said quietly.

"Okay?" Samuel hesitated, unsure of what to say. He expected Nyla to put up more of a fight.

"This is for the best." Nyla squeezed her eyes shut. "I can feel the hunger even now." She opened her eyes, looking straight at Samuel. "Samuel, last night . . . the power, it was amazing. Like nothing I've ever felt before. Samuel, I loved it, and that's what scares me the most."

"Nyla, we'll work on controlling it." Samuel moved from his chair to the bed, sitting next to her. Nyla nodded and took a deep breath, the events of the night before replaying in her mind. After they had gotten back to her room, the last thing she remembered was taking off her robe and . . . begging Samuel to get into bed with her. She looked at Samuel, her face reddening with embarrassment.

"Um . . . Samuel." She bit her lip, blushing. "Before I fell asleep and you brought me in here . . . I remember exposing myself to you." She took a deep breath. "I didn't, um . . . we didn't . . ."

"You really don't remember that? I didn't think it was that bad." Samuel shrugged nonchalantly. Nyla's mouth dropped open. Seeing the look on her face Samuel laughed.

"Nyla, I'm kidding! We didn't!"

"Oh, okay. I think I would have remembered if we had. That's good." She looked away and then realized what she said. "It's not like I wouldn't. Well I . . . I mean . . ." She looked away, pearly pink spreading across her porcelain face. "Don't get me wrong, I mean . . . you're obviously . . . you know." She smacked her forehead with the palm of her hand, not knowing how to recover.

"Nyla, it's okay." Samuel laughed. "I know what you're trying to say."

She cleared her throat. "Well, I clearly need to compose myself. Excuse me." She laid back down on her bed, pulling the covers up over her head. Samuel chuckled, glad that she was acting more like herself. Nyla's stomach growled from under the blankets. Nyla pulled the covers down slightly, uncovering just her face.

"I'm hungry."

"No problem. I'll send for some food." Samuel stood and started for the cell door.

"Wait!" Nyla bolted out of bed, running to Samuel and grabbing his arm.

"Nyla, I'm not leaving. Dominic is right down the hall. He isn't right outside the door, because he wanted to give you privacy."

"Yes, of course." Seeing she was in a nightgown, Nyla went to the wardrobe by the stone wall. Samuel went to the edge of the cell and asked Dominic to have food sent down as Nyla shifted through the few dresses that had been brought down for her.

"Ugh! There's nothing good in here. I need to be able to move and be free, not weighed down by these carpets! I can't move in any of these." She bent down, inspecting the drawer at the bottom of the wardrobe. She smiled as she pulled out black, stretchable pants, a black tank top, and a pair of boots. Samuel turned toward the cell door as Nyla changed.

Nyla walked over to the vanity, examining her appearance in the mirror. She let her hair down from the bun, and it flowed in perfect waves down her back. She bent her face close to the mirror, examining her glowing, torch-lit face. She gasped, when she saw her teeth. Her canines weren't full fangs, like she had felt before, but they were still permanently pointed and sharp.

"What?" Samuel looked worried as he came over to her, turning her toward him and examining her face. Footsteps echoed from down the hall and Nyla looked toward the bars of the cell, her heart pounding.

"Nyla?" Julia approached the bars, a cautious smile on her face. She held a covered tray of food in her hands.

"Julia!" Nyla ran over to the bars. "Julia, I'm so sorry for everything!"

"It's okay, Nyla. How are you?"

"Um . . ." She paused. "I'm just fine. Better than fine." Samuel's eyebrows knit together at her light, alluring tone.

"That's good. I brought food." Julia smiled brightly.

"Thank you so much! I'm starving." Nyla held on to the bars, putting herself as close to Julia as possible. "Come here." Nyla beckoned to Julia through the bars, holding her hand out. Julia started to walk toward the bars as if in a trance, her eyes locked on Nyla.

"Julia, don't!" Samuel warned, running to the bars. He turned Nyla toward him, frowning at her black eyes. Nyla bared her fangs at him.

"Nyla!" Samuel's tone was dark. He stared right into her black eyes. "Nyla!" he said again, moving his hands to either side of her face. Nyla blinked, her eyes returning to normal. She sucked a breath in as realization swept over her.

"Oh no. Julia." Nyla turned toward Julia, who had come back to herself. She stared at Nyla with shock on her face. A single tear slid down her cheek.

"Um, I better go." Julia cautiously set the tray of food down on the floor outside the cell door and turned to leave.

"No! Julia." Nyla willed Julia to turn around.

"It's okay, Nyla." Julia turned, her face filled with sorrow. "It's okay," she repeated, softer. She shook her head. "It's just not helping you for me to be here right now." Julia turned and strode out of sight, the sound of her footsteps echoing down the hall.

"Ahhh!" Nyla screamed in frustration. "What's wrong with me? Why can't I control this?"

"You will. Give it time." Samuel put a hand on her shoulder.

"You shouldn't be in here." Nyla faced Samuel, but cast her eyes down in shame. "I don't want to hurt you." Nyla whispered.

"You won't." Samuel reassured her. He tipped her face up with his finger. "I trust you, Nyla."

"How can you trust me if I can't even trust myself?" Nyla shook her head.

"You won't hurt me." Samuel looked her straight in the eyes.

Nyla nodded, hugging Samuel, breathing in his scent. The hunger bubbled low in her stomach, but she pushed it down.

"Okay, let's get some food in you." Samuel let go of Nyla and called to Dominic, who came and unlocked the door from the outside. Samuel picked up the tray of food and brought it to Nyla as Dominic locked the door again, turning and walking just out of sight.

"You don't have a key?" Nyla frowned at him. "What if I try to hurt you? You wouldn't be able to get out unless Dominic let you out."

"Nyla, like I said, I trust you." Samuel set the tray down on the table and sat at one of the chairs. He took off the cover for the tray, revealing two plates of food. One had a rare, bloody piece of meat with a side of Nyla's favorite scrambled eggs. The other contained another steak, less bloody, and fried eggs. There was also a bottle of red liquid.

"Come. Eat." Samuel beckoned toward the food.

Nyla sniffed at the air, the scent of food making her mouth water. She reluctantly sat in the other chair across from Samuel. Her stomach rumbling again. She grabbed the plate with the bloody steak and quickly cut into the rare meat. She sighed as she chewed the tender meat, the juice and blood running down her throat.

"Here, this will help with the cravings and blood lust." Samuel uncorked the red bottle, setting it in front of her. Smelling the metallic scent of blood, Nyla seized the bottle and drank deeply, gulping down the whole bottle. The warm liquid rushed down her throat, warming and calming her whole body. Nyla breathed deeply, relieved that her hunger subsided.

"Better?" Samuel smiled at her.

"Yes. Much better." Nyla gave Samuel a half-hearted smile. She paused, frowning. "This is disgusting. This isn't human blood, is it?"

"No, no." Samuel shook his head. "It's cow's blood. If you consume blood regularly the hunger won't be as bad. We'll work on breathing techniques and expose you to other people gradually, and soon you'll be able to control it and you'll be out of here in no time." Samuel smiled reassuringly.

Nyla nodded. Although she didn't feel too confident at the moment, she hoped that it would be that easy.

Julia came a few times the next day to bring her meals. Like the day before, the sight of another human being made the hunger bubble in Nyla's stomach. Each time Nyla had to struggle to remain herself and not give in to her vampiric urges. As soon as the world turned colorful, Nyla would shut her eyes tightly and breathe in and out slowly through her mouth. Nyla was relieved to find that it got easier each time she saw Julia or Dominic. At dinner, the queen came to visit. Although she stayed a safe distance from the bars, she sat in a chair and talked to Nyla as Samuel had to see to his duties as head of the guard. Not once did Nyla have the urge to suck the life out of her mother, which made her feel ten times better than she had before. At least she wouldn't be a danger to her mother.

The next two days were about the same. Julia or the queen would bring Nyla and Samuel meals, clean clothes and a basin and sponge for Nyla to use to cleanse herself, for which Samuel would politely exit the cell and stay just out of sight for. With each meal, Nyla would drink the bottle of blood. It got easier and easier to hold back from gulping the whole bottle down and Nyla got better and better at sipping the blood, making it last longer each time. On the fourth day of being in the cell, Nyla was getting antsy. She longed to get out and run in the sunshine, but she knew it was in everyone's best interest if she stayed locked up until she could fully control herself. Julia came again at lunch, bringing a tray of fresh fruits, along with the usual rare piece of meat. She sat outside the cell and talked to Nyla and Samuel as they ate.

When they were finished, Nyla stood and stretched out her limbs. She turned to Samuel.

"Can I see Jamin? There's a lot that I need to ask him."

"Are you sure you're up for it?" He walked up to Nyla and put his hands on her shoulders, looking into her eyes. Julia looked at the ground when she saw his concerned face. She fiddled with her skirt, uncomfortable.

"I'm sure. I need to talk to him, and soon, because I'm dying to get out of here!"

"I'm sure you are." Samuel chuckled.

"Do you think you could sit by yourself for a few minutes while we go get Jamin?" Samuel asked Nyla. "If you don't feel comfortable that's fine, but I think it would be good to try." Nyla thought for a moment.

"Yes, I can handle myself." Nyla nodded with confidence.

"Okay, we'll be back soon." Samuel waited as Dominic unlocked the door. Samuel gave Nyla a positive nod as he locked the cell door and he and Julia disappeared down the hall of the dungeon.

"Well, she's sure chipper today." Julia raised her eyebrows at Samuel, unsure whether that was a good thing or not.

"Yes, she's definitely getting better at controlling the bloodlust. Drinking the cow's blood helps." Samuel followed Julia up the dungeon steps and toward the library. Since Nyla was put in the dungeon, Jamin had been spending extra time there. He was reading book after book, trying to find any information he could about vampires and tellers to see if there was a way to subdue Nyla's vampire side again.

Nyla sat on the couch in her cell. Her heart pounded and a dangerous hunger bubbled low in Nyla's chest as she sensed the presence of the two guards just out of sight beyond her cell. She closed her eyes and listened to their heart beats, one she recognized as Dominic as she had memorized his steady strong pulse over the past few days. Dominic was the usual guard outside of her cell until he had to take a break and a different guard replaced him. Kristy had been removed from her duty of guarding Nyla and the other two guards that cycled through rotation outside her cell were Eli, who had guarded her with Samuel before, and Sahar, a strong, dark skinned woman who could easily crush anyone's skull with one blow from the battle axe she chose as her weapon. Nyla opened her eyes, the thermal world, reflecting bright light from the torches on the walls.

"No." Nyla whispered to herself, closing her eyes and shutting out the colors. She thought about Samuel's face. The way his blue-gray eyes bore into hers when he helped to calm her. "Breathe. Breathe." Nyla repeated Samuel's words to herself and breathed slowly in and out through her mouth. Nyla smiled as she opened her eyes to the dark, torch-lit room. She stood as she heard familiar footsteps echoing toward her. She smiled brightly as Samuel, Julia, and Jamin came into view.

"Jamin." Nyla smiled at her tutor.

"Nyla," Jamin nodded at Nyla, looking her up and down. He met Nyla at the bars.

"You are looking very healthy, Nyla." She nodded and Jamin examined her face with his eyes. "Do you think we could come in?" Jamin asked. "It would be better for me to get a closer look at you. We brought a bottle of blood in case you need it." Nyla looked at Samuel. His positive expression gave her confidence.

"Yes, I think I can control myself. Samuel will be here if I can't." Jamin nodded and Samuel opened the cell door.

"Julia, would you mind getting my mom?" Nyla asked.

"Of course." Julia nodded and left.

Jamin and Samuel entered the cell. Samuel closed the door, but kept it unlocked, just in case Jamin needed to make a quick exit. He opened the bottle of blood and handed it to Nyla. She held it close her body, comforted by the fact that if the blood lust overtook her she would have a blood substitute instead of Jamin. Jamin came to stand in front of Nyla.

"Yes, you're looking good, Nyla. How are you feeling?" Jamin peered at her through his spectacles.

"Well, other than the hunger that I get in my stomach, I'm feeling great." Nyla smiled. Jamin nodded.

"May I?" Jamin beckoned to her mouth.

"Um, yes." Nyla clutched the bottle harder and opened her mouth.

"Hmmm." Jamin felt the tips of her canines with his fingers. "Teeth are normal. They will always stay their sharpness even when they aren't full." He took a few steps back and pulled out a small knife. Suddenly he hurled it at her face, but she caught in with ease right before it hit her between the eyes.

"What the hell, Jamin?!" Samuel stood up.

"Reflexes are good." Jamin smiled at Samuel's surprised face. Samuel calmed down. "Can I try something?" Nyla nodded and Jamin took the knife from her. Turning her hand over, he ran it along her palm.

"What are you doing?!" Nyla looked alarmed, but it didn't even affect her skin.

"It's okay." Jamin put the knife back into his pocket. "Your skin is just like her father's, strong as diamonds. It's expected of a pure blood."

"What do you mean a pure blood?" Nyla sat down on the silk couch. Just then the queen and Julia came into view.

"Your father was an original vampire. His family became the first vampires ever." The queen entered the cell and smiled proudly at Nyla. Julia also entered the cell, but stayed a step behind Samuel,

"So what does that make me?" Nyla looked at her mother.

"Well, if my theory is correct, and I think it is," Jamin pushed up his spectacles, "then your father's pure vampire blood canceled out your mother's human blood. So the moment that blood touched your lips, you were turned full vampire."

"So what does that mean? How does that work?"

"Well, see I don't know. Your father let me study him. However, he didn't give me any real details about his lineage, or his powers, but you will be powerful Nyla. The original, pure-blood family is very powerful. They have abilities that no other vampire can have, like being able to be in the sun freely. Unfortunately that is all I know."

"Well, it's more than I knew a few days ago, Jamin. Thank you." Nyla nodded at him.

"I must tell you though, you have changed Nyla, and not just in your fashion sense."

Does everyone only notice my clothes? Since she had been in the dungeon Nyla hadn't touched a single dress and only wore the training outfits that were brought for her. "I know I have Jamin. I can feel it. I'm more . . . powerful. I feel amazing."

"You'll feel that way until you need to feed again. Well, you won't feel too different, you'll just be hungry." Nyla's brows furrowed and she took a sip from the bottle in her hand.

"Don't worry, honey." The queen knelt in front of her, taking her hand. "We've figured out a way for you to feed whenever you need and not have to hurt anybody. You can hunt animals in the forest whenever you need and we'll save any blood from a cow, sheep, or pig that we slaughter. As you've probably noticed, it won't taste as good as human blood, but it will work just the same." Nyla processed this, satisfied.

"So how often will I need to . . . feed?"

"Well, I'm not exactly sure," Jamin answered. "These first couple weeks you'll have to feed every day or so like you have been. After you can fully control the blood lust, from what I know about vampires, probably about once a week."

"However," the queen cut in, "I do know that Richard mentioned he didn't have to feed as much as a normal vampire. The originals can get away with a couple weeks without having to feed while retaining their full strength."

"But," Jamin added, "it's always good for you to have blood probably every few days, or a little whenever you want to. It keeps you strong all the time and you'll never feel hungry."

"See, we've already started to get this figured out. And we'll all do everything that we can to help you until you adjust and get a hang of it." Samuel smiled at Nyla.

Julia put a hand on her shoulder. "Nyla, we are all here for you."

"Including me." Nyla froze as Kaden walked into the cell. He stood next to Samuel. He stared at Nyla. She was more beautiful than ever in her tight, training outfit. His heart pounded as he studied the flawless, porcelain face of the creature in front of him.

Heat rushed through Nyla's veins and a burning crept into the pit of her stomach. She stared into Samuel's eyes. Focusing on the brilliance of them, she refused to look at Kaden. The memory of his horrified face and how scared he was of her surged into her memory. She had pushed it out of her mind until now. He had run away from her. He had been so afraid of her that he hadn't wanted her to touch him. Even now she could feel a hint of fear coming off of him. She tried to focus on Samuel's protective feelings and affection toward her, but she couldn't get Kaden out of her mind and the pushed away feelings welled up inside her again, drowning her in sorrow. She clenched her fists as she felt her eyes changing. Her vision began to go red, and then colorful as the thermal vision kicked in.

"Kaden. I don't want to talk to you."

"Nyla." Kaden said, concern in his face. Nyla felt more fear rolling off of him. Samuel moved toward her and she tried to focus on him alone. No fear came from him, only concern and protectiveness.

"Get him out of here." She growled through her growing fangs. The queen and Jamin jumped into action. Jamin grabbed Kaden's arm and tried to pull him out of the room.

"No!" Kaden shook him off. "Let me help her!" Nyla turned away from Samuel, focusing Kaden in her heated vision.

"Kaden, I can't control myself when I'm angry. If you don't leave now I will probably hurt you."

"Get out of here!" Samuel turned toward the queen, Jamin, and Julia, and they retreated out of the cell, but Kaden didn't budge. Nyla tried to breathe as she focused on Samuel's back. Samuel took ahold of Kaden's arm and dragged him out of the cell.

"Samuel, stop!" Kaden struggled but couldn't shake him off. "I can help her. I should be the one helping her!"

"Kaden, don't be stupid!" He looked into his friend's stubborn face. "Can't you see that you're making her angry? Every time she sees you, all the emotions crash into her and she can't handle it. We've almost got her blood-lust controlled! So don't ruin it!" Kaden stopped struggling. He looked past Samuel. Nyla's eyes were completely black and empty, but he could tell that she was staring right at him in anger. She bared her fangs at him, and a low hiss emanated from deep within her throat. Samuel turned and strode over to Nyla. He took her shoulders in his strong hands.

"Nyla," Samuel said calmly, "look at me." He could tell that she was looking at him as her body started to relax. "Breathe." Nyla tried to concentrate. She looked into Samuel's eyes and breathed deeply. After a couple deep breaths, her fangs shrank back into her gums and her vision began to return to normal. Kaden stared helpless at her. Samuel was right; he was making her angry and hurting her. She didn't need him, she needed Samuel. He had had his chance to comfort her and he couldn't. He understood that as he watched her relax to Samuel's touch.

"That's it. Keep breathing." Samuel rubbed his hands up and down her arms. She continued to breathe. *In . . . out . . . in . . . out.* She closed her eyes and when she opened them again her eyes were back to bright blue. When she looked back at the cell door, the others were still there, standing cautiously behind Dominic and Sahar, but Kaden was gone.

"Dammit, Kaden!" Nyla looked at her mother's sad face. Guilt seeped into her chest, but her heart still stung from Kaden's fearful feelings toward her. Samuel brushed the hair away from her face.

"Are you okay?" he asked her, concern on his face. She covered her face with her hand for a second and when she removed it, her face was calmer. She took a big gulp of the blood bottle she still clutched in her hand.

"Yes, I'm fine. I just really do not want to talk to him right now." She stared at the door.

Jamin walked past the guards to the bars of the cell. "Nyla, you are not the same person you were before. I mean, you are the same person, but you will notice subtle differences. Right now you are more irritable and vampires tend to be more stubborn and hard headed." Nyla opened her mouth to speak.

"Nylina." Lydia looked at her daughter, an unhappy look on her face. "Don't judge Kaden too harshly, okay? I know you're angry, but like Jamin said, you are feeling things differently because it's in your nature to be more . . . well, what Jamin said. I know Kaden feels bad about how he reacted and you should try to find it in yourself to forgive him." Nyla's mouth was in a hard line, but she nodded her head.

Jamin nodded. "Did anything happen with Kaden that you, well, want to talk about and forget?"

"Yes," Nyla looked down, "he, um . . . when I attacked Kristi he kind of freaked out. When I realized what I was doing I tried to reach for him and he . . ." She sighed, reliving the memory. "He flinched away from me. He was scared of me. I could feel it. Then when he saw me in the barn he was terrified of me. It's like he didn't even recognize me. I was just a monster with bloodlust to him. He couldn't get away from me fast enough." Nyla couldn't shake the image out of her mind.

Jamin nodded his head. "It makes sense then, why you would be enraged with him, especially because of what you felt for him before. When there is attraction of any kind, then it always makes all of this harder. It feels as if he betrayed you." Nyla nodded uncomfortably.

The queen looked Nyla in the eye. "But, Nylina, you do realize that it's not that he hates you or is terrified of you. His family was attacked by vampires. They killed his mother and brother, so it's understandable what he's feeling." The queen hesitated. "And . . . you did kill people, Nyla. I know you didn't have control, but we can't forget about that." Nyla nodded and looked down, tears threatening to spill over her eyelids.

"However," the queen continued, "yes, Kaden could have acted differently, and I'm sure he knows that and feels horrible about it." Nyla nodded, biting her lip. She didn't want to talk about this anymore.

"You're lucky that you have Samuel through all this," Jamin pointed out. The queen nodded in agreement.

"You've really helped her through this, Samuel." The queen gave him a smile of gratitude. "Thank you. You have a connection with Nyla and I'm very grateful." Samuel nodded. Nyla looked at him out of the corner of her eye and smiled to herself. She did feel connected to Samuel.

"So what can we do to help you, Nyla? Kaden is one of your best friends." The queen broke the silence.

Nyla chose her words carefully. "I want all my friends with me and I admit it would suck if I could never be around Kaden again."

Jamin cleared his throat. "If I may suggest something, I would say to just talk to him in a few days. You don't have to fully forgive him right now. As you adjust to your new life and come to accept what and who you are, then you can start to acclimate yourself back to Kaden's presence as you see fit. Take your time."

"Okay." Nyla would definitely try. She wanted Kaden around her just as much as she needed Julia and Samuel. She would make it work.

CHAPTER 14

Nyla thought about how to approach her problem with Kaden. She figured she would give it a day or two so that she could get over it and then talk to him. She kept getting the feeling that she should make him grovel and beg for forgiveness, but she knew that was just her temper talking. After the next two days, Nyla was doing much better with controlling the hunger. Julia, the queen, and Jamin were able to be inside her cell with no incidence.

Samuel suggested that they go on their first hunting lesson, but since Nyla was supposed to be "sick" and she couldn't be seen out by Lamar and the others, they thought it was best to wait until nightfall. Nyla was irritable the rest of the day and impatient for night to come. As soon as the sun started to set, she began to bug Samuel about going to the woods.

"All right, all right. Let's go." Samuel finally gave in after the third time Nyla asked him.

"Thank you!" She stood up from where she had been sitting on the couch. She gave him a bright smile and headed toward the cell door.

"Now, wait a minute." Samuel stopped her. "We don't want anyone seeing you sneaking out of the castle, especially Lamar, so we need to be extra careful and sneaky."

"Easy." Nyla shrugged. "Remember last time we had to sneak through the castle? That was pretty darn sneaky." She laughed and Samuel grinned.

"Oh, ya. Very sneaky!" he said sarcastically. He had Dominic open the cell door, and they both quieted. They were silent as they walked down the hallway toward the front doors. Nyla was surprised that they hadn't run into any maids this time and was a little disappointed. It kind of took the fun out of "sneaking" around if there was nobody to watch out for and have to actually sneak around. They exited the castle doors and Nyla took a big breath of fresh air in through her nose. It was nice to be out in the open air. She twirled around with her arms out, smiling up at the sky. The moon was only about a quarter full and the sky was alive with glittering stars. Samuel smiled at Nyla as she danced in the darkness. She looked more alive and free than she ever had and it gave Samuel joy to see her that way. Nyla continued to smile up at the sky as they neared the rose bush garden, but was startled when Samuel suddenly yanked her down by her hand. She gave him a questioning look and he pointed ahead of them. Nyla peaked her eyes over the top of the rose bush in front of them and cursed silently as she spotted Lamar taking a stroll just ahead of them.

"Do we just have the worse timing ever?" Nyla ducked back behind the bush. She looked at Samuel. "So this way?" She pointed to their right and Samuel nodded. Adrenalin started to surge through Nyla and she smiled with excitement. Finally, they could actually sneak past somebody!

"Quiet." Samuel mouthed to Nyla and pointed at her accusingly. She squinted at him and he grinned. Staying in a crouch behind the bushes, he began to move to the right and Nyla followed him. They followed the path that lead to the stables. Nyla kept poking her head up from the bushes every once in a while to check their status of where Lamar was, but they weren't in any danger of being discovered. They continued the pattern of moving and checking their position until they reached the edge of the garden. The half-burnt stables were just a few yards away. Nyla checked behind them and frowned. She could have sworn Lamar was farther away than that the last time she checked. He was definitely getting closer. She turned to Samuel.

"Lamar is headed in this direction," she said in a hushed voice. Samuel gave her a mischievous grin.

"I guess we better run then."

"What?" But it was too late. Samuel sprang out of the bushes and took off in a run toward the stables. Nyla took off after him and she smiled as she sped up, zipping past him into the stables. She stopped in front of the second stall.

"I win!" Nyla grinned. Samuel sprinted inside, but didn't stop when he saw Nyla and he crashed into her. He pushed her into the empty stall and they both tumbled to the ground, landing in a pile of clean straw. Samuel braced himself on his elbows so that he didn't crush Nyla as he landed on top of her.

"What—" Nyla began, but Samuel covered her mouth with his hand.

"Someone's coming." He laughed and turned his head, his face coming just inches from hers. Samuel stopped laughing and uncovered her mouth with his hand. Nyla's heart pounded as she stared into Samuel's gorgeous eyes. His breath softly tickled her mouth and his body slightly pressed against her.

"Hello?" Samuel snapped his head toward the voice. "Captain?" A big, burly guard stood there, illuminating their faces with a torch he held in his hand.

"Carl." Samuel rolled off Nyla.

"Oh!" The guard's eyes grew wide as he spotted Nyla. "Pardon me, Princess." He gave Samuel an uneasy smile and turned away.

"Oh, it's not what you think." Nyla called after him, but he was already gone. She stood up and looked after him just as he rounded the corner of the stables. She turned to Samuel, who was still lying in the straw, trying not to laugh.

"Great. I can just imagine the rumors." She rolled her eyes and smiled as she helped Samuel up. "Let's hurry up and get out of here before Lamar catches us." She put a bridal on one of the four horses that were left in the stables. The others had been put out to pasture after they "escaped" from the stables. She turned and stopped in her tracks as she peered into the rubble that was left of the stall that she had left Jimmy's body. She grimaced and tried to shake the memory away. She hurried past Samuel, who had bridled his own horse and was leading it out of the stall.

"Let's get out of here." Nyla didn't bother to grab a saddle. She peaked out of the stable, looking left and right, but Lamar was nowhere to be seen. She led her horse out and pulled herself up. Samuel brought his horse up beside hers and swung himself up onto its bare back with ease. He pushed his horse into a walk and Nyla followed him as they headed toward the gate. Samuel nodded to the guards on duty and they raised the big, metal gates. As soon as they were out, Nyla and Samuel pushed their horses into a cantor and headed toward the forest.

As her horse loped beneath her, thoughts of Samuel raced in her mind. Her heart pounded as she remembered how his toned body had felt against hers as they had laid in the straw. She bit her lip as she imagined Samuel's hot breath against her face and how his eyes had born into hers. Heat broke out over her face as two different types of hunger burned in her stomach and chest.

Nyla and Samuel pulled their horses to a stop at the edge of the woods. Samuel dismounted his horse and walked around it, holding his arms out as he approached Nyla's horse. She swung her leg over and slid off of her horse and into Samuel's arms. He held her firmly in his arms for a few seconds before he set her down on the ground. Nyla turned toward the woods and smiled. *Apparently what had happened in the stables was still on Samuel's mind too.* Nyla stopped and waited for Samuel as he passed her. He gave her a grin and nodded his head for her to follow him. She started after him, walking beside him, but letting him lead the way.

"So what's it going to be?" Samuel asked.

"What?"

"Rabbit . . . deer . . . any preferences?"

"Oh." Nyla giggled. "Whatever we run across first. I'm starving." Samuel nodded. They walked through the forest a ways before they heard a rustling in the bushes. A big, brown jackrabbit burst out of the bushes to their right. Samuel grabbed the bow that was slung around his shoulder and quickly hooked an arrow into place. Drawing back, he let the arrow fly no more than a second later, and the arrow pierced the rabbit.

"Nice!" Nyla nodded. "I've never seen you hunt before. I'm impressed. You didn't even have to aim. Even in the dark."

"Well, the moon is pretty bright tonight." Samuel chuckled as he shrugged.

Nyla followed him to the rabbit. Samuel bent down and picked the gangly body off the ground and pulled the arrow out.

"It's not much." He held the limp body out to her. "But it'll do." She reached out and took it from him. Although her mind told her to throw it and run away, her stomach grumbled. She glanced at Samuel and then turned around. Although she knew Samuel wouldn't be disgusted with her, that didn't mean she had to parade her eating habits around right in front of his face. She sunk her teeth into the soft fur of the rabbit's neck and sighed as the warm blood ran down her throat, cooling the burn in her stomach. When she was finished she wiped her mouth with the back of her hand. She turned back to Samuel.

"I'm still hungry." She gave him an apologetic smile. Samuel gave a small laugh. He reached out and wiped a drop of blood from her bottom lip. Nyla gulped as she looked into his eyes. He took his hand away and gave her that heart-breaking smile.

"Okay, we'll find you another rabbit, but that should be enough."

"Okay," Nyla agreed. They started meandering back toward the edge of the forest and Samuel halted as he spotted another rabbit just ahead of them. It hadn't noticed them yet and sat on its haunches, ears up and alert. Samuel slowly moved toward Nyla, watching his footfalls. She shivered as his breath tickled her ear.

"This one is all yours." He gave her a grin and she raised her eyebrows at him. He nodded and pointed to the rabbit and Nyla took a deep breath, accepting the challenge. She took a step forward, but the jackrabbit spotted her right at that moment and took off running to their left. Nyla punched Samuel in the arm when he started laughing and she took off after the rabbit. She sped up and within seconds was just few feet away from the it. In one smooth movement, she leapt into the air, pouncing on the rabbit, and rolled into a crouched position the animal tucked into her arms. She looked behind her, but

Samuel wasn't in sight. Nyla sighed. She really wanted to share this triumph, but she wasn't going to wait for him to catch up with her. She looked behind her again, feeling a strange presence, but nothing was there. Suddenly a howl split through the night. Startled, she let go of the rabbit and it took off in a sprint. She stood and looked around her.

"Samuel?" she called into the darkness. There was no answer as there was another howl, sounding closer this time. Nyla took a few steps forward.

"Samuel?" she called again. She heard a twig snap and she whirled around, but nothing was behind her. She immediately took off in a sprint toward the edge of the forest and the horses. As she neared the edge of the forest she caught the scent of something that resembled wet dog and she slowed to a walk. Her heart pounded as she reached the last couple trees bordering the forest. Suddenly, she was yanked behind a tree. She almost screamed, but shut her mouth as she came face-to-face with Samuel.

"We need to get out of here now," he whispered to her.

"Werewolves?" Nyla's voice was barely a whisper. Samuel nodded and Nyla's heart surged with fear. Samuel led Nyla forward and they heard a commotion ahead of them. Samuel pulled her into a run, but Nyla stopped dead in her tracks as they broke out of the forest. One of the horses was lying bloody on the ground and the other was being circled by a giant, snarling wolf. Nyla gasped and the wolf turned in their direction. It growled and crouched low. Just as it was about to lunge at Nyla, Samuel shot an arrow, piercing the wolf in the shoulder. The wolf whimpered and took off running back into the woods to their right. Nyla let out a breath she hadn't realized she had been holding and looked at Samuel in panic. He ran to the horse lying on the ground.

"This one is dead." He stood and walked to where Nyla stood frozen. "We're fine." He took hold of her shoulders. "The wolf is gone, but we need to get back to the castle." Nyla looked at him and nodded. "Come on." Samuel took Nyla by the hand and led her to where the other horse was waiting for them now that it was safe.

Samuel swung himself up on the horse's back and pulled Nyla up behind him.

They were silent as they galloped to the castle. Nyla couldn't believe what had just happened. The werewolf was only a few feet away from her and if it had not been for Samuel, Nyla could be dead. She couldn't believe that she had just stood there frozen in fear. She tightened her arms around Samuel, hugging him.

"Are you okay?" Samuel turned his head and glanced back at her.

"Ya, I'm fine." Nyla nodded. As they entered the palace gates Nyla was relieved to be back. The encounter with the werewolf terrified her. She could sense that it wasn't a real wolf from the moment she smelled it and she never wanted to smell that scent again. She was silent as Samuel stabled the horse. A werewolf that close to the gates couldn't have been a good sign.

"Come on. We need to inform the queen and Fulcan." As they reached the steps Samuel stopped walking and turned toward Nyla, grabbing ahold of her arms.

"We are never splitting up like that again. I will never let you out of my sight when we are outside the palace walls again. That was too close." He ran a frustrated hand through his hair. "How could I have been so stupid?! I should've known better with everything that's been going on with Ridia."

"Samuel, that wasn't your fault. There's no way you could've known." Nyla shook her head.

"I should've been more prepared. I let my guard down and you could've been hurt. If anything would've happened to you . . ." Samuel shook his head in anger and frustration.

"Samuel, stop." Nyla looked him in the eyes. "There was no way you could've known. If it weren't for you shooting that wolf I could be dead right now. Don't beat yourself up about this." Samuel shook his head, but let it go and they continued into the castle.

"What?!" Fulcan slammed his fist on the table, making Nyla jump. "There was a werewolf in the forest? This close to the castle?!"

"We expected this sooner or later, Fulcan." Samuel stood across from him in the council room.

161

"Yes, but not this soon." The queen shook her head tiredly.

"You're lucky that neither of you were killed!" Fulcan scowled at Samuel. "You were foolish to go anywhere outside the castle walls at night without a party of guards!"

"Fulcan, it's not his fault," Nyla interjected. "I needed to hunt and we couldn't go during the day with Lamar and the others walking about. We had no idea there was going to be a werewolf so close to Galacia. Samuel saved my life."

"He wouldn't have had to if you two hadn't been frolicking through the woods in the middle of the night!" Fulcan seethed.

"Fulcan, give Samuel some slack. He is the captain of the guard and he knows what he's doing. None of us could've known there would be werewolves coming this soon." The queen kept her voice calm.

"Do you think it's a scout from Ridia?" Nyla asked.

"I wouldn't doubt it." Samuel shook his head. "I should've been more careful. I take full responsibility for this, General." Samuel looked at Fulcan.

"Nothing happened!" Nyla shook her head, feeling a prick on her lower lip. She took a deep breath, her fangs sliding back in. "We were both fine. We know better for next time. We'll be prepared."

"Oh, there won't be a next time!" Fulcan raised his eyebrows. "You shouldn't even go outside the castle walls for your own safety!"

"Fulcan, I need to hunt." Nyla took a deep breath again, feeling herself becoming unstable. She glanced at Fulcan, relieved when he didn't notice. "I have to go outside the walls sometime. We will just be more prepared."

"Well, since the wolf wasn't killed we will have to be cautious. Now Rothgar and Gafna know that we know they are watching us." Fulcan shook his head.

"I was more concerned for Nyla's safety and getting her out of there. I should've killed the werewolf." Samuel shook his head, frustrated.

"Samuel, you did what you could and I just thank you for getting my daughter back safely." The queen put a hand on his shoulder.

"Well, we'll just have to be more careful now and more importantly move our training schedule and battle strategies up. We need to be prepared for a war sooner than we may have originally thought." Fulcan looked at the queen.

CHAPTER 15

CHAPTER 15

Nyla spent the next couple days shut up in her room and in lessons with Jamin. Since the hunt with Samuel, the council agreed that Nyla was stable enough to be back in her room with guards posted on her balcony and outside her bedroom door. Normally, Nyla was excited for her vampire sessions with Jamin, but since the werewolf encounter the other night, Nyla was restless. Samuel had immediately rounded up scouting groups to hunt for the werewolf. Samuel and Fulcan figured there were probably more not too far off and they wanted to be prepared. Kaden, of course, was in one of the scouting groups and Nyla didn't have a chance to talk to him either. Nyla felt left out. She had asked to go on a scouting mission as well, but both her mother and Fulcan had vetoed that idea.

Nyla was ready to get out there with everyone else and be done with her fake "illness" that the queen had told Lamar and the others she had come down with since she had fully turned. The queen and the council had agreed that Nyla was able to control herself, but part of Nyla suspected that it had taken some convincing from Samuel. Well, whatever the reason was, Nyla was just glad she could walk freely around her own home without having to be afraid of ripping someone's head off. Tonight she was going to celebrate her next day of freedom by having a girl's night with Julia. She felt like she could control her hunger now that she had, had a couple more days to work on controlling the hunger.

Nyla ran around her room, straightening the pillows and blankets, making everything comfortable. She heard a knock on her door and sped over to it, opening it with a smile. Julia stood in her long, pink, cotton nightgown with a huge paper sack full of popcorn and a glass bottle of orange liquid.

"I have orange punch and our weight in the cook's kettle corn!" she squealed, running into the room. She jumped onto the big couch, sinking into the piles of blankets Nyla set out. Nyla smiled, glad she was finally alone with her best friend. She grabbed a straw and a bottle of blood from the cooler Fulcan had brought in. She poured the deep red liquid into a glass and joined Julia on the couch. Julia eyed Nyla's glass.

"Is that stuff even good?" She grabbed her own glass and poured herself some punch.

"Well, this is animal blood from a deer Fulcan shot the other day so it's not as good as the real stuff, but yes, it's good enough." Julia made a face at her.

"Does my blood count as real stuff?" Julia half-joked.

Nyla shook her head. "Sorry, I didn't mean it like that. I'm sure this is grossing you out . . . we'll talk about something else."

"Oh no! Nyla, this is who you are and I'll get used to it." She smiled, hoisting the huge bag of popcorn onto the couch between them. "Let's dig in!" They ate their popcorn in silence for a couple minutes as Nyla got out a deck of cards. She began to shuffle them absentmindedly.

"So you got the glorious job of getting to know Adrian huh? How's that going?" Nyla took a sip of her drink.

"Ugh! It's horrible! You have no idea." Nyla laughed, putting her glass down on the maple coffee table next to the couch. "No, she eats with her hands! She barely ever talks, I have to do all the talking, and half the time I think she just ignores me. Oh, and listen to this. I'm pretty sure she is worse than a dog when it comes to her attention span. She literally cannot finish a sentence without getting distracted by something in the sky, or an animal on the ground!" Julia started to imitate Adrian acting like an excited dog and Nyla was laughing so hard, her ribs started to hurt. "It's awful!" Julia exclaimed. She joined in laughing until her eyes watered.

"It's good to be back." Nyla wrapped her arms around herself, holding her sides.

"Believe me, it's good to have you back! I've missed this." Julia picked up her glass, taking a sip. "So . . . how've things been going with, um . . . Samuel?" An awkward feeling suddenly spread through the room. Nyla took a deep breath, the image of Samuel putting a smile on her face. Julia had always had a crush on Samuel and everyone seemed to know it. Now that Nyla's feelings for him were growing each day, she didn't know what to say.

"Well, it's going good. I don't have to depend on him so much anymore. I mean, I still feel like I need him, just to help me through, like, the hunger, but it's getting better."

"Okay, but, Nyla"—Julia scooted closer to her—"you know that we are all here for you. I'm here for you. I can help you through this too."

"Yes, but . . . it's different with Samuel. I feel closer to him. Like he knows what I'm going through somehow. He feels what I feel and he makes me feel better. I don't know it's hard to explain." She looked down, studying the cards she was shuffling again.

"Okay, but what about Kaden?" Julia looked Nyla in the eye. "He really cares about you, you know. And it crushes him that he can't help you like . . . Samuel can. I mean, how can those feelings that you had for Kaden just go away? He told me about what happened in your garden hideout." Nyla bit her lip, thinking about that moment in time before her world changed. Julia studied Nyla's confused face. "I just don't want you to give up on Kaden, okay?" Julia hesitated. "I know that spending so much time alone with Samuel, and him helping you, is bringing you closer together, but please just give Kaden a chance." Nyla wasn't sure if Julia was giving her this advice because she really wanted to help her, or if it was just because she liked Samuel.

"Okay." Nyla nodded her head. "Julia, yes I spend a lot of time with Samuel, but I don't even know if I feel anything, like that, for him." Julia gave Nyla a skeptical look. "Julia, I'm serious. I mean, yes, Samuel is . . . pretty amazing. He is so kind, he listens . . . his smile and eyes—" Nyla cleared her throat. "But despite all those things, Kaden still means something to me, and just because Samuel and I are closer than we were, and I trust Samuel with my life, it doesn't mean that I'm in love with him or anything. Besides, he doesn't feel that way about me anyway. He's just helping me through this. We're just friends."

"Okay." Julia sat deeper into the comfortable couch, satisfied. Secretly she hoped that Nyla and Kaden would work out. She felt they were right for each other, and it might work out better for both her and Nyla.

They continued to talk, play rummy, and eat popcorn until a knock came at the door. Nyla got up and answered the door, smiling when Samuel stood there. He looked her up and down, appreciating the sight of her in her short, skimpy, silk nightgown.

"Hey." He grinned at her as she stepped aside, letting him in. "You ladies have a fun time?" He gave Julia a smile as she waved at him from the couch, carefully pulling a blanket on her lap, hiding her own plain, cotton nightgown.

"Yes, we did." Nyla grabbed her empty glass, filling it with more red liquid. "Is the moon up already?" She looked toward the balcony.

"Yep." He turned to her. "That was when you wanted me back wasn't it. We are still training aren't we?" Nyla ignored Julia's hurt expression.

"Yes." It was true; she hadn't realized it, but she felt safer now that Samuel was back.

"Well, I better get to bed." Julia stood, taking her almost empty bottle of orange punch. "Can I take the popcorn?"

Nyla laughed. "Yes." She gave her friend a hug. "I'll see you tomorrow, okay. Bright and early so don't be late. We have to find something awesome to do and have a blast! Plus, we need to learn everything there is to know about these potential . . . 'werewolf' newcomers." Julia gave her a funny look. "What? You never know. They could be just waiting to pounce on all of us in the middle of the night." She laughed as Julia turned her head, looking out the open balcony doors to the night sky.

"Thanks! Now I don't want to walk to my room." She laughed halfheartedly.

"Well, we can walk you down if you need to." Samuel pulled out his sword. "With a guard and vampire on your team, you're bound

167

to be safe from any werewolf that wants to eat you for desert." He winked at her.

She eyed Samuel and laughed. "No thanks, I think I've got it." She hoisted the half empty bag of popcorn over her shoulder and smiled at Nyla as she left the room, shutting the door behind her.

"So you ready to train?" He sat on the chair next to her bed.

"Oh, yes." She sat on the bed, facing him. "I'm more than ready to work on getting the hang of this vampire thing."

"Good." He smiled at her. "The next thing we need to work on, other than controlling your hunger, is being able to control your ability to sense emotions. It could really become helpful in battle, or an interrogation, or anything."

"Samuel." She looked him in the eyes. "How do you know so much about vampires?"

He hesitated for a moment. "Well, ever since I found out what you were, Jamin has been teaching me about this stuff. I, um . . . I also used to know a few."

"What?" Nyla scooted to the edge of the bed. "You never told any of us that. When? Who?"

Samuel laughed. "I'll tell you about it sometime, just not right now, okay?"

"Okay." Nyla looked at him suspiciously.

"So," Samuel changed the subject, "I see you've started to consume blood regularly." He nodded to her glass. "How do you feel? Is the animal blood Fulcan brought you still working?"

"Oh, ya. I like it. Well, it's obviously not as good as the human stuff, but it'll do." Samuel nodded.

The conversation with Julia came back to Nyla's thoughts. "Samuel, I want to ask you about something."

"Yes?" Samuel sat forward, propping his elbows on his knees.

"This is kind of weird to ask." Nyla shifted on the bed. "Can vampires . . . love? I mean . . . do they still have the same feelings as humans?" Samuel opened his mouth but shut it again. He thought for a moment.

"Um, I would assume so, they're not that different from people. Why?" He studied Nyla's face.

"You know what, it's nothing." Nyla blushed, embarrassed. She took a deep breath. "Okay, it's just ever since I turned I feel . . . different. The way I've acted in certain situations makes it seem like maybe my heart has changed . . . become closed. I don't feel exactly the same way about things that I used to." Samuel nodded his head.

"You mean Kaden, don't you?"

"Maybe . . ." Nyla looked down. "But it's not just that. I'm . . . I don't feel bad about what I did to Jimmy anymore. I mean I feel bad about killing him, but I've accepted what happened and I feel like it's how it had to happen . . . and I can't stand that! I should be rotting in guilt for the rest of my life, but I'm not. You know what, I lied. I don't even feel guilty anymore for killing Jimmy. That's a horrible thing to say." Nyla frowned, closing her eyes.

"Trust me, Nyla, I've heard worse." Samuel spoke in a soft voice, almost to himself. "I mean, I'm a soldier, I've killed tons of people." Nyla looked at him.

"I'm afraid of what I'm turning into, Samuel."

"Nyla, you are still you, but you are a predator now. You will feel differently about things like killing and bloodshed, but you are still who you are at heart. I'm not going to lie to you. Vampires . . . lose a lot of their humanity when turned. It's a curse, and it's just the way it is. You're just beginning to find yourself and discover who you are." Samuel paused, looking her in the eyes. "You know what, don't worry about Kaden. You have a huge heart and things will fall into place where they are supposed to be."

"You're advice and words of wisdom amaze me." Nyla gave a small smile.

"I've come to learn a thing or two about life." Samuel looked away. Nyla got the growing suspicion that Samuel wasn't telling her something, but she let it go.

"Well," Nyla broke the silence. "So let's train." Nyla smiled eagerly. She rushed to her closet and shut the door before changing into more reasonable clothing than a silk nightgown. "Okay, let's get started." She emerged from her closet to find her room reorganized. "What did you do to my room?" She looked at the furniture that was pushed up against her bed.

"Well, we are going to need room to move around." Samuel took the sword and sheath from his belt and placed them on the bed.

"No weapons?" Nyla asked, confused.

"Although you'll have a sword at times it's always good to learn to fight without one. You're faster now and stronger so most of the time you might be better at close hand to hand combat anyway."

"Well, if I'm faster and stronger won't I kick your butt?" Nyla grinned at him.

"Don't underestimate me too much," Samuel countered. He removed his shirt and placed it beside his weapon. He grinned at her raised eyebrows. "Just get into position." Samuel laughed. Nyla stood across from him and stood with her feet apart, readying herself. Ten minutes later Samuel had Nyla pinned to the wall for the third time.

"You're not focusing, Nyla." Samuel stepped back, letting her move into position again. "You need to anticipate my movements. Watch your opponent carefully. You have fast reflexes and if you concentrate and stay focused you will be able to predict my movements and react to them." Nyla took a deep breath. It wasn't like she wasn't trying to focus she just couldn't concentrate that well with Samuel's shirtless body distracting her.

"Again, and this time concentrate." Samuel ignored Nyla's glower in his direction. Nyla closed her eyes, took a deep breath, and tried to clear her head. As soon as she opened her eyes Samuel attacked her. She dodged him just in time, but he came back around and thrust her arm behind her back. She twisted out of his grip and stumbled back a few steps. *Focus.* She lunged at Samuel and he anticipated her move, but she was too quick and zipped behind him. She grabbed him from behind and he grabbed ahold of her arms, flipping her onto her back. The breath was knocked out of her as she struck the hard floor and Samuel was on top of her before she knew what was happening.

"You're lucky I'm not a werewolf." Samuel breathed, still holding her down. Suddenly Nyla moved her hips, strengthening her core, and did a backward summersault, bringing Samuel with her and flipping him onto his back. She sat on top of him, holding him down with her arm gently across his throat. Samuel let out a surprised breath.

"You're lucky you're not a werewolf." She grinned triumphantly.

"Yea." Samuel's heart pounded beneath her. Nyla bit her lip as she looked into Samuel's blue-gray gaze just inches from hers. She quickly rolled off of him and stood, composing herself.

"Well," Nyla said nervously, "I'm going to get some sleep. Might as well quit on a good note." Samuel nodded and stood. He retrieved his shirt and weapon from the bed.

"Want me to straighten out your room again?" He motioned toward the couch against her bed.

"Oh, sure. Thanks." Nyla nodded, giving him a small smile. Samuel moved her furniture back into place and looked at Nyla.

"Um, good job. That was better." He nodded at her. "We still need to work on it though. Well, I'll be outside the door . . . if you need me."

"Okay." Nyla nodded. Samuel moved to open her bedroom door. "Good night Samuel." Nyla called to him.

"Good night, Nyla." Samuel closed the door behind him.

Nyla lay awake in her bed, reviewing what had just happened between them. She closed her eyes, listening to Samuel's uneven heartbeat outside the door.

CHAPTER 16

Nyla woke the next morning with a giddy excitement in her belly. She was so ready to get outside. She smiled, sitting up and looking toward the door. She heard a heartbeat outside her room, but it wasn't Samuel's. She spotted a white slip of paper tucked into the frame around the mirror on her vanity and she got out of bed, ignoring the coldness of the hardwood floor from the decreasing temperature of the upcoming winter. She grabbed the slip of paper, smiling at the words written in Samuel's fancy handwriting. He had gotten up early to oversee the guard, but he would be back shortly. She was to get dressed in warm, hunting appropriate clothing and skip her blood ration for the morning.

She placed the note on the vanity counter and dressed in her favorite training clothes, lacing up knee high boots. She worked her hair until it was in a thick, golden braid that hung to her waist. Looking at herself in the mirror, she approved her look and turned just as Samuel walked in through her bedroom door. He looked her up and down, smiling.

"You ready?" He smiled, beckoning toward the door. She eyed him with a suspicious smile and grabbed a maroon cloak from her closet. She draped it over her arm and followed him out the door.

"What are we doing?" Nyla smiled, taking in a deep breath of fresh air as they exited the castle, heading toward one of the stables next to the training grounds.

"We are going hunting. We need to get you well fed for today." He smiled at her.

"I thought Fulcan forbade us from going out by ourselves?"

"Well, we never found a trace of the injured werewolf or signs of any others so I think we'll be okay. And what Fulcan doesn't know won't kill him. I'll be there next to you the entire time and we'll keep a look out for them." Nyla nodded in agreement. Samuel continued, "But this time, instead of me telling you what to do, you get to catch your own meal without my help. I'm not taking any weapons, except for my sword. You're on your own for this one."

"Okay, should be easy enough." Nyla was up for the challenge. She was feeling extra energetic and longed to get out and run free.

Samuel laughed. "We'll see."

"Hey! What's with the lack of faith, huh?" She laughed, elbowing him. "You don't think I can hold my own?"

"No, I do." Samuel grinned down at her. "It's just a matter of if you can keep up with an animal on your own without sneaking up on it and shooting it like regular hunting."

"You think I'm slow, do you? Well let's see if you can keep up with me now?" She crouched, preparing to go into a full out sprint, but Samuel caught her by the arm and swung her around. She smacked into his body and gasped in surprise. Samuel burst out laughing, taking in her startled expression. She looked up at him and warmth flooded her body. His attractiveness stunned her and she was totally aware of her body pressed against his. She turned around abruptly and started walking.

"Let's go."

Kaden had been watching Nyla and Samuel as they walked outside the training ground walls. He was told that Nyla was going to be over her "illness" today and he had been waiting for her, going over what he was going to say in his mind. He smiled slightly at how happy she seemed. He was glad that she was beginning to return to herself. His smile had faded as he saw Samuel pull her back and her body press against his. *But she had turned away from him right away.* Kaden thought, trying to keep hope.

"They look happy, don't they?" Kaden jumped slightly and turned toward Lucas, who had crept up behind him.

"Um . . . ya, I guess." Kaden glanced back at them, jealousy creeping into his chest.

"I thought you and her had a thing. That's the impression I got anyway."

"Apparently not." Kaden turned, walking toward the archery range.

"You're not going to do anything about it? You're not going to fight for her?" Lucas followed him, irritating Kaden. *Why won't he just leave me alone?*

"Why should I? She seems happy enough without me." Kaden looked toward the direction of Nyla and Samuel bitterly.

"It's just as well, I suppose," Lucas said absentmindedly. He picked up a bow, weighing it in his hands.

"Why's that?" Kaden gave him an irritated look. He turned, taking a bow and aiming at the target.

"Oh, it's nothing. It's just that I've seen them together a lot lately. They're always strolling outside the castle together at night."

"What?" Kaden let the arrow fly, missing the target. Kaden had thought that Nyla couldn't leave her room at night because it wasn't safe. That's what he was told.

"Oh, you didn't know?" Lucas gave him a look of sympathy. He looked toward the direction of the stables. "If it were me I would follow them." He shrugged his shoulders at Kaden's disapproving frown. "Well, don't then." He set his bow down. "Then again, trust me, it's for the best."

"Excuse me?" Kaden turned toward Lucas, but he was already almost out of the training ground entry way behind him. Kaden put down the bow and strode off toward the stables. He stopped just outside of the doorway, watching Nyla and Samuel as they saddled their horses. He glared at Samuel as he helped her onto her horse. *She is more than capable of getting up onto her own horse!* Kaden thought fiercely.

"Kaden?" Kaden spun around to come face-to-face with Julia. "What are you doing?"

"Shhh!" He shushed her, looking into the stables watching as Nyla and Samuel trotted their horses out the other doors.

"What are you doing?" Julia stood in front of Kaden, blocking his view.

"Nothing." He moved around her and started to saddle his own horse.

"Kaden!" Julia put her hand on his arm, stopping him from getting up onto the horse.

"I'm spying, okay, Julia? Are you happy now?" He looked down, avoiding her gaze.

"Kaden." Julia gave him a disapproving look. "Really? Why are you going to spy on Nyla and Samuel?"

"I just . . ." He gave a huffed sigh, running his hands through his dark hair. "I hate not being with her! I want to know what they're doing. I know it's bad, but I just need to know why she can't be with me. She wanted me just two weeks ago and I know that couldn't have changed. I want to know why they are going off on their own. I . . . I want to keep an eye on them." He was ashamed of how bad that sounded.

"Kaden . . ." Julia gave him a sympathetic look. "Just stop this. You can talk to her when she gets back."

"No, Julia!" He calmed himself at her startled look. "I'm sorry. It's just . . . I'm in love with her Julia." He looked up at the roof, clenching his jaw.

"Then tell her how you feel, Kaden!"

"It's not that simple, Julia!" Kaden mounted his horse, but Julia grabbed the reins.

"Tell her how you feel! She'll listen. She has feelings for you too!"

"Look!" He stared into Julia's brown gaze. "If it were that easy, I would tell her, okay? She probably has feelings for him too! They spend every minute together, how could she not? We don't live in a perfect world Julia! If we did Samuel would be interested in you instead of spending all his time with Nyla, but he's not!" Julia let go of the reins, giving Kaden a hurt look. Kaden sighed, looking away and turning his horse swiftly, and headed in the direction Nyla and Samuel had gone.

Nyla stayed crouched in the tall brush of the forest, silently watching the small deer. She looked across to where Samuel sat in the shadow of a bush. He gave her a smile that fueled her confidence. She took a deep breath as Samuel gave her a nod. She sprung from the brush, moving to pounce on the deer. Startled, the deer jumped and Nyla missed, hitting the ground. She quickly stood, brushing dirt from her hands as the deer ran through the bushes in front of her. She looked at Samuel, who was laughing, still seated by the bush. He stood, clapping his hands together in applause.

"Nicely done," he teased, looking in the direction the deer had gone. "Well, what are you waiting for? Go and get it!" She shot him a look and he laughed as she took off in a sprint after the deer. She stopped next to a tree and sniffed the air, the scent of the deer filling her nostrils, spurring her hunger. She snapped her head to the right, squinting to see the deer running in the forest ahead and took off after it. She caught up with it easily and pounced, grabbing the deer around the neck, and sank her teeth into it as they rolled. The deer stilled and Nyla drank deeply. She raised her head when she heard Samuel coming toward her through the brush. She smiled at him.

"See, I can take care of myself." She stood, walking toward him.

"Clearly." He grinned. He lifted his hand and wiped a trickle of blood from her lip and she blushed. He wiped his finger on her nose, smearing the crimson liquid down the center. "You're messy," he teased, laughing. She looked down at her bloody hands.

"So are you!" She wiped both hands on his face and down his neck, stopping at his shirt collar.

"Don't." He smiled down at her. He raised his eyebrows at her smirk. "Don't." She grinned as she smeared her hands down his shirt, staining the fabric. He gently pushed her away and chuckled, heading toward the deer.

"Okay." He bent down next to the deer.

"Samuel." Nyla took a few steps toward him. He wiped his hands on the deer's neck, covering them with blood. He stood up, a mischievous smile on his face.

"You wouldn't!" She gave him a disbelieving smile as he slowly walked toward her. She took a couple steps back, but he ran toward her, pinning her against a tree. "You wouldn't!" Nyla giggled, trying to turn her face away from him.

"Oh, I would." He chuckled, taking her face in his bloody hands.

"Samuel!" Nyla squealed as he rubbed blood on her face and into her hair. He stepped away and laughed as she stared at him, open-mouthed. She began to laugh.

"I can't believe you just did that! How am I going to get this out?" The image of them riding up on their horses, covered in blood, made Nyla laugh even harder. "What will everyone think of us covered in blood?" Samuel laughed, giving her a handsome grin that would make any woman in the kingdom weak in the knees.

"There's a lake just that way." He nodded his head to the left. "We'll just wash up there." He smiled again, and Nyla was surprised when her heart did a flip. Samuel turned, walking toward the lake, and she followed. After a couple minutes, the trees cleared, opening to a small, sparkling lake that was fed by a beautiful, flowing waterfall from the cliffs above. Nyla stopped a few feet from the trees, taking in the view. Her eyes traveled down the shimmering falls and landed on Samuel. He was standing at the water's edge, looking out over the water. Nyla's heart began to pound as he pulled off his shirt, exposing the muscles along his back. He turned, smiling at her stare as he began to unbuckle his belt.

"You might want to turn around." He grinned as she blushed.

"Right." She spun around, wanting to run and hide back in the woods. She heard a splash and glanced behind her.

"Well, are you coming or not? Don't tell me you like being covered in dirt and blood." He grinned and she bit her lip, her heart in her throat. He raised his eyebrows. "No? Okay, suit yourself." He began to swim backward.

"Okay, okay." Nyla walked toward him. "But turn around, okay?" She turned her face away, blushing at his grin.

"Okay." He turned, treading water. She smiled at his head, making sure he wouldn't turn around before she unbraided her hair, letting the blood dried curls flow freely to her waist. Glancing at Samuel, she stripped off her clothes and dove off of the bank.

Surfacing, she pushed her golden locks out of her face and turned to face Samuel.

"There. Feels better already doesn't it?" He dunked his head under the water, rubbing the rest of the blood off of his face. Turning, Nyla swam to the waterfall. She found a spot where she could touch the bottom, and keeping her body safely under water, dunked her head into the falls. She rubbed her scalp, smiling at the coolness of the water. Wiping excess water from her face, she opened her eyes and blushed as she caught Samuel staring at her.

"What?" She smiled, biting her bottom lip.

"Nothing, nothing." He shook his head. He grinned at her, making heat rush to her face, and swam closer. "It's just . . . you missed a spot."

"Where?" She touched her flawless face.

"Right . . . Here!" He splashed water at her and swam backward, laughing.

"Hey!" She laughed, swimming after him. She kicked off the bottom, launching herself at him and grabbed ahold of his shoulders. She pushed him down, dunking him underwater, but he spun out of her grasp and turned, grabbing ahold of her wrists. Nyla squealed and tried to pull away, but he pulled her closer, holding her wrists together. She gasped, staring into his gray-blue eyes, suddenly aware of how close their naked bodies were to each other.

Her heart pounded and heat rushed to her face as a burning filled the pit of her stomach. She could feel Samuel's breath on her face and his breathing quickened as his gaze fell to her lips. He inched his face closer, feeling the heat radiating off of her lips and she closed the gap, softly pecking his lips. She pulled back slightly, looking into his gorgeous eyes and was suddenly lost in them. She met his lips again and her hand touched the back of his neck as his arm moved behind her waist, pulling her closer. A twig snapped and they both turned their heads to the left, looking toward the source of the sound. Nyla's heart sank as she looked up, meeting Kaden's shocked, green gaze.

"Kaden!" Samuel and Nyla sprang apart. "What are you doing here?" She swam toward the bank.

"What are *you* doing, Nyla?" Kaden took a step back, hurt in his voice and face.

"I . . . we . . . we were . . ." She looked at Samuel.

"Save it, Nyla." Kaden turned, stalking away.

"Wait, Kaden!" Nyla splashed through the water, ducking down into the shallows when she remembered her clothes were on the bank. She looked at Samuel and he turned around, stunned. *What just happened? What did I just do?* He had begun to feel something for Nyla as he had gotten to know her better, but he had not planned on this happening. He might have just jeopardized his friendship with Kaden forever, not to mention Nyla's friendship with Kaden as well.

Nyla pulled on her clothes and boots, running after Kaden. *This can't be happening. This can't be happening!*

"Kaden!" Nyla ran to the edge of the trees, scanning the forest for Kaden. She spotted him untying his horse from a tree and sprinted to him, grabbing ahold of his arm. "Kaden . . ."

"Nyla!" He spun around, wrenching his arm out of her grip. "What were you doing?"

"I . . ." she was at a loss for words. She ran her hand through her wet hair. "We . . ."

"No, Nyla! I'm not listening to this." He turned and mounted his horse, pushing it into a gallop.

"Kaden!" She yelled after him, but he was already too far to hear her words.

CHAPTER 17

Kaden kept his horse at a gallop until he was well out of the woods, only slowing it to a trot, and then a walk when he feared for the horse's health. *I can't believe Nyla! How could she?* Just two weeks ago, everything was going great. He had confessed his feelings for Nyla and he had thought that she returned the same feelings. He had apparently guessed wrong. He clenched his teeth together, wanting to turn his horse around and beat the crap out of Samuel. *I thought Samuel was my friend. How could he do this?!*

He pushed his horse into a cantor and didn't stop until he was inside the castle gates. Dismounting his horse, he quickly led it into the stables, not even bothering to hand the reins to a young stable boy. When he stormed out of the stable doors, he spotted Julia reading a book on a bale of hay, clearly waiting for his return. She stood up when she saw him, setting her book down and walking toward him.

"Kaden?" She stopped when she saw his angry face. "What's wrong? What happened?"

"Nothing." Kaden grunted, storming past her. All he wanted to do was go to the training grounds and slash the crap out of a dueling dummy with a sword, and then go up to his chambers and sulk.

"What happened?" Julia had a worried tone in her voice. "Where are Nyla and Samuel? Did something happen?" She started to walk behind him, trying to keep up. "Are they okay? Did you—"

"They're fine! Okay, Julia?" Kaden spun around, almost yelling into her face. Julia stepped back away from Kaden's angry face.

"Wha—"

"They were together, Julia! They were kissing in the lake!"

180

"What do you mean?" Julia shook her head, her heart sinking to her feet.

"They decided to go skinny-dipping at the falls in the woods! Nyla and . . ." He didn't even want to say the name.

"Oh . . ." Julia mumbled, putting two and two together.

"Ya." Kaden ran his hands furiously through his hair. "I was so sure . . . but . . ." He let out a growling sigh and turned, stalking to the training grounds, leaving Julia staring at her hands.

‹‹‹○››

Samuel sat on the bank at the water's edge, watching Nyla with a somber expression. When she had come back from the woods, she had dropped down onto a big rock, putting her head in her hands. She had been there ever since, and Samuel had no idea what to say. He stood, rubbing the sand from his hands on his pants, and slowly walked toward her.

"Nyla." Samuel sat beside her on the rock, keeping a small distance between them. "I . . . I'm sorry." He lifted his hand to place it on her shoulder, but put it back down. "That's not how I wanted things to happen." Nyla looked up and Samuel's heart ached when he saw her wipe a few tears away.

"Nyla, I'm so sorry." He gave her an apologetic look.

"No, Samuel." She gave him a small smile. "I'm sorry. I shouldn't have kissed you." She looked him in the eyes, making him want to take her in his arms. "I just." She looked Samuel in the eyes, but found she couldn't concentrate on what she was going to say when she did, and looked away. She took a deep breath and blurted jumbled thoughts out.

"I shouldn't have kissed you. It was just in the moment and it was stupid. It meant nothing and I shouldn't have done that. You know that there was something between Kaden and I before I turned. I still have feelings of some kind for him, but I need to figure out what those are. Believe me, I did not want this to happen, and I just think that just because I turned, I still can't give up on him. I need to see what this is and where it can possibly lead." She looked up into his eyes and her heart throbbed when she saw the sadness in his face.

Samuel was taken aback. Nyla had felt something when they kissed. He could feel it, and now she was saying it meant nothing? He quickly composed himself and any emotion was gone.

"Okay, I understand." He lied.

"I'm so sorry, Samuel! This shouldn't have happened and it was wrong. I just . . . I need to find Kaden and explain things."

"Well," Samuel stood, avoiding her eyes. "We should get going. We need to hurry if you want to catch up with him and explain that kissing me was a mistake." He walked past her into the forest.

"Samuel, I . . ." Nyla realized she had hurt him. "Samuel." She caught up with him.

"Let's go, Nyla."

When Nyla and Samuel arrived at the stables, a frozen rain had begun to fall. Nyla pulled the hood of her cloak up around her head so that it framed her pale face. She could faintly hear the sound of steel hitting wood and she turned her head toward the sound.

"He's in the training grounds." Nyla looked at Samuel. He nodded and looked up as Julia came running up to them.

"Nyla! I've been waiting for you, guys. Kaden . . . he told me what happened." Julia kept her eyes down.

"I . . . it's not what it seemed like. We kind of got into a . . . blood war." Nyla paused at Julia's confused expression. "Well, we were playing around and we both got covered in blood from the deer that I hunted and we were washing it off in the lake. Kaden kind of came at the wrong moment." They began to walk toward the training grounds.

Julia shrugged. "So you didn't kiss Samuel?"

"No, I . . . I did, but, it was a mistake. It shouldn't have happened." Nyla avoided Samuel's eyes.

"Well, Kaden's real upset. He's been out here slashing up that training dummy since he got back." They stopped at the training grounds entryway and watched Kaden attack the dummy like it was a monster that wouldn't die. Nyla sighed, her heart throbbing with guilt at the sight of him.

"I need to talk to him." Nyla took a deep breath and started to walk toward him.

"Wait!" Julia grabbed ahold of Nyla's arm. "What if you attack him? The last time you saw him, we kind of had to restrain you, remember?" Kaden turned, spotting them. He stared hard at Samuel and turned around, leaving the sword on the ground and stalking off toward the other door.

"Kaden! Wait!" she yelled to him. He turned toward them again, stopping when he saw her coming toward him.

"Nyla, are you sure?" Julia looked worried.

"Yes, I need to talk to him. The only way that I will ever be able to be comfortable around him again is if I talk to him and get everything straightened out. Jamin said I need to forgive him in my heart before anything else."

"Okay." Julia looked unsure.

"And . . . I need to explain what he saw . . . at the lake." Julia nodded at Nyla, her heart sinking when she recalled the image she had formed in her mind when Kaden had told her what he had seen.

"I trust her." Samuel nodded in Nyla's direction, but didn't return her thankful smile. "She needs to do this." His voice was hard and his face impassive, but Nyla could feel the hurt from him. Julia kept her eyes down, not wanting to look at Samuel.

"I promise I can control myself." Nyla looked at Samuel and he nodded when he saw the truth in her eyes. She looked away from Samuel's hard face and turned around to look at Kaden. Seeing that he had turned and continued out of the training grounds, she sped up.

"Um . . ." Julia tightened her hood around her face, looking at the ground. "I'm going to . . . go make sure Nyla's room is nice and warm." She spun around, hurrying toward the castle. Samuel looked to where Nyla was catching up with Kaden and he turned, slowly following Julia.

"Kaden!" Nyla put a hand on his shoulder when she caught up with him.

"Nyla, I don't really want to talk right now."

"Kaden, please. Let me explain." Kaden stopped, but didn't turn around. His heart felt like it was going to rip apart.

"Nyla. Do you love him?" He almost whispered, not wanting to know the answer.

"I . . . no. Kaden, what you saw at the lake . . . it's not what it looked like."

"Then what was it, Nyla?" Kaden turned toward her, looking her in the eyes.

"We were just swimming and washing blood off of ourselves from hunting. Nothing happened!"

"It sure looked like something was happening, Nyla." Kaden raked his fingers through his hair. "What would have happened if you hadn't seen me? Would you have . . ." He couldn't say the words, the thought making him sick to his stomach.

"No, Kaden!" Sure the thought of doing more than just kissing Samuel gave Nyla a giddy feeling in the pit of her stomach, but she pushed it down. Nyla bit her lip, thinking of Samuel's warm lips on hers and the look on his face when she told him it was wrong.

"See, Nyla! I know you're thinking of him!" Kaden started walking again.

"Kaden! I . . . I like you, Kaden. I have feelings for you and . . . we need to figure this out!"

"No, Nyla!" He spun around, pointing his finger at her. "*You* need to figure things out! It's either me or him Nyla, and I'm not going to sit around and pretend that everything is okay when I can't even think about you with him without wanting to . . . punch something!" Nyla stared at him, not knowing what to say. Kaden ripped his hands through his wet hair. "Goddammit, Nyla! Silence is all I get? Whatever! You and Samuel have fun together, okay?" He turned, starting to walk off.

"Ugh! Really, Kaden? I swear sometimes I could just k . . ." She cut off, fuming.

"Say it!" Kaden spun toward Nyla, looking her in the eyes.

"Sometimes I could just kill you! Are you happy now?" She glared at his back, tears starting to fall as he strode off toward the castle. She turned, sprinting toward her balcony. She quickly climbed the vines and jumped up onto the balcony, disappearing into her room.

Kaden reached the doors to the castle, but turned away instead of going in. "Dammit!" He sat on the top step, pounding his fist against his thigh. He wiped wet hair back off of his forehead, looking

184

out into the pouring sleet. He looked to his right as Adrian stepped around the stone pillar next to the steps.

"You all right?" Adrian sat beside him. "I kind of . . . heard everything." Kaden frowned at her. Adrian held up her hands. "Not that I was eavesdropping! I just, well you guys were practically yelling. Are you all right?"

"No." Kaden looked down at his freezing hands.

"What can I say? Lucas tried to warn you."

"What?" Kaden looked at her.

"Listen, I know what she is and, trust me, you don't want to get entangled with someone like her."

"How do you know what she is?" Kaden stood up, defensive.

"Calm down! I won't tell anybody!" She tugged Kaden back down on the steps. "It's actually good to have her on our side. However, I know what things like her do to the hearts of men. They play around with them, and then when they least expect it, they rip their hearts out . . . literally. Listen, creatures like her don't love. They can't! They aren't human beings and they can't feel things like we do." Adrian paused, letting her words sink in. She put her arm on his shoulder, scooting closer.

"You're wrong," Kaden said quietly, not wanting to accept her words.

"You know I'm not." Adrian put her hand on Kaden's cheek, turning his head toward her.

"She's a monster. You can't love her, because she won't love you."

"You're wrong!" Kaden stood up, escaping her grip. "Get away from me! What do you know?!"

"Listen, I—" Adrian stood, but Kaden pushed her away from him.

"Leave! I don't want to hear this anymore!"

"What's going on here?" Lucas came around the pillar. Adrian turned toward him.

"I was just trying to explain that a thing like Nyla isn't capable of love." She walked over to him.

"Ya, and I am telling you to leave!" Kaden glared at her. Adrian looked at Lucas and he nodded. Turning, Adrian took a last look at

Kaden, then went back the way Lucas had come. Kaden sat back down, putting his head in his hands.

She's wrong! She's wrong! She doesn't know anything! He tried to keep telling himself in his mind.

Lucas came up to him. "It's better this way, trust me. You probably weren't even really in love with her. You just thought you were, but she's been playing with your heart this whole time."

No, no, no, no! Kaden screamed in his mind. He looked up at Lucas, squinting his eyes against the freezing rain.

"Trust me. She's meant to be with him. Let her go, it's hopeless. She's not capable of loving you." Lucas gave him a sympathetic look, holding out his hand. "Trust me."

"No." Kaden knocked Lucas's hand away, standing up on his own. "You're wrong! I know you're wrong!" Kaden turned, retreating into the castle.

"Suit yourself. You'll see." Lucas said to himself, watching the castle doors close.

∽⚬∾

Nyla sat in the freezing rain against the stone railing of her balcony. Holding her knees against her body, she silently cried into them.

"Nyla?" Julia stood at the doorway of her balcony, holding her cloak around her.

"Julia." Nyla raised her head, wiping tears and rain away from her face. "I didn't even hear you come into my room."

"Oh, I've been here the whole time. I just . . . when you got onto the balcony I thought I would give you some time."

"Oh." Nyla gave her a fake smile.

"Are you okay?" Julia asked the useless question she already knew the answer to.

"No!" Nyla stood, running into the room and embracing Julia. She pulled back as Julia's appetizing scent started to fill her nostrils. "Julia, I think I screwed everything up!"

"No, Nyla." Julia held her soaking friend at arm's length. "You couldn't screw things up. It will be okay, Nyla. He'll come around. You'll see."

"I don't know, Julia." Nyla walked past her, pacing. "I . . . I tried to make things right and now Kaden hates me!"

"He doesn't hate you, Nyla!" Julia stopped Nyla before she could soak any of the furniture. "Here." Julia helped Nyla take off her saturated cloak and got her a towel.

"No, he does." Nyla disappeared in her closet, coming back out with the towel around her. Nyla started pacing again, wiping tears away from her face.

"Come on." Julia put her hands on Nyla's shoulders, directing her toward the huge bathroom. "Take a bath and clear your head. Everything will be all right. If you really do care for Kaden then it will all work out. He'll come around."

"Okay," Nyla sauntered to the bathroom with her head hanging low. She turned. "Oh, when Samuel gets here, can you just let him know?"

"Um, Nyla," Julia looked down, heart sinking at the mention of Samuel's name. "He got called for duty tonight. He'll be here in the morning. I'm sorry, I thought you knew that." Julia hated lying to her friend, but Samuel asked Julia not to say anything. He just wanted to give Nyla space tonight to think about things. He couldn't deal with being around her this soon after what had just happened between them and her swift rejection.

"Oh . . ." Nyla nodded her head in a zombielike fashion. "Okay." She turned toward the bathroom again, shuffling along.

"Dominic is outside the door, but I can stay if you want me to."

"Okay." Nyla didn't turn around as she shut the door to the bathroom. Julia sat down on the couch. She picked up a thin book that Nyla had sitting on the table and flipped through the pages, lying down on the comfortable cushions. Nyla stayed in the bathroom for hours and Julia eventually fell asleep on the big couch, not even waking when Nyla came out of the bathroom and quietly laid in her bed, staring up at the ceiling.

CHAPTER 18

CHAPTER 18

The next morning went pretty smoothly. Nyla woke up after sleeping for a few hours, feeling well rested. She smiled at the fact that vampires needed little sleep, if any at all. She also loved the fact that she wasn't even a little hungry after her meal yesterday and was in an optimistic mood. Maybe she could talk to Kaden again today and they could make up. She still didn't know exactly what she wanted, but she hated the fact that Kaden was angry with her.

Samuel had shown up early, as Julia had said. As soon as he entered the room, Julia made an excuse to leave, saying she would meet them outside the castle. Samuel nodded and greeted Nyla with a polite smile. Nyla knew things were going to be different since their kiss in the lake, and she hoped things between her and Samuel would be all right. She knew how much Samuel cared for her and her feelings, at least in a protective sense, and she was grateful for that. She wished that she hadn't said the hurtful things about their kiss the other day, and she knew deep down that none of them were true, she just couldn't admit that right now. Nyla hated herself and her stupid heart for not being decisive. When she saw Kaden, her heart smiled, but at the same time, every time she saw Samuel her heart seemed to call out for him and she longed to be with him. She had no idea what she was going to do.

Samuel made her put on a pretty, pink dress, although she protested. She gave in with Samuel's warning of "looking normal" and her and Samuel headed outside. However, her whole mood changed when she met up with Julia, Adrian, Lucas, and Felix.

"Now, just be careful around them." Samuel warned Nyla as they spotted the group by the training grounds. "They are very snoopy and not as well mannered as your mother seems to think they are. I don't know how she trusts them."

Nyla squeezed his hand in reassurance but frowned when he pulled his hand away. "I'll be careful I promise." She giggled, trying to lighten the mood. "Plus, if they give me any trouble I can always just rip out their throats." She stopped, staring, open mouthed, at Samuel, surprised that those words even came out of her mouth.

Samuel gave a small laugh. "Don't worry that's normal when you're a newborn, but not funny." He gave her a half grin, but she still felt his distance from her. Julia waved them over and Nyla started toward them again.

"Well, we're finally graced with the lady's presence." Adrian gave a poorly faked bow as Nyla and Samuel approached them.

"Excuse me?" Nyla gave Julia a surprised look. Lucas stepped forward, blocking Adrian from Nyla's line of sight.

"What my rude partner meant to say was that we are all glad to actually get to spend time with you face-to-face. After all, we will be training and maybe even fighting side by side if the time comes. Which is lucky for you." He held his hand out to her. Samuel gave a sarcastic snort from beside Nyla, but Lucas ignored him. Smiling, Nyla ignored his hand, walking past him to greet Felix and a reluctant Adrian. Samuel smirked at Lucas and he rolled his eyes, turning and standing beside her.

"So should we take a walk?" Lucas beckoned toward the direction of the garden.

"Sure." Nyla started ahead and Lucas walked beside her as Felix trailed behind, followed by Julia and Adrian. Samuel walked on the other side of Nyla.

Nyla could hear Julia and Adrian talking behind her and she was surprised when she heard Julia laugh. Julia had apparently been over-exaggerating when she told Nyla that hanging out with Adrian had been awful.

"Nyla?" Samuel nudged her with his elbow. Breaking her concentration.

"What?" She looked at him.

"Lucas was asking you a question."

"Oh"—Nyla looked at Lucas sheepishly—"sorry, what?"

"I was just saying that it was very welcoming here in Galatia. It's probably the most welcoming place I've been to. I asked you if you've ever visited anywhere? Have you've ever been out of Galatia?"

"No, I've always wanted to visit the sea, but I've never been out of Galatia. The farthest I've been is in the woods hunting."

"I see, well, maybe sometime I will have to take you on one of my travels. Ridia is deep in the forest, surrounded by woods and mountains, and Genora is on the plains, but the castle Valdora is right by the sea."

"Oh." Nyla frowned at the mention of the vampire kingdom. "I didn't know that."

"Your father was from somewhere by the sea, right?" Lucas looked at Nyla and she swallowed.

"Yes, he was." She cleared her throat, looking away.

"You've been out that far, to Valdora and Genora?" Samuel looked at Lucas in interest.

"Uh, yes." Lucas continued to look at Nyla. "Gafna and Rothgar expected us to know every aspect of the kingdoms for military purposes."

"I see. So you never had to come here for the same reasons?" Samuel gave Lucas a suspicious look.

"No, we left before any scouting groups were sent out here, but I do suspect that if there haven't been any groups yet, there will be in the next few days."

Nyla thought for a moment. "Why would you need to go out to Genora? Isn't the castle abandoned?"

"Yes, it is." Lucas took a breath. "Gafna is planning on claiming Genora completely as his own."

"So there will be scouting groups coming soon?" Nyla looked at Samuel and he nodded.

"We've been sending our own scouts out every day just in case. We'll be ready to ambush them when the time comes." The group continued to talk and discuss battle plans as they made their way through the garden. Nyla found herself getting more and more annoyed as Julia and Adrian continued to be in their own little conversation and when they stopped by the fountain she pulled Julia aside.

"Since when did you and Adrian get so close?" Nyla eyed Julia curiously.

"We're not. It's just, well I'm trying to get to know her and determine if there's anything suspicious about them." Julia looked at her innocently.

"Well, it sure seemed to me that you two were having a good time in your own world the whole time we've been out here."

"Nyla, relax. She's actually not bad to talk to when you get to know her, and I mean you and Samuel have been pretty preoccupied doing your vampire stuff together, so I've been hanging out with her to pass the time."

"What?" Nyla was taken back. "Julia, I've tried to spend as much time with you as I could."

"I know, it's just . . . she's not that bad, okay? Let it go, it's nothing."

"Okay," Nyla hesitated but went back over to Samuel and Lucas, suggesting that they head back toward the training grounds and castle for lunch.

When they made it to the training grounds Nyla began to turn toward the castle, but Lucas continued on.

"So since we are going to be training together, we might as well get to know each other's moves. Well, you should get to know my moves anyway. I can teach you a thing or two, I'm sure." He grabbed a dull sword from the rack, swinging it in his hands expertly. "I want to see what you've got."

"Okay." Nyla shrugged and grabbed another training sword, weighing it in her hands. It felt lighter than a feather. "Let's go."

"Um, Nyla." Samuel walked up behind her, putting his hand on her shoulder. "I don't know if that's such a good idea."

She turned toward him. "Come on, Samuel, I can control myself. Plus I want to teach him a lesson." She grinned up at him, twirling the sword in her hands. "I've got this."

"Okay. Just be careful. If you feel like you're starting to lose control stop and breathe, okay?"

"Okay." Without thinking, Nyla winked at Samuel and instantly regretted it. She turned around, sizing Lucas up as she approached him.

"Don't you want to change first? We wouldn't want to get that pretty dress dirty." Lucas smirked at her, getting into a low stance.

Nyla stayed upright and her posture was relaxed. "Mmmm . . . nope. I think I'm good, thanks."

"Suit yourself then." And with that, Lucas lunged at her, swinging his sword, but she blocked it with ease and swung around to face him.

"Too slow." She laughed, blocking another jab at her. This time, Lucas put all his strength into the blow, taking Nyla by surprise and knocking the sword out of her hand. She stepped back, surprised, but quickly rolled and grabbed her sword from the ground. Lucas smiled and sped toward her, she blocked the blow and swung her sword at him, but missed as he dodged to the right. She turned, and he crouched, flipping over her and hitting her in the back. The hard blow stung Nyla's back more than she thought it would and she sucked in air through her teeth.

Samuel flinched as the sword hit Nyla's back. He could tell she was in more pain than she should be in. He watched Lucas intently, studying every swift move. He was superbly agile and moved with the quickness and ferocity of a wolf, but Nyla was like a cheetah. She was quick and nimble on her feet, dodging blow after blow. No matter how quick she was, Lucas was one step ahead of her. He seemed to anticipate every move.

Samuel looked over at the others to his right. Julia was biting her nails in anxiety, jumping every time Lucas's sword almost came in contact with Nyla's body, but Felix and Adrian were the opposite. They both studied Nyla intently, grinning maliciously with every move Lucas made against Nyla.

Lucas's sword came in contact with Nyla's leg with a blow that would have broken a normal human's bone. Nyla grunted and fell to her knees, swinging her sword upward. Lucas laughed as he dodged it. He quickly looked over at Felix and Adrian, grinning at their looks of approval. Rage flared up in Samuel's chest. Lucas was egging her on and testing her! Samuel looked at Julia, and she gave him a panicked stare, as if reading his mind. Samuel trained his eyes on Nyla, praying that she could sense his feelings of warning.

Kaden entered the training grounds as he heard swords clashing. He stopped dead in the doorway when he saw Nyla and Lucas dueling. They were amazing, moving like two animals fighting over a piece of meat. Nyla was more beautiful than he had ever seen. She blocked almost every move that Lucas threw against her. He leaned against the wall in awe until he saw Samuel watching her intently. The sight of his "ex-friend" gave him a gut wrenching jealousy and he frowned. Adrian spotted him and waved, a smile on her face. Kaden didn't smile, but waved back in politeness. She started walking over to him.

After the second bone-crushing hit to her leg, Nyla had just about had enough. *I should be stronger than this. I am stronger than this!* She flipped in the air, one hand on her dress, and took a swipe that collided with Lucas's back. He went to one knee and Nyla landed in a crouch on her feet, smiling in triumph. Suddenly Lucas whirled around and his sword smacked Nyla hard on the side. She doubled over, falling to her knees. Kaden clenched his fists, wanting to run over there and choke Lucas out himself. Samuel held his breath, targeting as many calm feelings as he could toward Nyla as she held her side, looking at the ground.

Nyla's blood boiled, and her vision started becoming red. *Breathe . . . breathe.* She thought to herself. She tried to picture Samuel's face in her mind, but all she could hear was the low chuckling sound Lucas made as he touched his sword to the ground. She felt triumph and arrogance wafting off of him and the burning in her stomach started to grow. She focused on his even beating heart. He laughed again and Nyla completely lost it. Her vision turned thermal and her fangs shot out to their full length.

"Dammit!" Samuel cursed under his breath as Nyla raised her head. Her eyes were completely black, and a low, growling hiss came from her throat. Samuel glanced at Felix, but he didn't seem to notice anything. As fast as cheetah, she leapt to her feet. She sped around

Lucas and grabbed his neck, crashing him to the ground. Flipping over him, she sat on his chest, resting her sword against his throat.

"Scary, isn't she?" Adrian whispered in Kaden's ear. She smiled at his troubled expression.

Kaden had noticed that Nyla had shifted into the vampire part of her, and fear crept up on him as he watched her take Lucas down. Images of the vampires attacking his mother flashed through his mind.

"Practically an animal," Adrian continued. "You're better off with someone . . . better." She ran her hand along his chest and smirked at him as his gaze switched to her golden eyes.

Nyla looked down at Lucas's smiling face and all at once her fangs shrank back into her mouth and her vision returned to normal. She quickly got up, putting her sword back on the rack and walked over to Samuel, realizing that she had exposed herself. Samuel met her halfway, looking into her eyes.

"Are you okay?" He gently grabbed her chin, examining her eyes. Satisfied that she was all right, he looked over her shoulder at Lucas, who was still lying on his back in the dirt. He was laughing as Felix ran over to him, helping him up. Lucas smiled when he saw Adrian talking to Kaden and he patted Felix on the shoulder as he helped Lucas up.

"Wow! What a rush!" Lucas smiled at Nyla as she turned around to face him. "Bravo!" He dusted himself off. Nyla nodded and tried to hide her contempt. Julia ran up to Nyla.

"Are you okay?" When Nyla didn't respond, Julia looked to where Nyla was looking. Her gaze fell upon Kaden, standing in the other entrance of the training grounds, talking with Adrian.

"Do I need to make him leave?" Julia asked, looking at Nyla.

"No. I . . . I need to talk to him." She hadn't seen him since he had seen her and Samuel in the woods and then refused to talk to her at the castle and she had told him she could kill him. "What's he doing with her?" Nyla glared at Adrian.

"I don't know." Julia looked at Nyla's glare.

"Well, I'm going to talk to him." Nyla nodded her head in determination. Julia looked at Samuel and he nodded, his hand still on Nyla's shoulder. Nyla tore her eyes away from Kaden and turned to Lucas.

"Well, I think I've met my match." Lucas smiled at her. "That last move was pretty fast. I thought I had you beat."

"I guess you underestimated me." Nyla didn't look him in the eye. *What had he seen? He had to have seen my eyes.* Samuel gently squeezed her shoulder.

"Nyla, I think we need to go look at your injuries. You took a few hard blows."

"Likewise," Lucas said, holding his back. "We'll both rest and meet in the dining hall for lunch?"

"Agreed." Nyla breathed, her ribs aching. She looked at the other doorway again, but Kaden was gone and Adrian was walking back toward them. "We'll see you then." Nyla nodded at him and started walking toward where Kaden had been standing. She ignored Adrian as she passed. Julia and Samuel started after her.

"Nyla, are you sure you're okay? He was hitting you hard!" Julia struggled to keep up.

"I think he knows something. He wanted you to show your vampire side. He was egging you on." Samuel looked at the girls, "We need to figure out what they are really doing here and how much they know, but we have to do it subtly."

"I'm sorry, Samuel." Nyla looked at him. "I really tried to breathe and focus, but he just pushed my buttons. Apparently I'm not doing as well as I thought at getting a handle on this."

"It's okay, Nyla. He was doing it on purpose."

"Should we tell Fulcan and the queen?" Julia asked.

"No." Nyla kept her eyes at the ground. "They would be angry at me for even accepting the duel. No, we need to be sure first, and then we can tell them if we find anything against them." They reached the end of the training grounds and Nyla looked around, spotting Kaden heading toward the castle.

"Kaden!" She strode toward him, ignoring her sore body.

"Nyla, the last time you talked to Kaden, it was a yelling match and you well . . . practically threatened to kill him." Julia stopped

Nyla, grabbing her arm. "Are you sure you want to do this right now?"

"I know . . ." Nyla frowned, remembering the night before. "I didn't threaten to kill him! I just said I could kill him." She ignored Samuel's amused expression. "I'll be fine. I need to talk to him." Julia nodded, looking at Samuel. He looked at Nyla, but kept his face emotionless.

She turned and rushed toward Kaden again. "Stop, Kaden! I need to talk to you!" When he didn't stop she sped up, zooming in front of him. "Stop." She held her side and caught her breath as she looked him in the eyes.

"Are you sure we can be this close? You might kill me remember?" He looked Nyla in the eyes.

"Kaden, stop."

"Nyla." He tried to move around her, but she stepped in his way again.

"Kaden, don't do this again. Don't shut me out. Please, talk to me."

"Okay." Kaden looked at Julia and Samuel. "So let's talk." Nyla turned to Samuel and Julia.

"It will only take a minute. I need to talk to him alone." She looked at Samuel.

"Of course." Samuel nodded, a hard look on his face. He avoided Kaden's eyes. "But please make it short. You're a pure blood, and you shouldn't even have a bruise, but for some reason you need to heal and we need to figure out why."

"Yes, I do need to heal!" Nyla rubbed her sore legs and side.

"We'll be over here." Samuel and Julia headed to the door, waiting by the big stone pillars beside it.

"So," Kaden said as Nyla headed toward him.

"So here's the deal." Nyla sat on the low stone wall that led to the entryway of the garden, taking weight off her hurt leg. "This is how it's going to go. I'm going to talk and you are going to listen." Kaden nodded. "These past few weeks have been hell for me and you couldn't even be there to help me through them. Do you know why?"

Kaden shook his head. "You didn't need me. You needed Samuel." The image of Samuel and Nyla in the lake made Kaden sick. Nyla looked toward Samuel and smiled, but forced it away when she saw Kaden's hurt look.

"Kaden, I couldn't be around you because . . ."

"Yes, I know. Jamin told me everything. You couldn't be around me because I was there when you first lost control of yourself, and you wanted to forget your first kill, and I acted like an idiot and ran away from you and hurt you even more."

"Okay." Nyla processed this. "Kaden, I could feel every feeling of horror coming off of you. You flinched away from my touch and yes, you ran away from me. How could you not believe in me? You doubted me so much that you thought I would actually hurt you . . . how could you think that?"

"Nyla, I'm sorry about that. I really am." Kaden looked her in the eyes. "I don't doubt you, I just . . . I was scared yes, but I was in shock too. I wasn't afraid of you."

"Bull, Kaden!" Nyla called his lie, reading his emotions like a book.

"Okay, Nyla. Yes, I was afraid of you! Is that what you wanted to hear? Vampires killed my mother and brother, and I'm terrified of them! I absolutely hate them!" He sighed as she turned away, obviously hurt. "I'm sorry for that, Nyla. I really, truly am! I know that I can trust you always and I'm so sorry. I'm also sorry for following you yesterday and . . . well, you know. You can sense that I'm sorry, can't you?" Nyla nodded. "Can you forgive me? Please? I can't live with you wanting to rip my head off for the rest of my life."

Nyla looked at him. "Kaden, I would never . . . rip your head off. Don't be stupid."

"I really am sorry, Nyla." He stood up. "But . . . I still can't get you and Samuel out of my head."

"I know, Kaden . . ." Nyla hesitated, trying to find the right words to say. "We were caught up in the moment and . . . the hunt and the blood . . . it's seductive and alluring and . . . I don't know what happened, okay? But I don't want this to come between us.

I know I need to search my heart, but I can't have you angry with me . . . or Samuel." She looked him in the eyes.

"Well, I can't promise anything about Samuel."

"Well, please try. You guys used to be friends, and I hate that I'm coming between you two. It's not right." Her heart throbbed when she thought about hurting either man, but she knew she had to figure things out soon. Her thoughts settled on another subject.

"Hey, what were you doing with Adrian? Was she bothering you, because if she was I'll tell her to back off."

"No." Kaden ran his hands through his hair, thinking about Adrian's warnings about Nyla. "She's not bothering me." He thought about telling her that Lucas and Adrian knew about her, but he decided against it. Something in his mind kept telling him to keep his mouth shut for now.

"Oh . . ." Nyla bit her lip, looking down. She knew she shouldn't be feeling jealous, but she couldn't help it. The fact that now Julia and Kaden were hanging around with Adrian bothered her greatly.

Kaden broke her thoughts, holding out his hand. "So . . . are we okay? Can you touch me now?" She took his hand and he pulled her into a hug. She held her breath, being this close to him still gave her that dangerous, burning feeling in the pit of her stomach, but she knew it would go away with time.

"Ouch!" She jumped out of his grasp and held her ribs, "Apparently I can't touch you." She laughed. Turning, she hobbled over to Samuel and Julia, her hurt leg starting to stiffen on her. Kaden grabbed her arm and helped her over to them.

"How you doing?" Samuel searched her face.

"Better." She smiled at Kaden. "And worse." She grabbed her ribs again as they throbbed.

"We need to get her to Jamin." Kaden moved to pick her up.

"No." Nyla stopped him with her hand. "I don't need Jamin, and I'm not a cripple I can walk." She looked at Samuel.

"She's right, she needs blood." They slowly made their way up to Nyla's room, following a hobbling Nyla, but Samuel finally swooped her up in his arms.

198

"We can't take all day." He teased and carried her the rest of the way up the stairs and down the hall to her room, followed by Julia, and a pouting Kaden. He was more than capable of carrying her.

They reached her room and Samuel set her in a sitting position on the bed, sitting next to her. Julia sat on the chair next to the bed and Kaden stood awkwardly in the corner. Samuel unlaced Nyla's dress from the back and pulled it slightly forward, looking at her ribs. Kaden silently glared at him, surprised that Nyla actually let him look at her like that, then again he had no idea what had gone on during the past few days in the solitude of Nyla's room. They had also been naked together in the lake. The thought made him want to punch something, mainly Samuel.

"I think you have a broken rib." Nyla sucked in a breath through her teeth as Samuel touched the blue and purple flesh. "Sorry," he said, giving her an apologetic look. He lifted the bottom of her dress up to the top of her thigh, examining the purple lines on her leg.

"How am I bruising so fast? I thought vampires could only be killed by getting stabbed in the heart and pure bloods pretty much can't die."

Samuel chuckled. "Well, that's kind of true. Ripping the head off of a normal vampire works too." Nyla touched her throat, sick at the thought. "Also, a werewolf can kill a vampire."

She swallowed. "Oh that's comforting, we aren't fighting werewolves any time soon, or anything."

"Relax," he said with a smile. "They have to literally rip your heart out of your chest or rip the head off for them to kill a vampire." He turned back to her bruises. "Right now, I guess you are bruising fast because you're not to your full strength? Animal blood isn't as good as human blood. Yes, it's a good alternative to live, but you won't be at your full strength. That's the only explanation I can come up with, unless Lucas is a werewolf, but I doubt that. You should be able to tell if he was because vampires can smell animals."

"Here." Julia got out of the chair, grabbing the bottle of animal blood from the cooler.

"No, that won't work for healing this time, it's too weak. Usually the animal blood would work as good as any, but right now, she needs fresh, warm blood. It'll heal her faster."

Kaden jumped at the opportunity. "Here"—he held out his wrist—"take mine." *This will make Nyla trust me again.*

"No!" Nyla shook her head. "Sorry, but I can't handle that with you yet, and I might kill you."

"You can have mine." Samuel rolled up his sleeve. "It'll work the best for you anyway."

"What does that mean? You have super healing blood or something?" Kaden glared at him.

"Something like that." Samuel gave him a condescending smile and Kaden huffed, turning around and stalking back to the corner.

"Okay, will you two stop? I'm hurting here."

"Sorry." Samuel held out his wrist. Nyla's still heart did a flip and she eyed Samuel's wrist wantingly.

"What if I can't stop?" She looked into Samuel's eyes and support warmed her like a blanket.

"You will. I trust you." He smiled at her and her heart did another flip. She stared into his eyes, taking a deep breath. Kaden wanted to pounce on Samuel and slam him in the face, but he kept quiet for Nyla's sake. Nyla looked at Samuel's wrist and it seemed to warm in her hand. Her vision went thermal and she bit her fangs down into the soft flesh of his wrist. Samuel didn't even flinch as she took a gulp, letting the warm blood run down her throat, filling her with a tingly power. Instantly the throbbing in her leg and side subsided and Nyla felt her rib stitch itself back together. Nyla took one more, replenishing drink and let go of his wrist, satisfied. She smiled up at him, her vision returning to normal instantly.

Samuel chuckled. "Better?" he asked, wiping a trickle of blood off her chin. She nodded and adrenaline surged through Samuel when he saw a new hunger in her eyes. She stood up, going over to her oversized bathroom.

"I need to make sure everything is healed right." She stopped in the doorway. "Samuel, will you help me a minute?" The look she shot into his eyes made his body tingle with a new excitement.

"Yes." He stood up abruptly and passed Nyla, going through the door.

"One second." She smiled at Julia, who looked confused, and shut the door. She spun around and pushed Samuel up against the wall, holding her face close to his, her fangs protruding through her slightly open lips. He grabbed her by the waist and moved her so that she was pressed up against the wall. Nyla longed for him to kiss her and her pulse pounded out of her chest.

"Nyla." Samuel shut his eyes. "We have to stop. This isn't right." He took in a deep breath and opened his eyes, looking at her disappointed face. Nyla remembered Julia and Kaden sitting just outside the door and was suddenly embarrassed about her behavior.

"I'm sorry." She rubbed her palms on the front of her dress nervously. "Drinking your blood just gave me a huge rush. Is it always going to be like that?"

"Yes, I think it will be." He hesitated. "Not all the time, but with . . . human blood, yes." He stepped back, rubbing his hands over his face.

"I'm not going to ask you how you know that." She gave a small laugh, still self-conscious and regretting what she had just tried to do. That wasn't fair to Samuel, but at least he had stopped it. She looked at herself in the mirror. Her cheeks were flushed and her hair was a mess from fighting with Lucas. She grabbed a brush, smoothing down her hair and Samuel laced up the back of her dress.

Kaden glared at the bathroom door, jealousy flooding his chest. Lucas and Adrian's warning words replayed over in his mind. *She isn't meant for you . . . she is meant to be with him. She can't love you . . . your love would be doomed . . .* He ran his hands over his face, silently hating Samuel. *No!* He refused to believe them, but the sickening feeling still coursed through him and he longed to know what was going on behind the door.

Don't be silly, he thought to himself. *Samuel is just checking to make sure she is all right.* He ran his hands through his hair. *Ya, just like he was "just hunting" when he found them in lake together.* A voice from the back of his mind said. He shook his head, sighing heavily.

Julia looked at Kaden's grim face and looked back at the closed door. She felt sorry for Kaden. What Nyla was doing to him was cruel. It seemed like she was going back and forth between the two men. It was as if she was playing with their feelings and Nyla needed to know what she was doing. Nyla opened the door and smiled at Julia. Samuel stood beside her.

"All's well. She's fully healed." He glanced at Kaden, who didn't look convinced.

"Let's go, shall we?" Nyla said, heading toward the door. "We said we would meet Lucas and the others in the dining hall."

Julia rubbed her stomach. "Yes, I'm hungry. Let's grab something to eat."

Nyla gestured toward the door. "Well, technically I got to eat, but yes, you guys need to." She glanced at Samuel and headed out the door. Julia rushed in front of the men, stepping in place beside Nyla.

"What just happened?" Julia asked her with raised eyebrows.

"I'll tell you about it later." Nyla gave Julia a smile.

"No, Nyla." She pulled her aside, waving the men ahead. She gave Kaden and Samuel a reassuring smile. "I just need to talk to Nyla for a moment." She turned back to Nyla as the men passed.

"What are you doing?" She looked Nyla in the eyes.

"What do you mean?" Nyla gave Julia a frown, removing Julia's hand from her arm.

"You know what I mean. Nyla, you told me you were into Kaden and now all the sudden you're acting like Samuel is the sun. And what were you doing naked in a lake with him?! You know you're hurting Kaden, don't you?"

Nyla sighed. "Julia, I didn't know he was spying on us." She sighed at Julia's angry expression. "It's hard to explain. I didn't think I felt anything like that for Samuel, but, in the lake . . . I don't know. It was the heat of the moment and I didn't know what I was doing. It was a moment of weakness. I don't know anymore . . . things have changed and it's complicated."

"Well, you need to try to explain, because lately you've not been acting like yourself. I didn't say anything last night because you were upset, but you need to know. You've been putting me on the backburner and you've been treating Kaden like he's not even meant anything to you."

"I have not!" Nyla was appalled that Julia would accuse her of treating her friends like dirt. "You're the one who's been ditching me for Adrian! Kaden is even talking to her on a regular basis now."

"That's because she's actually been there for me. I can talk to her and she will actually listen to what I have to say, and you know what, Nyla? If you're not going to take Kaden seriously, then he might as well find somebody else, and maybe Adrian is the best thing for him right now!"

"Well, fine!" Nyla stepped back. "If she's such a good friend to you then go be her best friend. You are dismissed and I'll fetch you when I need your services, Lady Julia." Julia gave her a hurt look and Nyla instantly regretted her harsh words. She had never treated Julia like her lady in waiting and Julia had always done everything Nyla asked without a word. She had always been more than just a lady in waiting to Nyla and now Nyla was treating her like dirt.

"Julia, I'm sorry."

"No, Princess Nylina." Julia gave her an exaggerated bow. "I'm forever in your services." She turned and followed the men down the hall.

"Julia, wait!" Nyla ran to her and matched her pace, walking beside her. "Julia, I'm sorry. I shouldn't have treated you like that and . . ."

"Nyla." Julia stopped, turning toward her. "I will always be your friend, but right now you have some things that you need to sort out for yourself. You need to be honest with Samuel and Kaden both and you need to figure out what you want."

"I wish it were that easy." Nyla gave a sigh, but deep down, she knew the decision in her heart might be easier than she was making it.

"Well," Julia looked her in the eye. "Obviously, I don't know everything that's going on with you. You can tell me when you're ready, but I won't stand by and watch you continue to pretend like the world will stop and wait for you to decide who you are and what you want. Whatever you decide, I will be here for you, but until then you need to decide things for yourself." She turned, continuing toward the dining hall.

Kaden and Samuel walked side by side, but kept a few feet between them. Samuel could feel Kaden's glare on him from time to time, but he kept his eyes down. He felt guilty; this wasn't fair to Kaden and Samuel knew that. He just couldn't help what he felt for Nyla.

"Okay, listen up." Kaden stopped Samuel in the hall, keeping his voice down. "I love Nyla and I'm not about to give her up to you. Now that I can be close to her again I will fight for her and I want you to know that." Although Kaden tried to forget it, what Lucas and Adrian had told him earlier about Samuel and Nyla still disturbed his thoughts.

"I know." Samuel looked down at him, glad that he was a few inches taller. Samuel shook his head and sighed. "Kaden, I didn't plan for this. I didn't want this to happen and it's not like I meant to feel this way. But it's too late for me to turn back now. I'm going to fight for her too. However, I won't let this feud between us affect, or hurt Nyla in any way. Her needs are above my own, and I would do anything for her. Whoever she chooses, that will be the end of it. If she chooses you I will back off."

"Good." Kaden nodded his head and turned, following the girls toward the smaller dining room beside the great hall. What Lucas said couldn't be true. He was the one meant for Nyla and he would fight for her. They entered and headed straight for the table in the middle of the room. It was always stocked with fresh food through-out the day, which was very helpful for everyone's busy schedules. Julia and Kaden went to work, grabbing rolls, cheese, and veggies off the table.

"You're not hungry?" Nyla gently nudged Samuel with her elbow.

"No." He smiled at her. "I'm used to eating later in the day with the other guards, so I'll eat later."

"Okay." Nyla shrugged her shoulders. "Um, Samuel, I need to talk to you about something. About what's been happening between us."

"Okay." Samuel looked at her and she gave him a small smile. She looked around the room.

"Later?" She smiled as he nodded.

Lucas, Felix, and Adrian walked through the doors and grabbed food as well, joining them at the table. Anger rushed over Nyla as she saw Adrian sit beside Kaden, but she let it go. Julia's words rushed inter her mind. *Maybe she is good for him right now.*

"I think I'm done dueling for the day." Lucas rubbed his back. "You're a mighty fine opponent."

"So are you." Nyla smiled at him, all feelings of suspicion and distrust gone for the moment. They ate their meals in silence and Nyla eventually got up to grab a piece of ham to ward off anyone's suspicion to why she wasn't eating with everyone else. After they were done, Dominic showed up, pulling Samuel aside and the others parted ways. Lucas explained that he needed some more rest and he and Felix started in the direction of the doors. Nyla didn't protest and she wanted to talk to Kaden more.

"Adrian and I are going to go back to the training grounds," Julia told Nyla as they were exiting the dining hall. "She's going to show me some moves so that I can defend myself when the time comes."

"Well, I can do that." Nyla looked at Adrian, waiting by a column in front of them. She wanted to make things up to Julia.

"Well, she just knows more about the werewolves, so . . . You can come with us if you want."

Nyla hid her disappointment. "No, it's fine. I'm going to talk to Kaden." Remembering their conversation from before, Julia nodded, giving her a small smile.

"Good luck." She nodded and went to join Adrian. Nyla watched them for a moment, trying not to glare, and went over to Kaden.

"Hey. Do you want to take a walk? We should talk about things a little more." She gave Kaden a smile.

"Ya, sure." Kaden's eyes met Lucas's where he had stopped in the doorway, clearly listening to everyone's conversations, and Lucas gave him a nod, giving what Kaden thought to be a mischievous smile.

Kaden looked away, wanting to push what Lucas had said out of his mind, and glanced over to where Samuel stood, talking to Dominic. Samuel walked over to them.

"Dominic and Kristi need me to oversee training some of the new recruits." He looked at Nyla apologetically. "You'll be okay for a while?"

"Yes." She smiled at him. "Kaden and I are going for a walk. I'll be fine."

"Okay." Samuel looked between the two and nodded, joining Dominic. He looked back, regretting having to leave her alone with Kaden.

"Later?" Nyla mouthed to him and he nodded, returning Nyla's reassuring smile.

"Well, shall we?" Nyla started walking. "Where should we go?"

"Um . . . I know a place." Kaden grinned at her and Nyla smiled, glad that the tension between them was lightening.

When Nyla and Kaden made it to Nyla's hideout it had begun to lightly snow.

"It's starting to get colder every day." Kaden pulled his jacket tighter around him. "Ya, it is." Nyla didn't really feel cold as much anymore and was secretly excited to be out doing activities in the beautiful snow without freezing her butt off.

"So . . ." Nyla sat across from Kaden in the cave that was now made up of cold, hibernating shrubs. She looked into his sparkling green eyes and smiled. Suddenly, Kaden grabbed her arms.

"I've missed you so much." Nyla stayed silent with surprise as he smiled into her eyes.

"I . . . missed you too." Nyla searched for the right words. "Kaden, so much has happened since my change and I don't even know where to start."

"I don't care about any of it, it's all in the past. I just care about being with you right now." Suddenly he moved in and kissed her, his lips pressing firmly into her own. Nyla stilled in surprise then loosened her mouth a bit, letting him kiss her. She waited for the giddy emotions to hit her like they had with Samuel's kiss. Nyla opened her eyes and pulled back. She couldn't get Samuel out of her mind and guilt flooded her chest.

"Kaden, wait." Kaden sighed and looked at Nyla, dreading what he was about to hear. He shook Lucas and Adrian's words out of his mind.

"What is it?" His heart pounded and jealousy flooded his chest.

Nyla searched for the right words. She had hoped that her first kiss with Kaden would be everything she had hoped, but her heart squeezed painfully as the truth sank in.

"It's Samuel, isn't it?" Kaden frowned at Nyla's silence.

"I . . . what Samuel and I have is complicated, I can't explain it to you and I just feel that you should know . . . that I do have feelings for him." Although Kaden knew something was obviously up between them, and after what Lucas had said, hearing it from Nyla stung Kaden more than he thought it would.

"Nyla, I know you have feelings for him, but it doesn't matter to me. I want you, and whatever you and Samuel have is nothing compared to what you and I had before you turned. I know that. It's just a crush from him being able to help you when I couldn't. It's not a big deal." He moved in to kiss Nyla again, but she looked down. "There's something more, isn't there?"

Nyla nodded. "I have more than just . . . simple feelings for him."

"What, you're telling me you love him?" Kaden rolled his eyes, but his face fell when Nyla didn't answer.

Kaden stared at her, open mouthed, unable to comprehend what she had said. "So the other day when you said you didn't love him and that you didn't want anything to come between us . . . that was all a big lie?!"

"No! I don't know if I love him . . ." Nyla thought back to that conversation she had with Kaden. She was so caught up with her old life and trying to make things work with Kaden that she had silenced her heart when she had kissed Samuel in the lake. As soon as their lips had met, she knew the burning in her heart was more than just a simple crush or fling.

"Why wouldn't anyone tell me this?!" Kaden was enraged. "Here I am making myself look like an idiot trying to love you and you have been falling in love with my friend all this time!" Kaden's heart constricted. He couldn't believe that what Lucas and Adrian said was true.

"Kaden, I didn't lie to you when I told you I didn't want things to come between us. I didn't, but I can't ignore what I feel! I . . . I don't know. I guess I just wanted to see how things went between me and you, but I couldn't change what I felt for Samuel. But that kiss we just had, it wasn't . . . And I . . . I had to tell you." She backed up as Kaden stood, his head brushing against the plants overhead, and he let out an angry growl, leaving the shrub cave.

"Wait!" Nyla ran out after him and grabbed his arm. "Kaden, wait! I . . . I still care about you. I don't want things to end this way!" Kaden spun around. He wasn't going to give up.

"Nyla, we can still make this work! I . . . I love you, Nyla and I know you would be happy with me. I know you love me too!"

"Kaden, I can't and won't lie to you. I care about you so much. You are one of my best friends, but . . . I don't think I love you . . . like that."

"Nyla . . ." He grabbed her by the shoulders and pushed her up against the wall-like bush. He kissed her passionately, his hands traveling down to her waste. She put her arms to his chest, wanting to push back and trying ignoring the burning in the pit of her stomach. She could hear and feel Kaden's heartbeat through his chest and she could feel the blood pumping through his lips. Still, something felt off. Like the one before, the kiss wasn't right and as much as she wanted to feel the love for Kaden that he felt for her, she knew she couldn't. She tried to push away, but he held on tighter and the burning hunger from his scent and passion was too much. She moved her head to the side and Kaden's lips moved to her neck. Nyla opened her eyes and the world was bright with thermal colors. The world and that moment was gone. She pulled back Kaden's head and he looked into her black eyes, fear creeping into his chest.

"Nyla . . ." But it was too late; Nyla sank her fangs into his neck, feeling the warm blood run down her chin. Suddenly, she realized

208

what she was doing and pulled back, her vision returning normal, and she pushed Kaden away from her.

"Oh my gosh! Kaden, I . . ." She looked into his terrified green eyes as he held his neck with his hand.

"Nyla, you . . . you bit me!" Kaden backed up, disbelief overtaking his face.

"Kaden." She took a step forward, but Kaden backed away from her. Dread filled him. Lucas was right.

"They were right. You are a monster . . ." Kaden hissed through clenched teeth. "I tried to accept what you were and love you even though I was afraid of you. I tried to love you and be with you, but you are meant to be with another man and I knew it, but I wouldn't accept it. My judgment was clouded with what I thought was love and now I realize that I was wrong all along. I can't be with you, it's hopeless."

"Kaden, don't!" Tears ran down Nyla's face. "I . . . I do love you, it's just . . ." *Just not in the way you want me to.* But she couldn't say the words.

"No, you don't, Nyla. You love him, and whatever you think you feel for me is you confusing love with hunger and lust. Vampires can't love like that and sooner, or later Samuel is going to figure that out too."

"Kaden!"

"Stay away from me, Nyla!" Kaden turned and started running toward the castle, leaving Nyla crying behind him. She couldn't believe what had just happened. She had let the hunger overtake her and she hurt her best friend, the man she cared for with all her heart. She refused to accept what Kaden said about her being a monster and that vampires couldn't love. Every time she was around him, she could feel the fear, but she had just pushed it aside and ignored it. She had been willing to try to work things out with Kaden, even though she knew in her heart it could never be and she had feelings for someone else. Look what had happened. It had cost her a friend.

No, no, no! She couldn't afford to think like that. He would see, he would come back to her. He would accept her for who she was, he had to if he was truly her best friend and if he "loved her." She got up, wiped her tears away, and walked numbly in the direction of the training grounds, needing to talk to Julia. Wiping blood from her chin, she searched for her friend and her heart sank when she saw her laughing with Adrian. Nyla turned around and walked in the direction of the fountain. Sitting down at the stone fountain she washed her face with the cold water. She looked up at the stone face of the angel, surrounded by the falling snow, and sighed. She looked down, closing her eyes and stretching out her hands, feeling the flakes drop onto them. She felt a presence and looked up, jumping as she saw Lamar sitting next to her.

"Isn't it nice to just enjoy the snow? I love this time of year." He smiled at her.

"Yes, it is." She shifted uncomfortably beside him.

"What's the matter, child? You look distraught." Lamar looked at her with concern. Nyla looked at him, searching for any reason not to trust him. She looked at her hands.

"I made a mistake. I hurt someone I cared about. I feel like my best friend is pulling away from me and I just don't know what's right and wrong anymore. I feel so alone."

"We are never alone, no matter what we do. You have friends and family that care for you and you of all people shouldn't feel alone."

"I know, but I just do." Nyla sighed. "It's like I don't know who I am anymore."

"Princess Nylina, no matter what you are, or what you do, you will always be you. Believe me, I know. I've had to deal with losing and finding myself. I . . . I lost my family because I couldn't see things clearly and now all that I had is gone, but I made it through. I have to stay strong for them. Sometimes I still don't know if I've truly found myself, or not. You just have to remember who you are and have confidence in your heart. That's the best advice I can give you. Follow your heart." There was a pause and Nyla thought about his words.

"I didn't know you had a family. How do you know so much about losing and finding yourself?" Nyla looked up, but Lamar was gone. She stood, peering around the statue and watched him as he walked toward the castle doors. She sat down again, staring in the direction he had gone.

"Hmmm . . . follow my heart," Nyla said to herself. She leaned over, resting her chin on her hands. Nyla didn't know how long she had sat there, immersed in her own thoughts. She had always thought she knew who she was. She was strong and confident. She would do anything for her friends and she knew they would do the same. First, she needed to apologize to Julia. She realized she really had been putting her on the backburner. After that she would somehow work things through with Kaden. She would apologize and somehow, it would be okay and they could be friends. *It has to be okay.* She stood, turning toward the training grounds.

"Princess Nylina." A young maid walked up to her, looking distressed. "The queen requests your presence in the council room immediately."

CHAPTER 19

CHAPTER 19

"Mother, what is it?" Nyla rushed into the council room, followed closely by Julia, Adrian, and Kaden. The queen was talking intently with Fulcan, Samuel, Jamin, and Lamar, her face very serious. Behind them were Lucas and Felix. Jordee, the royal scout, was also talking in a group with Dominic, Kristi, and a couple of other guards. Nyla caught Kristi's eye, but she looked away from Nyla's gaze abruptly. Nyla hadn't seen Kristi since she had attacked her, and apparently Kristi wasn't going to forgive and forget easily, if she even ever did.

"Nyla." The queen waved her over. "There's been an attack on our closest neighboring town, Libia. It was Rothgar and Gafna testing out their new army. So far none have been found alive. Our scouts on the west end say that there is no advance on Galatia yet, but it could be just days away."

"What?!" Nyla couldn't believe her ears. She was nowhere near ready for a battle in only the span of a couple days.

The queen continued, "Everyone who is able, is to train intensively for the next few days. That includes all of you. We need to be ready for anything."

"My queen," Lamar spoke up, "Ridia's army, combined with Rothgar's, is at least twice the size of this army. Even with Libia's help, like we planned, we still wouldn't have had enough to stand up against their werewolves." The queen thought for a moment, completely frustrated.

"We'll have to draft." Fulcan looked at the queen. "It's our only hope. With the help of our able subjects, above the age of fifteen, we should stand a good chance. Galatia is a big kingdom, Your Majesty. We could do it." Julia sat down in the nearest chair. She had never actually trained for battle a day in her life. She was just a simple lady in waiting. She couldn't hurt a fly.

"Mother, we can't draft everyone able in the castle and in the kingdom! It would be impossible to train everyone in time!" She looked at Julia, who was close to hyperventilating.

"Nyla, Fulcan is right! We have to start . . . immediately." The queen noticed Julia's white face.

"Are you sure, Your Majesty?" Jamin looked her in the eyes.

"I'm sure. All able men will be drafted. The women will be volunteer." Julia looked at her, somewhat relieved. Nyla nodded, shocked at how much had just happened in so little time. Her brain could barely keep up as the queen went right into action.

"Fulcan, you and Lamar will go into town, posting draft notices. Gather all the able men and bring them to the castle while there is still daylight. I'll get the maids and extra guards setting up camps within the castle walls." She looked at Kaden, "Kaden, will you help oversee this project?"

"Yes, Your Majesty." He stood up a little taller, taking on the responsibility she had bestowed on him.

"Samuel, as head of the guard, there is another task I ask of you." He became attentive as she addressed him.

"Anything, Your Majesty." He bowed his head.

"There have been many sightings of large wolves over the last few hours along the west side of the castle. We suspect that they are part of the scouting groups that Lucas and Lamar had talked about. I need you to lead a group of soldiers to that area and eliminate all that you see. Try to keep at least one alive for interrogation if you can. You are to leave immediately, as soon as you are ready."

"Yes, Your Majesty." Nyla admired the sincerity and respect with which he addressed her on the issue. As for Nyla, she couldn't believe her ears. Everything was happening so fast.

"Dominic, Kristi, I'll take you two, along with a couple others, if you are willing." Samuel looked at the two of them. Dominic looked at Kristi.

"We would be honored." He nodded at Samuel.

"Felix and Adrian are to go with you as well. They know how to face these wolves and they will be much help." The queen looked at Lamar expectantly. He looked, at Lucas, who nodded and then looked at Felix and Adrian. They looked at each other and nodded in agreement.

"I'm going with you too." Nyla put her hand on Samuel's arm.

"No!" Kaden looked at the queen. Nyla wanted to turn around and smack Kaden's face right off. *Why does he even care anyway? He thinks I'm a monster.* She balled her fists and refrained from hitting him.

"No, Nyla." The queen looked her daughter in the eyes. "We can't risk that. You, Julia, and Lucas are joining Jamin on the training grounds. You're going to become familiar with all weapons and battle strategies, and Lucas is going to show you everything you need to know about facing these creatures." Nyla looked at her mother, astonished. Her mother either didn't trust her, or she didn't have enough confidence in her to send her to hunt down a couple wolves. Seeing Nyla's expression, Samuel turned to her.

"Nyla." He bent his head down, speaking in an attractive, low tone that Nyla couldn't ignore even if she wanted to. "It will be all right. You need to go with Jamin. You'll be able to help train recruits if you know all about what we will be facing. You are next in line for the throne. You'll be able to stand as a leader." She nodded, still half unconvinced, but she would obey.

"Does everyone know exactly what is expected of them today?" The queen looked around and everyone nodded. "Then, let's get to work." Samuel opened the door, going out first and Nyla followed him.

"Wait, Samuel!" She rushed after him and pulled him behind a marble pillar, cloaking them in shadow. "I . . . I don't want you to go." She shook her head.

"Nyla, I have to go. This is my duty as head of the guard, to your mother, and to the kingdom." He smiled at her. "I'll be fine. Trust me, I'm stronger than I look." He winked at her and she punched him in the arm.

"Samuel, I need to tell you something. What I wanted to talk to you about earlier. . . . I'm not sorry." She smiled at his confused expression. "I mean, I'm sorry for how I've been dealing with things between me, and you, and Kaden, but . . . I'm not sorry for kissing you at the lake. I'm not sorry for kissing you, because I like you. I didn't realize it, but spending so much time with you, I've gotten to know you and my feelings have grown for you."

She shook her head. "I've been acting so selfish, and I shouldn't have led both of you on like that. But after that kiss, I realized that I feel so much more for you than I thought and I can't ignore that anymore. I just didn't want to lose Kaden, but I almost lost you both. What I said at the lake was a lie. Kissing you wasn't a mistake. I do have strong feelings for you, and I need you to know now. I just hope I'm not too late."

"Nyla." Samuel took her face in his hands, staring into her crystal eyes. "I was being selfish too. I knew that there was something going on before. I was just only thinking of myself and my feelings for you. After we kissed, it's all I've been able to think about." Nyla smiled at the fact that Samuel had been thinking about their kiss at the lake. He laughed, "Whatever your decision was going to be, I would never have left you no matter what. I can't."

Nyla beamed up at him. "Samuel, please be careful! I don't know what I would do without you. I'd literally go insane so you better come back." She couldn't lose him, not now. If she did, she might give into her vampiric side and never find herself again.

"I will, Nyla. I promise and I wouldn't promise if I didn't completely believe what I was saying. I'll be fine." He bent down, lightly brushing his lips against hers. He let her go, giving her a smile and turned, leaving her in the hallway. Nyla took a deep breath, still mesmerized by Samuel's soft kiss. She turned around the pillar and came face-to-face with Kaden.

"Kaden." She looked down, away from his hurt face.

"So obviously I was right. You want him and you always will. Nice to finally know." He pushed past her, stalking down the hallway.

"Wait! Kaden!" She ran her hands over her face, unsure of what to think. She opened her eyes, stressful tears threatening to run down her cheeks, and stared up at the ceiling. Looking down, she saw Julia standing in the hallway, looking lost. No matter how weak Nyla felt, she needed to be strong for her friend. She took a deep breath, mustering up strength.

"Julia!" Nyla ran up and hugged her.

"Nyla." Julia looked up at her, her eyes watery. "I . . . I've never fought a day in my life, Nyla. I thought that I would be prepared after learning from Adrian, but I won't know what to do." Nyla took hold of her shoulders.

"Julia, you don't have to fight. You can stay and take care of things here. It's okay."

"Is it?" She looked up at her friend. "I feel like everyone will be doing their part except me."

"I'll tell you what. Adrian already showed you some moves and I'll show you a few more. You'll stay and help with things here, and that way you'll know how to protect yourself and the people around you if you need to, okay? But right now we need to go with Jamin and Lucas."

∽o∾

A couple hours in, Nyla tried to concentrate on Lucas as he told them strategies and showed them moves that the army and wolves would be using, but her mind kept straying to Samuel and Kaden and what Lamar had said. *Follow your heart . . .* Her heart felt ripped into two pieces. She now knew whom she really wanted to be with, but Kaden was her best friend, and she was losing him.

"Nyla . . . Nyla, are you even listening?" Lucas looked her in the eyes. "This is important! Wolves rarely feel comfortable out of their packs, so they are always in groups. If you aren't careful, they will surround you and overtake you. Your best weapon against them is a sword, but not a huge sword because the wolves are fast and a big sword would take longer to swing. A bow is good at long distance, but you only have one shot. If you miss a vital spot, they will be on you before you can grab another arrow. So don't get caught with just a bow. It will also be better for us all to stay in groups. Alone we are helpless against a pack, but together we are just as strong." He proceeded to give them valuable information and Nyla pretended to be interested in what he was saying. She nodded when it was appropriate and rarely took her eyes off of him. They started dueling and Nyla was still having a hard time concentrating.

"Nyla!" Lucas exclaimed as he put her on the ground for the fifth time.

"What?" Nyla pushed herself to stand.

"You're not focusing. You can't let your thoughts, or emotions get in the way, or it's going to get you killed," he scolded her. "We're done for now. We aren't going to get anywhere with you like this. Let's review." Lucas looked at her as she moved to stand by Julia, "What are the main kill points on a werewolf's body?"

"Oh." Nyla cleared her throat, searching for the moment in her brain where she might remember hearing that information. "Obviously its heart and . . . head."

"Nyla." Lucas stood right in front of her. "You need to know this stuff, okay? The only kill spots on a werewolf, if you don't have a silver blade, are to cut off its head, stab it in the eye, or stab it's heart. If you have a silver blade, then any normal kill shot on a regular person, or animal will work." He sighed. "Well, for now that's all the information that I can give you until we start training the recruits tomorrow. We're done here."

"Nyla." Jamin stood up. "Would it help if I went to see if we got word from Samuel yet?" Just then Kaden came up to them.

"Jamin, we have just about gotten the first and second infantry camps set up on the South side near the training grounds. Will you check our progress before we continue?"

"Yes." He looked at Nyla. "I'm sure he's fine Nyla, but if you want I will have a guard check in with you every so often."

"Thank you, Jamin." She looked at Kaden and gave him a small smile, but he just looked at her, nodded, and followed Jamin out of the training grounds.

"Kaden!" She followed him. "Can we talk?"

"It can wait." He kept walking.

"No!" She zoomed in front of him and he almost walked right into her. She put a hand on his chest, pushing him back. Kaden looked at Jamin, waving him to keep going. "Kaden, we need to talk. You need to hear me out." She looked at the small bandage on his neck and swallowed, regret and guilt filling her.

"I get it." He tried to go around her, but her hand kept him in place. "You want him and not me. I was right, I don't know how your heart could change so quickly, but I guess everything we've been through didn't matter to you." He looked her right in the eyes, ignoring their intense, blue stare.

"That's not fair. I do care for you . . . but my feelings are different. I'm a different person now. Things have changed. You said I wasn't the same, and you know what? You were right. I'm not who I was, and I'll never be that same person again. Samuel keeps me on the ground. He knows who I am now and . . . you just don't understand. You can't accept me for who I am."

Nyla's words stung Kaden and Lucas's words fueled his anger. "Nyla, I'm sorry, but I don't know if I will ever be able to accept you for who you are. I try to see you, but I can't. All I can see is the thing you are. I know that makes me a jerk and a complete idiot, but I don't know what to tell you. You need to let me move on Nyla, and I can't do that if I'm around you. So just stay away from me." Kaden knew he didn't mean the words as they spewed from his mouth, but he didn't care as long as they stung.

She looked up at him, frowning. "Kaden, you gave up on me before I could even give you a chance to think otherwise. When Samuel found me, he didn't hesitate and he wasn't afraid. He comforted me and didn't flinch away from my touch, or run away from me. I felt no fear off of him whatsoever. Even now, I feel hints of fear coming from you."

"Nyla! I can't change what I feel! I try, but I just can't. All I see is a . . ."

"A monster?" She grew her fangs from her gums and Kaden turned into a heated form of colors. She looked him in the eyes, not moving a muscle. She didn't blink or breathe, making her look more like a beautiful, dangerous creature. Kaden held his breath as he stared into her pitch black eyes, drawing him in. His heart pounded painfully and he had to look away. Nyla sighed, turning to normal.

"You still can't even look at me. Kaden if you ever loved me at all, even as a friend, you wouldn't be afraid. I am your best friend. I'm not a monster. This is who I am and who I will always be. I will always be the same Nyla you knew, just with little changes. You just refuse to see it."

"I know, Nyla, I just . . ." He didn't know what to say, his stubborn defenses shattered. She was the most beautiful creature he had ever seen, but when she turned into that beast, he couldn't get a hold of himself. All he could see was Jimmy's bloody body and his mother's lifeless, bloodless body in the forest.

"Kaden, you're one of my best friends, and you always will be. You know I love you, but you pretend that this part of me doesn't exist, and you can't stand to see me for who I really am."

"Nyla, I can try. I really can. I just . . ." He ran his hands through his hair.

"You can never accept all of me. It's okay, Kaden. I know who I am now and . . . I will always be your friend, no matter what." She stepped aside, her eyes on the ground. He looked at her in pain, her words of rejection sinking in this time. He took a last look at her then turned around and left. Nyla wiped a tear off her cheek and smiled as Julia came up to her.

"You okay?" She put a hand on her shoulder.

"Ya. How much of that did you hear?" Nyla sniffed.

"All of it. Nyla, I'm so sorry! He's an idiot! You are not a monster and I will always be here for you . . . so will Samuel." She put her hand on Nyla's shoulder. "Nyla, I'm sorry I've been so distant lately. I was jealous of you for being with Samuel so much, and that he had feelings for you, and I felt betrayed and scared and I should have been there. Adrian is cool, but she isn't you."

"It's me who should be sorry. I put you in the background. I was so caught up with everything that was happening that I didn't even realize what I was doing." They hugged each other and Nyla wiped away another tear.

Julia gave her a small smile. "Let's go to the council room. You need to see if there's been any word from Samuel." She turned and almost bumped into Lucas. *How had he gotten behind us?*

"Sorry," he said as he backed up. "What was that all about?"

"None of your business." Nyla pushed past him. Lucas had, had enough of her stubborn disrespectfulness.

"Princess"—he came up behind her, following her closely—"you really should pay more attention to what I'm teaching you. It would benefit you greatly. I know what you are and I can say, I think it would benefit the people greatly to know what their future queen will be. They will probably appreciate the knowledge that their future queen is a bloodthirsty monster." Nyla swung around, grabbing Lucas by the throat, and slammed him against the ground.

"Don't you dare!" She glared at him with black eyes and bared fangs.

"Nyla." Julia came up beside her. "Don't, he's just egging you on like a jerk."

"Why is that, Lucas? Huh?" She tightened her grip and Lucas laughed. A low hiss came from deep in her throat and she squeezed harder.

"Okay, okay!" He choked out. She released him and he gulped at the air, clutching his throat. He coughed, "Okay, yes. I've known you're a vampire for a while, but in my defense it was only because I could sense you."

"What?" Nyla's face became normal. "What do you mean you could sense me?"

"Because . . . I'm a werewolf." Julia's eyes widened and she stepped back. Nyla transitioned again and went for his throat, but he grabbed her hand. "Wait, wait! I'm a werewolf, yes, but I was turned before I could leave Gafna's army. I was turned against my will and the first chance I had, I got out of there." Nyla stared hard at him, listening to his even heartbeat. After a few seconds she backed off, returning to normal.

"Are the others werewolves too?"

"Yes." Lucas admitted, getting to his feet. "But we all left for the same reason. We wanted to be free. Gafna pretty much cages the wolves. They aren't allowed to do anything and Gafna and Rothgar force them to do their bidding day and night. It's disgusting. All we want is to free them." Nyla thought for a moment. It sounded like a believable cause.

"Okay." Nyla squinted at him. "I'm giving you a chance, but you're not out from under my radar. If you make one move against anyone I care about, I will kill you, no matter where you go. Got it?"

Lucas nodded. "Loud and clear."

"Good." Nyla turned and started walking toward the castle, Julia quick on her heels.

"Do you really think that's a good idea?" Julia looked back at Lucas, who was rubbing his throat and watching them as they left.

"I don't know what to think anymore, but I did mean what I said and I think he knows that. He's seen me in action, and he knows what I'm capable of."

"Let's hope that he sticks to his word."

"We'll see. I'm going to be keeping an eye on him though." Nyla shook her head. "We need to tell my mother and the others."

When they reached the council room, Nyla's stomach was twisted with anxiety. Regular wolves were dangerous enough to hunt, but werewolves were a whole different level of dangerous. With their human intelligence and wolf instincts, they were one of the greatest predators next to the vampire. At least Adrian and Felix had gone with the group, but then again Nyla wasn't so sure that was a good idea. Although Nyla believed that Lucas truly did want to free the werewolves from Gafna and Rothgar's clutches, they still couldn't be trusted.

"Mother, is there any word from Samuel yet?" She went over to where Lydia was talking with Fulcan and Lamar.

"Not yet, but we have a lookout stationed on our highest tower, so we'll know as soon as they are seen." Lydia looked at Nyla. "Don't be too worried honey. Samuel can more than take care of himself and the others, plus Felix and Adrian know the tactics and strategies of the wolves."

Nyla eyed Lamar. "Felix and Adrian don't need protecting. They are werewolves too." The queen's eyes flew to Nyla's serious face and

Fulcan moved into action. He pulled his sword, putting it to Lamar's throat.

"So I guess you found out." Lamar looked at Nyla calmly.

"You mongrel! How could you betray us like this?!" Fulcan growled.

"We didn't betray you." Lamar looked at Fulcan without moving his head.

"He's right, Mother." Nyla moved in Lamar's defense. "All they have done is help us. I trust Lamar." Nyla remembered their conversation at the fountain. The queen looked at her daughter, studying her face.

"Fulcan, lower your sword. He's no threat to us right now, but make him sit in the corner and have guards watch him until Samuel and the others return." Lamar sat in a chair in the corner and two guards stood on either side of him. She turned to another guard standing to her left.

"Go and find Lucas and bring him here."

"Yes, Your Majesty." The guard left hastily. Nyla looked at the map the queen was studying intently.

"So this is the plan so far." The queen pointed to a spot in the woods on the west of the castle. This area is where Samuel and the others are, but this." She pointed to another spot south of that, in between Libia. "This is where we will station ourselves. We don't want them making it to the castle, so our plan is to meet them halfway, but to take them by surprise, we will stay just inside the forest beyond Libia and they will hopefully not even know what's coming. They won't expect us to come for them. They will think that we will want to fight from inside Galatia's impenetrable walls, so we will have the element of surprise. A small army will stay here, just in case some get around us, but we are hoping to take them off guard and overtake them."

Nyla took all of the information in. "Okay, so who's staying behind? I'm going with you." She looked into her mother's eyes.

"Very well. We will need your speed and strength." The queen pushed her hair back. "We need Fulcan and Samuel with us. Kaden will probably volunteer either way, so he'll be with us too, and Kristi will stay behind to lead the army here. Dominic will be with us. Of course, Jordee will be staying behind with his lost hand and all, but he will be able to fight if need be." The queen sighed. "I think that's all we have for now. Now we can just wait until Samuel gets back."

"If I may ask, your majesty, why aren't we just staying inside the safety of our walls?" Julia piped up.

"If it was just a regular army we would." The queen shook her head. "But werewolves are a whole other story. I don't know if we could keep them all out while having to fight them for a long period of time. At first the walls would hold and we would be fine, but over time the werewolves would find a way to get in. This way we have the element of surprise and we can catch them off guard." Julia nodded in understanding.

Just then, the guard came in with Lucas in tow. He sat him beside Lamar and Lucas looked at Nyla.

"I figured you'd tell them. Oh well. I guess it's time everyone knows what we are." Lucas didn't take his eyes off Nyla.

"Yes, well, it's lucky Nyla spoke in your favor or else you would be in a world of hurt." Fulcan glared at Lucas and Lamar. Lucas remained silent, but the act looked pained for him.

Nyla paced back and forth. They still hadn't heard a word about Samuel and it had been well over a couple hours. Lamar and Lucas had remained silent since being brought in and Julia sat at the other end of the room as far away from them as she could get. The queen stood from where she had been sitting and placed her hand gently on Nyla's shoulder.

"Dear, you need to calm down and sit. Samuel and the others will be fine. I know they will."

"Okay." Nyla sighed as she sat down. Lydia walked to the window and looked up at the moon in the middle of the night sky.

"Happy eighteenth birthday, Nyla." The queen turned to Nyla and gave her a small smile. Julia whispered something in the queen's ear. The queen nodded.

Julia smiled. "Nyla, we are throwing you a party. With everything that's happened, everyone forgot that your party was supposed to be tonight."

Nyla shook her head. "No, no. I don't need a party this year. Really, it's okay. There is a lot more going on than just my birthday."

"Nyla, Julia is right. Right now a party would be a perfect happy distraction from everything that's been going on. Plus, you forget that at your eighteenth birthday is also a celebration where you are named the official heir to the throne of Galatia." The queen gave her daughter a hug. "We need this right now. It signals hope. Especially if something happens to me." She pulled back, giving Nyla a small smile.

"My queen." The guard turned toward her. "We've gotten word that Samuel and the others have returned. They are coming in the main gate as we speak. They have a prisoner with them."

Nyla looked at Julia and spun around, running as fast as she could until she reached the courtyard at the main gate. She spotted Samuel, leading a mangy looking man tied up with a rope. As soon as he saw her he handed the rope to Dominic and took a step forward. She flew into his arms, hugging him with everything she had. After a few seconds of breathing him in, she pulled back, examining his face. The others had scratches on their faces or arms, but besides looking dirty with a few blood streaks, he was untouched.

"I guess you did tell me the truth when you said you could take care of yourself." She smiled at him.

"Told you so." He grinned.

"My queen." Dominic stepped forward, leading the man toward the queen, who had just stepped outside the castle doors. Nyla gave Samuel a small smile and turned around, walking toward her mother.

Samuel stepped forward and took the man from Dominic. "The wolves were a group of scouts from Ridia. We left this man alive, but the rest didn't go down without a fight." He beckoned to the other's wounds. "One man got away, but Felix went after him and killed him before he could get too far."

"Speaking of which." Fulcan signaled to a couple guards behind him and they moved to grab Felix and Adrian.

"What is this?" Felix tried to shake the guard off him.

"We know everything." The queen glared at the siblings and nodded toward the castle.

"Take all of them down to the dungeon." The queen turned toward another guard. "Take Lucas and Lamar down there as well. Everyone needs to be there."

As they went down into the dungeon, the queen filled Samuel, Kristi, and Dominic in on everything that had happened since they headed out. Nyla walked beside Samuel, sending warmth shooting through her entire body.

When everyone had arrived, the werewolf man was kept tied up to a chair in the middle of the room. Lamar, Lucas, Felix, and Adrian stood behind him, surrounded by guards.

"So"—the queen looked at the group of wolves—"Lamar, you and your group are not going to speak unless spoken to. Understood?" He nodded, looking sideways at Lucas, who also nodded. "Good," the queen looked at the grungy man in the chair. "What is your name?" The man looked at her through stubborn eyes.

"Nigel." His voice was gruff.

"What were you and your group doing so close to Galatia's walls?" The man looked at the queen but kept his mouth shut.

"The queen asked you a question." Fulcan got in the man's face. When he still didn't speak Fulcan looked at Samuel who went up to the man with a silver dagger in his hand. Samuel knelt in front of the man, looking into his eyes.

"What were you and your group doing so close to Galatia's walls?" The queen asked again. He shook his head and Samuel slammed the dagger into his leg. The man let out a small scream and looked at Samuel in hate. Nyla looked at Lamar, who looked pained and Lucas had his jaw clenched.

"I will ask you one more time." The queen paced in front of the man. "What were you doing?"

"We were scouting your land and walls. We were trying to find any weaknesses you might have." The man continued to glare at Samuel.

"When is the attack on Galatia supposed to take place?" The queen stopped pacing, looking Nigel in the eyes.

"Why should I tell you? You are just going to kill me anyway," the man spat out.

"Samuel," Fulcan commanded. Samuel grabbed hold of the knife, twisting it in the man's leg, causing him to whimper.

"Okay, okay!" The man had his eyes squeezed shut. Samuel let go of the knife. "Gafna and Rothgar are planning an attack in two days at nightfall." The queen nodded. Nyla could hear Julia's heart beat fearfully beside her and she squeezed her hand. She looked over to where Kaden stood and caught his eye.

"How many men?" the queen asked the man. She looked at Lamar.

The man gulped. "More than five thousand men." Lamar nodded at the queen and she kept her face impassive.

"Why didn't you tell us you were werewolves?" she spoke to Lamar.

He looked her in the eyes. "Because we wanted you to trust us. We wanted to tell you at the right moment."

"And when did you feel that the right moment was?" Fulcan asked him, his voice stern.

"With all due respect your majesty, you were keeping something from us too." Lucas pointed his chin at Nyla. "We should have been informed of something that dangerous. How many people did she kill again?" He eyed Nyla with a small sneer.

"You flee-bitten mongrel!" Samuel wrenched the knife out of the prisoners leg, causing him to scream, and held it against Lucas's throat. Fulcan stepped back, not even trying to intervene. Lucas let out a small laugh and Samuel tightened the knife on Lucas's throat.

"Wait!" Lamar called out. "Lucas is running his mouth. We never suspected princess Nyla of ill intentions and we have all been there. We know the struggles of being freshly turned."

"Okay." The queen nodded at Fulcan and he put a hand on Samuel's shoulder. Samuel lowered the knife, but his expression was still one of malice.

"We were going to tell you soon, before we went to battle." Lamar spoke to the queen in a polite, innocent voice. "We meant no harm, we really are trying to help you." The queen looked around the room at each person. Nyla eyed Lamar and nodded in their favor and Kaden nodded and looked at Adrian. Jordee nodded, and then Samuel nodded. The queen looked at Fulcan.

"Are you sure we should trust them?" Fulcan looked at the queen.

She sighed. "Yes, they have helped us this far. I think we should trust them."

"Very well." Fulcan nodded to Samuel, who nodded to his guards. The guards stepped away and Lamar and Lucas came to stand beside the queen, while Adrian and Felix stood beside Kaden.

"What should we do with this one?" Samuel turned to the queen.

"We'll leave him for now. He can't harm anything. We may need him later." She turned to leave the room.

"Filthy traitors!" the ratty man spat at Lucas and Lamar. "Consorting with indecent vampires." He looked at Samuel repulsively. "Disgusting blood-sucker!" Nyla looked at Samuel in confusion and his eyes shot to hers.

"What is he talking about?" she asked him.

The man looked at the queen. "They'll get you, ya know. It's just a matter of time and then I'll laugh at your bloody, mutilated bodies. You just wait they'll . . ." The man gasped as Lucas ripped his heart out. He looked at the queen, who had fury on her face.

"Forgive me, My Queen. He talked too much." He threw the heart onto the dead man's lap and walked past the queen and Fulcan.

"Lucas, disobedience is unacceptable. However, since we are so close to war we will review this incident after battle." The queen raised her eyebrows at Fulcan and followed Lucas out. The rest followed silently. Nyla kept her eyes down, her heart twisting in knots. *What was that werewolf talking about?* He had looked at Samuel, not Nyla. As soon as they came out of the dungeon and into the main corridor Nyla grabbed Samuel's hand pulling him back onto the dungeon stairs.

"What was he talking about?" She looked Samuel in the eyes. "I know you have kept things from me for a while and I let it go. But I'm done letting it slide. Tell me."

Samuel sighed, looking into Nyla's crystal eyes. "I'm a vampire, Nyla."

Nyla stared at him at a loss for words. "No, no. I would've known. You would have told me." So many thoughts rushed through her mind. *I have never seen him actually eat food, he never really needed sleep, and then there was the time when I had drank his blood. It had tasted so sweet, so different from Jimmy's blood. He knew so much about vampires. I should have known, but it couldn't be true!*

"No! I . . . I don't believe you." She took a step back, astonishment on her face.

"Nyla." His eyes turned black and the fangs grew from his mouth. He looked more handsome and deadly than ever and Nyla hated that she longed to touch him, even in her anger. Her heart ached from sadness and rage all at the same time.

"Why didn't you tell me?!" She stepped past him, but he grabbed her wrist.

"I wanted to, but your mother wanted you to recover from your transformation on your own. No one else knows but the queen and Fulcan, Nyla. After the vampires betrayed your father, the kingdom went into a rage and Queen Lydia knew it wasn't safe to let anyone know I was a vampire for my safety. I went into hiding for a while and came back as captain of the guard. That way, no one suspected a thing. I told her we should tell you, but she wanted you to discover who you are first. I was not the best vampire Nyla, and you shouldn't know how horrible vampires really are. I . . . also wanted you to make a decision about Kaden and I without knowing what I was."

"How dare you?!" Nyla didn't even hide the shock and hurt in her face. "How dare you not tell me?! You knew what I was going through and still you let me think I was alone in this!"

"Nyla, you were never alone, I was always there for you without having to be a vampire around you."

"It's not the same, Samuel!" Nyla threw her hands up in the air.

"I know. I'm sorry." Samuel shook his head.

Nyla wasn't ready to accept his apology yet. "And you thought I should create my own opinions about you and Kaden? I don't even know what to say to you right now! You should have known I was falling for you, you dumb idiot! Couldn't you sense it? From the moment we kissed in the lake you should have known!"

"Nyla, you told me that kissing me was a mistake!"

"Yea, well, I didn't mean it!" Nyla shook her head.

"How was I supposed to know that? You looked like you meant it and . . . wait. You just said you're falling for me." He looked at her, a smile coming to his lips. He was making it hard for Nyla to be mad at him and she huffed an annoyed sigh.

"Oh, I could just . . . ugh." She drew back and punched him in the face, frowning at the fact that it probably didn't even hurt him even a little. She smiled when she saw his shocked, but amused face.

"Feel better?" He tried to hide his smile and suppressed a laugh.

She forced a frown. "No, you jerk." She sighed. "You should have told me."

"I know, and I'm sorry. I really am, Nyla. You have no idea how hard it was not telling you. With you not knowing what we could do together because we had no limits." He paused. "You really feel the same way I do?" Nyla glared and moved past him, out of the room.

"Don't think you'll make me not mad at you." She felt him follow her out the door, but she stopped as she saw Kaden and Julia's shocked faces.

"Did you hear everything?" Nyla looked between them. They nodded and suddenly Kaden's face turned to fury.

"Are you kidding me?! You are both vampires? I never even had a chance." He looked at Samuel. "I thought I knew you. Now not only are you going for the girl I love, but you have been a blood-sucking vampire this whole time?!" He moved toward Samuel with vengeance in his eyes, but Julia and Nyla stepped in front of him.

"Okay, there's been enough punching for one night." She looked right at Kaden. "I need to talk to you alone. She pulled him down the hallway and partway up the stairs to the next floor. "What are you doing? I thought we were passed all of this. You can't love me, Kaden. You said so yourself," she spoke in a hushed, angry voice.

"Nyla, I want to try. I can love you, I just need time." He looked at Nyla's face, hurt all over his features. He wasn't going to give up that easy.

"Kaden." She took hold of his shoulders. "It's too late, okay? You are one of my best friends, but it's too late for us. You have to accept that."

Kaden shook his head. "Nyla, do you see this?" He pulled back his collar, revealing the bandage over her bite. "I would take this any day if I could be with you. I can make myself not be afraid and I can get used to the idea of you being a . . . vampire." He had a pleading look on his face and Nyla felt guilty.

"Kaden. You have always been my best friend. I don't want to lose you, but I can't do this." She motioned between them. "Kaden, neither can you."

"Do you love him?" Kaden asked in a hurt voice.

Nyla sighed. "Kaden, I don't know. I . . . I really like him."

"Nyla . . . how can you just throw us away just like that. After all that we've been through. After all we had?"

"Kaden, we've been friends forever and we will still be friends. It's not like we were in love."

"Nyla, I was in love with you." Nyla stared at him a moment, tears welling in her eyes. Kaden sighed, not taking his eyes off of her. "Nyla, look me in the eyes and tell me you didn't feel something for me and that you still don't."

"Kaden, I can't do that." Nyla squeezed her eyes shut.

"Then come back to me." He stepped closer to her and took her face in his hands. "Give us another chance. I love you."

"Kaden." A tear slipped from Nyla's lashes and she stepped away from him. "I've changed and . . . my feelings have changed. I won't lie to you and tell you I don't feel anything for you, but I don't love you like you love me. What we had . . . it was what it was, but it wasn't love. I'm sorry, but I can't give you what you want."

"Fine." Kaden backed up. "I'll back off then, but I still don't believe you and you know you don't fully believe it either." Kaden lowered his eyes and left, walking past her up the stairs. Nyla followed him up into the main hallway, but he didn't stop and continued out of sight. Nyla backed down the stairway again and sat on the second step. Pushing her hair back from her face, she took a deep, calming breath. She heard footsteps approach and Julia came around the corner, sitting beside her.

"Well, that was intense." Julia looked at Nyla. "You going to be okay?"

Nyla gave a fake smile. "Ya, I'll be fine."

"Nyla, I know when you're lying and I know when you're hurting."

"I just hate what I'm doing to him. I don't want to hurt him I just . . . can't give him what he wants." Nyla shook her head.

"Nyla, if you don't love Kaden the way he wants then that's not your fault. Yes, he's going to be hurting for a while, but he will survive. You guys were friends way before all this happened. He'll get over this."

"I hope so." Nyla stood up and walked into the empty hallway. "Where's Samuel?"

"He left the other way. He wanted to give us some time alone and he wants to give you some space to sort things out and think things through."

"He must have heard everything. Was he mad? I . . . I told Kaden that I couldn't say I don't have feelings for him. I hope he doesn't think—"

"Nyla, Samuel knows how you feel and he's okay with that. He's not mad at you, but he knew you were still angry with him."

"I should go find him." Julia nodded and Nyla gave her a small hug. "Thanks. You're a good friend." Julia smiled and made her way up the stairs as Nyla started in the direction Samuel had gone. She found him walking in the main corridor, toward the front doors. He turned as he heard her approach and let her catch up.

"Samuel I'm sorry about—"

"Nyla, you don't need to apologize." Samuel cut her off. "You and Kaden have a long history and I understand."

"But about what I told Kaden. You have to know that it doesn't change the way I feel about you." She looked up at him.

"I know, Nyla. Kaden is a part of you and you can't just let him go. You shouldn't have to and I want you to know that I don't want to rush things. I want to go as slow as you want and I will wait for you. I'm not going anywhere." He took her hand. "And I am so sorry that I didn't tell you about me."

"Thank you. Although I wish you would have told me I understand why you didn't. I'm not going to waste time holding it against you. At least I know now and I really don't want there to be any more secrets."

"Neither do I." Samuel looked into her eyes and bent to kiss her on the cheek. Nyla smiled at him.

"So you're really a vampire?" Samuel nodded at her. "Wow! How did I not know? How did nobody ever figure that out?" She shook her head in disbelief. "So how old are you?"

Samuel laughed. "Pretty old."

"How old?" Nyla pleaded.

"Okay, okay. I was turned about 105 years ago."

Nyla looked at him in astonishment. "Holy crap, old man. It's a good thing I'm eighteen now." She gave a small laugh, trying to forget about Kaden. "Oh, by the way, we better get some rest, it's almost dawn. If we're going to get any rest before the celebration today, we better do it now. We are going to celebrate today, then head off to war the next night, so it's going to be some party."

"It's a good thing we don't need sleep then." Samuel smiled at Nyla and she grinned back. "Speaking of your birthday and your naming ceremony, I have something for you."

"You didn't have to get me anything." Nyla smiled as he held his hand out, placing something in hers. She looked down, holding up the necklace in awe. It was a simple, strong silver chain with a black stone pendant on the end. Nyla admired the swirling symbol that was carved into the center, revealing a sparkling, red-jeweled interior.

"It's from your father. It's the symbol of the pure bloods, the Valdoras, your family. He gave it to me right before he and your mother went to negotiate with Vallira. He wanted me to give it to you on your eighteenth birthday if anything happened to him."

"Really?" Tears sparkled in her eyes. "Thank you, Samuel." She turned and he fastened it around her neck.

"This necklace means that you are an heir to the throne of castle Valdora. Every member of your pure-blood family has one and this one was your father's. From now on, every vampire that sees you will know you are of pure blood and will respect you." Nyla turned back to Samuel and smiled up at him.

"Thank you." She stared into his amazing gray-blue eyes and lost her breath. She reached on her toes and kissed him and he pulled her close to his body. When they pulled apart Nyla could barely speak, a burning in the pit of her stomach.

"Are you guarding me again tonight?" She grinned at him.

He sighed. "Unfortunately, I have to see to the housing situation and then go through battle plans with Fulcan, but tomorrow, I'm all yours. I'll walk you to your chambers, though." He smiled at her and they made their way to Nyla's room.

CHAPTER 20

Nyla sat at her large vanity, staring at her reflection in the mirror. Although vampires didn't need sleep, they still sometimes needed to rest their minds and get away from the world. She had lain in bed anyway and eventually fell asleep, but her dreams were plagued with nightmares of the upcoming battle. She had woken feeling jittery and nervous. She had contemplated going down to the training grounds to see how the new recruits were doing, but was too nervous that she wouldn't like seeing the old men and young boys who were barely fit to fight in a battle. Now she had been sitting in her robe, staring at her reflection for some time now. So much had happened the past year and she felt way older than eighteen. It was weird thinking that from now on she would never age a day, no matter how many birthdays she had. The thought of an eternity made her nervous, but thinking of an eternity with Samuel excited her.

She sighed. Although it was her birthday and in a little over an hour everyone would be celebrating life and would be happy, she couldn't stop thinking of all the lives that would be lost the next day in the battle. Just then, Julia skipped into the room.

"Hello, birthday girl, or should I say official heir to the throne of Galatia!" She smiled at Nyla in the mirror, but then frowned. "What's wrong?"

"Oh, nothing." Nyla forced a smile, "It's just . . . I can't stop thinking about tomorrow."

"Nyla." Julia turned her around, making Nyla look at her. "You do remember that we have two vampires, a whole army of soldiers that are mostly experienced, and four werewolves that know every battle strategy Gafna and Rothgar are going to make against us, right?"

"Yes, I guess so." That thought made Nyla a little cheerier.

"Good. Starting now we are not going to worry about tomorrow, and celebrate your birthday and the beginning of your new life, okay? So cheer up and get dressed already!" She pushed Nyla toward her closet. "Come on. We don't have all day and Samuel will be waiting for you." That made Nyla smile and she searched her closet, looking for her favorite dress.

"You really are okay with this, aren't you?" She poked her head out of her closet and looked at Julia.

"Of course." Julia smiled. "At first, yes I was a little jealous, but I can tell you really like him and he obviously feels the same way and you two are meant for each other in soooo many ways. Besides, there are so many fish in the sea and Kaden will get over it."

"Well, okay. I just . . . It's so weird thinking of how things are turning out." Nyla continued to look for a dress and paused. "I mean, I guess I always thought it was going to be Kaden . . ." She trailed off. Thinking of what Kaden thought of her made a knot form in her stomach and she continued shifting through dresses.

"Nyla, he'll come around." Julia appeared in the closet doorway, a small smile on her face. "He doesn't hate you, he just . . . he's torn between fear and love I guess? Well, and he's hurting because you don't love him in the way he wants you to. It'll take time, but he'll come around."

Nyla hoped Julia was right. "We will always be friends, if he wants to, but . . . My feelings have changed and his will too." She pulled out a dark green, satin dress that shone in the light.

"Here." She gave the dress to Julia. "You wear this tonight. You will look amazing in it." She smiled at Julia and helped her put it on. "See?" She beamed at Julia's reflection. "It fits you perfectly." Nyla went back into her closet and pulled out a gold shimmery dress that sparkled with every beam of light. She pulled it on and smiled when it fit every curve of her body perfectly.

"There." She emerged from her closet and looked at both of their reflections in the mirror. "We are both royalty tonight." Nyla smiled and touched the black and red pendant that hung from her neck. She looked at the door.

"Where's Martha?" The maid never missed a chance to pretty somebody up.

"Oh, she's putting the finishing touches on the party down in the dining hall."

"Okay, well let's get to work then." Nyla sat Julia down on the cushy chair at her vanity. "Up, or down?" She started brushing Julia's hair.

"Oh, I can do my own hair. It's okay." She started to stand.

"Julia, sit." Nyla sat her back down.

"Okay." Julia smiled at her. "Um . . . up." Nyla worked Julia's hair until it was up in a pretty, messy bun with curly strands hanging around her face.

"Your turn!" Julia smiled at her reflection and got up. She sat Nyla down in the chair and went to work on her hair. By the time she was done, Nyla's hair was in a half up hairstyle with perfect curls to her waist.

"Now for the makeup." Nyla stood up. "Um . . . I think less is more." In about fifteen minutes, the girls stood side by side, looking at their reflections in the huge mirror. Julia went with light brown eyeshadow and had ruby lips while Nyla's face sparkled with shimmery eye shadow and rosy lips.

"Perfect." She ran to her closet. "Come pick which shoes you want to wear." She held up a pair of strappy heals.

"Um . . . no." Julia laughed. "I don't think I could walk in heals." Nyla shrugged and put them back, pulling out a pair of sparkly flats that had rhinestones and emeralds sewn into them. "Better." Julia smiled, slipping the flats on. Nyla put on a pair of gold and diamond jeweled heals, and admired her feet in the full-length mirror beside the closet.

"You ready?" She turned to Julia, her face shining with radiance. They made their way down to the main hall, listening to their footsteps that echoed off the quiet halls. Julia rubbed the silky fabric of her dress between her fingers.

"Thank you, Nyla. For everything."

"No." Nyla stopped walking and looked at her best friend. "Thank you. You have always been there for me, no matter what I have done and I thank you for that. You truly are a good friend." She gave Julia a hug and they continued walking until they heard voices coming from the main hall.

"Well, here goes nothing." Nyla smiled at Julia as the guards opened the big oak doors. Nyla walked in first, Julia dutifully walking just behind her. As they entered, the hall went mostly quiet and all eyes were on them. Nyla caught Lamar's eye seated next to Lucas, Adrian, and Felix. She gave him a small smile and continued walking. Nyla and Julia headed for the big red thrones that stood at the end of the hall. Queen Lydia was standing in front of her throne with Jamin on her left, holding a pillow with the gleaming crown of the princess of Galatia. Next to Jamin stood Kaden. On the left of the queen stood Fulcan and Samuel, standing loyal and proud. As they approached, Nyla caught Samuel's eye and smiled at him before turning her gaze to her mother. She stopped in front of her and Julia went to stand beside Jamin. She beamed at Nyla proudly. Nyla and the queen turned, facing each other so that the whole hall could see them. The queen gently picked the crown up from the velvet pillow in Jamin's hands and held it in between them.

"Ladies and gentlemen," she spoke to the crowd, "today, my daughter, and the daughter of King Richard, rest his soul, turns eighteen. This day signals her leap into the world and womanhood as well as her right to be named the rightful heir to the throne of Galacia." She turned to Nyla.

"Princess Nylina, do you accept this crown, and your title as the rightful heir to the throne, in front of your queen, the royal advisor, and the people of Galatia?"

"Yes, I do." Nyla smiled at the queen and she nodded her head, signaling Nyla to kneel. Nyla knelt and the queen held the crown over her head.

"Then by the power of me, Queen Lydia Galatianti, wife of the late King Richard, King of Galatia, place this crown on your head and name you Nyla Galatianti, heir to the throne of Galatia." She placed the crown on Nyla's head and grabbed her hands, helping her stand. They turned toward the crowd and everyone cheered, standing and applauding their queen and princess.

"Let's eat!" The queen clapped her hands together, kissed Nyla on the cheek, and they both sat in the thrones. Julia moved to sit in the velvet chair next to Nyla and Jamin and Kaden sat next to the queen. Fulcan stood behind the queen, Samuel stood behind Nyla, and all at once servants began bringing in platters of food. A table was brought up in front of the thrones and food was set on each table.

"Sit." The queen motioned for Samuel and Fulcan to join them at the table. They moved and Samuel took the seat across from Nyla. She beamed at him and he took in her wonderful glow. Samuel smiled handsomely back and Nyla's heart almost leapt gleefully out of her chest.

"So." Nyla took a deep breath and tore her eyes away from Samuel's gorgeous face. "What time do we head out tomorrow?"

"Well"—Fulcan chewed his steak—"according to the prisoner Samuel brought in last night, the attack is planned for the day after tomorrow. We will continue to train troops in the morning and head out tomorrow at nightfall and we will travel all night until we reach our camp point just inside the forest outside of Libia. We will get a little sleep and prepare so we are ready to catch Gafna and Rothgar off guard before they reach Galatia at nightfall. We still don't have as many men, but we will have a greater chance if we get the element of surprise." Nyla processed the information and chewed on a piece of turkey for a while.

"Okay, that's enough talk of war. This is a festive occasion and we are going to take advantage of this time and be joyous, understood?" Everyone nodded at the queen. She clapped her hands together. "Maestro, music please!" The band of stringed instruments in the corner began to play a joyful tune and the mood began to lighten. The queen got up and offered her hand to Fulcan.

"Come, dance." He stood and joined her on the dance floor. People began to get up and dance one after another. Samuel stood and smiled at Nyla.

"May I?" He took her hand and pulled her onto the dance floor. He brought her body close to his as the band began to play a slow tune.

"You look beautiful." He whispered in her ear, making shivers race down her spine. He smiled down at her and made her heart throb as he leaned in, kissing her on the forehead.

"I have to admit, I didn't expect to feel like this. You're perfect, and I of all people definitely don't deserve you." She could feel his hot breath on her face and she stretched up, bringing her face closer to his. His hands tightened around her waist. She looked into his gray-blue eyes and felt like she could get lost in them forever. She smiled, biting her lip as she pulled his face closer to hers. Samuel's gaze fell on Kaden's glaring face and guilt crept over him.

"Not here." He kissed her cheek and pulled back, smiling as they continued to dance.

Julia looked at Kaden. He stared at Nyla and Samuel with contempt on his face.

"Kaden?" Julia stood up. "Get up, let's go." Without saying a word he stood up and walked to the dance floor with her. "Kaden, it's going to be okay. You'll get through this."

"I don't know, Julia." He took his eyes off Nyla and Samuel. "I've loved her since we were kids. I really did, but I blew it." He sighed, wanting to punch something.

"Maybe it just wasn't meant to be." Julia gave him a comforting look.

"No, Julia. She was the one. I could feel it."

"Listen, I'm not going to tell you that there's hope, but I'm not going to tell you to lose hope either. You can't help who you love and if you two are meant to be together then you'll find a way. But no matter what I know you'll find somebody amazing one day." She hugged him. "Come on. I'm your friend too and I do know some stuff." She smiled. "Let's just have a good time. Let everything go tonight before we head out tomorrow."

Kaden sighed. "Okay, but I'm not giving up on her. Not yet." He twirled her and she laughed.

"May I cut in?" Adrian smiled at Kaden and Julia. Her slim, athletic body was adorned in a yellow gown that accented her wolf like eyes, and her blond hair was up in a tight bun.

"Um . . . sure." Kaden smiled at Julia and took Adrian's hands.

"Are you ready for the battle?" She had a hunger in her eyes like a wolf ready to hunt its prey.

"I guess so, yes." He shrugged. "I will be when the time comes."

"I don't know." Adrian sighed. "It might come sooner than you think. Time flies when you're having fun." She winked at him and sighed. "Even the idea of a battle gets me going. It makes me . . . hungry." She smiled dangerously at him and brought her face closer to his. "You know . . ." She brought his face close and whispered in his ear, her lips barely touching his earlobe. "I could get your mind off of her."

"Uh . . . no." He gently pushed her away. "I'm sorry."

Adrian shrugged but kept her arms around him as they continued to dance. "Suit yourself. I just hate to see that handsome face of yours in a frown. You know, it would be better if I was at least close to you to ensure your survival." She gave him a wicked smile, bearing sharp teeth, and he gulped nervously. She laughed. "Don't worry. I'll give you your space, just don't expect me to let you out of my sight."

The party lasted well into the evening. Before he knew it, Kaden was laughing and dancing along with everyone else. Nyla blew out the candles of her four-tiered cake and everyone was having a joyous time, the battle and upcoming horror forgotten for the moment.

∽◌∾

"Princess Nylina?" Lamar tapped her on the shoulder as she was taking a sip from her crystal glass.

Lamar eyed the red liquid. "Is that . . ."

"Oh." She set her glass down. "Yes, it's blood. Sorry if it grosses you out."

"No, no. Never be sorry for who you are." Lamar smiled at her. "May I have a dance?"

"Yes." She followed him and he placed one hand on her back, taking her hand in the other. After a few seconds of dancing he looked her in the eyes.

"Princess Nylina, there's something I need to tell you." He glanced at Lucas, who was watching him intently. Lamar spun Nyla so that she was facing Lucas and he couldn't see Lamar's face. "You should be careful in who you put your full trust in the next coming hours."

"What?" The music shifted to a happy tune and she had to lean closer to hear him to hear.

"It's . . ." Lamar was tapped on the shoulder.

"Excuse me." Lucas smiled at Nyla. "May I cut in?"

"Of course." She looked at Lamar, wondering what Lamar was about to say. Lucas nodded at Lamar, who gave him a half smile and turned, bowing to Nyla. She nodded at him and took Lucas's hand.

"What were you and Lamar talking so seriously about?" Lucas asked Nyla. She thought for a moment, a weird feeling in the pit of her stomach.

"He was just . . . wishing me a happy birthday." She looked at him, a smile on her face.

"Oh, yes, happy birthday." Lucas smiled and brought her hand up, pressing it gently to his smiling lips. Nyla gave him a small, polite smile, feeling suddenly uncomfortable.

"Excuse me. I need a drink." She put her eyes down and stepped away from him, walking toward Samuel.

"He still creeps me out," she whispered to him, taking a sip of her drink. He chuckled, watching Lucas walk over to Felix and whisper something to him. Nyla looked to where Julia, Adrian, and Kaden were talking with a few of the maids.

"I'm going to go talk to him for a moment." She nodded toward Kaden and Samuel nodded, going over to where Dominic and Fulcan stood. Nyla took another drink, letting the red liquid flow down her throat, tingling her stomach pleasurably. She took a deep breath, preparing herself, and walked over to Kaden and Julia.

"Hey!" Julia smiled, clearly a little tipsy from the glass of wine in her hand.

"Hey." Nyla laughed. She turned to Kaden. "Hey, do you want to dance?"

"I don't know, Nyla." Kaden shifted his feet.

"Come on, Kaden. Tomorrow night we are headed off to battle and who knows who will make it out. It's just one dance with your best friend."

"Right. My best friend." Kaden gave her a look and turned to Adrian. "Want to dance?" He held his hand out to her and she took it, smirking at Nyla as she followed him.

"Ooo, she just pushes my buttons." Nyla clenched her fists.

"Come on, Kaden will lighten up and Adrian's really not that bad. Everyone knows vampires and werewolves naturally don't get along." She laughed. "Earlier she was joking about having me turned into a werewolf. I just laughed at her. I think she's had a little too much to drink." Julia swayed and Nyla's eyes widened.

"I hope not!" She took the glass of wine away from Julia and set it down. "I think you are the one who has had a little too much to drink." She giggled.

"Yes, I think I have." Julia laughed and pointed to the dance floor. "Come on. One more dance?" All of a sudden, the music stopped and the queen spoke.

"Thank you all for coming and making this night one to remember. It is getting late, and we better all retire. Everyone needs to rest up and be ready tomorrow. We will take the fight to them and make sure they know who we are. We will not falter and they will see they cannot overtake Galatia!" The room was alive with cheers and hugging. A large man with a long beard lifted his beer mug.

"To Galatia! And to the princess and queen!" Everyone raised their glasses and cheered.

"Thank you." The queen smiled proudly at all of them. "Good night to everybody." She motioned to Samuel and Fulcan before turning toward Lamar, and then Nyla and waving them over.

"Everyone get some rest. We will be up at the break of dawn to get ready and will head out at nightfall to make camp and take our positions." She nodded at all of them and gave Nyla a hug. "Good night and happy birthday, my beautiful daughter." She then turned and left, followed by Jamin and Fulcan. Lamar turned to Nyla.

"Princess, we must speak." She nodded, but Samuel grabbed Nyla's hand, smiling at Lamar.

"I'll escort you to your room. Even though you're a big bad vampire now and can take care of yourself, you still need a guard." He winked at her, making heat rush over her face. She nodded an apology to Lamar before she turned to Julia, giving her a hug.

"Good night." She squeezed her friend, making her grunt. "Sorry." Nyla smiled apologetically.

"You two have a good night." She raised her eyebrows at Nyla and giggled. Kaden turned, not wanting to hear anymore. Nyla looked at him.

"I don't think he'll talk to me. Would you make sure he's all right?" she asked Julia.

"Of course." Julia gave her another hug and turned, following Kaden out.

"Shall we?" Nyla turned toward Samuel, smiling.

"Absolutely." He grinned at her and she blushed, starting toward the door. Samuel fell into step behind her, followed by Dominic.

Nyla's heart was going a hundred miles an hour and threatened to leap out of her chest. She bit her lip, thoughts rushing through her mind. Although Samuel had been in her room many times before, this time was different. She could sense every wave of heat off Samuel, and she blushed. When they arrived at Nyla's bedroom door, Samuel held the door open for her and she went in and stopped, standing just inside the door by Samuel. He turned toward Dominic.

"I think I can take the watch here tonight. Why don't you and Nyla's other guards get some rest? You're going to need it and now that my secret's out, you know I don't need sleep." Nyla's heart leapt when she heard this and the thought of Samuel in her room without anyone else around made her jittery.

"Yes, sir." Dominic addressed the head of the guard formally and gave him a smile. "Have a good night." He raised his eyebrows at Samuel with a smile before turning and walking down the hallway.

Samuel turned toward Nyla, closing the door behind him. He gave her a grin.

"So." She smiled up at him.

"So." Samuel stepped in closer so that his breath tickled Nyla's face. A delightful shiver ran up her spine as he leaned in. He looked into her eyes a moment before softly brushing his lips against hers. He drew back slightly, taking in a slow breath, not wanting to push her. Heat rushed through Nyla's body and she reached up, bringing his face to hers again. She kissed him deeply as he pulled her up against his body and she let him slowly push her back until she was up against her bed rail. She reached up, wrapping her hand around the back of Samuel's neck and his hands traveled down her waist.

Nyla's heart beat faster and she turned him around, pushing him down onto the bed. She hovered over him for a moment, smiling into his eyes. She gazed at them as they turned from gorgeous blue-gray to stunning jet black. She could feel his breath on her face and the burning in the pit of her stomach swelled. Samuel's form turned brilliant blue as her vision changed and she stared at him, wondering how she never noticed how cold his body temperature was in her enhanced vision. She slightly pulled back, distracted.

"Samuel, can I ask you something?" She slowed her breathing and shifted, sitting next to him on the bed.

"Anything." He sat up and kissed Nyla's nose, giving her butterflies, and smiled back at her.

"Actually, I have a lot to ask." She looked into his warm eyes, wishing he would kiss her again.

"I'm all yours." He smiled at her, reaching up and tucking a strand of blond hair behind her ear.

She bit her lip. "So when you said you knew a vampire did you mean yourself?"

"Well, yes and no. I used to live in Valdora. I knew your father."

"Oh . . ." Nyla remembered that he was over 105 years old.

"We weren't exactly good friends, but . . ." He paused. "He actually saved my life." Nyla gave him a questioning look. "You see, his sister, Daniella, turned me. I was a soldier for one of the Kingdoms on the coast back then and I was still living with my family. She saw me one night while I was on a hunt and fell in love with me. She continued to watch me every so often, but I never saw her. She approached me once while I was in the market, but I didn't realize who she was. We barely talked, and . . . I wasn't interested in her. So one night she came into my house and killed my mother, father, and three younger sisters, turning me to be with her. I hated her for killing my family and there was never going to be any attraction from my end. I um . . . I was with someone at the time, but I kept it a secret from her. Your father was planning to leave the castle Valdora at the time when he realized your mother was pregnant with you. He took pity on me and brought me here with him and I was going to join the army here. After the fight at Valdora I went into hiding, not sure if my being at Galatia was safe. I kept in touch with Fulcan and Lydia and eventually I came back. They trusted me and made me the head of the guard, and that's my story."

Nyla didn't know what to say. He had such a tragic life and had gone through so much. Not only had he known her father, but her father had saved him. Standing up, she wrapped her arms around herself as she looked at him with tears in her eyes.

Samuel spoke again. "I really wish I had gone with them to Valdora to try and make peace, but your father wouldn't let me. He feared what Daniella would do, because she didn't know I had gone with your father. She thought I had just run away, but I should have been there. I could have helped him."

"No." Nyla sat down again and stroked his cheek with her thumb, looking him in the eyes. "Don't put that on yourself." She thought for a moment, so many other questions racing through her mind.

"You said you were with someone at the time." She paused.

"Yes." Samuel looked down. "But when your father helped me, we didn't have time to get her away. I was planning to go back for her, but somehow Daniella found out about her and . . . she was gone when we got there."

"I'm sorry. That's horrible."

Samuel gave her a smile. "That was a long time ago." He stood and pulled her up against him again, tilting her chin up. "I found the one I'm meant to be with."

Nyla sucked in a breath, starting to lose herself again. She pushed him back with a grin, not wanting to get distracted again, but suddenly stopped.

"So how can you walk in the sunlight like I can? You're not a pure-blood original."

"Well, the pureblood originals can turn anyone by draining the person to the point of almost completely dry and then feeding them their blood to revive them. No one else knows this except for the originals, but when an already turned vampire drinks the blood of an original again, they can also walk in the sunlight. When your father brought me here he gave me his blood to protect me."

"So can you only walk in the sunlight, or do you have all aspects of an original pure blood now?"

"Your father said I would have almost every ability that a pure has, I'm still not as strong as you and I still have to feed a little more often than a pure, but as for invincibility, as far as I know, only an original and a werewolf can kill me." This made Nyla smile. Although a werewolf could still kill him, it would take a lot and Samuel was a 105 year old vampire and also the captain of the guard. He could more than take care of himself. She would have one less person to worry too much about in the upcoming battle. Samuel gave her a sexy smile and pulled her onto the bed, hovering his body above hers.

"That's enough talking for now, I think." He began to lower his mouth to hers and she smiled as butterflies raced into her stomach.

Her smile faded as ghostly howls flooded the night sky. Chills ran up Nyla's spine and she looked wide-eyed into Samuel's alarmed expression.

"Something's wrong." Samuel stood up and turned, rushing toward the balcony. Nyla hastily followed him and leaned over the stone rail, looking out into the eerie darkness. In the distance hundreds of tiny lights poked out through the trees. Suddenly, the battle horn from the main watchtower blasted through the sky, joining the sickening howls that continued to ring through the night.

"No." Nyla's breath caught as realization swept over her, flooding her stomach with a gutting terror. "They're coming."

Samuel sprang into action. "I need to get to the training grounds. Fulcan is already there. He was stationed there all night until I was supposed to take his place at daybreak."

Nyla turned. "No! This can't be happening! It's too soon! We're not ready!" She paced as thoughts of werewolves storming the castle rushed through her mind. *The battle couldn't be here.* She stopped pacing and turned to Samuel, wide-eyed.

"Samuel! Julia and Jamin, and . . ." She ran her fingers viciously through her hair.

"Breathe." Samuel put his hands on either side of Nyla's face. "It's going to be all right! As long as we stand our ground at the walls nothing can penetrate through them." She shook her head, looking into his calming eyes.

"Now." He grabbed a bottle of blood from the cooler and took a gulp before handing it to her. "Drink this. We'll need you at full strength. I've got to get to Fulcan and the Queen. Suit up and meet me in the command tent on the training grounds." He gave her a quick kiss before he turned, bolting out the door. Nyla gulped the blood down and threw the empty bottle in the trash. Taking a deep breath, she grabbed her battle gear from the corner of her closet and began to dress. Suddenly Julia burst through the door.

"Nyla!" Julia looked as if the castle had been bombed.

"Julia, do you know what's going on?" She laced up a knee-high boot.

"No, I haven't talked to anybody yet. I was making sure I had everything ready for tomorrow when I heard the horn, but on my way here I heard servants talking about a surprise attack. Is that true?"

"I think so." Nyla turned to her scared friend and cocked her head a bit, listening to the approaching howls with her enhanced hearing. "They're getting closer." She turned around, holding her long blond hair over her shoulder. "Lace me up?" Julia tightened the leather laces and tied them into a tight double bow.

She gasped. "I hear howling!" Her fingers turned to stone on Nyla's back. Nyla could sense the waves of fear rolling off her friend.

Nyla turned toward the door, braiding her hair. She looked back at Julia, who was still standing by the bed, frozen in fear. Nyla walked over to her, gently grabbing Julia's shoulders.

"It will be all right, but we need to move now. We need to get to the command tent on the training grounds." She looked Julia in the eyes. Julia nodded her head, taking a deep breath. "Okay, let's go." Nyla opened the door and they entered the hall. It seemed to be eerily empty and quiet except for the howling coming from beyond the walls. Nyla and Julia hurried toward the castle doors, occasionally passing a panicking maid. Once they opened the big, castle doors, they entered into chaos. Every way they looked, there were people running to follow orders. Nyla scanned the scene of running people, searching for Samuel or the queen.

"This way." Nyla pulled Julia toward the white command tent. They entered and headed for the round table in the middle of the small room where Samuel stood with the queen and Fulcan.

"What's going on?" Nyla looked at the queen.

"Rothgar's army is advancing on the castle."

"I don't understand. They weren't supposed to attack for another day." Nyla shook her head. *This can't be happening. We aren't ready. This wasn't the plan.*

"Well, either the scout we found gave us false information, or word got out that we knew." Samuel scowled. "The problem is we already sent scouts out and about a quarter of the army is on their way to the rendezvous point. Chances are they've already been intercepted."

"How much time do we have?" Nyla looked at Samuel, dreading the answer.

"We are inside the walls so as long as they hold and we fight back we'll be guarded inside. They'll be at the wall before the moon reaches its apex. We have to make sure the wall and all access points are well manned. The archers should do good work of them." More howls split through the sky.

"They're getting closer. We need to move now!" the queen urged.

Fulcan moved into action. "Samuel, go see to the archers and make sure all entrance and access points are heavily manned." He turned to Dominic, who had just entered the tent. "Dominic, take all the maids and other women to the bunker. Make sure they lock it tight from the inside and use the escape tunnels if they have to. Nyla, go with him and try to keep everyone calm."

Nyla nodded and took one last look at the queen and Samuel before following Dominic with Julia in tow. They split up in the castle, Dominic taking the left wings and Nyla and Julia covering the right. Every maid and woman they found in the castle, Nyla ordered to get to the bunker. After they did the first round, Nyla did a last quick sweep before following the last couple stragglers to the bunker. Dominic was already there giving orders to a few male servants armed with daggers and a few swords.

"Lock and barricade the doors tight. Don't open them until the queen, Princess Nylina, General Fulcan, Captain Samuel, or I come for you. If the wolves get to the doors use the escape tunnels and get everyone to the Ieldra Forest." They nodded and Nyla walked over to calm a few young maids panicking in the corner.

"It will be all right," she reassured them. She turned to Julia who was frozen in terror in the center of the room where Nyla had left her.

"Julia"—Nyla took ahold of her shoulders—"breathe. It will be all right."

"How can you know that for sure?" Julia asked in a shaky voice.

"Because I do. Have faith. Remember all that we have on our side."

"Princess Nylina!" Dominic beckoned her toward the door. Nyla nodded and turned back to Julia. She hugged her fiercely before turning and following Dominic into the hall. They shut the doors and made sure they were tight before rushing toward the main doors.

"I'm joining Kristi and Kaden at the southern gate. You should join Samuel and the queen at the main gate." Nyla nodded as they opened the main door and went outside. Nyla stopped in her tracks as she tried to collect her thoughts. The howls now screamed through the darkness and flooded her mind. She took a deep breath and forced any fear down. Adrenaline surged through her body as she took off toward the main gate. She spotted Samuel on top of the walls with the archers. Nyla raced up to him.

"Samuel." Nyla stopped as she surveyed the scene before her. Blazing lights from handheld torches danced through the darkness as their carriers came closer and closer to reaching the walls. Behind them were masses of dark shapes. *There are so many wolves!*

"Nyla." Samuel walked toward her. "They'll reach the walls any second. Go grab your sword from the command tent and join me back here." She nodded and ran down the steps as he turned away, barking orders to the surrounding archers.

"Archers, ready!" The archers readied their bows and aimed into the darkness. Some of them had flaming arrows. "Light the beacons!" The few with flaming arrows let their arrows fly and big fires blazed on the ground, lighting up the darkness and masses of wolves below.

"Fire!" Samuel bellowed. Hundreds of arrows flew into the air. Nyla reached the command tent as whimpers sounded into the night.

"Fire!" Samuel yelled again and another round of whimpers were heard as the arrows hit their targets. "Fire at will!"

Good. Nyla thought as she grabbed her sword from its place on the empty rack. Hopefully the archers would do good work of the wolves. She exited the tent and started to head toward the steps to the top of the wall where Samuel stood.

"Princess!" Nyla whipped her head to the right as Lamar rushed up to her. He was limping slightly and held his hand to a bleeding gash on his arm.

"Lamar?!" Nyla rushed to meet him.

"I'm sorry! I'm so sorry! I tried to warn you! I tried to stop him!" Lamar gasped. A sinking feeling gripped at Nyla's insides as she looked into Lamar's panicking face.

"Where's Lucas?" She whipped her head to the side as a commotion broke out on the other side of the castle. Lamar looked toward the direction of the south gate and instantly Nyla knew something was wrong. She took off, leaving Lamar hobbling fast behind her. *Kaden is at the south gate!* She heard Samuel call her name from behind her, but she didn't stop. She skidded to a halt as she rounded the corner and a shriek almost escaped her lips as she saw the wolves and men spewing into the courtyard through the open gate. Nyla pulled out her sword and instantly swept the scene with her eyes.

Kristi was on top of the wall, shooting incoming wolves with a crossbow while Dominic slashed at them on the ground. Soldiers and wolves collided everywhere as blood covered the dirt-packed Earth. Nyla rushed toward the wall, readying her sword as she went. She was prepared for the first large wolf that lunged at her and she thrust her sword into its side as it fell to the ground. She plunged her sword into its heart and the next wolf was upon her in seconds. It pounced and knocked her to the ground, but she rolled before it could pin her down. She sprang up and readied as the wolf turned on her. She dodged its attack and buried her sword into its neck, decapitating it.

She made her way toward Dominic as two wolves rushed her from the side. She rolled to avoid the first wolf, but the second pounced on her. She struggled as the wolf snapped at her face. She gathered strength into her torso and brought her legs up, kicking the wolf off of her. She got to her feet and flipped over the wolf as she struck it in the side, her sword penetrating its heart. Before she could react, the second rushed her and clamped its jaws down on her forearm. She cried out as her sword skidded across the ground out of her reach. She punched the wolf in the side of the head and it let go of her arm. She went to move toward her sword but the wolf pinned her to the ground again. It's teeth sunk into her shoulder and she screamed as blood soaked her leather armor. She tried to reach for her sword, but was unsuccessful and she struggled to throw the wolf off of her. Suddenly the wolf went limp as blood covered the ground. She rolled the wolf off of her and nodded at Lamar as he pulled his sword out of the wolf's body.

Nyla stood and looked at her arm where the skin was smooth and freshly healed. She felt her shoulder and smiled as the skin knit itself back together. She heard Kristi cry out and looked up to see a wolf pinning to the ground. Nyla spotted a crossbow lying a few feet away. She leapt at it and yanked a bolt out of a body next to her. She loaded the crossbow and shot it at the wolf on top of Kristi, hitting it in the eye. Kristi nodded at Nyla in gratitude as she reached her.

"Where's Kaden?" Nyla looked down from the wall to where bodies clashed together and littered the ground.

"He was manning the other side of the gate, but he went off with Adrian a few minutes before the gate was down. It was Lucas!" Kristi shook her head in anger. "He overtook me before Dominic got here. Felix took out the guards manning the levers and started to lift them before we even knew what was happening. We didn't expect it. Those bastards!" Kristi spat. "As soon as the gait was lifted even a little, the wolves started to crawl under."

"But Kaden went with Adrian? Why? You didn't see Kaden, or where they went?" Nyla kept surveying the ground.

"Adrian said they needed more men at the northern gate." Kristi shook her head. "Watch out!" Kristi pushed Nyla out of the way as a wolf approached them. Nyla leapt down from the wall, landing in a crouch. She stood as Lamar rushed up to her.

"We need to get to the northern gate. They probably have Kaden already." Nyla beckoned for Lamar to follow her. She rushed toward the northern gate, Lamar following behind her. Nyla was relieved to see that the northern gate was still closed, but bodies still littered the ground as soldiers fought for their lives against the hoard of wolves.

Nyla spotted Samuel fighting with a large red wolf while another one circled him. Samuel was covered in blood that Nyla hoped wasn't his. The wolf lunged at Samuel while the other charged him from behind. In one swift movement, Samuel flipped over the red wolf, slashing at its neck. He spun around as it collapsed on the ground and quickly sank his sword into the other wolf's chest. Samuel turned and spotted Nyla and Lamar. He rushed over to them and looked Nyla up and down.

"What happened?" he breathed. "Wolves are storming the castle grounds. How did they get in?"

"It was Lucas." Lamar held his arm. "I tried to stop them, but they overtook the southern gate. They betrayed you."

"Dammit!" Samuel swore angrily.

"I think they have Kaden. Adrian said they needed more men here." Nyla pushed loose hair back with a blood dried hand.

"I thought I saw them here, but as soon as the wolves started coming from the South end, Kaden headed back toward the southern gate," Samuel responded. Just then Nyla spotted the queen fighting off a pair of wolves.

"Samuel!" Nyla screamed. She went to move toward her mother, but Samuel stopped her.

"Go to the southern gate and find Kaden! I'll help the queen!" He took off toward the queen and Nyla took a deep breath before turning toward Lamar.

"This way!" Nyla pulled Lamar toward the east side of the castle. Nyla tried to run as fast as she could, but so Lamar could still keep up. *I have to find Kaden!* As they neared the southern gate, Nyla slowed. Only a handful of men were left battling the wolves swarming them. The gate still remained lifted and Kaden stood at the top of the wall, but Nyla didn't see Kristy, or Dominic. Kaden stabbed a wolf and kicked it off the wall before rushing down the steps to aid the last few soldiers.

"Kaden!" Nyla rushed toward him, stabbing a wolf in the chest as it approached her. She reached him and he turned just as a wolf charged Nyla from behind.

"Nyla!" Kaden stepped in front of her and the wolf stopped dead in its tracks before it reached Kaden. Nyla pushed past Kaden and slashed the wolf in the throat. It collapsed on the ground, Nyla took off its head, and turned toward Kaden. She looked him up and down. Although blood spattered his clothing and armor, he had no marks on his body. The wolf had stopped before hurting Kaden and he had killed the wolf on top of the wall with ease. It was as if they were purposely trying not to hurt him! Suddenly the wolves stopped attacking, leaving only them and two other men alive.

"Where's Lucas?" Nyla looked around, but the three traitorous werewolves were nowhere to be seen. She turned toward Kaden again. "Where are they?!"

"What's going on, Nyla?" Kaden frowned at the wolves standing patiently nearby.

"Lucas betrayed us! Felix and Adrian were in on it too! They've been playing us the whole time!" Nyla fell silent as a chuckle sounded behind them.

"Bravo!" Lucas sneered at them. "Aren't you a smart one?" Felix and Adrian laughed from behind him. Still partially in their human forms, all three barred sharp, wolf-like fangs, and long, deadly claws.

"No." Kaden shook his head. "Adrian?" He frowned at her.

"Oh, it's true." She grinned, her fangs stained red with human blood. "We've overtaken the great castle of Galatia. And it was so easy." Nyla raised her sword as they approached and Lucas stopped beside Lamar.

"Oh, you don't need that, sweetheart. I'm not going to hurt you . . . yet." Lucas sneered at her before turning toward Lamar. "As for you." Lucas grabbed Lamar by the shoulder before taking his sword and thrusting it into Lamar's torso. He buckled and fell to the ground.

"No!" Nyla rushed to Lamar's side. She glared up at Lucas. "Why?"

"Why'd I kill him? He got soft and became a liability. But you were probably asking why we betrayed you?" Lucas started pacing. "Well, for a couple reasons actually. We are loyal to Rothgar. He gave us one of the greatest powers we could have. He taught me everything I know, which was more than my own father ever did. He wants this kingdom and we are helping him to overtake it. As for why I volunteered for this specifically . . . well, I came to reunite myself with the only family I have left." He smiled at Kaden. Kaden was taken aback for a moment, then dread flooded his chest.

"Kale?" Kaden's voice was barely a whisper.

"Hello, brother." Lucas walked toward Kaden. "Did you miss me?"

"Kale, what happened to you? You're body was never found. We all thought you were dead."

"No, little brother. Fortunately for me, Rothgar took pity on me and spared my life. He took me with him and turned me into the glorious creature I am." Nyla took Lucas's speech as an opportune moment and slowly began to move toward him.

"Now I'm here to take you back with me so that you can be given this gift as well. It's a shame about Mother and Kane, but at least you and I will be together again."

"Not if I can help it!" Nyla lunged at Lucas, but he turned away and a different wolf intercepted Nyla, knocking her to the ground. He snarled into her face, but didn't touch her.

"Nice try, sweetheart, but you weren't quick enough." Lucas began to walk toward her and the wolf moved out of his way. He knelt down in front of her and took her chin in his hand, squeezing hard. "I was hoping to spare you for my little brother's sake, but I can see you're going to be a problem. Unfortunately you're a vampire and can't be turned by Rothgar, so I'll just kill you."

"No!" Kaden cried. He tackled Lucas away from Nyla and she sprang into action. The other guards grabbed their swords and charged at the wolves surrounding them as Nyla advanced on Adrian. She swung at Adrian with her sword, but she dodged it and tried to make a counter move on Nyla. Nyla brought her sword up and wrenched the blade out of Adrian's hand. Suddenly, Felix grabbed Nyla from behind. He twisted Nyla's arm and knocked the sword out of her hand.

"Gotcha, Princess." Felix breathed in her ear. Nyla threw her head back and struck Felix's nose. He let her go and she pounced on Adrian before she could go for her sword. Nyla sped around Adrian and grabbed her from behind. Nyla sank her teeth into Adrian's neck and she let out a howling scream. Nyla drank deeply, but was suddenly yanked off of Adrian. Nyla was flung to the ground and she looked to where Lucas and Kaden wrestled. Nyla rolled out of the way before Felix could grab her and she sprang to her feet. A wolf charged her and she flipped over it before rushing to grab her sword. She spun around just in time to sink her blade into the wolf's chest. Nyla looked over the wolf to where Kaden lie on the ground. Out of nowhere, Nyla was grabbed from behind and dragged to a standing position. Her attacker twisted her wrist until she dropped the sword. Nyla tried to struggle out of his grasp, but he grabbed her around the throat. Kaden came to and sat up, looking into Nyla's eyes.

"Sorry, little brother," Lucas said from behind Nyla, "but, like I said before, she's not meant for you. She'll destroy your life and hold you back from your true potential as one of us."

Struggling to get out of Lucas's grasp, Nyla looked to where Felix crouched beside a bleeding Adrian. Suddenly, Lucas whipped his head to the right as multiple arrows whistled through the smoke filled air. They pierced through the hides of two of the wolves flanking Kaden, and they yelped, falling to the ground. Nyla seized the moment and brought her leg up, kicking back with all her strength. She heard a sickening crunch as it collided with Lucas's knee. Lucas howled in pain and fell to the ground, his leg broken. Nyla looked to the right as a group of guards, led by Samuel, rushed toward them, swords raised. Nyla turned, spotting her own sword, and made a dash for it. She retrieved it from the dirt as the guards and the wolves collided. For a brief moment, time seemed to move in slow motion before Nyla's eyes. Only the pounding of her own heartbeat reverberated through Nyla's eardrums as she scanned the bloody scene before her. All at once, time and sound caught up with her as she sped to join the battle.

As Nyla fought the wolves around her, she kept a lookout for the others. She spotted Samuel and Kristy amongst the chaos. They stood back to back, working together to take out the advancing wolves around them. Nyla spun around and felt relief as she glimpsed Kaden fighting alongside four other guards. Nyla stayed alert as she slashed and stabbed at wolf after wolf, not letting her guard down.

Nyla looked around as the snarling seemed to thin throughout the crowd around her. They were winning! Nyla spotted Lucas just ahead of her as he struck down a guard. She pushed past the battling men beside her, making her way to him. He turned and sneered at her with his deadly wolf fangs as she reached him, her sword ready in front of her. Nyla stayed in a calm stance, sizing up Lucas, waiting for him to make the first move. Although Lucas's leg was broken, he stood strong, his injured leg slightly bent. Lucas swung at her, but she blocked his sword with ease. Quickening his pace, Lucas dodged Nyla's thrust and counter attacked, his sword just missing her neck by inches. *That was too close.* Nyla took a deep breath as she searched

Lucas's eyes, trying to anticipate his next move. She saw a black shape hurtling toward her out of the corner of her eye and at the last second she turned, swinging her sword into the wolf advancing on her. The blow threw the wolf toward Lucas and he dove to the ground. Nyla rushed at him, taking him by surprise. She knocked the sword out of Lucas's grasp and held her own sword to his throat as he lay on the ground.

Nyla looked to her right to where Felix and Adrian stood back to back, surrounded by guards. *Victory will soon be ours!* Nyla looked back down, meeting Lucas's vengeful stare. Her brows knit together as a small smile crept onto his face. She looked around her as the fighting suddenly stopped. The wolves seemed to freeze in place before slowly turning toward the open gate. Keeping her sword aimed at Lucas's throat, Nyla shifted to face the gate. She squinted, the beacon fires lighting the air beyond with a hazy, brown and orange hue. Nyla's eyes widened as a figure came into view, just a silhouette in the smog. The figure continued toward them, arrogance and fierceness in every stride. Nyla jumped, startled, as the wolves all let out howls into the night. The figure outstretched his arms to the sides, welcoming the echoing howls. Nyla took in shallow, cautious breaths as the figure came into view.

The man stood before the crowd, keeping his arms raised as he surveyed the scene before him. His striking, yellow-brown eyes glowed red in the firelight and sharp canines protruded from his smiling lips. Curly, dark brown hair strayed wildly from a long braid that fell alongside the two curved daggers crossed at his back. All at once, the wolves stopped howling and everyone stood still, staring at the beastly man before them. Nyla barely dared to breathe as the air was too still and quiet around them.

Nyla sucked in a startled breath as the man threw his head back, letting out a bloodcurdling howl into the smoky, dark sky. The wolves joined in with his howl and the man brought his head back down, yanking the daggers on his back out of their sheaths and charging into the crowd. Terror chilled Nyla's veins as he headed straight toward her, malice on his scarred face. Before Nyla could react, Samuel stepped in the way. He attacked the man with a speed and ferocity Nyla hadn't seen. Samuel managed to knock one of the daggers out of the man's grip, but he was too fast. The man swept the air with a deadly, clawed hand, sending Samuel flying through the air. Nyla cried out Samuel's name as he hit the stone castle wall, falling unconscious to the ground.

Filled with fury, Nyla rushed at the man, seeing Kristi also bolt toward them from the corner of her vision. Nyla dove to the ground, rolling to her left, barely avoiding the sharp blade in the man's hand. Nyla looked up just in time to see the man stab the blade into Kristi's chest. Kristi's eyes widened, blood oozing from the corner of her mouth. Her terrified eyes flew to Nyla's as the blade was yanked out of her chest and her last breath escaped her crimson lips.

"No!" Nyla screamed. She stood, rage overtaking her body. The man's body transformed into bright colors and Nyla's fangs shot out from her gums as she charged him. Although Nyla swung and jabbed at the man with everything she had, after three dodged blows, the fourth hit Nyla square in the chest. Nyla was thrown backward as the air was forced painfully out of her lungs. She hit the hard ground and she squeezed her eyes shut as ringing reverberated through her skull. She coughed as she tried to force air back into her burning lungs and struggled to prop herself onto her elbows as she heard Kaden calling her name. Nyla opened her eyes just as she was dragged from the ground, the man holding her firmly against his body in his steel grip. A chill ran down Nyla's spine as a hot, rotting breath ran against her cheek and into her nose. She struggled as Kaden's eyes widened.

"Rothgar." Kaden breathed in fear, finally speaking the name that everyone feared to even think. Nyla struggled harder and Rothgar tightened his grip. Nyla looked at Kaden. He slowly reached into his boot.

"You won't kill me." Nyla breathed, still wheezing as her lungs sucked in air greedily.

"We'll see if you survive after he rips your head off." Lucas sneered. Sometime during the struggle, he had managed to stand beside Rothgar. Nyla looked at Kaden and he nodded. Nyla thrust her elbow back into Rothgar's side as hard as she could and twisted out of his grip. She dove to the ground out of reach as Kaden stood.

He flung a dagger in Rothgar's direction, but he caught it before it plunged into his chest. Kaden was ready and charged at Rothgar. Rothgar was faster and threw Kaden backward. Kaden hit the ground with a grunt.

"Lucas." Rothgar motioned toward Kaden. Kaden stood up, trying to catch his breath. Nyla looked to where Lucas started to move toward Kaden. He smiled as his teeth shifted to the fangs of a wolf.

"Kaden!" Nyla screamed, but she was too late. Lucas was on him in one swift moment. He pushed Kaden toward Rothgar and Rothgar grabbed hold of Kaden's shoulders from behind. He pulled Kaden's head to the side and sank his teeth into Kaden's shoulder. Kaden let out an agonizing scream. Nyla sprang to her feet and charged Rothgar, but Lucas intercepted her. She took hold of Lucas by the neck before he could grab her and sank her fangs into the soft skin. Lucas shrieked and Nyla was dragged off of him as Rothgar now held her in his grip. She screamed as Rothgar bit down on her shoulder. He threw her on the ground next to Kaden and licked his lips.

"The blood of a pure blood is the best I've tasted." Rothgar said satisfied. Nyla crawled to Kaden, who lay on the ground. He was breathing heavily.

"Are you hurt?" Kaden asked her weakly. Blood poured from his shoulder.

"I'm fine." Nyla shook her head as tears mixed with the blood on her face. "Kaden." She caressed his face with her hand. "Stay with me, Kaden. Please." Nyla cried out as Lucas yanked Nyla back by her hair. He grabbed her by the throat.

"Please let me rip her throat out!" Lucas spat into her face as he held the wound on his neck.

"No," Rothgar objected. "We can't kill her. There is still use for her."

Lucas frowned in anger but then grinned maliciously at her. He lifted her up and bit into her shoulder where the previous wound hadn't healed yet. Nyla screamed as pain spread through her shoulder, into her chest, and down her arm.

"Master!" Felix called. Lucas dropped Nyla and her head hit the ground. She turned her head to the side to see people running at them from a distance. Felix helped Adrian to her feet and she began to follow the retreating wolves out of the gait.

"Come, Lucas!" Rothgar commanded him. Rothgar bent down and picked Kaden up. Kaden hung limp in his arms. Lucas smiled down at Nyla and kicked her hard in the ribs. She curled up and cried out in pain.

"Nyla!" She heard voices coming closer to them.

"Come, Lucas!" Rothgar commanded more insistently. Lucas began to follow Rothgar out.

"Kaden!" Nyla pushed herself weakly to her feet and charged at him. She was tackled from behind and hit the ground.

"Go! Go!" Felix yelled at the wolves from on top of her. The others started to run as the group of people got closer. Lucas turned and threw a lit match on a patch of flammable oil lining the outside of the gate.

"Kaden!" Nyla struggled against Felix. "Kaden!" Suddenly Felix was dragged off of her and Nyla stood. She ran toward the fire, but Fulcan grabbed her.

"No, Nyla!" He held her tightly but didn't hurt her.

"Let me go! I can get to him! I'll be fine! I can get to him!" She struggled against his grip as tears poured down her cheeks.

"Not without getting burnt to a crisp you can't! Nyla you can't help him. It's too late!"

"Fulcan, let me go!" Nyla screamed. "They took him. Rothgar bit Kaden and they took him." She sobbed. She tried to struggle again and Fulcan swung Nyla around and she looked to where Samuel now stood holding Felix in a death grip. She closed her eyes against his pained expression and relaxed her body, giving up.

CHAPTER 21

Daylight started to stream through the clouds as the feeling of death settled over the castle grounds. After the werewolves had retreated into the forest, the castle gates were secured and all entrances were guarded with double the men. Right away, the bodies were gathered in the infirmary and their families were let in to identify their loved ones. The bodies that weren't claimed were prepared for a mass military burial. The werewolf bodies, now mostly in naked human form, were gathered and were to be burned outside the castle walls.

Although they were safe and the werewolves had retreated, many lives had been lost and the kingdom was in a somber haze. After the fire had burned down, the South gate had been closed. Samuel had taken Felix down to the dungeon before he could make any moves or do any damage. Since Felix had stayed behind he was now a prisoner, only kept alive for information. Fulcan had kept ahold of Nyla until after the gates were closed, but she hadn't tried to resist. She just cried into his arms. When they had brought Nyla back to the castle steps she thought she had cried herself dry, that was until Samuel had retrieved Julia from the bunker and told her the news about Kaden. Nyla and Julia now sat huddled on the palace steps.

"I'm fine, Samuel," Nyla said weakly as he checked her wounds for about the eighth time. They had almost fully healed, but still ached a little. "Really, they feel better."

"Okay." Samuel gave her a worried look before brushing his lips against her forehead and going back to his duties. Although he hated to leave Nyla alone, at least she had Julia for comfort.

"The big funeral is tomorrow," Nyla said absentmindedly. Julia nodded. Among the fallen were Kristi, Jordee, and a few guards that Nyla had seen with Samuel or Fulcan and Nyla hadn't known too well but still wanted to honor and remember.

"We might as well be honoring Kaden at the funeral." Nyla scowled as a tear slipped through her lashes.

"Nyla! Don't say that! Don't ever say that!" Julia paused, lost in her own thoughts. "We have to keep hope."

"You didn't see him, Julia! He was limp, lifeless! He's probably dead!"

"Then why would they take him with them?" Julia looked at Nyla.

"I don't know." Nyla sighed. "But if he is still alive out there I'm going to find him. He wouldn't give up on me and I won't give up on him. I just hope he's alive."

"He's still alive, Nyla. He has to be. I can feel it."

"How's she doing?" Fulcan looked at Nyla somberly as Samuel joined him.

"She just lost one of her best friends, Fulcan. How do you think she's doing?"

"I know." Fulcan shook his head. "I know she's angry with me. I just couldn't let her go out there. She would have gone straight through that fire. She could've gotten herself killed."

"She'll understand. It was too late. He was gone. He is gone." Samuel scowled at the ground.

"I don't think he's dead, Samuel." Fulcan looked him in the eyes. "Nyla said Rothgar bit him." Samuel's eyes widened and he raised his eyebrows.

"I guess that's why they took his body with them." Samuel shook his head. I don't know what's worse. We have to find him and get him away from Rothgar."

"That might be hard to do now, Samuel." Fulcan took a deep breath. "He might not want to come back with us." He hesitated. "If Lucas bit him then Kaden isn't dead . . . he's a werewolf."

ABOUT THE AUTHOR

Mariah Hayes grew up in the tiny town of Augusta, Montana. From when she first started to form the silly sounds of baby babble, Mariah has loved to read everything from Dr. Seuss to Harry Potter. That love of reading soon turned into a love of writing and Mariah took every creative writing class she could in high school. Her first published work was a poem titled "The Secrets of Time," entered in a Montana literary art magazine showcasing K–12 students.

After graduating with a music education degree from the University of Montana in Missoula, Mariah decided to pursue her love of writing even further when she finished the manuscript that would become *Bloodlines*.

When she's not reading or writing, Mariah's other interests include, fishing, hunting, spending time outdoors with her family, singing, playing computer games, and playing musical instruments, like guitar and piano.

CPSIA information can be obtained
at www.ICGtesting.com
Printed in the USA
FSHW010525170519
58228FS